'It's a big book, the w   g
concepts: birth, life, death – and those puzzling bits in
between – time, religion, God and resurrection. The plots are
beautifully pulled together to create an almost palpable sense
of tension. And like the best science fiction, or writing in any
genre, this is stimulating, thought provoking, haunting. And
totally spellbinding. *Something More* may be an ambitious
title – but the book thoroughly lives up to it. And something
more besides.'   *SFX*

'Cornell's writing feels loaded with uncertainty at the best of
times, and his evocation of that spooky feeling you get when
you might have heard something outside your bedroom
door in the middle of the night raised all the hairs on the
back of my neck . . . Cornell writes very well indeed and
deserves praise for trying something just that little bit more
challenging and off-kilter.'   *Infinity Plus*

Also by Paul Cornell in Gollancz:

BRITISH SUMMERTIME

SOMETHING MORE

Paul Cornell

Copyright © Paul Cornell 2001
All rights reserved

The right of Paul Cornell to be identified as the author of this
work has been asserted by him in accordance with the
Copyright, Designs and Patents Act 1988.

This edition published in Great Britain in 2002 by

Gollancz
An imprint of the Orion Publishing Group
Orion House, 5 Upper St Martin's Lane, London WC2H 9EA

A CIP catalogue record for this book is available
from the British Library

ISBN 1 85798 959 7

Printed in Great Britain by
Clays Ltd, St Ives plc

Acknowledgements

Thanks for help, research, support and critical comments to: Lou Anders, Clayton Hickman, Gerard Johnson, Matt Jones, Jo Kemp, Rebecca Levene, Penny List, Claire Longhurst, Steven Moffat, Amanda Murray, Stephen O'Brien, Nick Setchfield, Felicity Shea, Viv Turner, and to the Goodfellows, Saint Etienne, and Who Ink. Also to my wonderful editor, Jo Fletcher, literary agents John McLaughlin and Don Maass, my brother Terry for introducing me to science fiction, and to Mum and Dad, for bread and butter and honey.

For Caroline Symcox

. . . the world can never be seen again as harmonious, orderly, full of profundity, connection, and meaning, so much as being a cross between a snuff-film made for a commercial break, a skin-flick made in a concentration camp, and a scenery disaster in the end-of-term play.

Colin Bennett, review of *Amok Fifth Dispatch*
in *Fortean Times* issue 132

A manifestation, an event develops quickly and magically into an image of the universe. Even as the beloved and ever-sought-for form fashions itself, my soul flees toward it; I embrace it, not as a shadow, but as the holy essence itself. I lie on the bosom of the infinite world.

Friedrich Schleiermacher, *On Religion:
Speeches to its Cultured Despisers*

Rock me, Amadeus!

Robbie Williams, celebrating beating Mozart in
the HMV 'Best Songwriter of the Millennium' poll,
It's Only Us (Live Version)

Prologue One: Rebecca Champhert

Autumn, 2248.

Rebecca was lying in the back of a cart as it clattered along the cobbled streets of Charlton. Heading home at last. She'd gone off on her own as soon as they'd entered the gates of the Manor. She needed, after travelling so far, to be by herself. She was coming out of the end of a two-day hangover, full of new energy, needing to escape. She had her phone out, and was trying to work on the start of a novel, an idea she'd had during the wine-fuelled dreams: another historical work, but something set much further back than her previous books, something she could do to keep her sane in those few moments when she wasn't required to keep the biographical journals going. The bouncing of the cart kept throwing her around, her fingers messing up the keys on the phone, so a lot of what she was writing was gibberish. She'd felt a tremendous need to do this during the drunken night before, but now she wasn't as sure of her material.

She'd wanted to write about how things had been before the General Economic Collapse, before 2042. She'd wanted to write about nations, and companies, about how people had lived before the families: the Hawtreys, the Campbells, the Mandervilles, the Singhs and all the others, had divided Britain into territories and turned the islands into the map of civil wars and rebellions. She'd wanted to write about unity, about the church then, about communicating with other nations, even going to them.

She'd wanted to write about deep time. How whole dynasties and revolutions and political movements and gods and their followers got reduced, from a distance, to a handful of joke references that were all supposed to have happened at the same time. But how, when you were in the middle of it, one soldier from one of those dynasties walking into your kitchen could mean everything. People lived and died for tiny causes across history, but to them they always seemed huge.

She'd seen a lot of this during her drunkenness. She hadn't had the energy to write it down. Now she did . . . she stared at what she'd typed. It didn't seem to mean much after all. She was just looking forward to getting back to her bed at the court. To seeing some folk she knew, even if they didn't want to see her. To be someplace for some reasonable length of time.

But there was something there, something she might work on in time. She just couldn't get her head around it yet.

Frustrated, she hit the erase button on the phone. She was only twenty. She had at least another thirty years of writing in her. She'd keep it in her head, mull it over, give it time to stew.

She knew that somewhere in all that nebulous stuff, there was something for her to work with. Something more.

They were passing the big doors that led to the court.

Rebecca leapt up and started shouting at the driver to stop.

Prologue Two: Booth Hawtrey

Winter, 2043

Booth threw his coat on to the floor and sat down by his father's bed.

The old man looked up at him. 'I suppose you'll never find out what this is like. You bastard.'

Frank Hawtrey was dying of lung cancer. He was a hundred and nine years of age. He'd been confined to this hospital for six months – except that Booth wasn't sure if you could really call it a hospital any more. The draughty, broken-plastered room was being paid for by Dad's company, paid for in food. That was all that kept the concept of the hospital going here. Similarly, the company had stepped in to pay the handful of doctors and nurses who'd decided to stay on after the GEC. When the old man passed on, perhaps they'd go too. Or perhaps their other patients would keep them here by guilt. Booth had no idea. He didn't think the company itself could last much longer. Not that he understood the economics. He could just feel the way things were going.

The hospital was surrounded by Hawtrey security people, a fortress on the edge of Hampstead Heath. In these six months, the situation had deteriorated to the point where it felt like the world outside was dying alongside the old man. When Booth had come here at night, he'd sometimes heard the sounds of distant gunfire and explosions, seen the red roses of flame reflecting on the glass. At the start, right after the GEC, there had been euphoria in the air, the British love of disaster. People like Dad had waited all their lives for something like the GEC. The spirit of the Blitz was back. The pain brought comfort, so the pain was pleasure. Fucking masochists. But the smiles and the happy greetings were few and far apart now, as the chaos started to genuinely rear up from under the pavements.

Thank Christ.

Booth walked the emptying streets and wanted the houses demolished. Wanted just rubble, so they could start again from that. But maybe that was just because of what he was, now. Maybe he just wanted to kick on to the future and be done with all this bullshit.

While his dad was dying.

He hated the anger he always felt around the old man. Even now. Nothing he could do. He reached out his hand and smoothed the hair back from Dad's brow.

Dad coughed, long and painfully, the jerk of his head knocking Booth's hand away. 'Did you hear about what happened to your brother?' he gasped, when he'd finished.

'Yes.' Booth knew he'd bring it up.

'Kids. He's got a—' He gestured jaggedly down his cheek. 'He was getting out of his car. Could have killed him. They're going wild, they're becoming like dogs. That's the next generation, that's who's getting the world. Animals!'

Booth pursed his lips for a moment before he answered. 'Same as always.'

Dad didn't seem to hear. 'They're vicious now. Vicious. Are you saying that it's right, them just attacking folk for whatever they've got, food or . . .'

'Things change.'

'When you were a teenager, you were always finding excuses for the way the world was going. And look at it now!'

Booth knew he should be silent. But this was his dad. He couldn't shut up. He leant closer to Dad's ear. 'When I was growing up you were angry at graffiti and vandals and football hooligans. Now you're angry at this.'

Dad gestured violently at the window. 'Aren't you?'

'I think something better's going to come along.'

'It's the end of the world!'

'It's not the end of the world.'

'Not for you, eh? Just for us real human folk, those of us unfortunate enough to remember the War.'

Booth sat back, taking a deep breath. Finally, he just repeated himself. 'It's *not* the end of the world.'

Booth set off in the rainy night, marching down the street away from the hospital, intending to cross the city on foot, down through Kilburn and Shepherd's Bush, to get back to the family home in Chiswick in the early hours. The emptiness of the A40M appealed to him, particularly at night. He knew it was a journey nobody else would dare make, and that appealed to him too.

But he was tired.

He stopped by a bus shelter, turning back to look at the lights of the hospital compound. He could get an armoured limo to take him home.

Just pride. He had to make some peace with his dad now, it was demanded of him. But he couldn't. He was going to take that weight of guilt and history on into the future with him. The buildings of London were never gonna be rolled flat. They would just stand and haunt him.

Suddenly, he turned and kicked and kicked at the fake glass pane of the bus shelter until it broke from its frame and shattered into a thousand pieces.

Prologue Three: Simon and Edwin

Spring, 1922.

They walked down from the folly together, and paused to look down the forest path at the completed house, shining and white in the sunshine. The monumental masons were hauling their gear into their little van on the driveway, and the first of the moving vans had arrived.

'However are you going to fill it?' laughed Sir Edwin, his little round glasses sparkling in the sunshine.

Trent managed a smile. He wanted them all to go, so he could finally be alone in his new house. But it had only seemed right to invite the famous architect to see the completion of his work. 'With me, and the servants, and family furniture from all over the place. Amazing what one accumulates.'

'Good luck to you, I say. A fresh start, a chance to get away from the past, eh?'

Trent didn't manage to say anything.

Lutyens turned and looked at him, his balding brow furrowed. Those sparkling eyes looked straight into Simon's own. 'That is the purpose of all this, surely? I'm sure you'll never forget Alisdair, but—'

'I'd rather not talk about it, Edwin.'

'Oh, don't talk rot! I've built your house, man! To those ridiculous plans of yours, yes, but there's quite a lot of me in there too! There are tens of thousands of people like you in this country now. Everybody's lost someone. Now, how are we going to *deal* with that?'

Trent inflated his cheeks, trying not to be angry at his friend. He still couldn't think of anything to say.

The architect bunched his hands up into imploring fists. 'By a better life, that's how! By turning towards the future and going there, full tilt. Making something sensible out of the sacrifice. If I'd thought you were just going to rattle around that big new pile, old chap, like a man without his marbles in a jar, I'd never have built it for you!'

6

'What do you know about losing someone?' He regretted the words as soon as he said them.

But Lutyens was nodding violently. He took off his spectacles and wiped them, continuing to nod. 'Oh, I don't know death as well as you do. But consider Emmy for a moment, Simon. She and I . . . we are married, but because of what she believes, what she needs from her life . . . we are not husband and wife, have not been for several years now. I would not dream of saying it's the same, but . . . I know of what I speak. Don't live in the past.' He put his glasses back on and smiled. 'No house for you there. Just that one. In the future.'

Trent managed to smile back at him. He wished he could tell the man everything about the house he'd just built. But Lutyens would never have believed him.

Weeks later, when the servants had arrived and the rhythm of life at the house had been established, Trent decided that it was time.

As he'd been instructed, he'd saved the final brick until this point.

He chose the middle of the night, and walked down and down the stairwells until he was in the cellars by the waterwheel that eccentrically powered his house.

He found the single gap that the builders had left for him, mixed some mortar, and carefully slid the brick into place.

As soon as he stood up, he felt the difference.

And he remembered the words of Sir Edwin Lutyens, and knew that, for him, living in the future was going to be the task of a lifetime.

One: Communicating at an Unknown Rate

For a long time, the land seemed empty. The coast of white cliffs and the dark sea defences of spikes and mines had ridden up suddenly out of the sea, and there had been the mossy ruins of a town, with its cloud of seabirds in the dawn, come and gone in a moment. But no people. Farm buildings here and there, and of course the roads and the hedges, now being erased back into the green, but no vehicles or lights. Every field looked full of dark crops, because the only harvest now was the frost, and the edges of each great patch of land had started to blur into the next.

A glow to the north-west would be Bristol, the first artificial thing that spoke of life. The composition of the glow was changing as the early light grew brighter.

Beneath swept the spire of a church, a weathercock spinning on its side, the stained glass beneath it frost-cracked and gapped. Around the building twined a mass of green: elm trees and weeds, root systems spreading through the graveyard and slowly lifting the building from its hill.

A river covered a village destroyed by fire, had fattened on it like a snake, leaving dark second storeys as islands in a lake. A supermarket stood on the edge of the water, with a beach of detritus in front, as tides had washed through its aisles, year in, year out. The interior would be a place for frogs and water-loving trees.

A low row of hills shot up on the horizon, the folly still standing at lookout on the first of them. And then the wooded valley of Heartsease lay below, the lake shining up at the sky, the details of the maze now visible, becoming clearer. The great expanse of the driveway was still white and open, the lawn kept short by grazing animals. And there was the house itself, proud behind its ornamental gates. The huge, clear windows, the flat expanse of the roof with its water-weary pool, the battlements and flagpole and gardens.

There were lights about the great house! In the bedrooms, in the stables, in the kitchens, in the library. The place could have been home to all its old inhabitants, all the hundreds of staff and guests and family that had ever lived there, waking up together in the dawn.

But it was truly only home to a few.

The last few, in one of the last dawns.

But they didn't know that yet.

At a window in one of the upper bedrooms in the south wing, a woman was standing, black against the light, staring out at the empty world in autumn.

She gripped the sides of the alabaster window frame.

She was crying as she looked out.

Her eyes were very blue.

'God?'

Jane Bruce waited for a moment, like she really expected an answer. Then she slapped her brow with the tips of her fingers, and inhaled deeply through her hands. She rubbed her face vigorously, bashing away at the tears, chiding herself.

She'd woken from a dream crying, and had kept on crying. She really didn't know why.

And then she'd thought she felt something coming at her through the dawn sky. Like she was being looked at.

It must be the drugs, she thought. So many little side effects. One never quite got used. She'd been having strange dreams since she got here. This was just another sad one. Perhaps.

She looked back to the corner of the room, the pristine golden wallpaper warping under her gaze.

Her dad still stood there, one arm outstretched, his finger reaching towards her. It was like he was running out of the wall. He was wearing his full dress uniform, including his medal ribbons. She took a couple of steps closer and looked hard at the finger. That was an Ornamental Detail, almost certainly. Something that had ridden in from associations to obscure and overwrite the detail that had been forgotten. Dad was reaching out for her like God in Michelangelo's *The Creation of Adam*. She could see in her memory the little cherub under the wing of God's cloak who was looking back. 'Abandon God!' her father had used to say when he looked over her shoulder and saw that picture on her phone, like 'Abandon ship!' Then he'd make a boom noise in his cheeks, anticipating God hitting the hillside in the picture like a crashing airliner.

As she understood that, the finger wavered, skidded through half a dozen different positions.

Jane popped another green from the little dispenser round her neck and swallowed it. She'd taken the first pill as soon as she'd woken up, a reflex of her training, to keep the sad and powerful dream image in her mind. There had been all sorts of things in her dreams. The twins had been there, that day they'd gone to see the fishes under the bridge. But her father was the main thing, the thing she wanted to check on. She closed her eyes for a moment, then looked again. This time the finger was more certainly her father's, with a tiny scar that she either deeply remembered or had just made up.

'Better, Dad,' she told the apparition. She'd have to be certain that she'd got all the details of this thing clear in her mind in the next hour, before she went over her green limit for the day. She'd taken a long look at it already. The procedure now was to walk away, let the green play with what was already there, and then look back.

So she could go and get a shower.

It was probably nothing. If there wasn't some obvious message from her unconscious or the divine – she gave a bitter little sneeze and blew her nose on a tissue – then there probably wouldn't be one on closer inspection, but she was pledged to look.

She put the dispenser down on the night table beside her dog collar, and was about to pull her nightgown over her head when an awkward sensation stopped her.

She looked back to the open mouth and staring eyes of her father, and headed for the door of the en suite bathroom, clothed. 'Don't go away,' she called to him as she closed the door.

The shower was of a piece with the bath, a single ceramic unit that surrounded Jane in a white art deco half-tube. Five brass taps down the right-hand wall of the apparatus controlled everything that the aristocracy might have wanted from a shower back in 1922 (the date was designed, not even stamped, into the plughole grid). It was, like everything else, still perfect in every way, and worked exactly as it should. An unexpected grace, right on the edge of miraculous.

Jane showered at length, taking small pleasure as she always did in the swell of her tummy, the fond weight of her breasts. Her chubbiness had always made her stand out at court, a shape the soldiers whistled at and then pretended it hadn't been them when she looked around. Plump as a partridge, they said. In many ways she was unconcerned that men found her beautiful, but perhaps it had opened a few doors. And the attention made her feel confident and strong. The argument from design was rubbish, of course, but it had always pleased her emotionally. If God's hand could be seen anywhere, it was in the details of her flesh, making her smile at the few grey hairs in the brush.

Jane had been looking for God in everything she did lately. He wasn't coming out. She believed He was there for other people, but not for her at present. She was usually so happy. She still did, on occasion, seem happy. But frustration and doubt had put weight under her eyes and changed her nature.

The green had put a distant noise into her head like it always did, an awareness of something whispering away at the edge of hearing, like a song in the next room. It wasn't unpleasant and she'd got used to it. It went well with the sound of the water.

She blinked suds out of her eyes and glanced at her watch, which she'd placed on the Lutyens dais beside the bath. If she was going to interrogate the dream figure further, it would really have to be shortly.

Jane grabbed the brass fitting marked 'plunge' and yanked it forward.

She hollered with laughter as the mass of cold water hit her, and jumped out of the bath shuddering and going 'brrrr', entirely for her own amusement.

The thought slowed her at the door. Once she'd have been certain of a constant audience at every step.

Wrapped in her dressing gown, Jane sat on the edge of the bed and studied the apparition again. Details of it had changed, of course, while she'd been in the bathroom. Her memory of the vision had started to refer to itself, to the story it was telling, rather than to the original event. That was the natural process which green acted to prevent, the frighteningly swift change from stored information to oft-told story. She'd left it a little too long, so the normal brain processes were going about their business again. She'd have to do something about that.

She remembered a story she'd been told at college in Wells, the tale of Rory Fitzwaller, a British colonel in India during the days of the Raj, who had always told his dinner guests an elaborate ghost story. He'd been served on several occasions, he said, by a young boy who always insisted on leaving the room before one of the other servants entered. The punchline was that the other servant turned out to be his mother, and the boy turned out to be dead. In his old age, he'd written it all down for publication in *Pall Mall* magazine. The week after the story appeared, he suddenly realised that, decades before, when he first told the story, he'd made it all up. He did the decent thing and wrote a letter to the magazine, wondering not at ghosts now, but at the splendour and mystery of the human memory.

It would have taken a lot of green to help him climb down into his memory that far, if it had become so powerful as to trick him. He'd have had to become a vicar, and to have learnt mnemotechnics. So there might have been some grace in his sudden realisation.

Either that, or he'd secretly known, and had just been lying to himself all along. That one was definitely a case of the sacred or the profane.

Still. Jane clapped her hands together to make herself focus, and took three sudden sharp breaths, flooding her system with oxygen. She brought to mind her memory theatre, the imaginary building that, at the start of her training, had been like a village hall, but these days was more like one of the great abandoned buildings of old London. She stood in the middle of a stage, very like Shakespeare's original Globe.

During her training, Jane had learned that some scholars thought of the Globe as a physical reconstruction of a memory theatre. The concept had been very popular in Shakespeare's day. Giordano Bruno, a contemporary of Galileo, burned at the stake by the Inquisition, had been the first person to link the memory theatre to the divine, and the Globe was, perhaps, the realisation of his vision. The theatre as tool of transcendence, the idea that onstage a performer had at hand, in his catalogued and sorted audience, the experience of all the world, and was able to use that knowledge as a sort of fuel to go beyond it. To reach, in the limelight, for something at the heart of the human condition.

Or, as one of Jane's tutors had put it, 'All the world's a stage he's going through.'

Her calling was thus referred to, these days, as Brunian Anglicanism, or the Brunian Heresy as the Catholics saw it.

There were five hundred and twenty rows of seats in Jane's memory theatre, each row identified by a letter, from A to 20A. From where she stood onstage, a rainbow of coloured lights was projected on to those seats. The red, at the left, shone over the oldest experiences, and the violet, at the right, over the newest. There were exits on either side and at the back, which memories no longer required were allowed to leave through. Ten boxes contained things of special importance.

There was a box for Jane's family and one for dreams, because dreams formed a special part of Jane's duty. In the latter box sat images of emotional resonance, surrealism and sex and horror. Most nightmares were very silly in retrospect, though, with fear showing up only as a sort of marker, a reminder that the experience had, for some reason, included that.

She'd placed Dad, unconsciously, at the edge of the dreams box nearest to family. So everything in her head was ticking over as it should be.

She concentrated on the green, in the way that she could never really explain to anybody. Accessed it. And emphasised that particular box to it. And then there was Dad in the room again, the vision from the dream moving again against the wall where he'd appeared in her sleep, his mouth opening and closing in speech, his hands beckoning urgently to her.

Don't do that, he seemed to be trying to tell her. It's dangerous. Leave well alone. She could hear his voice saying these things, but she was fairly certain that was just her memory of his voice, filling in the gaps. Her brain seemed to want to make up stories even more than anyone else's.

That was all she was going to get. The complete sideshow. No clue as to why she was seeing this now, what had made this bubble up out of her brain.

It just *felt* meaningful.

She breathed the green out, contracting the muscles around her neck, letting it go. The vision started to fade. She opened her eyes, and let the memory theatre go too.

She went to her bedside table and checked the EM meter's recordings from the previous night, which had been archived on her phone. No spike at all, just the same unusually low background figure of just under one milligauss. No DC field. This was the sanest room she'd ever slept in.

That was so wrong, but it had to be true. She'd checked every connection in the blessed thing. So it looked pretty unlikely that Dad was anything other than a rather odd dream.

There was a knock on the door. Jane called enter. It was Ruth, looking scrubbed despite the ground-in mud on her camouflage jacket. There was something even more intimidating about the young woman in the mornings. Duty shone from her. Her boots were freshly shined.

'Breakfast,' she said.

'Lovely,' said Jane. 'I'll be down in a minute.' She went to get her suit from the wardrobe.

14

By the time she was dressed, Dad had vanished completely.

But the green still played in her head. It played on the reaction she'd just had to Ruth.

It took her back to the awkwardness between them.

Jane's party had landed a week before at the little tower airstrip in the Bristol docklands. The dirigible they arrived in had Campbell markings on its tail and fuselage, in case anybody in the countryside thought of taking a potshot, or there were any patrols from the other families wandering across their route. The Cormorant in white in a blue circle with the red circle on its breast said that the Campbells would call retribution for such an attack. Even this far from their own lands. Well, hopefully. That was how the Campbell court boasted. But in truth, much of this land was ruled by whoever happened to be around at the time, and the boundaries between those lands claimed by the great families were vague and changed from map to map. The families earned much of their power through symbols: flags, badges and favours. The journey had taken two days. They had slept in the cabin and flown on through the darkness, navigating by compass. Jane, not used to such expeditions, had stared down at the empty landscape beneath the dirigible, wondering at such acres of nothingness. How terrible it must be to live in the outback, far from the protection of one of the families. Or worse, in thrall to one of the more savage families, like the Hawtreys. The land was dark and empty, and at night, the occasional distant light, driven by some lonely generator far below, made her shiver at the foolish bravery of whatever farm or isolated fort that was. She expected to find it hard to sleep, but the gentle whirring of the electric motor had lulled her so easily, her last thought before dreaming was a worry that it would send Ruth, at the controls, asleep also.

Bristol claimed to be a free city, so there was some delay at the bottom of the steps that led from the tower where the dirigible was docked. They were met by some self-consciously aggressive local militiamen who wanted to check their Campbell family papers and health certificates. Their own soldiers had bridled just as they should until Ruth told them to shut up. The local militia swore their civic oath that there were currently no representatives from any of the other families in the city. But they would say that, of course. Jane was certain from the tales she'd heard that there'd be someone on the airstrip staff reporting back to every one of the other families' intelligence-gathering operations.

Once they'd reached the airstrip offices, their party now

ceremonially confirmed as being no threat to the city, the red carpet was literally rolled out, and a band of children had played the Campbell March.

The Mayor of Bristol, Jack Tembe, had knelt and kissed the Campbell ring on Major Ruth Crawshay's knuckle. Ruth was the leader of their little team, and the ring indicated that she was a pilot, one of the more prestigious trades. Jane saw a look of pride in Tembe's eyes as he bent: our city is ready for you. Bring the Campbells west if that is your eccentric wish, everything's waiting. Jane had the impression he'd even be willing to let his city become the battlefield that a Campbell push here would result in it being. But perhaps that was the impression he gave all the families.

The eight of them were each put into an individual cycle rickshaw, and taken to a hotel in the town centre, as far from the city walls as it was possible to be. We're as good as Chester. You aren't in the boondocks down here.

Jane had had a vast hot bath that lasted an hour.

The militiamen, she supposed, were used to this feeling of dislocation, of starting the day in one town and ending it in another. But to her it was a bit of a shock. This was only the third such mission she'd been sent on in twenty years as Campbell house chaplain. She'd been glad of it, in a way, in that it was a mark of her seniority over Frances, who now seemed to be visiting Georgina Campbell on a regular basis. The younger vicar was intense and driven, concerned with every detail of their mistress's dreams, more so, even, than her own. And Georgina had the most extraordinary dreams, enough to lead any chaplain into the error of studying them endlessly, especially one as inexperienced as Frances. Jane had talked to the younger cleric about it several times: one's own mind is the only mind that one can even begin to know. Others' dreams are translated to us by their intelligence and personality, and are deformed and futile as a result. But the admonishments seemed to fall on deaf ears. So now Jane's gentle whimsy was no longer flavour of the month with Georgina. It had occurred to her then that this strange job might have been entirely designed to get her away from the court. Georgina certainly had the power to send her on such an assignment. She'd heard from the soldiers that Ruth had had to pull strings to get her and her team assigned to accompany her. That Ruth hadn't been the first choice, but had marched up and down the court campaigning to do so. It was as if the court wanted Jane to go, but it had been Ruth who had wanted desperately to accompany her. And Ruth seemed to know all the

16

mysteries of the journey, so surely Jane wasn't being sent into danger.

Whatever would happen would happen. Jane would merely return to find herself pensioned off to one of the outlying communes. The court didn't like fuss. They'd want to have Frances set in place and her own rooms relocated by the time she got back.

She'd stifled the thought. What would happen would happen. Her duty wasn't about playing Campbell politics. Her duty was to God.

When He was about. He hadn't been about for a while.

The bath water had grown cold by the time she got out.

There had been an official reception that evening, in a hotel function room that overlooked the city. Things looked blooming, as far as Jane could see from the big picture windows. There was actually new development. The lights of construction sites shone outside the walls in the wasteland of demolished suburbs. But things had bloomed before, she knew from her history. As soon as a place like Bristol started advertising its wealth, it attracted forces that would rip it apart to eat what was inside. Tembe must know that too, hence the guard posts and the heavy guns that were stationed about the walls.

Jane raided the buffet during the speeches. There were jugs of apple juice and cider, ceramic bowls of curried shrimp and stirfry and chopped cabbage. She filled her cracked old mug, which had been Dad's before it was hers, with cider and took a plateful of the goodies.

Each member of Ruth's six-man team was then personally introduced, and did their party piece. Matthew, a gunner with a little carpet of orange hair flat on his head, had a martial poem that he performed, with great whoops for the artillery and handclaps for the slap of bullets around him. Jane noted that he had rolled up his sleeves to show off his tattoos, particularly, she suspected, the thorn on his wrist, which indicated he had experience of combat, in the Third Singh War. Jane liked the energy of his performance.

Joe, a huge engineer with a face that looked as if it had been deformed by a careless sculptor, did coin magic, so badly that the applause afterwards was more for the fact that such an obviously military man had tried his best to entertain. That was what such ceremonies were for, Jane had thought. We're all normal people, here, see what we do. She knew that barracks set aside time on Saturday afternoons for militiamen to practise such party pieces.

After their introductions, the men were sent to mingle with a crowd that consisted of civic workers and a number of single women, hostesses for the evening. A chaperone sat discreetly in the corner, with a velvet bag to collect favours and a phone to note contact details.

Poor old Ruth, Jane had thought, must feel very left out at times like this. The young woman had made a short and direct speech, thanking the Mayor for his hospitality and listing the fertilisers, food and fuel that they'd brought as gifts to the city. 'The Campbell family will remember your hospitality,' she concluded.

As leader of the team, Ruth wasn't obliged to entertain. Jane couldn't imagine what she would have done if she had been. Ruth had retired as early as custom allowed.

Jane had discreetly snaffled a further plateful of pie and curried eggs, and had followed shortly after, leaving the gathering to get more raucous and beery.

Jane had always felt a kinship with militiamen. She'd grown up with them being there, amongst the family. She'd gotten to be familiar with the members of her dad's unit. Her first crush, when she was thirteen, had been on Stuart, a wonderfully muscular, highly decorated man under her father's command. He'd had the most powerful, tattooed arms. He hadn't laughed when she'd taken a risk and told him her real first name was Alice. He hadn't even made a soldier's joke about her being a real farm girl or asked if she was an Alice by nature or if she had a friend called Zoe. He'd just thought about it and carefully nodded. She'd waited for days to get him alone, and then had let him know how she'd felt. Asked him if he wanted to kiss her. She still winced at the memory. Stuart had looked at her with an agonised expression, and, stepping back from her, had adopted a tone of voice she'd never heard from a soldier before. Very formally, he had promised her that when she attended her first ball, they would have the first dance together.

It was a very minor promise, and the chances of Jane ever making it to a ball, then, looked pretty small, and even so it wouldn't have been for another year or so. She'd been very angry.

She'd been even angrier when Dad had made a joke about it that night. Stuart had told him straight away.

She never spoke to the soldier again. But now she understood that he couldn't have done anything else. Not with the daughter of his commander.

The double standard by which soldiers lived their lives was interesting to Jane. They would carouse in private, devise the cruellest and most dangerous games, talk with rough honesty about women. But in public they were all working for their commissions, so they could pass into the officer class and hope to marry into the family. Rude but honest underneath, prideful and mannered above. That was the form. They read improving texts off the net, novels like *Russell for the Flag*, or manuals such as *You Shall Go to the Ball (But what do you do when you get there?)*. They mochaed their hair into hard cliffs and waves and furls, anything that was original, macho and eye-catching. And the tattoos! Family crests and flags, names of women, slurs that famous soldiers of other families were homosexual, huge fighting animals . . . A number of Ruth's lot, who had been under her command for several years, had her name written above their hearts, indicating that they would die for her, and in official company they would declare loudly that they hoped to marry her when they had earned their commissions.

Unless, of course, it was taken as read, a lady from the family appeared first.

These contradictions had made Jane smile when she was a girl, watching Dad's troopers as they painted a wall or dug a ditch, and they still made her smile now.

She'd finished the evening with another bath, anticipating mud.

The next morning, when Ruth's team had checked in, assuring her formally and, mostly falsely, that they had slept safely in the assigned place, they were rickshawed to Temple Meads.

At the great depot under the roof of what had once been the railway station, they found the armoured car. The great echoing hall was full of the shouts of gangs unloading produce, and the low buzz of electric engines. Little steam carts chugged to and fro, with crates of vegetables and corked jugs of milk from local farms. The produce would be loaded on to the funicular railway that led down through the markets.

There were papers to sign, and small gifts of food to be given to the smiths who had kept the vehicle and maintained it to the instructions of the Campbell family. A cart chugged up with the various provisions that had been requested and laid aside. Ruth's team opened the back doors of the armoured car and started to load it with the provisions and their own kit bags, weapons and ordinance, throwing the items to each other rhythmically. The vehicle had a long black cabin, more than enough room for seven people to live and sleep over several days. Its armour plating was welded on to its sides, extending down over the wheel arches to stop only a few inches from the road surface. The windows were made from shockproof glass. The driver, navigator and gunner sat in an enclosed turret at the front, mainly made from that glass, assuring a wide field of view. The reins looked like they were made from some sort of strong plastic that Jane hadn't seen used in harnesses at the court. Elements of this thing, she thought, must date back to before the GEC. The car had been refitted and refurbished until it was like the proverb about the axe and the handle. If you replaced the stock and the blade, was it still the same axe? The farrier brought forward six large horses in their own armour, which Ruth insisted on having introduced to her individually, and had a bundle of foodstuffs put on to the roof of the vehicle while the horses were fastened into their harnesses.

The Campbell team's work song was a marching rhythm that made ironic comments about Ruth's – apparently voracious, though Jane doubted that very much – sexuality. But it was all couched in terms of in-jokes, so that outsiders wouldn't recognise it as being disrespectful to their commander. She was referred to throughout as Three Cuts, which Jane didn't understand, though Matthew had, reluctantly, recited the full lyric to her on the dirigible. Jane boggled at the sheer effort over beer that must have gone into the creation of such a song, all for Ruth to raise a wry eyebrow and tolerate it. Very military.

The song joined with the other resounding noises of Temple Meads to produce a joyful uproar. The sound of good work. The soldiers would join their kit in the armoured car after they'd finished. Jane had been quite looking forward to riding with them. She liked the odd mixture of courtesy and laughter that the militiamen displayed in her presence. They wouldn't be able to tell their stories about last night, at least not without using courtly euphemisms. 'I've been seeing a lady of the Bristol court recently,' they would have to say. 'But I don't expect to see her again, although our discussions were fruitful.'

But Ruth, perhaps mindful of her men's need to express themselves freely, had then invited Jane to ride beside her and navigate. Matthew, his machine gun attached to the pinion on the roof, was to be their gunner.

The soldiers had closed the rear doors, and Jane, Ruth and Matthew had climbed up to the high seats, Ruth spending a few moments familiarising herself with the reins before jerking them and calling giddyap. As the horses started to move, a woman in the uniform of the Bristol watch had jogged up to their running board, clipboard in hand. She hopped on, grabbed a strap that had obviously been installed for just this purpose, and thumped the side of the vehicle, calling for them to move off. With a harbour pilot's easy intimacy, she'd directed them through the maze of other vehicles under the great arch of the roof, and then out into the streets towards the southern gate. They turned left out of Temple Meads, and went over the great iron bridge that passed above what had once been railway tracks. Now the cutting below was filled with little allotments and greenhouses, running far off into the distance. The noise of the horses' hooves made a thunderous racket on the metal of the bridge as they accelerated to a trot. Other vehicles, rickshaws, steam-driven buggies and little electric bikes, rattled past, making the armoured car look huge and dangerous. They were heading outside, departing this little community where quaint civil life had taken root again so precariously. At the other side of the bridge, the official made sure that Ruth knew where she was going. Then she hopped off the running board and curtseyed to them before jogging off back towards Temple Meads.

There was a low autumn sun in the clear sky. It looked like it was going to be a nice day.

They got an occasional cheer from pedestrians responding to the Campbell banner that one of the soldiers had left sticking out of the rear doors, and as they passed the thriving Brislington market, hooves clicking on the cobbles, a great hallooing went up. Marketeers were never keen to show their colours, and Jane was sure that many of them would have shouted for any banner. But she waved back graciously. Matthew hadn't taken up his gun since they'd left the station. He gave the marketeers a clenched-fist salute: off to change the world. Jane decided she liked being so high up above things. She sucked in breaths of clean October air, enjoying the smells of fresh vegetables from the market.

As Ruth encouraged the horses to climb up the hill through Brislington itself, Jane realised that she had a tune in her head. It was something her dad had sung to her when she was little, that she'd later found out was a tune from one of the Public Information Films at the time of the GEC, passed down the generations. He probably hadn't been aware of the origin of it himself. Those little cartoons were the height of camp now, popular viewing on the phones, in a cynical sort of way. 'Manufacture,' the tune went. 'Manufacture, that's what we need. If we're going to be the best, if we're going to beat the rest . . .' That was back before 'beating the rest' became out of the question. She wondered why she'd recalled the tune just then, and realised that they'd clattered past a row of thriving potteries.

They turned left at Three Lamps Junction, where a single iron post supported three ornate electric lamps in a mock-Victorian design.

They weren't the original lamps, but the Mayor believed, as he'd said the previous night, in keeping alive the memory of what the city had once been, in the hope that, like a piece of metal deformed by pressure, it would naturally return to that shape in time.

The southern gate of the city was formed from two great metal plates, cast with the badge of the Free City, a bear on one side and an elm tree on the other. This had replaced the original solid-wood barrier twenty years ago, on the anniversary of the founding of the city. There was a machine-gun nest on the top of each supporting pillar, and militiamen sat on the walkway that led around the city walls. They called down to the armoured car as it stopped at the checkpoint barrier: courtly propositions to Ruth. Jane doubted they could have seen her from up there. The Mayor had probably asked them to do it. 'Return with this favour, lady,' they shouted, dropping Free City handkerchiefs, weighted down by coins, on to the roof of the vehicle behind the cab.

Ruth looked up from signing the passing-out documents and glanced at Jane. It was like she felt she should make an effort to talk to her.

'What do you think, Reverend? Should I entertain them?'

Jane shrugged, uneasy. 'Why not? They're obviously very sincere chaps.'

So Ruth had bent down to hand the papers back to the gatekeeper, and had then hopped out of the cab to stand atop the roof of the armoured car. She selected a favour seemingly at random, and bent to pick it up. One of the militiamen on the walls above punched the air with excitement, laughing and whirling his cap before his fellows. The others half-heartedly congratulated him.

Such panto.

'I know,' Ruth sighed, tucking the handkerchief into the top pocket of her fatigues. 'I doubt I'll have the time or the inclination when we come back this way.'

Jane heard something in that phrase. A moment of hesitation before the 'when'. She couldn't help but give voice to her own nerves. 'You sound like you're afraid we're not coming back.'

And that had been a bad mistake. Ruth had suddenly looked at her, all fellow feeling between them vanishing in an instant.

'I mean,' Jane back-pedalled, 'well, not *afraid*, but . . .'

Ruth had finally turned back to the reins, her eyebrows raised, as if Jane had committed some private misdemeanour that was too terrible for words. But Jane was certain she had not. Soldiers talked about fear all the time, on a professional basis. How to deal with it, what it meant, the consequences of it. Matthew was still smiling up at the guards, though he must have heard her words. It was only an issue when . . .

When they found themselves afraid of something they thought they shouldn't be afraid of.

It was then that Jane caught a glimpse of something that changed all her thoughts about Ruth.

As the Major fastened the pocket that she'd stuffed the favour into, for just a second another tiny scrap of cloth was pushed out. It was of a deeply faded violet.

Jane turned away before Ruth's eyes met hers, hoping that the soldier hadn't realised that she'd seen it. She didn't want one more thing to add to the distance between them.

There was a pause as Jane looked around the gate area, and shared a smile with Matthew.

When she looked back, Ruth's whole attention was on the horses, and the pocket was buttoned up firmly.

Ruth took the tension in the reins, and, as the barrier rose in front of them, sent the six horses clattering forward, into the world outside the walls.

They passed through miles of flatlands, where there had once been demolished buildings and where the vegetation was purged on a regular basis to give Bristol a clear view of its approaches. Every now and then the landscape was enlivened by a new smallholding, surrounded by electric fences, or a construction project, labourers working with picks in the October sunshine. You could tell the younger ones from the old, because the old ones always kept their shirts on, while the young ones weren't afraid of going bare-chested. Another of those tunes: 'You've got to slap, slap, slap on the sunscreen.' The whole business of camp, Jane supposed, came from memory. Big, scary things in childhood, deliberately mocked by the adolescent, the warnings of elders who were no longer aware of the way the world turned.

The workers looked up from their labour, and saw the banner and cheered them. Jane chanced a glance at Ruth, but her eyes were now firmly set on the road.

They took the armoured car east, initially, following the course of the old A4. The road was generally clear, but once or twice the team had to remove a fallen tree or Ruth had to slow the horses to avoid a pothole. Jane was sure of their destination from her maps, and the roads were still approximating what was described by them, but Ruth never once asked her for confirmation that they were going in the right direction. She seemed strangely sure of her course, as if she had brooded on it. Jane chided herself: she could not know the feelings of others.

They turned off the road before they reached Bath, and headed off along an overgrown track that had once been a B road. Bath had something of a bad name these days, although Jane had been in many places, in her youth, whose negative reputation turned out to be based on racism or simple lack of communication. But Bath was certainly cut off from the outside world, with no radio or net links to speak of, and a wall of rubble that had no gates. Jane was sure that there were ordinary people getting by in there, but whatever system they lived under or suffered through or just ignored, it was one that had decided to isolate itself.

The fields were rough and beautiful in the gold of the low sun, masses of what had once been crops, long ago, overgrown and full of wildlife. The sky filled with crows disturbed by the noise as they passed beneath overhanging trees festooned with nests. Birds still migrated to other places in the world. That thought had always made Jane wonder. Once, a partridge, followed by four of her brood, sprinted across the road in front of them. Jane felt the desolation start to prey on her, the weird feeling of emptiness the open spaces gave you, the knowledge that if you got out here, you might walk for days without seeing another soul. Hopefully.

Eventually, the surface of the road crumbled, then vanished into a muddy track. The trees hung in closer, the vibrations of the armoured car causing masses of golden leaves to come swirling down around them in the dark passage, illuminated by sudden bursts of sunlight through the branches above. Jane sighed with small pleasure at the lonely sight. The beauty of the outback. She reached out from her window and snatched a beech leaf from the air. Her father had always told her it was lucky if you got a leaf before it hit the ground.

After another mile or so, the vegetation became too solid, the grip of the tyres faltering and slipping as weeds snagged the axles. The militiamen unpacked bottles from the rear of the vehicle and sprayed weedkillers ahead. Then they marched forward with scythes, sweeping aside the swiftly blackening and crumbling foliage until something like a path was visible again. Matthew unfastened his machine gun and stood up with it, turning slowly, watching for any sudden movement in the lanes around. Jane was suddenly aware that she'd put her hands to her face as the burning smell of decaying vegetation had come to her. She'd been caught up in recall, the memory of bonfires on November the fifth, the smell of the leaves and the tasty, chilly air mixed with chemical fire. She lowered her fingers, bit her lip, and made an apologetic little suck of air between her teeth. A vicar thing, to be lost in the past like that, lost in the patterns of her dreams. She allowed her glance to drift back to Ruth.

Surprisingly, there was some response. The Major met her eyeline, leaned back in her seat and stretched, yawning as she did so. Perhaps this was going to be a break in the wall she'd erected between them since Jane had made her faux pas. 'You're thinking about bonfire night, aren't you?'

'How did you know?'

'A vicar's always remembering something. You get to relive it all. I wouldn't like to have your job. I try and live in the present.'

'We have to remember. The experience of the EM field is so subtle that recording equipment won't do. It registers in dreams more than in waking consciousness, so we need to remember those especially, because the information in them is so important that—'

'I didn't ask for a lecture, Reverend.'

She'd thought better of it. She was trying hard not to connect, Jane had now decided that her expression then meant, with someone who was not going to be involved in the forthcoming battle. When, as far as Jane knew, there was to be no battle. Ruth probably hadn't even imagined that Jane had seen that look before, in the face of her father before a battle in the second civil war. He hadn't wanted to talk to her, not wanting to recognise within himself the fear of never talking to her again. If Ruth had known Jane well, then she would have been flattered. But with strangers like the two of them, this irritated tension could only mean one thing.

Which was why she had asked her question at that moment. 'Is there something concerning the nature of this mission that I haven't been told about?'

'No,' Ruth had said straight away. 'Of course not.'

But she was already looking back at the soldiers.

Jane had been silent for the rest of the afternoon as they continued on their way, toying with her leaf.

Now she put her hand on to the leaf again. It was sitting atop her bedside table, its cells dying as it dried out, slowly losing the cellular memory of once having been part of a tree.

She'd replayed that whole sequence of memories twice now, and both times Ruth's words had leapt out of it, pinching at Jane's paranoia.

She wished she could be certain about the reasons why they were here. Why the Campbells, or perhaps just Georgina Campbell, wanted this house, so far from their lands, to be surveyed and blessed. It would take a standing army to secure it, that much was obvious. They were hanging out over the precipice just by staying here, in danger from the other families, from bandits, from the loose alliances of the countryside. But nobody was saying that.

She'd prayed for guidance about this matter last night, as best she could. It felt like shouting from the edge of a cliff. She'd got that dream of her father, shouting a warning she couldn't hear and couldn't decipher.

Jane adjusted her dog collar, smoothed out her black robes, and headed for the door. She'd be happy if it weren't for her brain. She'd like to be happy again, and find God again, and not worry. 'I could stand in a nutshell and hold myself king of infinite space,' she told the room before she closed the door on it. 'But that I have bad dreams.'

Two: The True Adventures of Booth Hawtrey

Several hundred miles away from Jane, under her bed in her bedroom in the city of Charlton lay the well-known writer Rebecca Champhert. She held her phone just above her eyes, the screen adjusted to a far-distant focus, and she was trying to type quietly with one hand.

It wasn't really necessary to be all that quiet, because the springs of the mattress above her were straining and relaxing with such speed that the noise was making her head ache. But she knew the nature of one of the individuals in the bed, and it would be just like him to suddenly stop and make a joke or ask an odd question or mention the weather.

It wasn't that she had first-hand experience of that individual's sexual mores. Just lots and lots of second-hand experiences like this.

The bastard.

She'd already noted for her ongoing biographical journal the basics of this encounter. Booth Hawtrey notices a serving maid at the ball, Booth Hawtrey starts talking to her. Rebecca, knowing what's coming, decides to have an early night. Booth Hawtrey, not knowing where his assigned biographer has gone (or not caring), and (famously) not having a bedroom of his own in the family manor, brings said serving maid back to Rebecca's room. Rebecca, on hearing the door kicked open by Booth Hawtrey (carrying serving maid), rolls calmly under bed and catches up with her biographical notes during coitus.

That was how her world tonight had come to be defined by a narrow band of ornate plasterwork, the bottoms of plush curtains, a chamber pot and the odd brass fitting, the pulsating bed above her, and the purple screen of the phone stretching off into a purely imagined distance.

She had suppressed a sigh, and made careful note when she

had heard Booth, through the mattress, promising this poor girl a permanent position in the household. As if he needed to do that, being the most famous person in the world. Rebecca's chapters of Booth's biography were going to be a fair and balanced account of him. That would obviously leave him looking pretty terrible, and the family would doubtless edit out all the damning details, but what did they expect? They had forced her into this job, after all. Forced her to take the silver ring that had become the symbol of Booth's travelling companions, passed on from one biographer to the next, sealed to her ring finger by the court smith so that only he could remove it. It had come down to either this, she suspected, or banishment. The choice had been put to her by Ben Hawtrey shortly after she had split up with David, though Ben had never been crude enough to put it in those terms. He had just strongly suggested that Booth might provide useful protection for her in a charged atmosphere. That travelling with him would get her out of court for long periods.

How the mighty had fallen. Her novels sold in the hundreds, for God's sake, and she had made *one* mistake, and had left one boyfriend.

The way of the world.

The Hawtreys had obviously wanted her to turn Booth into one of her ethical but complicated heroes, but that wasn't going to happen without her making her journal into an absolute work of fiction. Booth was simply not ethical and was in no way complicated, and since they'd asked her to be his biographer then his biographer she had become, genital warts and all.

To shout a warning about that to the poor girl being buffeted above would be interfering with the life she was recording: she had made a principle of that when she had taken this job three years ago. Booth was like a closed refrigerator to Rebecca. She would not open him up to see if the little light was on. Even if, in literary terms, she was now feeling bloody famished.

He said the warts were a thing of the distant past, before his transformation. She was keeping a page ready for the accounts of those he had infected.

She had finished getting the journal up to date during what passed for foreplay, wondered if she could sleep down here, decided against, and begun to catch up on her e-mail before the pounding began. Booth wouldn't want to pretend to fall asleep beside his latest conquest. He'd want to get back to the ball as soon as possible. After he'd dragged the maid back in that direction, Rebecca would bolt the door, see if she could repair the destroyed lock, chuck the linen in the washing chute, unpack her sleeping bag and go to sleep in it. She would be nowhere near as comfortable as she'd planned to be, on this, her first night back in court in six months. They had arrived back from their last trip, a hike through the Lakes, two days ago. She'd been hoping to have at least a fortnight without seeing Booth and especially without seeing his arse.

The bastard.

While they were here, back in the court of Ben Hawtrey, she really ought to petition once again to have herself replaced. Surely he'd have mercy on her after three years of disgrace? But Booth would ask for her to be retained, she knew from prior experience. He liked her.

The bastard.

She had an e-mail from David. She closed her eyes for a moment, suddenly making a nasty mental connection between her ex and the cries coming from above. She'd read somewhere that whenever a random memory drifted into your head it was your brain asking if you wanted to keep it. If you ignored the memory, then it was dispatched into the big black pit of forgetfulness at the centre of your brain, unless you were one of the clergy. Or Booth. If you dwelt on it, you kept it.

Rebecca felt that, having dwelt so much, she could probably enter the priesthood tomorrow.

Relationships were sort of like reincarnation. Each one made you better for the next, more yourself.

If only there had been a next.

David was like the callus she had on her thumb, caused by worrying and worrying at it. It was now made up of lots of layers of bruised flesh, and every time she tried to let it heal, the next layer down would start bleeding again.

The trouble . . . one of the many troubles . . . with following Booth around was that she never got involved with men. They always assumed that she was one of Booth's harem. And for some reason they were happy with that. And by the time she'd established that she was single and a person in her own right, and famous, he had dragged her off somewhere else, to visit another historic site and photograph it.

The only good part of this mobile existence had been that it put some distance between her and David. No roots, no baggage, getting on with it.

She'd first e-mailed him, post-separation, on her first night on the road. She'd just about managed not to ask him back, but not by much. She'd said how she still cared deeply for him, how that, now she was out in the wilds, she'd started to appreciate that their life together hadn't been suffocating, but comfortable. She'd said that she'd see him again when she came back south, that they'd see what happened.

As time went on, she'd recovered a bit, found that she really had been right to leave, got used to being single again. So her e-mails to David had become more conventionally friendly, more distant. And while his to her had kept on being intense and close, they'd never made her want to stop being in touch with him. Good of him to give her that lifeline, not to vanish and get himself healed in darkness. The noises above had reminded her that he was still her last lover.

She ought to get herself down to the ball again. It was actually cowardice, not wanting to be judged and either accepted or not by the family, that had made her retire early, that had made her avoid the court for those two days. She really should get drunk again, throw herself at some young soldier. They all wanted her, just to be associated with Booth.

That was probably why she'd never done that.

She opened the e-mail, and smiled at David's choice of words. His tone of voice that was quietly wry and tired and entertained at the same time. He was going through it too, he said. He and his unit were somewhere deep inside another family's territory, he couldn't say where in case the e-mail was intercepted, and were bunked in some godforsaken little village. Rebecca had been relieved, and guilty at being relieved, that he wouldn't get near the court in the weeks she hoped to spend here.

Above, the maid loudly pretended to have an orgasm.

A moment later, so did Booth. He liked to give the impression, Rebecca had already intimated in her journal, that for him, coming was an orgasmic experience. Unlike for other men, who put the experience on a par with fishing or target shooting. He shook and shivered and cried out, and looked all distant and lost.

Thanks to his alien physiology, Rebecca had implied to her future readers, Booth Hawtrey was the only man on the planet who could fake it.

There was a sudden crash, and the bed stopped bouncing.

Rebecca stopped typing.

Something random and non-routine had just happened. As it usually did in Booth's company.

The complete bastard.

*

Booth Hawtrey sat bolt upright, his head still woozy from the sex, and tried to focus on the men who had come crashing through the door. He ran a hand through his golden curls. The maid had screamed and dived under the covers, hiding her face.

'And you would be—?' he asked the men.

They laughed merrily at him, and one of them slipped his big grey greatcoat off his shoulders and handed it to him. 'Christopher, sir. In the service of Ben Hawtrey, personal guard. Sorry to disturb you, but several people saw you duck in here and we've been told to—'

'I see, Christopher, yes.' Booth took the coat, biting his lower lip, still trying to place himself. He forgot so many people's names at this point. And they never believed that it was the sex that did that, he'd just remembered that bit. And for some reason it was good to forget. Why? Was there something awful in his past that he was hiding from? No, that was a familiar question as well, and he was sure the answer was no. 'Why are you handing me your coat?' he asked the young man.

'Because your presence is requested urgently, sir. By Ben Hawtrey.'

'Well, perhaps if you could give me a few minutes to . . .' He flashed a grin at the soldier and slipped the coat on.

The soldier grinned back, but shook his head. 'No, sir, I was told right now.'

'But I'm not Ben Hawtrey's servant to order from place to place!' He tried to focus on the man's face again. 'Am I?'

The soldiers laughed once more. 'No, sir,' said Christopher. 'You're the one and only Booth Hawtrey, the Aurigan Ambassador, and a law unto yourself, but I, to my occasional regret, am such a servant, and I decline to brave old Ben's anger.'

A low wail came from under the covers. Booth suddenly realised that the girl desperately didn't want the men to see her face. And that the men, pleased by her discomfort, wanted to.

He leapt to his feet, and, bouncing on the mattress on the balls of his feet, shed the coat. The soldiers roared with approval at his nakedness. Everything he did seemed to please them. It always did, a part of him was already saying. He'd remember everything in a moment, and meanwhile he could entertain. He shook his hips to waggle his dick. They roared.

He bounced off the bed and headed for the door, ignoring his scattered clothes. 'Now then, let's go and see this person you say I have to see . . .'

'But, sir, you're naked!' Christopher and the other soldiers looked after him, concerned.

'So we'll find something on the way.' Booth blinked, and realised the full complexity of who he was, and straightened up a little. It was like waking after drinking, the few moments of bliss before the realisation. Lots of memories. All of them. The moment when they came back into full effect. He loved those moments of babylike, post-coital freedom, so full of excitement and potential. Always a shame to get back to just the same old him. Always horrifying to go through that moment of remembering. At least his autopilot had distracted the soldiers from trying to identify the girl for their sport.

'All come back, has it?' asked Christopher.

They knew everything about him, of course. It was all written down and broadcast, his every tic.

He nodded sadly and seriously at the soldiers for a moment, then whispered: 'Chase me.'

And, still naked, he sprinted out of the room.

With a collective cry of shock, they set off after him.

Rebecca waited until the maid emerged from the covers, then she slid out from under the bed like she'd been checking the axles.

'Name?' she asked, her hands poised over her keypad.

The girl shrieked and buried her head again.

'It's all right. This is my room. And I have no intention of letting your reputation slip. Except I think you should stay under there for a moment, because if they sent that lot for him they'll have sent someone looking for me as well, and—'

This time, they knocked at the door.

The maid sank back under the covers.

Rebecca hopped to her feet, and went to the wardrobe. 'I'll catch up with you at some point,' she told the maid. 'I'd appreciate it if you could give me a brief account of the sex. Just for the record. And if anything . . . nasty results . . . do let me know.'

Another whimper.

Rebecca smiled and yelled towards the door, 'Coming!'

Booth scampered down the hallway, making servants yell and point and call out after him. Some of the calls were joking ones, some scandalised, but a few were just oh God, same old Booth, stop being so tiresome. This lot knew him too well for this stuff.

Which was probably why he was doing it. He hated being summoned to Ben's presence, as well. As if he wasn't vastly senior to the old man.

He knew the building well, so his pursuers had a job on their hands. He'd played with his great-great-nephews in these corridors, shortly after the Hawtreys had demolished the walls between the buildings and turned the square into one of the earliest manors. Some of the stains on the bronze wallpaper were his fault. He'd plastered the roof on this section into those ornate swirls when the family were short-handed. He'd taken a Bible and shored it up into a new supporting wall when he was going through one of his religious phases. He remembered every single moment, every physical sensation, every smell of paint and stone and plaster. He knew this building with an intimacy and nostalgia that was almost sexual. At least, would have been sexual for anyone but him, for whom fucking was forgetting, and all the better for it.

He found one of the side stairwells that led upwards and took it, remembering how well he could always hide from the children, how their footsteps would thunder up this musty wooden alcove after him. Their ancestors of nearly eleven generations were in the service of the family now, a thought which sat at the back of Booth's consciousness now and always, too big to ever properly deal with, too big to ever go away.

But the most wonderful thing about Tiggers is: I'm the only one. I'm the only one! He heard his mother saying it, a trace memory that swung in and filled him, complete in every detail, every note.

He burst from the door out into the frosty night. The stairwell had been cold, but this was like diving into a freezing pool. His breath broke from his lungs in a great plume. But this sensation couldn't harm him. It was only the cold. Such pains were distant to him now, familiar experiences filtered from his thoughts like background music. Pain was no surprise any more. He was familiar with every ounce, and the remembrance of pain was pain, every time, so he'd had several lifetimes of it.

He stood for a moment, at the furthermost corner of the guards' walkway, looking out over the rail at the darkness of the ruined city. The dark, slanted bulk of the roof hid the lights of the manor and the landing strip from him. The building turned in on itself, showing no window to the expanse beyond. When it was being built, they said that was in case of missiles, but the emotional truth of it was that the family inside the manor didn't want to admit that the city existed.

They were on a hill here, and Booth could see the dim shapes of ruined buildings, housing estates, terraces, offices, down into the distance. The grey expanse of Blackheath showed the occasional pinprick of light, where various farming projects had been set up. The roads from the manor to the heath were full of traffic on a morning, but almost everything got pulled in at night, and the automated defences left to themselves. There were a few allotment holders who insisted on living out there and good luck to them. Booth's eyes unconsciously compared the sweep of lights to that of the last time he'd seen this view. Two missing, one new. Never a whole new spread of them. Never a blooming-out. Somewhere in that massed darkness was the ancient family home at Chiswick, not that anyone spoke of it now. It had been abandoned in haste when his father died, part of the running away that seemed like it had never stopped. This hiding from what was in the dark made Booth angry, though it was so much a part of the culture now. He was angry inside almost all the time. His own journeys, he had thought, should make people want to go out and embrace the world again, take it all back.

But they seemed just content to let him do it.

They were kicked animals. Push too far and everything falls apart and people die for want of food. The thing they feared in all those empty buildings was the dead, the creeping ecosystems of plants and birds and rodents and bodies. Even now, they were living amongst the grave buildings rather than bringing them down. They ought to have had a great fire, driven the ghosts before them shouting, brought bulldozers and had a priest declare the whole lot buried, over and done with.

He had had those thoughts when he slammed the door closed on his father's house.

But he was from another time, an easier way of thought.

He was always expecting them to get back to that, he had realised long ago. He was always wondering why it was taking so long. He was getting his first, tiny glimpse of how deep time worked, at the depth of the well, at how people lived amongst history all the time. And he knew every detail of that history.

He looked up. The stars above were in exactly the same positions, the usual relief of that. Just the ones that faded or grew brighter, caught in this moment of their cycles and compared to all the other moments he'd seen them by his ever-comparing mind: they couldn't quite disturb this fond moment of stillness. He wondered if eventually he would see that the stars had moved. Even the moon had the new crater. Well, new to him. Only the oldest people he met called it that. To most of them it was just Hawtrey, the sudden plume of white ejecta that had changed the face of his old, unchanging friend one summer seventy years ago.

They hadn't understood why he had protested so much about

them naming it after him. Some of the other houses called it by different names.

He heard noises from the stairs behind him, the distant music of the ball getting momentarily louder as the lower door was opened. He trotted along the walkway to the door at the other end.

He opened it and found another smiling soldier there. For a moment he wanted to tell him to fuck off and close the door in his face. But since he was naked on a rooftop, that would just make him seem mad and horrid and alien, all those things the texts and phone documentaries about him insisted he wasn't.

So he laughed and raised his arms, looking around at the city for a moment like he was lost. 'It's terribly cold out here, isn't it? Do you think I could borrow your coat?'

Rebecca and Booth, therefore, both arrived in the great hall at virtually the same time. They descended from upper doors down facing sets of steps, in fact. Booth caught Rebecca's glare across the room, and felt his usual mixture of regret and rebellion. She didn't understand, but the thought was always in the back of his head that one day she would. She was just twenty, for God's sake. These days, that was halfway to being a matriarch, but from his point of view she was a child.

She was still in her gown, he noted, only she'd undone a few of the fasteners so it showed off her cleavage. A sudden awkward thought crossed his mind – where had Rebecca got to since he'd got involved with . . . with that serving maid, whose name he hadn't asked for? She hadn't been with some boy, had she, who'd undone those laces for her? She was carrying a bottle of wine, too. Perhaps they'd been sharing it? And while they'd done so, what had she said about her job, about him?

A roar went up from the crowd below when they noticed him on the stairs, and the band momentarily stopped playing. The usher, at his desk in one corner of the hall, stood up and cried out: 'Mr Booth Hawtrey has returned!'

Booth considered throwing open his coat and pissing on them all. But they'd probably just hold out their glasses.

He raised a hand in a quick greeting, and the band struck up again. The dancers returned to filling the floor of the hall with their swirling colours. The men, these days, wore waistcoats of the most fantastic shades, and cut their hair into dramatic sweeps and waves, the more outlandish the better. The women's dresses were great tents of expensive fabric, which they were sewn into to make themselves the most precious, unreachable, untouchable prizes the world had ever seen. They each carried a handful of mass-stamped data disks in their sleeves and would, every now and then, 'accidentally' drop one in front of a likely-looking man. The disks contained a biography, lineage and CV, and often, again 'accidentally', and usually hidden behind a mass of code, photos of the lady in a rather greater state of undress. After the ball, the servants arriving to clean the hall would race to sweep the corners for any of the disks that had gone astray.

The ball was a demonstration of wealth and power, designed to show the country that the House of Hawtrey was big and strong and glamorous.

In comparison to all the other dying candles in the world, that was.

The band was playing 'Stewart's Dash', one of his favourite reels, and he thought for a moment of leaping the banister and joining in, maybe prising one of the richest women away from her husband, get in enough trouble to earn a fight or a duel or be just thrown out into the wilderness again.

But then he saw Ben Hawtrey, staring up at him from high table at the opposite end of the room from the band. That rattish little face was fixed on him, on the coat and bare feet.

Booth decided that he'd already been as improper as his image demanded. He surrendered to the pressure of the soldiers at his back, and headed down the stairs.

High table was on a stepped rise at the north end of the great hall, on an eyeline above the other tables, and right under the geodesic sky-lights in the vaulted ceiling. Rebecca had sat down by the time Booth got there, and was talking with Ben. They looked like they were speaking urgently about something. Ben was shaking his head. Was she asking for his permission to dance with someone? Perhaps that little shit Andrew, who was hovering a few feet away, his fingers playing with a favour in his waistcoat pocket, his eyes on Rebecca's breasts?

As Booth approached, they stopped talking and looked up at him. Rebecca looked dissatisfied as always. Good, the old sod had refused her.

Booth sat down and the soldiers departed. The only other person at the table was Franklin, Ben's bodyguard. The other chairs were propped aside where Justine and Kate and August and Justine's husband, Miles, were off dancing. Even the chaplain, the Reverend Jacob Anderson, was dancing.

Booth had never seen Ben dance. 'So,' he began, 'you suddenly wanted to see me again.'

'This ball was in honour of your return,' Ben hissed. 'You could have stayed for longer than an hour.'

'I always intended to return. I was catching up with some old friends.' He noticed Rebecca's smirk and crossed his legs. 'I wouldn't dream of mocking this most high and glorious honour, dear child.'

Ben glared at him further. The head of the Hawtrey family, Booth knew, hated being reminded that the man he regarded as a rebellious teenager had assisted with his birth. It had taken years of separation, as Booth toured the world, for Ben to adjust from seeing him as a parental figure to seeing him as a child. On that basis, Booth thought, perhaps his extended tours were necessary, to let people accommodate him in their thoughts. He could be father to the man and child to him, but if he'd stayed around, those functions would have become all tangled up, and everybody would see him as a terrible aberration, and they might try and hang him or burn him.

Or something. Ben had grown the most ridiculous beard, as soon as he could manage it.

'And the names of those old friends?' Rebecca had slipped her phone from her sleeve.

'I forget.'

'That is the one thing you don't do.'

'And what were you up to?'

'Oh, I got my head down.'

Their gaze held each other for a moment.

'Well, I didn't call you back down here simply for ceremony's sake,' said Ben, finally. 'We got a call from Greenwich.'

'Oh bollocks,' said Rebecca.

Booth too felt his heart sink. On Greenwich Hill, a few miles away, the Hawtreys, in the buildings of the ancient Royal Observatory, had built a radio telescope, entirely to receive messages concerning him. Messages, or rather, instructions.

'Your masters from Auriga want you elsewhere, extremely quickly.' Booth was certain that he could see suppressed delight in Ben's features. 'This was outside the normal transmission time, so they must think it very urgent. They probably want some more photos of pigeons.'

Pigeons. That was a famously meaningless mission that Booth had been sent on, amongst the lofts of buildings in Edinburgh, to record visual images of native British birds, with special emphasis on pigeons. Going there had been the most hazardous journey Booth had ever experienced.

Many theses, debates and works of fiction had been written concerning the manifestly eccentric desires of the Aurigans. Some people still thought that every assignment Booth was sent on was meaningful, that they were working towards some masterplan. Those sorts of people dutifully recorded every destination from the Hawtrey website. Some, if they lived close by, even came along to find him, interview him, check that he was doing just what he said he was. The families and the courts of Britain had rather grown up around his activities. The civil wars and house wars limited him, of course, but gradually a diplomatic agreement had been reached concerning his wanderings. A single person, detached and harmless and ridiculous as Booth was, was often of assistance when there was no other means to send a message, or take an item across a border. Apart from a few unfortunate incidents of imprisonment, ransom and torture, Booth these days was largely allowed to get on with it.

'So . . .' Booth arched his arms above his head in a big stretch. 'Pigeons it is.' The Aurigans had offered, and to some degree provided, the House of Hawtrey with significant technological knowledge in return for Booth's continuing services. The details didn't quite make up for the expense of his keep, Booth knew, the most recent acquisitions being a series of notes on how to make solar power systems more efficient, but put that together with the diplomatic and social clout of having the planet's most famous inhabitant on your side and . . . well, he supposed the books just about balanced. He didn't really care, actually.

There was a sudden shout from the dance floor and applause. Two boys in crimson waistcoats, cadets, had reached for the same disk at once, and had swiftly drawn long thin blades from their waistcoats. A space formed around them, and the crowd began to clap rhythmically as they circled each other.

'So where—' Booth began.

Ben held up a hand. 'Wait, I want to watch this.'

Rebecca was already looking eagerly towards the contest. The way she seemed to accept these horrors always irritated Booth. A child of her age. And being in his company hadn't changed her a jot. The band had stopped and were craning forward also, in the cartoon poses they always adopted for a situation like this.

Booth let his arms fall to his sides and slumped, waiting for it to end.

One of the young men lunged. The other brushed his dagger aside with a padded forearm, and swept his own straight into the first man's stomach. He twisted suddenly and violently and stepped back.

Clearly trying to control his emotions, trying not to scream as he died, the victim fell to his knees, then on to his face. A bloom of blood spread across the dance floor and servants rushed in to carry off the body and mop up. The killer, smiling, wiped his dagger across his white cuff, displaying the blood. The lady who'd been the subject of the duel looked on, pleased.

Ben chuckled. 'Young Andrew. He'll go far. And they were of the same school, so we have a good duel and no hard feelings. Excellent.'

'I have got to get some of those disks made,' said Rebecca.

Booth looked at his watch. 'If I may continue? Where are we going?'

Ben became businesslike again. 'South Wiltshire.'

'Oh. Trowbridge?'

'Further south.'

'Shit. That is the middle of nowhere. What do they want me to do?'

Ben took a folder from the basket on his desk and slid it across to Booth. 'They quoted a map reference. We found the place. They want you to explore an old house. It's probably a bit of a wreck. No plumbing, no heating, no roof . . .'

Booth heard Rebecca's forehead hit the table. He didn't look. 'Why the hurry?'

'Why the pigeons? They want you down there by Wednesday.'

'Forty-eight hours.' Booth took the folder, and glanced at the maps. Then he grinned. 'Good. I was getting cooped up here.'

Rebecca threw back her wine, smiled brilliantly at Ben, then leapt up and marched off purposefully towards the dance floor.

'Didn't even curtsey,' muttered the patriarch. 'Why I let you persuade me not to exile her . . .'

'Time of the month,' said Booth Hawtrey.

Rebecca lay with her eyes closed in the passenger seat as Booth's Bentley Electric shot along the road towards Blackheath. She had a sickly hangover and the autumn sun was far too bright, even through the antique car's polarised windshield. The upholstery was a comfort though, and she had tried to sink as far into it as possible, resenting, as she did so, the fact that the straight road gave Booth just about time to accelerate to full speed before he had to begin decelerating again. If they were to reach the airstrip intact, that was. The allotments and market gardens swept by on both sides, steam carts moving to the side of the road to let them speed past. Rebecca could hear the hails of their drivers dopplering in front of and then behind them.

The car was soft and red inside, and a gentle racing green outside. It purred softly. The only problems were that it could reach such speeds and that it belonged to Booth Hawtrey. He'd been given it as a present by the Winchester Chamber of Commerce, who'd plainly had no use for it and could find nobody rich enough to buy it. Since then, the Aurigans had (for some reason) taken an interest, and suggested various modifications. Rebecca supposed they thought this vehicle would enable Booth to carry out his duties more quickly.

She had indeed thrown herself into the ball last night, and, having mentioned Booth's name to the usher, had got on to five different dance lists immediately. But there had been something awkward or annoying about every partner, notably that many of them still seemed to remember that there was something not quite right about her, even if they couldn't recall exactly what. And she had got young Andrew, the killer of his cousin, who at least just knew that she was famous, but only wanted to talk about how good he'd been in the fight, and she'd felt Vanessa Crayford's eyes boring into her back every second. Vanessa was dancing absently with her own list, waiting until she and Andrew were both free, and she could properly engage with the man who'd blooded himself for her. A couple of the men had been interested in Rebecca, she was sure, but she hadn't put down enough wine quickly enough, and by the time the lists were completed and the dances were done and they'd switched on the EM compiler, she was sitting at a table, dehydrated, feeling the elation and lust and wonder that came from the box wash over her like drizzle. A few desperate leftovers had wandered over as the dancers paired off and discreetly made their goodbyes, and she remembered getting angry, shouting something about her reputation, asking if she was still taboo, breaking a bottle.

She was becoming an outsider at the court now, as much as Booth was, only not loved as he was. It was almost as if she *had* been exiled. At least she'd woken up in her own bed. At least they still assigned her one.

'Feeling a bit under the weather?' Booth asked as he narrowly missed another steam cart. Even so, the owner called happily after him.

'Piss off.'

'You ought to drink plenty of water at the end of the night. Did you stay for the end of the ball?'

'I remember only joy. Did you find somewhere warm and comfy?'

Booth guffawed.

*

Booth had promised Ben that he would go and sign himself up for a few dances, and had indeed gone to talk to the usher. But he'd used his advice to find the maid he'd encountered previously. Her name, he'd discovered, was Alice Dean, and she worked under Mr Aziz the butler. So Booth had made his way through the dancers, ignoring the calls and gasps and grasping hands and the total disruption of the list system his presence caused, and found the servants' door, and gone downstairs into the kitchens. He'd been relieved that nobody had followed. Only he had the licence for this. He'd found Mr Aziz as he was yelling at Alice in the centre of a circle of servants, gathered by the big table which had his initials on the underside, carved seventy years ago. Her gaze had risen to meet his, and she'd started to shake her head, but then everyone had seen him and the circle collapsed into a mass of curtseys and bows. He'd stepped forward, being utterly pompous and offensive, and said that he'd come back for the maid he'd been assigned. Yes, that one there. Why had she stopped waiting on him hand and foot? And they all knew what the real situation was, and they all smiled at him when their eyes were away from Mr Aziz, and the butler himself had coughed and raised an eyebrow, and said that, of course, he would release Alice to Booth for the rest of the night.

And Alice had grinned broadly at him, her reputation and job preserved at once. She had taken him back to her cold and tiny bedroom, and they had made love again, and in the morning, though she hadn't asked and they'd talked only of history and memory, he had gone to Mr Aziz with a glowing reference concerning her intelligence and wisdom.

Mr Aziz had promised Booth that Alice would get a contract and a position in the office, and cease being a maid at midnight.

Of course, he remembered every detail. And that the sex had allowed him to forget.

Booth would have to take care not to meet her the next time he was back, because she would have to start thinking about a husband now.

They swung through the gates of the airstrip, which had been cranked open ready as they approached. Their dirigible was waiting. Servants stood about, an under-butler ready to take the car back to the manor.

Booth let the car trundle to a halt, and turned to his passenger. 'I am a leaf in the wind,' he said to her. 'And I fall where I will.'

She glared at him with her eyes closed.

Three: Rebecca's Twentieth Birthday

David sat on the edge of the bed, his dress uniform half unbuttoned, staring down at her. His eyes looked beautiful beneath his fringe of straw hair. Beautiful and terribly scared.

Rebecca Champhert wished she could have done this on some occasion other than her birthday. A new reason why the date would be scarred for her. When every now and then she thought she had managed to put the last scarring behind her. That was horribly cyclic. Very her. She was doing this today because what would be the point of waiting one more day and doing it tomorrow? She wished she could have done it around four in the afternoon, when whatever was inside her head made her feel that people's emotions were just clouds that cast shadows on the ground.

But no, that was her being writerly. She could never have told David that she was leaving him without it being horribly painful. For both of them.

She was kneeling heavily between his legs, one arm on each thigh, the absolute picture of bad timing. She'd been about to unbutton his britches and take his cock in her mouth as she'd always liked to do.

But the thoughts that had been in her mind for weeks now had finally caught up with her, at this exactly awkward point, and had made her stop, just as her hands were at the first button, withdraw them slowly and carefully and look up at him.

He'd known as their eyes met then. So she'd lowered her head again and just looked at the ground, letting the familiar shape of his legs hold her up, formulating the words.

'I can't go on . . .' she'd said. 'You and I . . . Can't go on.'

And that was where they'd left it for a minute now, him just staring, not saying anything, as if his words would start time again and he wanted it to stop right there.

She looked up. 'Well?'

'Why?'

'We're not right for each other.'

'Yes we are!' He sounded taken aback, like he'd never thought of this before, bitterly angry.

Rebecca got to her feet, smoothing down her scarlet ballgown, and made her way to the window. The party was still going on outside, their friends dancing in squares, warmed by the bonfire, music from the small band she had hired wafting its way through the night. Who would have thought that, just two years later, everything would be forgiven and forgotten? At last she'd become the person the family wanted her to be.

Until now. She wondered how they would react to the ending of her and David.

No. It didn't matter what they felt.

It was typical of her to choose a celebration for something like this. The memory that she'd made such a mistake would be pinned alongside that tune now. But maybe that was another good reason for choosing her birthday. She only had one day of the year that was permanently fucked. David was a captain in the Hawtrey militia, they'd been around and about each other from before her wanderings in the outback, and he would be around and about still.

'Is there someone else?' he asked, on the verge of bellowing, getting up to join her to look down on all his potential rivals. 'I'll take him on.'

'There is no one else.' There were, actually, a great number of potential new suitors for Rebecca, if no one special. It was that she had started noticing them, started thinking about them. That had concerned her, that had made her start seeking out the frailties in David's cocksure disposition. She had started to compare him. And in even doing that, keeping that secret from him, she'd swiftly realised the two of them were lost.

They had never had sex, of course.

Now they never would.

He grabbed her suddenly, roughly, by the shoulders. 'I don't believe you! We have *history*, Rebecca!'

She couldn't be afraid of him. Only sorry. 'I just . . . need to go on. Need to get out there . . .'

'You've *been* out there. If it wasn't for me you'd *still* be out there! I haven't stopped you—'

'No. But I need to get out there . . . In my head. I need to be free.'

'Free? Free of what? Free of the court? The family? What's Ben going to say when he hears of this?' There was a threat implicit in his words. *You're going to lose everything I've worked so hard to give you.*

'Not free of all that. How can anyone be free of that?' Would that it were possible, she thought secretly. For any of them in this world, anywhere. She put a gentle hand to his face. 'David. I need . . . something more.' For a moment she thought he was going to hit her or try and kiss her or try and force her to have sex with him, but she still couldn't be frightened of him. That look behind his eyes was too small, too limited. 'Let's talk about this. Let me tell you how I feel.'

He let go of her, his gaze still examining her, but now as if she was something terrible, something he shrank from. He took a step back. 'No,' he said. 'You used me. You used me to get to where you wanted to be. This is the worst thing you could ever have done to me. The worst possible thing.'

He grabbed her finger suddenly. He found the engagement ring, wrenched it off her, nearly pulling the bone from its joint. His fist clenched around it.

Then he turned around and headed for the door, swiftly buttoning up his jacket. The ring went into his pocket.

She started to cry, feeling the harsh pain in her finger. There was an abrasion where the ring had been.

'David . . .' she said. But inside she was very glad he was going.

He didn't look at her as he opened the door. He closed it behind him without even slamming it. Immense control. He'd be back at intervals, do his grieving in quick visits over days, she knew. They'd get to say what they had to say.

She could tidy up all the business of their separate lives very quickly. She knew there was only one bagful of his things that she would have to send to the barracks. She had even picked out which bag she was going to give up to that cause.

She looked, giddily, back down to the party, aware that she'd started to cry.

A huge thing, something that had defined her life, done with in moments.

The night was full of bonfire smell and music and the laughing chatter of friends. So inappropriate. Nothing at all like an afternoon.

She went to the bed, sat down, and, unlacing her bodice, started to cry in earnest.

Four: Rebecca's Nineteenth Birthday

David carefully moved from one side of the boat to the other, placing each oar inside the craft.

Rebecca sat watching him, clutching her presents, trying not to move to the left or right for fear that they'd capsize, or that she'd send David toppling into the water. It was late in the year for this, there was such a chill in the air that she'd had to wear her heavy coat. But David was in shirtsleeves, despite the fact that he must have got chilled to the bone too.

He managed to sit down opposite her. 'Go on,' he said. 'Open them.'

Rebecca plucked a tiny pair of scissors from her charm bracelet and began to do so, saving the paper with the flecks of green in it that smelt of pine. They were on the lower Thames, at the edge of Hawtrey country. Indeed, Rebecca knew that further upstream there was a bridge with a sentry post on it and a gate system beneath, a levy and a search demanded of any who wished to pass that far. That was a reassuring thought set against the open river and the slow vulnerability of the boat. The water was full of fish, big ones, leaping for the last insects that dipped back and forth above the surface, anticipating the winter ice. David had made a show before they'd left the boathouse of sweeping the boat for fire ants. She adored these little cares he had, the attention to detail in his love.

They'd talked about marrying early next year. David said that he had to make sure that he was well regarded by Ben Hawtrey to be given leave to marry such a well-known figure as Rebecca.

That was him being sweet. More like leave for a promising officer to marry someone whose fame just about balanced the bad smell that still hung about her when she moved in certain circles. The family were proud of her, yes, but even with all the work she'd put in this year, all the being quiet on David's arm at all the right parties, all the sucking up, they still didn't think she was quite the thing.

Perhaps they never would. The way of the world. Fuck them. She had David.

She folded back the paper and found what David had given her: a small box. Inside the box was a golden ring, remelted and inscribed with the Hawtrey crest by their smith.

She looked up at him: 'So—'

He raised himself on to one knee, careful because of the violent rocking of the boat, and said: 'Rebecca Champhert, will you marry me?'

Five: All Tomorrow's Truth Games

Jane enjoyed walking down the main stairs of the great house. They were made of cracked marble, stained with age, with dangerous-looking ornamentations still just about balancing on pillars at the top of the rail. The rail itself was polished lacquer, polished further by thousands of hands, doubtless not those of the servants, who had their own, safer but less formal sets of staircases.

She wanted to wear a big frock and a hairdo and a favour from some captain, and swish down here to make a big entrance at a ball. Maybe when their survey was finished, and the Campbells moved in here, she could do just that.

And of course that was going to happen, of course it was.

Apart from the bit about the captain. Well, maybe there could even be that, if she gave up her calling.

Oh don't be stupid, Jane, what else are you? What else can you do? Just because you and God aren't talking—

That had been Dad's voice.

She stopped for a moment, screwed up her eyes, and shook her head violently.

Her training had made her aware of her internal voices in ways that most people never considered. Reformed Church of England vicars weren't encouraged to characterise these voices, to assign them individual personalities, because that way lay schizophrenia, and they'd lost a few like that. But, as Jane knew from her conversations with other clerics, it was only human nature to do just that. She herself had the Narrator, who selected a single apt phrase, the sort of thing that gets used as internal monologue in novels, and chewed it over many times, usually during repetitive tasks. 'Frustration and doubt have put weight under my eyes and changed my nature,' the Narrator had said throughout her shower that morning. Said it so hard that Jane had nearly felt obliged to write it down. But definitions of self like that just limit you. Why would you need definitions when God's looking at you, telling you who you are? That had been like a continual nice compliment, when it was being said to her. The sort of memory you replay for days. She missed it.

And another of Jane's voices, the one she'd just heard, was that of her dad, a practical guide that would pop up and say: now you must put a bracket under that shelf to hold it up. Dad had read her a lot of James Bond when she was a kid. The only books he had, ragged paperbacks, the only books she'd seen until she'd been given a passkey for the Campbell library. He'd never let her read them herself, just read her selected passages, obviously and dearly sparing her from sex and violence. So the voice of practicality for Jane, the one that had yelled at her to duck and cover when she was running from an unexploded bomb that had fallen out of a wall, was thus a mixture of Dad and Ian Fleming.

So Dad being struck dumb in her dreams was disturbing. It felt like it must mean something.

The last inner voice was the Lyricist, who played a familiar song in the back of her head. She'd only realise when she had been humming it for a while that the lyrics were often a comment on what she was doing at that point, sometimes a pun.

And right now, Jane realised that she'd sat down on the stairs, her head in her hands. 'You're sitting on the blessed stairs!' she said out loud. 'Get a grip, Jane! Don't you want any breakfast?'

Maybe if her own head would just shut up and let her listen more to other people, she wouldn't fret so much. Maybe then she wouldn't worry, and God could just breeze back in.

She got to her feet and followed the smell of baking bread to the kitchen.

The surface of the kitchen table was huge and round and made of angular blocks of beechwood that slotted together in a rosette. Lutyens again, according to the lengthy information about Heartsease that had been provided in the briefing. In the 1980s the table had been loaned to a museum in London, and, being kept in the warm lights of a public exhibition, had warped. At some point, therefore, thin wedges of wood had been inserted between the blocks to maintain an even surface. The effect was oddly charming. The table was just about getting by, like the kitchen and the world. It sat at the centre of a symmetrical chamber, under a turretlike lantern of windows high in the ceiling, the only natural illumination in the room. With the dustiness of those windows, and the gentle glow of the electric lamps, there was still something pleasantly womblike and domestic about the place. Three vast sinks stood side by side along one wall, with a huge black block marked by the impact of knives down the decades, and a single, huge pestle and mortar. It all looked too big for a normal person, and Jane found that the singing part of her mind was mulling over a nursery rhyme: fe fi fo fum. This was the kitchen of the giant.

An unsealed foil bag of bread was steaming on the centre of the table, and Eric was handing out plates to the other soldiers from a chest. Each man had a fork of his own and used the blade of his work knife to eat.

A row of vast utensils hung from hooks along the wall above the huge, cold fireplace. Their presence alone suggested to Jane that Heartsease had either been left totally unoccupied for centuries, which would be something of a miracle, or that, until very recently, it had been home to a whole community.

The team had been worrying about that since they got here two days ago. The soldiers were used to encountering decay and destruction and working to clear it. They'd arrived at night. Ruth, when she'd walked through the front door, without the need for the stubby battering ram the men had brought along because the door had been standing open, had sworn at length at the pristine sight of the entrance hall. That had meant drawing the heavy weapons from the armoured car, before the horses could even be stabled, and an immediate search through the rooms to secure a perimeter. Jane had had to wait, trying not to fall asleep, at this very table.

Until they were certain the house was empty, which they now were, the soldiers had maintained a twenty-four-hour watch. Perhaps it was fear of the animals that had kept people away, Jane had suggested, but Eric had laughed at her. Was it the animals that had vacuumed the carpet and dusted the curtains?

The consensus had been, in the end, that there had been a sizeable force of occupation until just recently, and that then they had . . . gone. Down here it would have to be the Mandervilles. And the Mandervilles always set booby traps. So the team were on standing orders not to open anything without running a detector over it, and to wash ahead of them for pressure detonators.

Jane's survey, thankfully, would clear all that up. Booby traps were never set without the soldier setting them leaving a powerful trace of fear and anticipation. Jane would be the only one in danger, and only then if she didn't pay attention to her EM meter or stepped too quickly.

But still, the weight of the empty house lay on them all, some mention of the cleanliness and tidiness of it popping up in every conversation.

Jane remembered the anticipatory laughter from the armoured car when they'd driven through the gates into the gardens of Heartsease, and passed the sign that said 'Safari Park'. The big predators were probably all gone, they'd been told at their briefing. Not enough food to sustain a breeding colony of lions. But this place had also boasted lynx, jackals and, most worryingly, wolves. They'd heard a little of that in Bristol: watch out for the wolves of Heartsease. They'd have to keep the stables secure. A gaggle of ostriches had rushed away from the armoured car as it had come to a halt on the gravel outside the house, but otherwise they'd seen precious little of the wildlife.

Jane took her plate from Eric, and pulled up one of the big wooden chairs.

'Good morning, Padre,' said Matthew. 'Am I right in thinking that you'll be starting the EM survey today?'

'Oh yes.' Jane looked carefully to Ruth. 'The Campbell family will want to sleep soundly in their beds when they get here, without hauntings or awful atmospheres.'

'If I may venture an opinion,' said Eric, who was a tall black youth with a fractal curl on his head, 'this will be an excellent summer house, and provide a most suitable base in the west from which to civilise the area.'

'Eric, you are so full of shit.' Ruth gently tossed a slice of hot bread to him.

The men all gasped in mock horror, glancing between Jane and their commander.

'What were you saying last night? That this place was a fucking Hawtrey pile of shit, and that we ought to leave it for them to find, so they could deal with the wolves and the apes and so on and so on . . .'

Eric put a hand on Jane's shoulder, and whispered gently into her ear: 'I can't think what she's referring to. I would never use language like that.'

Jane turned and took him by the hand, looked him in the eye. 'You don't have to worry about insulting me, Eric, really. I'm afraid I'm simply not free to marry you.'

The other soldiers howled as Eric slapped a hand over his mouth. 'Oh, you wound me, ma'am!' he wailed. 'You have, like, broken my fucking heart!'

'You're not the first, you won't be the last,' Jane vamped.

She reached for another piece of bread, feeling warm inside.

Ruth still had something in her gaze. Something held back. While they could relax for a moment, she would always be on her guard. So, Jane thought, the secret is not shared.

She would not green this in her room later. She simply would not. That would be giving in to her inner life completely.

After breakfast, some of the militiamen declared that they were going ostrich hunting to get some meat for the evening meal. Joe and the second engineer, Morgan, would be resuming their task of the previous day, working in the great switching room beside the boilers, updating the house's antique (but apparently very sturdy) electrical system. Heartsease had its own generator, run by a water-mill in a stream under the house. The stream had got rowdier since the place was built, but the system apparently still ticked over perfectly.

Jane got her meter, salt, Bible, candles, bell and holy water from her room, placed them in her satchel, and made her way to the front door. The traditional place to begin.

The Wiltshire sky was overcast, threatening rain. A bitter wind was cutting down the valley between the forested hills. Jane stood on the doorstep, still inside the long porch with its rough mats, and looked out to the horizon. The gates were on a rise, so the white expanse of the drive seemed to sweep up towards them and then stop at the sky, as if the world ended there. To the left and right were the gentle contours of the hills, the little folly to the south poking out from a gap in the trees. Jane would have to go up there, eventually.

Ruth stood outside the porch, huddled inside her parka. She was there in her official capacity, to welcome Jane into the house as the Campbell chaplain. She couldn't do a thing until Jane said the words. A wicked thought made Jane step slowly out of the house, shivering in her robes, and turn to look minutely up at the façade of the house, the wall of granite brickwork with the lion rampant over the door.

Edwin Lutyens, the great twentieth-century English architect, had designed this house, to the specifications of Simon Trent, a textile millionaire and the first person to live here. Where Jane stood, to the west, at the front of the elongated entrance hall, was the tip of a blunt arrow, two wings stretching back to the south and the north-east. The north-east wing was a grand piece of architectural tomfoolery, with battlements and the crosses of arrow slits and a great blank face of weatherbeaten granite on the north wall. There were only a few, austere windows here. The ground floor of that wing contained the kitchen and scullery, shielded by a curtain wall, and the upper floor the bedrooms. There were crenellations, but absolutely no guttering of any kind. The south wing, though, was smooth and refined, a modernist pun on Tudor architecture in fact, with a gentile simplicity to its flat roof. Still a castle, but a castle with a swimming pool on top. This wing was adorned with mullioned and transomed windows, illuminating the dark spaces of the family living rooms within. The two faces of the house merged so neatly that it took you a while to notice that there was any difference between them. This despite the fact that the sweep of the weather in this wooded valley had turned the north end black and left the south end white. The subtlety of the blend was probably down to the entrance tower that stood in front of Jane. Twin octagonal towers with a once-white flagpole between them stood over the mock gatehouse, that even featured, right above where Jane stood, the teeth of a wooden portcullis. According to their briefing, it was actually a real one. Jane wondered about decades of rot and how thick the supporting ropes were. Or perhaps, like everything else, they were as perfect as the day they had been fitted. At least the outside of the house seemed to be subject to the forces of nature.

Big drips started to pelt down off the face of the gatehouse. The wall was battered: inclined both at the base and at a level above the ground floor, giving any lonely traveller who arrived here a sense of looking up at a much taller, much more imposing barrier. Jane found that the first blustery strains of *The Funeral of Siegfried* were playing in the back of her mind.

She spent another delicious moment readying herself, then turned to meet that look in Ruth's eye.

'As house chaplain of the Campbell family, I am about to survey and bless this house for their future use, to make sure that it contains nothing that will disturb their minds, their souls or their dreams.'

'I'm aware of your work, house chaplain, go about it,' the young woman snapped. She spun on her heel and walked away, heading for the stables where she was now obliged to shelter with the horses. No one could set foot in the building now that Jane's survey had begun.

Jane smiled to herself, checked her equipment, and stepped into the porch out of the rain.

*

Video footage from 2013, Bishop Michael Swansley's address to the General Synod in Canterbury:

Swansley is tall and thin, with sunken cheeks, a receding hairline and a rather sensual mouth that constantly splits open to grin with big teeth. He grins at inappropriate moments, probably out of nervousness. He stands behind a simple wooden lectern bearing a cross, and glances down at his notes often in the early stages of his address. As he gets into it, though, he becomes more assertive. We know from his biography that he became certain of the truth of some of these ideas only as he spoke.

'Many of you will already have met Professor John Ruehl and his colleagues from Keble, who I've brought along to the Synod today.' (Murmurings of unrest already. Swansley looks up.) 'I felt they simply had to be here. The more I've explored his work, the more I'm convinced. Professor Ruehl's work with the human temporal lobes clearly indicates that the religious impulse within mankind is a reaction to . . . no, let me go farther, simply *is* what occurs when this part of the brain is stimulated by a strong electromagnetic field.' (He has to speak up now, to make his voice heard above the shifting of chairs, and the occasional shout from the room. You can clearly hear Bishop Moloki's cry of 'Blasphemy!') 'I believe that Professor Ruehl has discovered God's chosen means of communication with mankind, the medium He has used throughout history to speak to us. At this moment, when the most profound emotion amongst the population of the developed world is worry, even fear for the future, this gives us . . . this gives us a direct insight into— Yes, what about faith?' (He breaks off from his text to address a call from the crowd.) 'We're not talking about simple messages, but the kind of numinous experience familiar to us all from the Bible and the lives of the saints. My friends, this is not the end of faith, it's the start of it.'

Jane stood inside the porch of the great house, and took the salt cellar from her satchel. She sprinkled a line of the stuff across the threshold behind her. Then she took the EM meter out, connected it to her phone, and made her first official reading in this building.

Background standard. Just under one milligauss. Right on the same line as in her bedroom. Absolutely no deviation from the average magnetic field generated by planet Earth.

For one room, her own room, that was just a bit eccentric. For two, it was starting to look extraordinary. She ran a quick diagnostic from her phone. Like she'd confirmed last night, everything was apparently working fine.

The thing was, she'd had that dream of her dad in a room that was supposed to be background standard, and that had felt like it had come from the field, even if the meter and her drugs had told her the opposite.

How odd.

She recorded the level of the EM field, and used the automapping device on her phone to confirm the shape of the porch. The outline of the rectangular building with its arched roof glowed green over the grey map of the rest of the building, with a zero for the average EM level blinking away at the centre of it. She swept for point sources around the heavy wooden beams and the threshold of the inner doorway, but she didn't find any.

Video footage from 2013, Bishop Michael Swansley and Bishop William Kemp at Keble College, Oxford:

Kemp looks decent, white-haired, jovial, with an experienced face and a neat moustache. He's sitting in a modified dentist's chair, drumming his fingers on the green leather arm rests. He smiles at the camera. Around his head is a mesh helmet, wires leading away, with a broad metal band across the back of his neck. Swansley stands at the rear, looking pale and tense. The video is time-coded 10/10/13: 2102 and an ever-changing rush of seconds.

'Are you ready, your grace?' asks a voice offscreen, the gentle tones of Professor Ruehl, who's just set up the camera.

'Ready,' nods Kemp. 'Fire away.'

Swansley and a couple of lab technicians back away. There's the sound of a number of toggle switches being engaged, and the thrum of an engine starting up. 'We'll go in ten, nine, eight . . . try to relax, your grace . . . three, two, one . . . Begin.'

Another switch is flicked. Kemp visibly tenses, then relaxes again, cautiously looks around him. Nothing much seems to be happening. He closes his eyes, obviously making an effort to concentrate.

Video footage from 2013, Bishop Michael Swansley and Bishop William Kemp at Keble College, Oxford:

Time-coded 2130. Kemp is trying hard to get the words out between great breaths of air. His face is strained from weeping. 'I'm moving behind the Cross now. Great God, great God, this is real. I am here. This is real. He is a man, if I die here, you must know, He is a man. I can see the wounds on His skin. He seems to move in and out of consciousness. I can see His lips moving. Can't hear what He's saying. I can see the other two. I'm part of the crowd. They come and go, some have been here throughout, some just wander past. I've been here for five hours. I love Him. I want to follow where He's going, but I can't. I'm me, I have no knowledge that I'm anybody else. But I am physically here. I'm wearing my own clothes. All the historical details . . . There is more detail here than I have ever learnt, more than my brain can . . . could invent, I'm certain of it. Oh!' (He jerks in his seat, it's a physical impact, like he's been punched in the back. Swansley steps into view, concerned, as if he's ready to pull Kemp out of the chair.) 'The blood! Suddenly it's everywhere! This is what I'm here for! Michael, this is why I've lived, to be here for this! This is why I was born! I'm covered in His blood, it's spilling out of Him, washing all over the crowd, great gouts of it, and they're reacting, some of them ugly, distasteful, some of them embracing it . . . Oh, and I can taste it now!' (A long silence. Mouth movements.) 'Beautiful. Honey. Beyond anything. I know this is a taste, but I'm not thinking with my tongue . . . Reminds me of apples. And this is what my mother's milk tasted of, I know that, like you know things in a dream. But this is real, Michael, this is real. If I die, you have to tell them.'

Video footage from 2013, Bishop Michael Swansley and Bishop William Kemp at Keble College, Oxford:

Time-coded 2200. Kemp is still sitting in the chair, drinking something hot from a large mug with Snoopy on it, both his hands wrapped tight around it. 'I can remember, I think, everything, like I was actually there, rather than as if it was a dream. I can remember sounds and smells. There were distant things, too, the details of the city. Things that weren't relevant to the Passion. Which I now feel I was, in some way, genuinely present at.'

'Do you feel God talked to you?' asks Swansley's voice, off.

'In that I had a . . . terrifying, shaking religious experience, yes, Michael, I do. My life has been changed. But He didn't have any sort of message for me. No words. I just know that everything I believe in is literally, profoundly true.' (He breaks into a sudden, throaty laugh.) 'Isn't that great? Isn't that *great*?'

Jane walked between the massive oak doors, carved with lions, into the entrance hall proper, and ducked into the little cloakroom at one side, where the troopers had stowed their heavy-weather gear. Having got the same dull reading amongst the hooks and shooting racks, she went back into the hall. Still bare granite and black wood, very impressive. A luxurious carpet lay across the polished wooden floor, and metal torch holders stood either side of a broad fireplace. All was cold, musty with damp, and yet pristine.

The sanity of this building matched its state of cleanliness, Jane thought. It was like the place was a big model, a movie set. Except a movie set would show more EM activity. The big old doors were undamaged, the ceilings unmarked by the soot of campfires. Here was a place of great shelter, and, thanks to its waterwheel generator, even comfort to anybody with some basic engineering skills.

Yet it was clean, empty, and so sane you could probably murder your auntie here without disturbing the field.

Lord, am I being set up for some joke? Is this some test?

No answer to her whisper but echoes.

On either side of the fireplace stood a figure of a child, in medieval dress, made of thin, painted board. Jane went to touch the face of the little boy, and left fingerprints in the dust.

He would have been firewood, had this place been . . . real. She had been about to think *real*.

Zero on the EM meter here, too. Flatline.

She continued, pushing open a door to enter the library. The roof here was a great stone arch, with massive oak beams across it. A large fireplace dominated the room – when lit it would have smoked the place out unless the door had been kept open – and along every wall there were oak bookcases. Squinting in the poor light through the small and dusty windows, Jane went to read some of the spines. Volumes of Wiltshire history, a collection of *The Gentleman's Magazine*, a history of the National Trust, doubtless put here by some lonely curator in the last days of the great national institutions.

There was a section of the library, behind the glass, that, on close inspection, definitely wasn't real. Behind the panel was a sort of wallpaper of unreal book titles. Twenty volumes of *Arms and Heraldry*. Jane searched for a control that would unlatch a secret passage, like something out of Enid Blyton, but in the end came to believe that the effect was purely decorative. Somebody had decided they didn't have enough impressive books.

There was a roll-top desk by the window, an ancient table-football game on the tea table, with rusty little figures on bars, and, most wonderful of all, a 1930s radio, its dial marked for Luxembourg and Helvetia and the Light Programme.

And, according to the meter, this room was also background standard.

Jane nearly threw the machine down. Every EM map she had ever seen showed contours and levels on a metre by metre basis. One of the features that had persuaded Swansley and Kemp that the EM field was 'the voice of God' was that emotional events deformed, on a minute basis, the shape of the field. It was as if human brains and the field were designed together, as part of one mechanism. People tended to regard the same places as 'spooky' or holy, felt they had an 'atmosphere', depending on the geological processes affecting the local EM field. That was why, in the days before the GEC, the new movement had started to build new churches in very precise places. But also, people themselves could alter the atmosphere of a place. Murder, violence, drawn-out suffering changed the EM field. There had been no experiments into that phenomenon before Swansley and Kemp's movement had come along. That was why the bishops had, early on, funded a fairly inconclusive EM map of the Holy Land.

Jane plugged the radio into the bulky socket in the wall and slowly turned the dial as it warmed up. She wasn't at all surprised by now that the ancient device worked. Pre-digital, so there was, she supposed, no reason why not. She listened to the fizz and thump of Atlantic storms, the songs of the planets, the noises that human civilisation had once blanked with its own constant noise.

The alternative theory was that human brains had simply evolved in the EM field, and thus had a sense concerning it. Under great stress, instinct caused a brain to mark the field, modulating its own activity to interact with that of the planet. Other humans that came along, the evolutionary theory said, would recognise the warning and know better than to go there.

Jane found BBC Radio, and was instantly reassured. *The Archers* was just beginning. It was the only drama that the BBC service still ran, valued for both its practical storylines and the simple fact of its continuing run, a connection back to the civilisation that had once been here, the Commonwealth and even the Empire before it. Steven Archer, at the start of this episode, was talking to his grandma, Kayleigh, about the pros and cons of using a dump of artificial fertiliser he'd found. He was insisting that there was no need to declare it to Shirankha Goulden, the local farm commissioner for the fictional Parson family. The Campbells often playfully insisted that Ambridge was in their territory, but since the BBC was based in Hawtrey country, but had to seem impartial in order to receive its funding from the families, perhaps the Parsons were a wise compromise. The BBC was the only organisation Jane knew of that still called itself 'British', though she had never heard the word used on the air.

On a whim, Jane moved the EM meter behind a heavy iron

fireguard, hoping to interfere at least with the clear BBC signal that the radio was getting. And here, finally, there was a dip to put on her map. The house of no emotional resonance was at least subject to the laws of physics. Just barely.

Through an arch, Jane progressed, with her newly interesting EM map, into an ornate billiard room. No windows here, just a small chandelier, illuminating enamel roundels that were fixed at intervals around the tacked and polished upholstered walls. The roundels each displayed the classical perception of one of the seven planets, a star against the body of a heroic mythical figure.

The green baize of the Lutyens table was a little dusty, but untouched.

'Untouched.' Jane found herself saying it out loud. She could bloody have a game on this if she wanted to. No cues. A single white ball sat on a ledge above the fireplace. She took it and placed it at one end of the table.

It slowly rolled to the other end and stayed there.

There had at least been geological subsidence in this perfect world. She checked the meter again. Geological subsidence without a crack in the field.

She realised, with a little shock that made her gasp as the adrenaline hit her, that she had been listening to a noise.

The tick of a clock.

She looked wildly around her, and found it, a grandmother, standing in one corner of the billiard room.

It was even telling the right time.

Jane reminded herself of the soldiers. The soldiers had been through every inch of this place before her. She was just responding to the mythology that surrounded this process, the brave cleric venturing into the domain of ghosts, the first-footer over the threshold into mystery. There was every chance that Eric had playfully adjusted the balances and set that clock going.

And he'd re-laid the billiard table while he was at it, too.

The ticking followed her along the vaulted corridor that led to the drawing room. The billiard room had also been background standard.

Maybe this was a joke on the part of the militiamen? Maybe they'd fixed her meter and would be waiting at the end of her tour?

No, that was beyond a joke. They'd get punished for that. Perhaps even dismissed.

She passed a portrait of a young man dressed in the uniform of a

British infantryman in World War I. On the wall opposite him stood a copy of Bermejo's *Saint Michael*. One of Jane's favourite pictures. She bent to look closely at the saint's burnished armour, and found, to her satisfaction, the details of the reflection in it: the new Jerusalem, the eternal city, seen only at this extraordinary, deformed distance. All you could deduce about Jerusalem from Michael's armour was that it had some towers. But the dream of it was wonderful. Beneath Michael's feet lay an extraordinary Satan, a mouth in his stomach. She straightened and continued.

Sixteenth-century tapestries lined the lengths of granite wall in the corridor, each one depicting a scene from the Trojan War. Their Trojan Horse had a scythelike, ruffled mane, made of spears. She walked under a green ceiling dome of uncracked glass panes, each engraved with a spidery black flower.

The drawing room, with its chintz furnishings and delicate green walls and vast windows, was also perfect, uncluttered, terrifyingly sane.

Obviously, Jane laughed uneasily to herself, resting in one of the deep armchairs and gazing out of the window across the green of the lawns, the house had been recently occupied by a group of dedicated Buddhists, who had left the place spiritually pristine and tidied up before they left.

Tidied up before they left: the phrase kept repeating in the back of her head.

You could, in theory, exorcise every room of a house down to this level. You could use ceremony and mental discipline and electronic dampers. But you'd have to do it to the very door and then lock it behind you, as if you were painting the floor. And the team of soldiers would have traipsed their muddy emotional footsteps through the house when they entered. Her job normally was to advise on, and get rid of, any spikes or areas of intense background. Not to roll the EM gradient flat. The grand organisation and civilisation of this place seemed almost to mock the world she and her comrades lived in. It existed in spite of the chaos and danger of the countryside, defenceless, innocent and somehow pristine. That was the feeling that had got to them all: it was like watching a child walk blindly through a minefield. Here was a house without defences, without security . . . which was somehow secure by accident. Any moment the little girl would miss her step. Jane had found no sign of actual booby traps, any more than she had found a sign of anything else. Heartsease had less life than a museum, and therefore, some kind of shadowy non-life.

She closed her eyes. Yes. She could feel it just at the edge of her craft, an inkling across the back of her neck. It was as if the *shape* of an EM field stood here, without the field itself. The ghost of a ghost. That was her imagination, perhaps. But her imagination had been formed through a lifetime of experience.

There would be one room that would surely break the pattern, it suddenly occurred to her. She'd read about it during the briefings. She changed her route to go straight there. She walked swiftly through the echoing corridors, determined not to run.

On the upper mezzanine, in an awkward little corner where the two wings of the house met, and up a little flight of stairs all of its own, was Alisdair Trent's room. He was the young man in the picture downstairs. The wooden cross suspended on the wall by the door had once marked his grave.

Jane pushed open the door and walked in.

The interior of the room was a little shrine to Simon Trent's dead son. He'd died at Ypres in 1915, before this house had ever been planned, while Trent was still living on the south coast, according to one of the net texts. So the son having a room here was eccentric to say the least. There was a perfectly made bed waiting for him in the oak-panelled chamber, and a tiny window for him to look out of. Jane thought that if she'd been a servant here, she'd have hesitated to look up at this window from the gardens, for fear of seeing someone in here. There was a writing desk containing . . . Jane opened a drawer and held a watermarked sheet up to the light . . . this dead man had his own headed notepaper. Which was, of course, intact from over three hundred and twenty years ago. How long did paper take to decay? Maybe this was a reproduction for the National Trust, but even so . . .

One wall of the room was covered in school and college mementos. Alisdair had rowed at Eton. There was a photo of him amongst his crew, and the pressed pendant, behind glass, from his boat, the *Lucitania*.

A full-length photograph of the boy in uniform ran down one narrow wall. He had been twenty-six when it was taken, the age at which he'd died. The face was thin and the expression preoccupied. He had a neat moustache and charmingly gawky ears under his cap. He kept one hand behind his back, and the other in front of him, holding his gloves and a cane. The photograph, in the manner of the time, had been hand-coloured, and the artist had given Alisdair a ruddy complexion rather at odds with his anxious eyes. The rough woodland behind him had been rendered into a Turneresque swirl of pastoral greens and browns. There was a distant gap in the trees into some lovely grotto, the reflection of which glowed softly with a blue like the sky. It was, she thought, perhaps where the colourist had placed heaven. In the original photo, the gap probably led to the fields of mud and metal. Alisdair's expression certainly seemed to belie the country behind him. You haven't seen the half of it, he seemed to be saying.

The strangest feature of the room was in one corner, on a little work table of its own. It was a radio transmitter and receiver which Jane would have called amateur, but for her feeling that it dated back to a time when there was no real distinction between professional and amateur radio use.

She went to the narrow window and felt the chill of the autumn outside. Across the lawn, rough cattle of some ancient breed were grazing. She could imagine Simon Trent in the years of his distress, preparing this room, freezing his grief into something that he could come here and dwell on. He would have sat here and contemplated the whole length of his dead son's life.

This room, she had been certain from when she first read of it, would register high on an EM map.

She activated the meter once more, calibrated it from first principles, rebooted it and loaded the map she'd so far compiled.

Once more, background standard, right on the line.

'All right.' Jane looked straight up at the plaster rose from which hung the single light in the room. 'That's it. I've seen the strings. I've seen behind the curtain. The joke's over.' She could feel the eyes of Alisdair Trent, agonising with her over his own false painted background.

The door opened a crack. Jane just watched it. There was a pause.

A thin face on a long neck shot out of the gap and stopped an inch from her face, laughing. The thing had eyes full of blood, and fluff on its cheeks, and a mouth that had flattened against the arm that Jane had flung up to protect herself.

It was an ostrich head. It had two more heads, sticking out of the door.

Matthew walked into the room, laughing. He was carrying the three heads by spinal stumps, wrapped in gaffer tape at the base of their long necks. Blood was dripping on to the carpet.

'Get out of here!' Jane screamed. 'Get those things away from me! You're not supposed to be in here!'

Looking hurt and worried, Matthew stepped quickly out of the room, and ran off down the corridor.

Jane, seized by contrition, ran to the door and called after him at length.

But he had gone.

Six: Rebecca's Eighteenth Birthday

Rebecca stood outside the marquee erected in the centre of the Singh herb gardens, nodding to everybody as they passed, thanking them for the occasional compliment, trying to keep smiling.

This had been going to be the year that broke the pattern. The good birthday. The Singhs had been keeping her informed over the net as to the progress of the picture, had sent her scenes and stills. It was the best thing that had ever happened to her. It was strange, seeing Russell and Maud, indeed her whole house of Cumberland, played by Singhs, while the Lyles were white, as both houses had been in the novel. The designs gave the families initially equal grandeur, which, in the case of the villainous Lyles and their agent Bonnie, became more and more decadent and tattered, a visual thought which had never occurred to her.

Initially, she had tried to discuss the progress of the movie with David, but he had become irritable whenever she'd brought it up. At first, she'd thought that was just him being him, uncomfortable with her having success of her own. But she'd gradually realised, as conversations at high table were turned away from the matter of the film, and ladies at court gave her little looks, that she had done something wrong.

David wouldn't talk about that, either. It was only because of him that she was at court in the first place, so she felt the burden on his shoulders, feared that he might leave her because of it.

It was a relief when the film was completed. Anand announced a premiere in the Singh stronghold on Rebecca's birthday as a deliberate gesture. She'd confided to him, during their lengthy exchange of e-mails, that the day had horrible associations for her. So he'd arranged to wipe the board clean by making the most wonderful day of her life her eighteenth birthday.

When David had told her he wouldn't be coming, she ran into her room and slammed the door. He heaved it aside and caught her by the sleeve, made her turn to listen to him, told her violently that none of the family would be going to visit the filthy Singhs and see their insulting film. That she was not to keep pestering Ben about it, or she'd find herself thrown out and he'd lose his commission.

She understood, even as she sat there weeping.

But there was nothing to stop her going, quietly and without announcement, to the premiere. So she did. David didn't try to stop her doing that. She supposed that he felt trapped by what had happened on her birthday too. It was as if he'd made a bit of her, so it was the bit that disturbed him and the bit he couldn't stop. Not that he knew all the birthday burdens she kept on her shoulders.

Anand and his three directors met her off the stagecoach. They showered her in petals, gave her gifts, paraded her through the city, causing crowds of people to cry out after her, cheer, run along by the side of the processional carriage.

For a time that had made her feel utterly better. So the Hawtreys were out of step with the world. Let them stay behind in their enclave. This was going to be a unifying event, a moment that brought all the families together. Nobody was actually at war right now, though there were the usual tense border disputes, incursions and raids. This was the ideal moment. Discussions would begin, despite all the stony faces of the house elders. Ambassadors would laugh together at the sequence where Russell and Maud confessed their attraction to each other while hanging under the bridge by their fingertips. They would be moved by the ending, where Maud and Russell watched Bonnie's execution. Only love and war give life any meaning, and now the time for war is over.

They might even have enjoyed the dance routines.

But as she accepted the hospitality of the Singhs, and supervised the details of the premiere, gradually the messages began to arrive. The replies to the invitations that had been sent to the other families. Many of them replied curtly that they had already heard about the content of the movie, and regarded it as an insult. A few sent threats to take back territory that was rightly theirs. There were containers of filth, and things which Rebecca was certain Anand kept from her.

The Mandervilles sent the head of one of Anand's distant cousins, caught spying in their territory. Previously, he had been ransomed. Anand vowed revenge, but told her he would leave the whole matter until after she had departed.

By the day of the premiere it was clear that nobody else was coming.

Anand didn't say that to her, and she didn't say it to him. She allowed herself to be dressed in finery and driven through the cheering Singh crowds to the marquee. She felt like a trophy rather than an ambassador now.

She was lined up with the actors and the directors and Anand, and was now smiling and shaking hands as the elders and high ranks of the Singh family headed into the tent, thanking them for their patronage, for having made her movie. Inside the darkened space, a crew of engineers were making last-minute adjustments to the projector and the screen.

She no longer even felt excited.

The last one to come to the end of the line was Grandfather Singh himself. Her patron, the one responsible for all this. He was tall and imposing, with a long mane of white hair and eyes that looked balefully right into hers.

They looked at each other for a moment, and Rebecca was sure he read every emotion in her head.

A cruel smile curled his lip. He reached out and placed a fingertip on her nose. 'Victory,' he said.

Then he turned away and marched, surrounded by his retinue of servants, guards and performers, into the tent cinema.

Anand took her arm, and Rebecca found herself being led after him.

At the end of the film, the audience got to their feet and gave a standing ovation.

Rebecca remained seated. She had been crying. The film had been perfect. She hoped they thought that was why she was crying.

She looked across the marquee and saw that Grandfather Singh had remained seated too. He nodded at the applause, acknowledging it.

On the way out, Anand tried to take Rebecca's arm again. 'So—' he began.

She gently took her arm away.

He looked alarmed. 'You're not pleased with it?'

'It's exactly what I wrote.' She considered her words for a moment. 'I'm flattered.'

'So, stay. For a while.'

Rebecca glared at him. 'Love and war are the only things that give meaning to life.'

'That's the message of the movie.'

'Then let's get on with them and forget all this hopeful shit, shall we?'

And she walked off to gather her luggage for the stagecoach ride that would take her home.

Seven: A Capella

December 1998. Bill Parkinson ran out on to the pavement outside the Forum, Kentish Town, displaying a pink feather boa like it was the World Cup. 'I got it!' he shouted. 'I got Sarah's boa!'

An audience was pouring out of the venue from all four doors, the bouncers leaning back against the brickwork and letting them through. The heat of the crowd's bodies bloomed into steam in the winter air. People were carrying their coats, still hot from the concert. The lights of the street glared messages about many different kinds of fast food, and amongst the laughter and the singing there were conversations starting about finding the car in the back streets and getting some chips, and somewhere Cher was singing 'Do you believe in life after love?'

'Stop whirling it about,' muttered Booth Hawtrey. 'Somebody'll nick it.'

Amanda, Bill's sister, looked sidelong at Booth, pissed off. She worked with him at the insurance company, and had become friends with him, and when he'd broken up with Fee, six months ago, she'd started to invite him out to things, to cheer him up, because he'd become such a whingeing sod, and she knew he wasn't like that underneath. He would talk to her for ages at lunch about how he had all these plans for the future, about this sitcom about insurance brokers that he was putting together. He'd come out with things like: 'Do you know that, according to folklorists, Father Christmas is older than the human race?' He'd tell her tales that she took to be true, only to realise, a couple of seconds before he got there, that there was a punchline coming. But when they all went out to the pub in the evening after work, he'd just sit there in silence as bloody Alan ordered the waiters about and told everybody what they should be doing and was just obviously the leader of the pack. Booth resented that, she could tell, and he had his English degree and all that, and was about twenty times smarter than Alan. But he couldn't open up and show anyone else what was inside. That was why, she had concluded tonight, he was never going to be anything. Why he was stuck in this shitty little job, why somehow he was qualified for nothing else. He had these rich parents who he never talked about. And she liked the idea of that, of him wanting to be just one of the gang. If only he could just *be* that. She'd finally got it as she'd been bouncing up and down on her brother's shoulders tonight, her hands in the air, and she'd looked down and seen Booth staring at the band like they were some interesting cultural oddity he'd come across on TV. He'd been crushed by Fee, but he'd been crushed before Fee too. He'd been crushed by something at the start of the world, and she was tired of her friends looking oddly at her while she explained that he was nice. Conversations with Booth always began with: 'Since Fee left . . .' It was like his life had stopped at that point, and he was just going to keep on thinking deeply and geologically about what had happened.

Maybe he was discovering he was gay. That would be a bit less fucking unflattering, anyway. She'd frozen her navel and her legs on the way here tonight. Now she was certain she wasn't going to freeze anything more for him.

Just now, for instance, she'd tried to take his arm, but he'd slid into his big black coat and looked off into the distance, obviously still a million miles away, obviously still thinking about *her*. She'd stopped in the middle of the action, and turned it into a sort of shrug. Thank God Bill had been busy with his captured boa.

Tomorrow, Amanda told herself, she was going to have lunch with the gang, and if Booth didn't want to come along, then he could just go off and be alone until he sorted himself out. He was thirty-three, for God's sake. He was turning into a sad old man.

Bill carefully finished slipping the boa into his record bag. 'Anybody sexy for a kebab?' he asked.

'Do you know what they put in—' began Booth.

'Yeah, okay,' said Amanda.

That got a *look* from him, at least.

At that moment, two hundred kilometres above Kentish Town, at the point where the Earth's atmosphere started to become noticeable against the vacuum of space, an *event* occurred. Molecules split into their component atoms.

A thunderclap was conceived that would penetrate all the way to the ground and roll around the globe of the world three times.

The thing that hit the atmosphere was defined by it, as it hadn't been defined by its lightspeed journey of the last four and a half decades.

It flashed the air away.

It burrowed, in a blink, through to the surface of the Earth.

It centred itself on the head of Booth Hawtrey.

It hit.

Booth opened his mouth, a look on his face as if he'd finally started to understand. He was, Amanda thought, about to ask if she was angry with him. That question could be the start of turning him around, towards the human race.

Then Booth exploded.

He flashed into light and flame.

Then Amanda was lying on the ground.

There were people lying everywhere. A great noise. There were dead people. People mashed against the theatre wall. Dead.

She saw Booth. He was on fire. No, shining. On the ground. Something complicated was happening to the air above his head. Amanda stumbled to her feet, aware that blood was spilling from the back of her head. There were purples and blues splitting from the white inferno, and blacks that hurt her eyes because they had something in them that made her retinas fill with trails of stars.

'Booth!' she bellowed.

Then the big sound hit. It was so deep it took Amanda in the stomach and made her retch. It hurt the muscles on the sides of her face as they stretched under the force that suddenly slapped down on her from the sky.

Her eardrums burst and all sound stopped.

Silently, in great pain, she started to crawl over the moving, swaying bodies towards Booth. Everything on the ground threw stark black shadows against the white of the thing that was battering at him. She could see him in the centre of it, on his knees, that familiar shape of his shoulders rocking insanely as wave after wave of it entered him.

She loved him like she'd love a baby. She wanted desperately to save him. She had no thought yet to question what this was that was hurting him.

She felt the heat tanning her hands, making her face sore like sunburn.

Then it stopped.

She was afraid for a second that she'd gone blind.

Then her eyes found the darkness again, and saw Booth huddled on the pavement, smoking with heat, his head curled between his knees. The natural illumination of the street was back. The sudden normality shocked her.

She got to Booth as people started to run in towards the pavement. A huge circle of white scarred ground centred on him, the clothes and the backs of people who had fallen scarred white too, until the circle ran up the side of the building and melted the billboards and the marquee lights.

Booth was breathing shallowly. He was absolutely unburnt. And Amanda knew now that she was very badly burnt indeed, that she'd be feeling great pain in a moment, when her body let her.

She touched his cheek with the red lumps of her fingers, and felt the first hint of that pain.

He opened his eyes and looked at her, his lips moving as he asked a question she couldn't hear. His aftershave smelled like it always did.

He'd clawed at his face with his fingers, clawed so deeply that he'd broken the skin, and had drawn—

Blue jelly. The big holes in his cheek were full of glistening, solid blue jelly.

Amanda smiled at that, at the idea too big for her to cope with.

Then she pitched forwards on to Booth, unconscious.

'He's waking up. Go and get Croft.'

Booth blinked, and then realised that his eyes were open. The last thing he'd seen was Amanda, badly hurt.

Now he was in hospital. Around his bed stood a circle of doctors. They were all wearing masks over their faces.

They were staring at him.

He stared back at them. He felt fine. Very shocked. Deep inside. To come: lots of shuddering and stomach convulsions and whimpering. But right now his body was just pleased to be okay.

'Lightning,' he said. 'I was struck by lightning.' A nurse pushed through the circle of doctors and put a glass of water to his lips. He took hold of the glass and finished it off. Handed it back to her. 'Amanda and Bill. Are they all right?'

Nothing. Some of the doctors looked at each other. He put a hand up to his cheek, and found the dressing there. 'How long have I been here?'

Somebody approached, and the crowd parted. A bearded man in a tweed suit made his way to the side of his bed, gripped the rail and looked down at him, wetting his lips, as if wondering where to begin.

At least he wasn't wearing a mask. 'Mr Hawtrey, my name is Peter Croft. I'm the senior consultant here . . .'

Booth had started to panic. 'Please. Whatever it is. Just tell me what's wrong with me.'

'That's just it.' Croft glanced at his colleagues. 'We don't know. We can't even begin to guess. Are you in any pain?'

Booth thought about it for a moment. 'No. Yes, slightly. Under the . . .' He couldn't find the word. He pointed. 'My cheek.'

'I see.' Croft looked again at one of the other doctors. Booth saw now that the woman was holding a cassette recorder over him. The little red recording light was on. Everything he said was valuable. 'Please . . .' he asked again. 'Amanda and Bill . . .'

'I'm afraid they didn't survive . . . whatever it was.'

Booth was aware of the tape recorder. He shut his mouth, and felt the top row of his teeth with his tongue. His thoughts, of their own volition, slipped to nearby questions. There was something strange there. Something different. Oh Christ, he had brain damage, he could feel it. 'You don't know what it was? Didn't somebody say it was lightning?'

'For fuck's sake!' A young man burst into the circle, shouting. Another doctor. 'Can we have some of you down in A and E, please? Sorry, sir, but for fuck's sake!' He moved off again, and most of the doctors, chastened, followed.

Croft took the cassette recorder from the woman and sat down beside the bed.

As he moved, his eyes never left Booth's face.

They left him alone that night, had given him some pills to help him sleep.

He didn't want to sleep. His thoughts kept going to Amanda and Bill.

But they went there strangely.

He remembered the look on Amanda's face as she looked down at him on the pavement. And the moment after that. And the moment after that. The moment when she fell aside. So badly burnt. By him. But those weren't 'moments', he felt that he had had his whole idea of moments from film, from frames of film. He could see each action that Amanda took, and all the chaotic, blazing background behind her. And he was aware of every movement that she made, and every movement that the background made, and there was . . .

No breaking into moments. Just the dark circle of his vision, even the things at the edge of it, and the feeling of pain from inside his own head, the pain of his cheek, the smell of burning, of bonfires—

Bonfire night when he was fifteen, Mum and Dad standing in the back garden, Mum wearing scarf and strange fur hat that was too big for her, he could see now. No associations of anything about that, he'd forgotten it, not important, strange to see younger mother and something about her's not important. And Dad wearing the suit jacket that smelt of his skittles club, old tobacco, beery—

Him coming home late at night, walking through the door with fish and chips open for Booth, being allowed to stay up . . . he must have been ten or so, because here he was, little limbs, those *Star Wars* posters on his wall. He could feel the roughness of his blanket in his tiny fingers. 'Here you go,' said Dad. 'Here's what you stay up for.'

'You shouldn't do it every week,' said Mum. 'He comes to expect it.'

Ordinary conversation. This was new. He didn't . . . he hadn't remembered this. This was new. But it wasn't. He knew it was real. Only he'd forgotten it. Where—?

He found himself . . . going . . . back. It wasn't film. No backwards-moving people. Just going back, letting the . . . not the moments, the continuum of events slide backwards.

He could keep on going. School that day, he sped through some times, stopped to gaze on others.

He was suddenly at his desk, the tiny indentations inked in shockingly familiar against the flat of his hands.

He was a small boy. Everybody else had their heads down, working at sums. Mr Smith was looking down at something from his desk at the front. Outside, the trees rustled and a bird was calling. Big patches of sunshine on the floor in the stretched images of the windows.

He was a small boy. Who knew what it was like to be thirty-three. He remembered sex. He could see Fee's face. But he was here. He looked slowly around the classroom. Had he always known? Had this moment happened . . . last time it happened? When he'd lived through it?

He tried to look back to Mr Smith, and, with a jolt, realised that he wasn't controlling where his head was going. He was *inhabiting* this memory, not living it. He could feel the hormonal rush of arrogant, unbeatable, bullied tearful *mind* inside. He could *remember* every detail of that. But there was also him, beside this, around this.

The realisation connected, back along the shape of his life. It was all there. He felt it like the length of a limb. He was aware of every part, like his body, and he could . . . visit . . . any point.

And there was a danger there. At the end . . . at the *beginning*, rather. There was a point where this body of time didn't exist. If he went there, and remembered nothingness. This river had a waterfall at both ends.

With an internal yell, he went there. The attraction had reared up in him like any of those memories he had told himself to stay away from, and like any of them, the merest hint had sent him flying towards it. Thinking about something in this . . . *configuration* . . . was the same as doing it. This was memory: it flew him.

He was in the dark. Tiny limbs. Fighting. No. Didn't want to go. Pressure all around. All nightmares. All fear. All from here. Movement when there had been no movement. Connections to all other nightmares. Rushing down the tunnel. Finding out what rushing was. Like now he was finding out what dreamlife was. Like coming for the first time, you're scared to be taken over by something from—

And he was there. Coming in his bed, just a tiny dot of it, and he was staring at it on the end of his penis, thinking it was some sort of new blood, wondering why he'd had such a powerful urge to make it happen when he didn't know what *it* was.

And he found something cramping and powerful and involuntary that would . . .

Take him back. To now. To sitting in his hospital bed with his head propped up against the pillows.

He could still feel it in his head. The length of all his perfect memory. A river circle. No, it didn't run. A pool, then. A pool he couldn't resist diving into. That would pull him into it suddenly, several hundred times a day. It nearly did again: pool, pool in garden . . . He *clamped* on to the . . . *memory memories*. The little stories. What he'd used to have and called it memory. They were plastic and bright and startlingly unreal: he suddenly put all of them against the *real memories* and could feel them all compared, feel how they were fiction and lies and things he'd preferred to believe.

But they were . . . *beacons*. Base camps. Ways to navigate. He could clamp down on one of them and it would take him back here—

He did it swiftly. The bird outside the window in school. A cuckoo. A poster of cuckoos when he was a toddler. Being hit by an older boy. He had *remembered* himself standing up to him. He had not. He was back here.

And he could feel that whole sequence now written into him. He could go back and live back along just that little . . . *track*. Remember remembering. It was like music. Like tiny themes replayed and overlaid. He let himself fall back along the loop of experience again, familiar with it now.

It was all as familiar as wanking. It had never happened to you before. It was extraordinary. But it had been waiting for you. And this had been waiting for him. This was natural. Or it was brain damage.

This time when he came back, he . . . *impacted* on a sudden fear.

There was something weird about *now*. It was the . . . magician, panto, behind the curtain, church, altar . . . the numinous part of memory. He could feel the . . . *flame* of *now* producing the memories which he then was a part of and could see. The urge to move into the flame, beyond it, to—

Remember the future.

He nearly threw up. In the whispering gallery at St Paul's, the great space below, the sickening urge to throw oneself off, that natural suicidal thing, that primate can-I-reach-the-next-branch thing . . . This was like that.

Back in bed, back facing *now*.

He could almost see it in the dust patterns hanging in the air beneath the moonlight from the window. They moved. He could then live back through the pattern of them moving. That was one country, a country he was now lord of, that he knew every part of, could walk through at will.

But there was, *therefore, obviously*, the other country. The one just *here*, where those moving particles *were* before they entered *now*.

And then he couldn't help it. He was dragged into . . .

He was aware of a real moment. A sudden fictionalisation. He'd gone through a curtain, felt the veil drop from his eyes. He was suddenly in the presence of—

He was no longer in that presence.

Statues in his imagination. Curled muscles and grave eyes. No, this was what he was supposed to *remember*, what he would remember. This was the story. For a *moment* he had been connected to— Been one with—

Had he? Had he really?

He was still sitting in his bed, only he couldn't really see. He was remembering the last construction of photons in the room. So everything had stopped. There was only darkness around him.

He knew that there was going to be something wrong with space soon.

I've turned time into space. That's what's beyond now.

How did he know? He tried to use his new adroitness to move back to where he'd found that out, but found that he couldn't.

He could wait until the space around the hospital gave way. He could feel it inside. Something vast and sickening. Being part of something that was about to bend and break. At the highest point of an infinite rollercoaster. Hanging before the drop. The drop is coming. The room was hanging in its moment of no time. Of fictionality. Of now. The drop is coming.

Or he could let himself fly back into—

He let go.

The fear vanished, and he was back in his bed, and the dust motes swung and shifted and he enjoyed, suddenly, their music. He would be just a disciple of now. A watcher of now. If he tried to be more, he knew something terrible would happen. The universe would change.

He could just feel the volume of spacetime that was vulnerable to him, like a man on a frozen lake, looking out at all that could cave in should he miss his step.

A night nurse wandered in from the door beside his bed, smiled offhandedly at him. 'Try and sleep.'

He smiled at her, happily aware that the universe and he were intimate now.

He watched her walk to her desk, and then watched her again, and looped that for a while.

And then he went back and fucked with Fee again, that time on the sofa, with his hands inside her clothes, and his cock farther inside her than it had ever felt before. Or ever since.

He came back when a sudden awareness of physicality came over him.

Booth Hawtrey gently raised the sheets and looked down.

'Oops,' he said.

The next day, Booth's parents came to visit him. They were puzzled and angry, glad that he was in a room apart from everyone else, even with the hospital heaving with accident and emergency patients, but appalled that nobody was telling them why. Booth didn't want to tell them anything about how he felt. Their immediate reaction would be that he was suffering from brain damage. It was certainly what he thought. Good brain damage, a fantastic new ability, but probably the sort of thing that killed you. The light that burned bright but fast, and all that. Just looking at his parents was difficult: they kept reminding him of what they'd been like, like they were the top of vast columns of difference, stretching down into time. He had to force himself not to fly from the shadow of the now in pursuit of those memories, millions of which tried to catch his attention and pull him back into thought at the first sight of the two of them. But he was getting better at that. He hadn't slept, he'd been practising with his new world all night, trying not to come all the time. But he didn't feel tired at all. The sonic boom, Mum and Dad told him, had caused hearing damage all around the world. They'd said on CNN that a meteor had struck the atmosphere. Frank thought the Iraqis had come up with some new weapon, and he wanted to know how many of *them* were deaf right now. He took the tiny hearing aid out of his ear, tapped it proudly and laughed. Once again, he'd been ahead of the game. Mum had been in bed, under the covers, with the curtains closed. She'd just heard a loud noise and thought the dogs had knocked something over. Booth's brother, Charlie, and his wife and kids were fine. They'd gone a bit deaf, but were already improving. They'd been out on the water in Geneva when the concussion had hit, and that had apparently been one of the safest places to be, on a small body of water, because the water took the impact and you didn't have to be so worried about waves. There was flooding in the West Country, Mum said. All those poor people in Cornwall with their ground floors underwater.

Dad brought it up first, after almost exactly half an hour. When Booth was up and about, why didn't he take a holiday, come back home, take a look around the family business? The manufacturing side was suffering, for all the government's talk about supporting the industrial base, but they weren't helping themselves, and Booth would be a fresh face in that department, kick a few arses—

Booth just stared at him. Yes, he was about to say. I'll do just that. And I'll try not to destroy the Earth too. Okay.

And you know that my friends are dead, right?

But a nurse rushed past the doorway at that moment, turned, and came rushing back in as if required to tell this to everyone she met.

'Aliens!' she said. 'Aliens! It's on the telly!'

BBC1 had stopped its schedules, and had stayed with the lunchtime news. ITN were popping up with bulletins every half-hour. Booth and his parents joined a growing crowd of patients and staff in the day room of one of the big wards. The room was full of people, mostly in dressing gowns, some with terrible injuries. The sound on the television was turned up to maximum.

' . . . one which has been, so far, accepted as genuine by the scientific community.' On the wall behind the newsreader was a graphic of what looked to Booth like a DNA helix. 'The message was received simultaneously by every major radio telescope in the world at eleven twenty p.m. yesterday.'

Booth felt a sudden subsidence inside his body. He glanced up at his parents, wondering if they'd got the significance of that time. They were both still staring at the screen in wonder.

'The message seems to originate from the area of the star Alpha Aurigae, better known as Capella, the brightest star in the constellation of Auriga.' A graphic of the constellation, with Alpha Aurigae highlighted, filled the screen. Then it curled and flattened itself behind the silhouette of some suburban houses and a fence, with a compass indicating north in the corner of the screen. 'It took some hours for the message to be decoded, and the first news service reports that some sort of information had arrived with what now seems to have been a beam of energy, the same beam that caused the global atmospheric event that has caused so much destruction . . . those reports came in around breakfast time this morning. I'm being told we have on the line Patrick Moore from our studio in Winchester. Exciting times, eh, Patrick?'

Booth felt a hand on his shoulder. He looked up into the face of an intense, stocky man in the plainest suit he had ever seen. The man nodded towards the door, and Booth, like a puppy, followed him out, leaving his parents engrossed.

'Mr Hawtrey?'

Booth nodded.

'I'm from the Prime Minister's Office. Would you come with me, please, sir? We're expected.'

Booth opened his mouth, looked back towards the day room. 'Well, I'm in the middle of medical treatment, and—'

'Don't worry about that. We're going to a medical facility first. I've already checked you out.'

'Can you do that?'

'I can, yes.'

'My parents—'

'Will be told, sir.' He glanced at Booth's dressing gown. 'I've got a suit for you in the car.'

The car turned out to be a black BMW with a disabled sticker on it, which was parked in the doctors' car park at the side of the hospital. They were somewhere just off the North Circular, Booth realised, in Acton. He hadn't thought to ask.

'Crouch down now, please, sir,' the man said as they drew calmly out of the gates on to the main road.

Booth did so, and only straightened up when they were a distance away. Behind them, a traffic jam was forming in the opposite lane, as cars queued to enter the hospital.

'Just in time,' said the man. 'D'you reckon your parents will appreciate being on the front of the *Sun* tomorrow?' He gestured towards the glove compartment. 'Have a quick shot of Laphroaig, it'll stop you shaking. But don't overdo it. Tony will have my head if his alien shows up pissed.'

'Alien? Do you mean me?'

'Of course. You're an alien now, sir.' The man flashed him a grin. 'Didn't you know?'

Booth found the hip flask and swigged from it.

Eight: Rebecca's Seventeenth Birthday

Rebecca signed 'Happy Birthday' on the rough surface of the first page of the papermill edition of *Ambrose Triumphant* and discreetly checked the net printing allowance stamp. 'You too?' she asked the happy Singh woman in front of her.

'Oh yes.' The woman nodded fiercely. 'We're so alike. I can tell from your writing.'

'Really?'

'Yes! In *Ambrose* you have Judith training for the priesthood and failing, because she can't get over the guilty secret in her past, and I went through something very similar when—'

Rebecca listened for a while and then said: 'Great. Next, please.'

The line stretched across the little square in the middle of the Singh manor, all those people braving the cold. Rebecca was acutely aware of the guards looking down at her from all the towers. And of the four that were standing beside the little table they'd set up for her, who had marched her curtly out here and would march her back at the end of her hour, making sure that she didn't run off and spy for the Hawtreys.

She'd been surprised to get the invitation in the first place: she knew from her net credit rating that her work was popular up here, and that the Singhs had set up a papermill to produce actual physical editions, but to be *invited* to cross over into the territory of another family was an extraordinary honour. A dangerous one. David had taken her to see Ben when they received the invitation, and she had been given a list of things to look out for in the Singh stronghold. It was only David's concern for her that had stopped Ben from sending her on a full espionage mission.

'Don't the Hawtreys think of you as a traitor for coming here?' asked a gorgeous boy in a colourful robe.

'Oh, absolutely not. They're very pleased to make friendly connections with other houses,' Rebecca lied. 'Who's it to?'

'Anand Singh.'

'Oh. So you're—'

'Your biggest admirer.'

They went for a walk, the guards beside them, in the gardens that Anand's father had laid out to the east of the manor. They were formed from huge craters, where the Singhs had used explosives to clear buildings in the heart of the city. The horizon was still a mass of tower blocks and pylons and the sinewy track of the old motorway system. This was the image southerners always had in their minds when they thought of the Singh court, and it made Rebecca feel like she was seeing the world. She'd like to see more, she decided. The sight, and Anand's company, was raising her spirits although, it being around four, and especially four on the most terrible day invented, she was in her usual mid-afternoon trough. It was hard to be away from home on her birthday now. David had offered respite, a fellow sufferer from the oncoming birthday memories, though she suspected he exaggerated how he felt about the whole thing to make her feel better. There had been a lot of dark afternoons in the carriage on the way here, without him. The Singhs had specified she come alone, and it had taken severe diplomacy and hostage exchanges to ensure her safety.

Anand talked about movies. The Singhs had apparently decided that they would make a film! The net printing problems would be huge, of course, but that was only the start of Grandfather Singh's insane plan.

'He says that it will be the best film ever made,' Anand was saying. 'That in the future, people will think of it as better than *Empire of the Sun*. The mad old boy.'

'Erm . . . I don't really like *Empire*.' She hoped he didn't find her ignorant.

'You don't? How refreshing. It's good to meet someone who stands against accepted critical wisdom.' He reached inside the pouch that hung from his waistband and produced a tiny square of silk with a Singh crest on it. It was almost a token of a favour, a nod to the southern custom, just on the edge of parody.

Rebecca felt her insides lurch. She hadn't been expecting that. She was nowhere near pretty enough for that. It must be a ruse. And at home there was David. How could she—? Did she have to? Was this expected of her?

He'd seen her reaction. 'I'm sorry. Perhaps I've made a mistake?'

'No!' That was almost a shout. 'No, of course not. I'm—' She stopped herself from saying she was flattered. That was a feature of one of the *Russell* books, the emptiness of that word, and Anand would know. 'Honoured. And I'm blushing, because . . .' She looked quickly towards the guards. Anand waved them away and they went to stand at a comfortable distance. He hadn't seemed worried about them overhearing anything that passed between them. 'Because I really like you and you're beautiful.'

He laughed. 'Thank you!'

On an impulse, she took his hands in hers. Suddenly this felt like a scene from one of her books. 'But I feel a lot younger than my six . . . my seventeen years. I don't know who I am yet.'

He didn't show any sign of disappointment, continuing to smile. 'But surely you're of the same opinion as Maud in *Russell for the Flag*, that only love and war give any meaning at all to our lives.'

Shit. Could this man be any more perfect? And she was going to turn him down. Definitely something out of one of the books. She made sure of the words before she said them. 'That's what I think now, yes. Sometimes I get so . . . empty . . . that I just hit the bottom and think there's no point to anything, that only . . . opposition defines us, right?'

'And that surely applies to the human race as well as individuals . . .'

'I'm really sorry. It would put such a . . . weight on me. Confine me. If we were two children at our first ball, then . . .'

He nodded, accepting.

He carefully put the favour back in his pouch, not letting go of one of her hands. 'I'm very sorry too.'

His other hand returned to hers.

'So,' she said.

'I have another proposal.'

'Yes.' It wasn't a question.

He laughed again. 'This film we're going to make. Could it be of one of your books?'

'Fuck!' she said. Then she put a hand to her mouth. 'Sorry.'

Anand Singh laughed again.

Nine: Who Cheers the Cheerleaders?

Video footage from 2013, Bishop Michael Swansley and Bishop William Kemp at Hunstanton Priory, Dorset:

The time code indicates 31/10/13, 2350. Swansley and Kemp, in parkas, stand in a dark space, their breath billowing out into the darkness beyond the glare of the camera light they stand in. Swansley is carrying a primitive EM meter, a metal box with dials. They're both smiling, eager. The priory, they've already explained, is a famously haunted building.

'We're absolutely sprinting towards a greater understanding of man and God. It's dizzying,' says Swansley, by now becoming at ease in front of an audience. 'We're going to keep on distributing this evidence to those who're up in arms about what we're doing, because in the end we think you're just going to *have* to believe us. The weight of evidence is too compelling.'

From behind them comes a sudden thump. They both jump, then look around, chuckling.

Video footage from 2013, Bishop Michael Swansley and Bishop William Kemp at Hunstanton Priory, Dorset:

The time code indicates 0000. The shot is close on a monitor screen, a contour map of a room, the interior of the great hall of the priory, white lines on green. In the centre of the map, which is otherwise a carpet of waves and stalagmites, stands a tall, knotted pillar. Its shape changes with flashes of the screen, moment by moment. It's like watching the charge of a tornado towards a coastline.

'Can you see that? Can they see that?' Kemp is shouting. 'It's a static DC field, not an AC one. It's not mechanical interference.'

'I'm trying to find it in the room itself,' calls Swansley. The camera flicks up from the screen to find the tall figure, dark at the centre of a circle of light, walking towards the far wall. 'How close am I to it?'

'It can't be more than feet. Be careful.'

'I'm feeling. Oh no. I'm feeling real fear. And a presence. This is someone. Someone awful. I don't want to know them. I—' A sudden shout. The camera turns sideways with a jolt and watches the leg of a table.

Video footage from 2013, Bishop Michael Swansley and Bishop William Kemp at Hunstanton Priory, Dorset:

The time code indicates 0030. Kemp is trying to rub life back into Swansley's right arm, which he himself is holding on to. They both still seem excited.

'I feel very cold, still,' says Swansley, talking very fast. 'I had a sense of tremendous fear, of being lost in fear. I was reminded of the traditional condition of those in Hell, cut off from God, like there was the shadow of something between myself and God. That something had a personality, I feel. An intelligence. Tremendously negative. I think my arm has lost—'

He tries to keep speaking while Kemp feels the right side of his face.

'I can't feel anything in my face, either.'

'Michael, I think you've had a stroke.'

'Oh, have I? Extraordinary.'

Ruth stood in the rain, looking at the maze. She wiped her phone with her glove, checking for a third time. The maze was square, made from carefully tended box hedges. The tending, of course, seemed right up to date. No branch was outstanding, no bush overgrown. The entrance looked straight and cold at her. She could see right down it to where it took a sudden turn.

She'd walked right round the perimeter of this thing the first chance she'd got, alone, her handgun in the pocket of her coat. Now she'd come back to where she'd started.

It was good to do that. She'd been looking at the thing since they'd got here, ever since she'd checked the map of the grounds and realised what this thing had taken the place of. What it stood right on the site of. She'd kept silent, wanting desperately to go and see, not wanting to give anything away.

She ought to go inside and make absolutely sure. Make certain that the stories she'd been told, that had been passed down in her family for generations, were just a confusion of something, a garbled legend.

She ought to go in, but she couldn't make herself do it.

This place felt edgy. Like there was someone watching her, waiting for her to go in. There was fear waiting for her in there. A fear so big it made the journey into the wilderness seem like it had simply been a journey to come and meet it.

Something made her head turn, to look back to the house in the distance. Had there been movement at one of the windows?

She shivered. If one of the men was watching her, she'd better not hang around here too long.

That would be her excuse for not going into the maze, then.

She'd wait until the bloody priest had gone in, ask her what was inside. Then she'd take the men in, pretend it was a game on the last day. Just to make sure.

She switched off her phone and turned to begin the long trudge back towards the house. Her private reconnaissance wasn't nearly enough to make her content. But at least it would allow her to sleep.

Jane looked at the scar on Matthew's cheek with horror.

'You needn't have gone that far!' she whispered.

Matthew looked down into his ostrich stew, withdrawn into himself, defeated. The other militiamen laughed.

'Everybody has them,' said Ruth. 'Mine are on the underside of my left breast. Three straight lines, cut by my commanding officer on three separate occasions, because—' She looked sharply at Matthew.

'Because you disobeyed orders, Ruth,' the soldier replied.

The soldiers laughed again.

Jane felt the tug of the idea that this was just the boisterous stuff that militiamen did. She'd seen scars like this before, knew that they eventually became something to be darkly proud of, a mark of youthful exuberance.

But no lady would be seen in Matthew's company for several years now.

It had never been her fault, before.

She'd just offhandedly told Ruth about the encounter with the ostrich heads, doing her best to laugh about it. But Ruth had leapt up, and sent the others to go and find Matthew, and ordered Jane out of the kitchen while there were harsh words and then a rumpus as a chair was pushed over, a muffled shout through a gag, soothing words, a short, curt squeal.

Jane had stood there, listening from the pantry, her fingers numbly touching the wood of the door.

Nothing was supposed to disturb the survey of a house. Jane had tried to insist, in Ruth's initial rage, that she'd finished her work for that day, that the joke was thus fine, but Ruth had just ignored her.

The others seemed to relish the moment, as if they'd been waiting for this to happen to one of their own.

Now they were gathered for dinner around the warped table in the kitchen. Jane had been allowed back in, and had just gazed at the ugly red line, covered in clear field dressing. Eric was rubbing his knife on a wet towel, looking satisfied, done, justified in an ugly, sexual way.

She had started to apologise, but Ruth had silenced her with a curt command. The other soldiers ruffled her a little, trying to joke her out of her horror, but she couldn't help but stare at the wound.

On her way to the evening meal she had decided that she was going to share her mystery. She had been going to tell the others about the astonishing lack of EM gradient in this house. Perhaps even about Dad. If those puzzles had chimed with their own worries about the cleanliness of the house, then maybe they could all have gone forward together, seekers after truth.

But now she was going to hate them for a while, and didn't feel like talking.

She sat down and took some bread.

What on earth was she going to say in her official report to the Campbells? Not to mention the National EM Survey in Wells. The bishop there would send a team down to check the incredible nature of her results. The Campbells surely wouldn't want that, despite the discretion that the church offered to all the families. Jane wondered again what Ruth knew.

'So what do you have left to do, Reverend?' asked the Major, attending to the meal as if this day was like every other.

'The rest of the house. The cellars, the gardens and the out-buildings. The folly and the maze.' She couldn't take her eyes off Matthew's cheek. Then she felt that was obvious, and did so. The young soldier wasn't looking at anyone.

'Good. The sooner we can leave this place the better.'

'She'll get lost in the maze,' said Mark, who had three blue streaks dyed down his shaved scalp.

'I'll watch the exit and keep an eye on her.' Ruth looked to Jane. 'The map on your phone is good enough to get you through it, surely?'

Jane rubbed her brow and nodded her answer.

Matthew hiccuped on his stew, controlling what would become vomiting. The soldiers laughed again.

Jane lay in bed awake, listening to the animals calling to each other in the darkness outside.

Poor Matthew. How could she have let that happen?

It was another notch in the rope that was twisting inside her head. The blankness of her EM map had left her with such incredulity concerning the whole nature of reality in this house. If she told the others about it, they'd probably have a go themselves, and get all the normal results.

She could just decide to sleep. It was something vicars learnt to do, after a while. But the mysterious boundaries and limits of one's mind stopped one from doing the logical thing, the saving thing, quite often.

The animals out there in the forest just ate and breathed and reproduced. They didn't lie awake when they could sleep. They weren't always drowning in the whirlpool of just being themselves.

The feeling she'd had when she'd stood at the window, and something had sped at her across the fields.

She wasn't going to let herself sleep, that much was clear.

She got out of bed, letting the duvet roll on to the floor, and took her dressing gown from the brass hook on the back of the door. Perhaps she was going to go for a walk through the deserted rooms, with long squares of moonlight stretching in from their windows. She never got as far as deciding.

Facing the door, she was suddenly aware of something looking at her from behind.

She snorted in a deep breath through her nose as the fear hit her. The hairs along her spine were literally standing on end. She was aware of the centre of her back. Her body was yelling at her to turn round and get her back away from the predator.

Either that or don't look, grab the door handle, pull it open, run.

Something would slam the door shut.

She took control of her muscles and made herself turn.

The light hit her as she did so, a sudden red illumination that framed her against the door as if she was about to be hit by a car.

A great sound with it. A roar.

She flung up an arm to shield her eyes, but almost instantly lowered it again when she realised it was—

'Dad.'

He was pushing his way through the wall, his mouth contorting as if in great pain, his hands, formed from plaster, grasping at the air.

He made a great groaning cry. His eyes were roasting with pain. Behind him was the light and the twisted, squealing roar, like he was trying to pull away from the terrifying sound.

'What are you trying to tell me?' she shouted.

He continued to contort, fixing his agonised eyes on her, like he was willing her to understand.

He was real, conscious, alive in pain.

Jane was tremendously afraid of him.

She made herself step forward towards him.

Then, on a thought, she dashed to a chair and grabbed her satchel and pulled out the EM meter, and, her fingers slipping at the controls, switched it on.

Nothing.

She could feel things boiling in her brain as the red light pummelled in, but the machine said nothing and her ears rang with the roaring.

She started to sob, making her eyes stay open, feeling death throbbing from the wall, death which lit up the room.

Oh tiny human, you are going to die one day. I am from there. I am beyond that. I am not on your machine.

She was inventing those words, she was sure of it.

Oh Fortuna.

You should fall to your knees and splutter great orgasmic prayers.

But this is Dad. Touch him. You won't get the chance again, girl.

'What must I do?' She forced her feet forwards, one after the other, keeping her eyes locked on his, trying to pull out his pain. She reached out to an inch before the figure, pushed her fingertip through the gelatinous, sizzling air around him until it was a skin's width from his.

His mouth bared his teeth in a great effort to speak.

Then he vanished.

The whole thing ceased to be there.

The room was dark and cold and empty and a wall was just a wall. Jane fell back and hit the carpet hard.

She leapt up and threw herself at the wall, beating it with her fists and the sides of her face until the paper was ripped and there was blood with her tears.

In the early hours, she finished cleaning herself up. She'd vomited, suddenly and utterly, five minutes after the vision ended. Her nostrils were full of the smell of the experience again, as she bent over the toilet bowl. The smell nearly took her straight back there, as smells sometimes did if you'd greened that day. But, in absolute fear, she resisted.

It was a choking smell that had filled the room. It made her vomit again, in fear and disgust.

Sulphur.

Brimstone.

Fucking brimstone.

She'd cleaned the wall.

She was too afraid to green this, but she had to. What was her calling about if she didn't do it?

The light that had gone with the screaming had been beyond anything she had ever seen in her life, a light that could only have been produced out of her visual cortex, out of her ideas of light. But this light had rendered the air into a solid thing, had left a warmth about her upper cheeks and nose that had already started to itch.

The itch of flies, of deserts.

Oh fuck.

If it wasn't for the fact that the EM meter had persisted in saying zero, she'd have checked herself for radiation sickness.

But the EM meter wasn't built for this. Her calling wasn't ready for this. Her church had not been built in the name of this.

Oh fuck.

She threw water over herself from the sink, washed her mouth out with it, letting the cold of it shock her back to reality.

The green wouldn't have given her that as a side effect, a hallucination. She had soiled herself during that. She had been in the presence of . . .

Brimstone.

'Oh fuck.' This time out loud as she stared at herself in the mirror and tried to make herself face it.

It had been a shooting accident.

It had been. Everybody said so.

Dad had been happy, he had been surrounded by his men. He had had time for proud last words.

But they would say that, wouldn't they?

Jane left the bathroom and went to the tiny refrigerator where she kept her holy water. It sat on the floor of the bedroom, plugged into the fat socket in the far wall. She lay flat, her chin resting on the carpet so cleaned that her nostrils didn't even twitch, and flipped open the door.

The triangle of yellow light threw the room into shadow again, and

Jane flinched. She stared at the metal flask, and made herself think past it, to ignore what was before her eyes. She'd just wanted the comfort of the different light.

'Nothing and nobody can stop you talking to me, if you're there,' she said to God. 'If you are there, I need to hear you. I need to hear you now. Lord, I'm amongst my enemies. Please talk to me.'

She waited for two minutes, breathing as quietly as she could.

Then, shaking, she closed the fridge door and, scared by the darkness, stumbled towards the bed. She half expected the hellish light to come on again, and Dad to lurch from the wall once more.

She was alone.

But she could still do this, couldn't she?

She was brave. She was her father's daughter. Go on, girl.

She grabbed the dispenser from her bedside table and threw back a green.

She stared at the wall for twenty minutes, aware of how silly she must look, her dimpled cheeks creased with determination. She had overdosed on green today. But her brain wasn't going to get any more fucked up than it was already.

Come on, whatever you are. Come on.

When it didn't show itself of its own accord, Jane clenched her teeth and went after it. She went back to the memory theatre and hunted for it in the row of the unknown. She was so scared to find it that she just noted it sitting there in the corner of her eye and emphasised it without looking at it. It sat in the fifth seat beside the Too Big Owl, the Thing Standing over the Crib, the Scary Box with Eyes and the Stickman that Ran across the Road.

When she opened her eyes again, he was there. She felt the fear come back into her throat, expected the roar and the screaming and the fearful smell.

But this wasn't the same vision.

It was Dad again, but now he was like he'd been in the dream, poised and sculpted and reaching out from the wall. No crashing wave of emotions came with him, no physical distortion of the room or the air.

This resembled, if anything, a Banal Image, the sort of thing one found in undrugged, unattended old memories that one came across. Home was always painted like a charming sitcom set, it never rained on holiday, everybody who was nice smelt nice.

Dad, here, had a rugged sort of smile on his face as he proudly heaved his way through the wall.

'You are lying to me!' she screamed at the figure, pointing at it. Then she turned the point at the EM meter. Then, aware that she was play-acting for nobody but herself, but hoping she had an audience, but knowing that she didn't, she slowly turned the point of her finger right back between her own eyes.

She laughed at the end of her finger for a second. Laughed at what she was doing. She was alone, she could act as she wished. Even if it was mad.

With a flick of her tongue on her palate she flushed the lie-Dad image from her mind.

She started to shiver and found she couldn't stop.

She stopped pointing at herself and made herself move normally, swinging her arms to get some heat.

Jane crouched by her radio in the corner of the room. She'd pulled furniture close around her, making a little nest, and set the metal casing of the radio around the device itself.

The soldiers' rooms were some distance from hers, but somebody had probably heard some of the sounds of this mad night.

If what you did rather than what you thought was the definition, she was, she thought, probably mad now.

That was why she had shoved the bed against the door, to stop them from coming to disturb her.

The radio had been tuned to the BBC, of course, but now, with her back cold against the wall, Jane slowly turned the dial. She had her headphones on, she didn't want anybody to hear this, or even know that she was doing this.

This was her last way of taking a reading, the last thing to hold on to.

She found a place between stations where the white noise howled and wailed, spiralling between two points off to either side of her narrow world of sound. A place without distant voices in foreign languages.

She closed her eyes and waited to hear.

She thought about spikes as she listened to the howl.

The howl took on subtle shape and form in her mind. It became an ocean of crashing waves, then the bluster of air atop a hill, then a distant sawmill. She could change what it was just by thinking of each description.

The EM spikes were what had finally caused the split between Swansley and Kemp's new movement and the rump of the church hierarchy, so she had learned as a child. The lesson had been one of her favourite net texts, because it was very spooky. The video of the two founding bishops in Hunstanton Priory before the GEC had been shown on Jane's local network every Hallowe'en, when people locked their doors and sheltered by the fire and only the militiamen, adorned with talismans, stayed outside.

Spikes gave off modulated EM readings. They changed on a regular basis, obeying some unknown system like an untranslated alphabet. There was order to their howling. Spikes rose at night and retreated with day.

They were, Swansley and Kemp had hypothesised, signals.

Signals implied a station from which those signals were broadcast.

Signals implied Hell.

The spikes were what over the centuries had come to be known as 'ghosts'. The nature of personality in them was a highly disputed topic in the theological net journals that Jane subscribed to. Were the spikes persons themselves, or did they just stimulate feelings of being in the presence of personhood in those they encountered?

Was that Dad or was that her thinking of Dad?

Was he from Hell or was she in it?

The shadow that had swept between Swansley and his perception of God had intrigued her ever since she could remember. Her mental image of it had been like it was a tidal wave, a great thing rearing up, blotting out the sun.

When that wave had hit the bishop, it had swatted something in his brain, swept it away with it, leaving him half paralysed.

The thought came to Jane now that perhaps the thing that had grown between her and God was just the start of a huge wall of dark water. That it had shut off the EM field in this terrible place. Its first foaming messengers, gaining strength now, were visions of her father in torment. Its shadow was rushing over her, claiming her colleagues too, changing what they saw and experienced before the wave closed over them.

She wanted to hear through the wave, wanted to try and catch a glimpse of the real Dad. And, part of him, perhaps, her God.

She began to think of the white noise in her headphones as something different, now. Aware that she was treading beyond the city wall, she started to think of the noise as a voice. The white noise that swirled and scattered about her head was a blank canvas on which something could scrawl, something inside or out. Like ouija, a deliberate opening of oneself to the things outside the walls. Beyond the wave.

She considered the hissings and hustlings to sound like voices, and kept her eyes tight shut for so long that it was as if she had forgotten how to see. The roar of the sea turned into the sounds she needed to hear. And in the background of a great, whispering audience saying things like: 'sedimentary information' and 'it was good that the griel was left as a girl' and 'poisonous suffices' and, hard, right on the edge of hearing, very stern: 'infomeg', there was suddenly:

'Jane. We're going to need you.'

Jane leapt up and threw down the headphones, shouting.

She kicked the jack out of the radio.

She stood, howling at her own weakness and cowardice. The fear that had come with her dad's voice.

Things she couldn't see were fighting in the air around her.

Shuddering so hard she nearly tripped over her own feet, aware of how deeply cold she'd become, she threw apart the makeshift Faraday cage.

A knock came on her door.

'Breakfast.'

'Okay,' she called back.

She went to the windows and opened them wide to let out the smell of brimstone.

Two hours later, Jane stood at the entrance to the maze.

She had been silent at breakfast. She had to fight down a desire to ask for them to leave right now. She didn't want to spend another night in this place. Nobody had asked about the noise. Perhaps they hadn't heard it.

We're going to need you.

Was that Dad reaching out to her from Hell?

Or was that Dad trying to pull her in?

If it was anything beyond the confusion in her own mind and the white noise. The only sensible reason she could think of for the discontinuity between her own experiences and the readings of her equipment was that her perceptions were somehow at fault. That something was going wrong with her head. She felt herself surrounded by evil, and didn't know where Dad was placed in reference to that evil.

She was looking a mess this morning, she knew. She hadn't showered. She hadn't wanted to be alone in the bathroom.

The maze was a perfect square of box hedges. A clear gravel path.

She'd chosen to do this first this morning because she didn't think she could bear to walk through those perfect, empty corridors again.

Ruth was standing beside her, hugging herself as the autumn wind rippled the surface of her parka. There was something expectant about her, Jane thought. 'Are you going to get on with it?'

'About Matthew, I just wanted to say—'

'Don't. It's part of our life. You can't understand it, so don't go on about it.'

Jane looked at the ground and let the words out between her teeth. 'I wanted to say sorry. Just sorry. Whatever you know that I don't, I didn't want that young man to get hurt!'

Ruth raised an eyebrow. As if she couldn't bother with more than a token refutation of Jane's paranoia. 'Fine. Now you've expressed yourself.'

Jane glared at her, wanting to punch her. She took a moment to breathe deeply, and made herself settle. There was something about the situation that reminded Jane of . . . what? She couldn't take a pill here and now to seize it. It came to her. This feeling between her and Ruth was like Bonnie and Russell in *Russell for the Flag*. She was leaving him, she'd already made up her mind, and so she got irritated with his protestations of love and his gifts. Their parting had this sort of frustrated anger about it. Now the truth is on the surface, but the moment of separation has arrived too. So you and I will never share this truth.

The executioner, at the end of the book, grew similarly irritated with Bonnie's wit on the way to the scaffold. Your goodwill itches at my guilt. Be negative or rude or awkward. Stop trying to connect with me. Stop trying to grab me, you're heading for the bottom.

Goodbye, Mr Bond.

Jane pursed her lips. 'As house chaplain of the Campbell family, I am about to survey and bless this maze for their future use, to make sure that it contains nothing that will disturb their minds, their souls or their dreams.'

'I'm aware of your work, house chaplain, go about it,' said Ruth. And there was a little clip at the end of her sentence which said go about it now. Quickly. I want you to walk into the trap.

Jane took her first step into the maze.

She didn't want to look back to the house for fear that her eyes would find that little rectangular window, and there would stand Alisdair Trent, looking painfully down at her from Hell.

Video footage from 2053, Bishop Michael Swansley's address to the General Synod of the Reformed Church of England in Chester:

Swansley is an old man now, the right-hand side of his body locked solid, his right arm tight against his body. The setting now is more modest, inside a church hall, with no PA. We're post-GEC now. He speaks from a chair, his notes on a phone in his lap. He doesn't refer to it often. 'This will be the last time I will see you on earth. Say that every time, don't I?' (A big laugh from the audience.) 'I am confident now that what we made will go on. I've seen it change a lot down these decades, as we've found out more. God has bid us come closer to him. Continue to go there. The Brunian legacy to our church, the developments of the last thirty years . . . continue exploring.' (He refers to his notes again, lost for a moment.) 'A priest of the Reformed Church of England must be an adventurer into the human condition. He or she must remember everything of each encounter with the divine or the demonic. He or she must be especially sensitive to dreams. For there truths slip past our waking minds. Further, he or she must testify to the information thus revealed. He or she must be open to the extraordinary things that our God asks of us and tells us, through His chosen medium of the EM field. Follow the Lord, my friends. Listen to Him. Continue to be the agents of His plan. Continue to find out what strange and wonderful creatures we are, about the divine creation of our memory. Memory is the concert hall, electromagnetic radiation the instrument, dreams the great concertos. Seek the player. For some of you that will be very dangerous. The things God will demand of us as we get closer to Him are going to get more extreme. More terrifying. He will need certain priests, especially, to take great risks. But we must persist. Goodbye.'

He doesn't even close his eyes. It takes the audience of priests a full minute to realise that he is dead.

Jane spread her line of salt across the entrance of the maze, walked ten yards, took the first turning right, and relaxed a little to be out of Ruth's line of sight. The Major had watched her back all the way down that first stretch, like she might be going to vanish any moment. She took her phone from her satchel. The maze formed a neat little decal on the screen. Not a classical pattern for a maze, from her limited experience, but something that looked modernist and restrained. The miles of box hedges, locked into their square, led to a circular clearing at the centre. From there, a straight path led to the exit. So Jane, of course, could have walked in through the exit and gone straight to the centre. But a priest had to follow emotional gradients as well as EM ones. Much the same thing, especially in this case. People would have got lost in this maze, hidden in it, escaped here to have sex. The exit was the end of that story, not the start.

She hoped it would be a gentle, normal story. Not the mocking laughter of a falsely blank reading. No manifestations. No surprises.

She dared to take a first, general reading on the EM meter. She nearly yelled at the sight of the numbers spinning. They settled to an ever-changing rough estimate. The topographical EM map was a mess of little grooves and lumps and waves.

Jane wished that she had a wall to lean on that would take her weight. 'Fuck,' she said, with a sincerity that surprised her. 'Fucking fuck!'

She connected the meter to her phone and recorded the reading. The EM map of the maze contoured appropriately, and an entirely appropriate figure appeared at the centre of the new topography.

Perhaps the buggers had never liked the house and had lived in the maze instead.

She felt greatly relieved. She hadn't realised how much her composure had depended on the contours of EM maps. It was like the invisible foundation that she had always visualised underneath the world was back. She could just get on with this bit, and when she left the maze, maybe the rest of the world would have snapped back to normality as well.

She traced the path of the maze with her finger. It didn't matter if she got lost initially. She had to take readings in a variety of locations. Normally, she'd have found a place at the four compass points and then gone to do a last one at the centre, but, hungry for such normality as she was, she was going to record every inch of this damn thing.

She decided on right, left, right, and found herself walking along a long outside corridor. The hedges here were a little more overgrown than elsewhere. She had to keep her arms tight by her sides to avoid her coat catching on the twigs.

Her footsteps crunched on gravel.

She walked for a while.

Her footsteps crunched on gravel.

There were also footsteps crunching behind.

Jane stopped. The crunching behind didn't. She looked over her shoulder, wondering if for some reason Ruth had followed her in. Whatever it was was still back behind the far corner. She relaxed for a second, thinking that such open pursuit couldn't be sinister.

But who would risk another scarring? It couldn't be one of the soldiers.

Jane fixed her eyes on the green vertical lines of the corner far behind her. In a moment it would come round.

They were odd steps, not a straightforward march of two feet, but a shuffling. Random falls of feet. Like something large with lots of feet.

The fear from last night rose in her throat. She glanced at the EM meter. Higher, here. Appreciably.

Would this anomalous thing be wearing a First World War uniform, and have a fixed intensity to its eyes and bring with it a painted background that would rush towards her and take her?

She started to back away before she knew she was doing it.

Still nothing came round the corner, though the footfalls became louder.

Her courage failed her. She turned and ran.

The hedges snatched at her coat to one side and then the other as she buffeted along the narrow lanes, choosing pathways thoughtlessly, panting as she tried to gasp relief out of the chilly air. She couldn't hear what was behind her because of the noise of her own crashing, crunching and gasping.

Something was burning at the back of her head, a warning that she hadn't felt in years. An instinctive sense of things askew.

She came to an intersection of four pathways and stopped. She didn't want to go back the way she had come. But she felt like it had got behind her. That one of these lanes would take her straight to it.

She made herself stay where she was for a moment. She would hear it coming. Maybe see it coming. She didn't want to see it.

Fumbling, she reactivated the meter.

The local reading was suddenly larger.

That was the thumping that was coming from the back of her head. The instinct that she was running up a powerful EM waveform. She'd left the recorder on. She checked the map. A steep gradient from the entrance to here. A straight line. She'd been going back and forth across that line, establishing it for the machine, and now she'd just run straight up it.

But there were no point sources intruding on to the picture. No spikes.

Jane jerked her head up from the meter at a sudden noise. A howl.

And here came the crunchings and rustlings from the gravel too, from two of the intersecting paths.

She managed to keep looking at one of them.

Around the corner loped a wolf.

It took her a moment to register it. It wasn't what she'd been expecting. It was pattering gently forward like a domestic dog, but the gait had the confidence of something that expected to get its prey.

It knew there was nowhere to run. Its own run was about economy. An easy kill. Its eyes flashed in the low sunlight as they fixed on her. Behind it came another. And another.

A pack was coming down the opposite path too.

For a moment, Jane almost felt relief that it wasn't the fear she'd been expecting. Then, sickeningly, the adrenaline burst up into her throat and she found herself tottering off down one of the side paths.

The scattering footfalls of the wolves sped up behind her. They started yelping at each other, coordinating her pursuit.

She sped up, trying to look at the map on her phone as she ran. If she could find the way to the centre, then she could sprint out of the long path to the exit.

She could follow the EM gradient to the centre.

She threw the meter and phone into her satchel, and took each turn at a sprint in the direction that increased the thumping in her head.

Shit, this was getting intense. This must be getting up into religious ranges, into prayer meetings and book burnings.

The wolves must live in the maze. Their den. That was why the place was so emotive. All the pursuits and kills here. All the blood on the gravel.

She realised, with another lurch of her stomach, that if the field got more intense towards the centre, then that was where the horror was. Where the kills had been.

Was she running from them, or were they herding her?

But the calls of the wolves came from behind her still. 'Ruth!' she shouted. 'Matthew! Help me!'

There was no reply from Ruth. And after the scarring, the others would have given her plenty of space.

What a stupid way to die. After all this. She had a horror of predation, as most people did. All the energy of the little human communities, lost to the things beyond the walls. They must have kept wolves here, in the safari park. But now they were free, they must have started to spread. The hedgerows and ditches unsafe again. Another darkness outside the gates.

The frosty air was catching at her throat. She had a fleeting thought of how cold the gravel would be when she hit it. How warm the wolf. Fear of blood. Memories of scraped knees in child fights. Cold morning violence. Emotive breaths puffing in the air. Other children.

She came to a Y-shaped junction, and saw them bounding towards her down one branch, so she dashed up the other.

The back of her head beat more.

She came to a T-junction, and found them rushing down the top of the T.

Again, up the gradient.

Numinous, now. Great ecstasy or horror. Things of the beyond lived here. She could expect visions if her fight-or-flight system weren't blocking her brain to keep her moving.

Higher still, and she'd be helped by the visions. Phantom soldier. Mother Mary. They'd burn right through her adrenaline and give her divine martyr strength as she died.

She found herself at a new crossroads, and now they were coming down three out of the four paths.

They *were* herding her. They were pushing her towards the centre of the maze. Where their killing pit must be.

She took the only option left to her. I must run or they will kill me. *Run, child! Run!*

She tried to make her thoughts turn to God, now she was free of the shadow that had been between them in the house. But she couldn't reach up while her brain was full of the fear.

Come to *me*! Lord, please come to *me*!

She hoped there would be time before they tore her apart. When they cornered her, she would reach out to Him before they came with every shouted word and every forced posture of prayer.

The field strength would help her. The field strength would take her there. Anaesthetic. Holy death.

Good to know that. She was a good sacrifice, thrown straight at God. Catch me, heal me. She would find Him now, the hard way.

She hoped wolves went for the throat. Please let them kill me before they eat me.

The buzz of presence reared up in the back of her head. She had to look. She grabbed the meter from her bag. She was sprinting up a vast EM gradient now. Straight to the centre of the maze. The topographical map was like the side of a mountain.

Why was this place so open to the field, when the house was closed?

She knew she'd never find out.

She burst into the circle at the centre of the maze, and all she could see was the gap that led to the path to the exit.

And it was full of wolves. They were standing shoulder to shoulder, a living wall of them.

She burst out sobbing at the prospect of death.

She looked round the other exits, and found that the animals were trotting down all of them.

She looked over her shoulder. And behind her.

She was almost calm as she stepped into the centre of the circle, as her body allowed her to look around. The intensity of everything made every blade of grass, every detail important, her body screaming at her that she was really here, that this moment was as real as reality got. No blood on the grass. No killing pit. There was only a low lump. A swelling in the surface of the ground, like a barrow. But rougher than that. Like a building had once stood here, and had sunk into the ground. Jane stumbled to the top of the little slope, tripping over the uneven surface, the remains of brickwork beneath the mud beneath the grass beneath her feet. She turned slowly on the spot, like a weather vane.

The field was roaring in her brain. On the map it was off the scale. She could feel the air prickling with potential. All her hairs were on end. Her hair was rising from her shoulders. She would attract lightning. God would kill her with lightning. Spare her the wolves.

There was a glow about the edges of her vision. Brilliant spots sailed across the hedges and the wolves, burnt into her retinas.

Presence settled in the air about her. She breathed in presence through her lungs.

The most intense atmosphere she had ever felt.

She threw her head back and looked straight up, laughing and sobbing. She fixed her eyes on infinity.

She heard growling, growing in volume around her.

Barks and snaps and the snuffling of hunger for blood. They were willing each other to attack her. She could feel them. They were welling up.

Now, she willed herself. Before it's too late. Give yourself to God. God come for me. Deliver me. It's me.

There was a dark speck in the cloudy sky above her.

It was growing larger as it descended. Fast now, like a spaceship in a cartoon.

Jane laughed in great gulps, feeling the wetness of her face, darkness shunting her vision with each pulse. Her throat and wrists and forehead were beating.

It was a figure. A woman. *An angel?*

Yes. Take me.

The shape flew down smoothly at an angle towards her. It was a woman in a long, bell-shaped dress, with boots on. She wore a hat. She held a bag in her left hand. She held up an open umbrella in her right, and she was flying with it.

She smiled utterly and benignly at Jane as she descended. The smile fixed her in its love and she smiled back.

'God?' she asked.

The boots of the woman touched the ground, and she stood a few feet from Jane, regarding her. She lowered the umbrella, and furled it.

The wolves bayed low to each other in fear.

The woman approached Jane.

Jane reflexively fell to her knees. She could see only the impossible boots on the impossible feet. Some part of her confirmed that she was mad. She had left reason behind. That part of her joined with the others in released longing. She was having her religious experience and had met the divine.

'Stand up.'

The voice was gentle and firm. A warm, terrifying hand closed on Jane's, and helped her stand so her eyes met the universal smile again.

'I'm Mary,' she said. 'I am your magical helper.'

Jane dumbly nodded.

Mary clicked the gloved finger of her other hand.

The wolves turned and ran off down all the pathways.

'Together, Jane Bruce, if you accept, we shall go on a long journey,' said Mary.

Her voice was like Mother's.

'This journey will answer all your questions and will make you complete. This journey will kill you. Do you accept?'

'Yes,' said Jane.

'Then let me tell you what you must do.'

Ten: Rebecca's Sixteenth Birthday

David shook her, slapped her face, looked deep into her eyes. 'Rebecca!' he shouted. He shouted her name many times.

They were in her room. With the big black circles painted on the walls.

She bared her teeth at him and growled through the tiny gap between them. She could understand the urgency of why he was there, though she didn't feel it. She didn't know where he'd come from, though. Or what he'd been doing beforehand.

She suddenly recognised him. 'David! Oh! I was wanting to talk to you. I have a lot of new theories now. No, never mind the plate. Never mind the plate. Come and hold on.'

He'd gone to look at the plate where she'd had the toast that had the mixture of mushrooms on it. And the cheese sauce. She was beckoning to him now and he flashed back to her and held her, but he didn't hold her right. He held her like he was propping her up. She tried to fall backwards with him, but he wouldn't fall.

'It's because it's today,' he said. 'You're trying to forget, aren't you?'

'No, darling! I'm trying to bloody remember!'

'Remember what?'

'All this . . . stuff! Stuff from when I was a baby. Never sorted it. Hanging around. Never think about it. In trunks. Like elephants never forget.'

'You're not trying to kill yourself?'

'No. Have I still got—?' She put a hand to the bridge of her nose and found the wound there. 'Oh. I did that on the toilet.' Then she laughed. And stopped.

'So you threw it up?'

'No.' Very proud. 'Kept it all down. Bit of a fight.'

'Where did you get them?'

'I found them. There's a good book on the net. So I picked one for one thing and one for another. Oh . . . my . . . God! I've taken lots of mushrooms! No, no, David, that's a joke . . .' Sway. 'My real revelation. Same as the old. I *wanted* something more. But I didn't get it. Didn't go far enough. So I continue to think: it *is* all shit! No, no, listen. There's *nothing* behind the curtain! It doesn't mean *anything*! And that feels great now because we're free. But when I wake up. And the great thing is, we can get away from the memory of the things that make us. We can use them to make us and then just . . . say goodbye! Who we are is connected throughout time and space to the number of distant things that are half of us, but even then that's not a proper revelation, and anyone that says it is . . . I feel like a priest, like any moment I'm going to remember everything. God, I'm hungry. I want more. Got any more toast?'

He was looking at her with a mix of anger, adoration and now, just a bit, amusement. 'No. No more toast.'

'Time and again I tell myself,' she sang, high-pitched.

'You will feel better, you know,' he said. 'One day.'

'Ha ha ha,' she said, running a hand through her long, dyed red hair, wondering why it was like that, why she was bothering to follow fashion at all. Or what fashion was. Oh, another distraction. But it's better to make one's own fashions. If you're stuck here, part of the process, it's better to be in control.

'David,' she said. 'Find my notepad and take this pen from behind my ear.'

Eleven: And Did Those Feet

The interior of the church was decorated with branches garlanded with flowers. Tiny fish swam in the font. The pews had been shunted up against the walls, those not fitting into a rough circle upended to stand as a series of pillars. New-budded holly topped each one. Where the altar had stood, there was now a huge black metal cylinder, with tiny controls embedded in its casing. Monitor lights flickered in a rhythmic pattern on those controls.

The EM compiler just didn't fit with the look of the rest of the place, David Hawtrey knew. He had learned to love the look of old stone, of water-worn steps, of buildings turning back to nature. He was certain that one morning in his travels about the islands he would wake to see a view of decaying splendour that would be so perfect it would kill him. That was why he'd changed the look of the church, to make it a private space just for him. But in the middle of that the compiler looked invulnerable, modern, unforgiving. Unfortunately this was the very centre of the village, and the site of a windmill power link that had been used to light the church, so the machine had to be here.

He sighed. Despite the waves of awe and wonder rushing through him, he had let his thoughts wander. The machine always did that to him. It was his drug now, and he let it take him where it would. He had never been an enthusiast for compilers when they were used in courts. He would leave dances early to be out of their way. One knew the feelings they generated in one's brain were false, just phantoms. A man who knew himself and the world shouldn't allow himself to become the puppet of one. That was how he had thought. But that was before he had encountered the particular machine that he stood in front of now. Before they had brought it to the enemy village, and he had found the wonderful juxtaposition of compiler and nature.

The compiler directed highly localised magnetic and electrical fields at the brains of everyone within a certain radius. This compiler was designed to take that further, doubtless for one of the Manderville revels that ringed their entire court with garlands of ceremonial dancers. This compiler could whip nature. Could flatten it like a storm flattened corn. The pathetic fallacy no longer held. The skies could be cloudy and say that the year ahead would be bleak, and human life just a collection of boxes on the land. But the compiler would say life was worth living for life's sake.

The compiler, by happy accident, also made it much easier to provide the sort of recreations his men liked. Unwholesome as they were. His team did dangerous things in enemy territory, then David let them behave as they liked. It was their reward. He supposed they didn't feel the same sense of duty towards his family that he did. Why should they? They were only kept in line by opportunities like this. Chances to feast at the enemy's table. From which he had to keep himself apart.

He looked down at the fourteen-year-old girl who was sucking his cock. She looked back up at him, her eyes full of ecstasy and holy fear.

He gently pushed her head back. She looked aghast. 'I'm sorry, Charlotte,' he said. 'It just isn't working.'

She started to weep, great sobs of sorrow, cut off from her worship at his feet. Which annoyed David. Even though she was an enemy villager, he had become fond enough of her not to want to hurt her feelings.

He reached down and pulled his trousers up, fastened his belt, and did up the button beneath his dog collar. He glanced back at his 'predecessor', Reverend Norman, who sat limply, propped up against the font, his head a mass of insects. Initially it had seemed fitting to leave the body of the enemy priest there. But now it was getting too messy to live with. And while they were in this place, he did want to live here, with Charlotte, away from the others. 'Do something about him,' he told the girl. 'I'm just going to take a walk.'

She leapt up to obey, joyful again.

David smiled sadly, glad that he'd been able to please her, and headed for the door.

He wandered out into the village square, pulling the vicar's collar from around his neck and stuffing it in his pocket. Now that the compiler had locked off the emotional patterns of the villagers and was playing inside those patterns, he probably didn't require the symbolism of the disguise any more. He'd hardly slept in the six days they'd been here, though his head had been full of dreams. He felt restless, despite the fact that they'd stopped here to rest. He felt this was a place on the way to some other place, and the part of his mind that listed and kept note of orders kept telling him that he should be moving on to that new place, despite the fact that, now they'd planted charges against one of the three Manderville net pylons, his only remaining order was to take his team safely home to Hawtrey country again. With the compiler as their most precious booty. He kept tripping over the inconsistency about the orders, kept thinking there was something he'd forgotten that he should be doing.

Maybe that was a function of having an erection all the time.

He'd wanted to have Charlotte rename herself Rebecca, but that had seemed too much, suddenly, when he was just on the point of doing it. The sort of thing his men would do.

Nobody was getting any sleep, it wasn't just him. Not the enemy villagers or the rest of what for some reason they'd started to call David's 'Quire'. Perhaps they associated licence and revels with a group of men of that name, one of these local village rites that the Mandervilles allowed or more probably couldn't be bothered to do anything about in their vast territory. These particular bastards had had it coming, with only a fence of wooden stakes and a couple of old men with guns that didn't work. The village elders deserved everything they got for protecting their people so badly. David's men had been able to smash right in through the gateway with the battering ram. They'd started up the compiler on battery power before anyone had even approached them. The enemy villagers had come out of their houses in awed, swaying waves, enraptured, gazing at the Hawtrey soldiers like they were gods.

So they had behaved like gods. And the enemy villagers kept on giving. So much for the 'peace of the Mandervilles'. They couldn't stop a squad of Hawtrey soldiers from stealing their compiler from their convoy, they couldn't hunt them down afterwards, they couldn't protect their own people. They probably didn't even care what happened to the inhabitants of one small village. Unlike in Hawtrey country, where there was civilisation, and everyone could rely on the protection of the law. When other enemy villages discovered what had happened here, hopefully they'd start questioning the tithe they paid the Mandervilles. So they'd done some good work here, it hadn't just been a convenient hiding place. This wasn't just a meaningless orgy for the men's sake.

There was a band playing in the school hall. Over the music he could hear the cries of one of Alec's endless 'punishment beatings'.

The stolen wagon stood on the green, its harnesses lying on the grass, its plastic armour glinting in the low autumn sunlight, the sickly-green Manderville flag on its door defaced with blood and shit and formed into the rough shape of the Bloody Eagle. The body of an old woman lay under the wheel arch, the source of the materials. David climbed up the ladder to the cab, groaning as another wave of divine ecstasy rolled through him. It was like he was being led around by his cock and tongue and stomach. Thank God he'd had the good sense to pick Charlotte from the crowd, lead her away and ride it through with her. That way he'd kept hold of his sanity. There was something willing in her eyes that went beyond the compiler's power, he was certain. He wished he could take her back to Hawtrey country. He checked the instruments. They could get out of here at any point now. The horses had rested in the village stables. Their trail was dead, they could move by night, driving along back roads their enemies had probably never mapped, send the wagon running fast at some Manderville checkpoint in the middle of nowhere, or use the ram again under covering fire. They'd have to clean the Eagle off first, though. The Mandervilles would know who had taken their new toy, but they couldn't be allowed to officially *know*. Not their place to start a war.

But would the others go now if he ordered them to? What would be the best point to tell them to give all this up? When the villagers were all dead, and there was nobody left to serve them? He'd made decisions like this many times before. At what point would his men become his men again?

He sometimes had nightmares about units like his own loose in Hawtrey territory. All the families had them. Anyone who lived outside of the protection of the big cities was fair game. But at least under the peace of the Hawtreys, such attacks would be avenged, the perpetrators found and burnt.

Maybe a war against the Mandervilles wouldn't be such a bad thing. Bring peace to places like this. Defend them. Educate the villagers to Hawtrey standards. Make them a bit more human.

He looked up at a shout from outside the cab, and watched joylessly through the polarised windscreen as Steven grabbed a screaming, running woman and wrestled her to the ground on the wet grass of the green. Steven knew something about compiler programming, and had set up various of the enemy women to be fearful rather than ecstatic participants in the rape of their village. He'd hunted them like rabbits, having convinced them they couldn't leave. David watched Steven bouncing up and down on her as she shrieked, his fists beating on her back and then pulling up her skirts. The whole scene was washed out in the polarised light of the cab's armoured glass. Steven rammed his way home, then started thumping her head now, harder and harder, until her chin was bouncing off the ground too. Then her head was thumping at an odd angle. He finished, held her tight down against the soil, checked the pulse in her neck, then hopped to his feet.

He threw back his long black hair, noticed David sitting in the cab and saluted cheerfully. Then he proceeded to fasten his britches, glancing happily down at the dead woman. He too still had an erection, David noted.

He clambered down out of the cab and met Steven as he danced over to him. 'Heaven on earth, sir!' he cried. 'Manderville girls for the taking! Why has nobody ever used a compiler like this before?'

David fell in beside him, walking carefully rather than matching the man's ecstatic skips. 'Because that compiler is something special.'

'You're not wrong, sir. It's better than anything I've ever seen.'

'When we get it back to Ben, he'll give us land.'

Steven looked anxious for a moment. 'We're going to do that soon then, are we, sir?'

'When you've collected all your favours. Nothing lasts forever, does it?'

The look on Steven's face belied his words. 'No, sir.'

David pushed open the doors of the school hall and they walked into shadow. The music became louder. A noticeboard was still pinned with announcements of future events: a school concert, a dance. One of the dates was two days ago. They had stopped time for these people. 'Turn the settings up far enough, and the whole world would be like this, don't you think, Steven?'

'Yes, sir.' He sounded excited at the prospect.

They walked round a corner and pushed open another pair of doors to enter the main hall. A ragged band of three or four elderly villagers was frantically playing pipes and drums onstage, their eyes staring as they put their all into the tune. They were playing far too fast. They looked like they'd been playing for days, and would continue to do so until they dropped. One old man's cheeks were inflated like a leather bag around the mouthpiece of his pipes.

At the other end of the room, a naked young woman hung from two posts that had been nailed to a wall, her flesh a mass of lacerations and open wounds. Her face was turned upwards at an angle, her mouth forming words that might be those of prayers, her expression lost in ecstasy.

In the centre of the room there lay a mass of bodies. David's gaze picked out Frank and Little Bob, sitting on the polished wooden floor beside the pile. They were being handed bowls of food by a woman dressed in a splattered nightgown. Her face was ecstatic too. The men saluted David eagerly, big smiles on their faces. Little Bob had soup down his shirt, covering his beer belly in green lumps.

David returned the salute and went to inspect the bodies.

They looked to be all male, a cross-section of the men of the village. They'd been alive last night, when everybody was dancing. After David and Charlotte had retired for the evening, the soldiers must have made them fight each other. Jutting limbs and ripped throats. The smell was already terrible.

He looked back to the band, and saw something moving behind them. Alec. He was fucking something behind the curtains. David could hear the cries under the music and loud swear words in Alec's Scottish burr.

A terrible suspicion formed in David's mind. He looked to the other two. They were still busying themselves with the woman, making her wash her breasts in the soup and feed them to them. They hadn't noticed what Alec might be getting up to. David marched over to the stage, leapt up on to it, stalked past the band and threw back the curtain.

It was a boy, as he'd thought it would be. He was bent over a piano stool, his face red. Alec's head spun round, his eyes boggling at the sight of his commanding officer. 'Sir! Wait, sir—'

'You disgusting—!' David could hardly contain himself at the sight. He had feared that with all the licence the machine had given his men, it might come to something like this. 'You know what you're doing, Alec?' He reached under his armpit.

'No, sir, it's the machine.' The desperate man jumped back from the boy, his penis not wilting even during his terror.

The boy started to cry.

'Buggery is a capital offence. Even the Mandervilles don't stand for it.'

'No, sir. No!'

David took the gun from his shoulder holster and aimed at Alec's chest. 'If you can manage to end your life like a real man, I'll tell your family it was in combat.' He was aware of the others approaching the stage, realising what was going on. He felt their fear about what was about to happen. But he heard what they were saying to each other. That Alec had brought it upon himself. They sounded disgusted.

Alec looked wildly around. Another wave of emotion hit them.

He leapt at David.

David fired as he hit him, the impact of the man sending him stumbling back to crash into the band, who fell with a squeal of bagpipes.

He was back on his feet in a moment.

But Alec was dead, lying on his face, the exit wound having opened up his back.

The others stepped up on to the stage and gathered round.

The boy leapt off the stage and ran, sobbing.

'What are you going to tell his family, sir?' asked Steven.

David turned to look at them. Filthy as they were, there was still respect in their eyes. He could afford to be generous. 'That he died in the taking of the compiler. Now tidy this mess up. We'll be staying here two more days. We use that time to plan our escape home, starting tomorrow morning. Bob, have Alec buried.'

He stepped down off the stage and headed for the door again. 'If anyone wants me in the meantime, I'll be in church.'

As the doors of the hall swung closed behind him, he found that he was mentally composing his next e-mail to Rebecca. I don't know how to tell you this. I know you were close. But Alec did a very heroic thing.

He gave his life for his friends.

'Everything I've done so far is absolutely normal.' Jane slapped her phone into Ruth's hands. 'The usual ups and downs, but nothing disturbing. When I've finished, you'll get the full report, of course.'

They were inside the orchid house that stood to the west of the house, in its lee from the prevailing winds. An utterly uncracked geodesic dome of glass that stood amongst a tidy herb garden. The rain made a thundering sound as it cascaded off that roof and on to the garden, and inside the dome the air was humid and lardy.

She'd emerged from the exit of the maze to find Ruth standing there, her hand on her holster. No wolves. The look on her face had been as guarded as always. Not that Jane had looked at Ruth's face for any length of time, then. In that moment of walking out of the maze, she had been bulletproof, filled up with certainty.

'I heard animal noises,' Ruth had said. 'Are you all right?'

Jane had just smiled at her.

Ruth had led her to the orchid house. Once there, out of sight of everyone else, which in the past was a thought that might have scared Jane, the Major had demanded to see what she'd come up with so far.

That was horribly prescient of her. Jane had spent twenty minutes inside the maze restructuring the EM map on her phone, creating an artificial version with a couple of small hotspots, one in the maze itself. She had signed it, and added all the official seals that would have earned her exile and defrocking at the very least.

Would have. Mary had looked over her shoulder as she'd prepared it, her fingers, with clear nail varnish, suggesting how to make the lie work.

Jane realised now, with a shiver, that in a discontinuity between two periods of feeling like herself, she'd actually changed allegiances, from her church to her God.

Or to His direct representative.

Put that way, it was what people who sealed themselves off from the world with supplies and guns did.

The move from object to subject, from one's religion being around one, to one's religion being . . . *about* one.

She looked desperately round the orchid house as Jane examined the display, full of a giddy sense of coming down.

Had that been real?

A big butterfly detached itself from one of the blooms and flapped lazily in her direction. The rain slid down the glass. Everything was in place as it had been in her childhood, her memories, her grounded sense of a continuing reality. The movie was now carrying on. But Jane had leapt across scenes, jumping in a clumsy edit. The vicar doing her job – chup! Now the vicar had had a religious experience. Jane hadn't been there in between. I was drunk, she'd heard soldiers say. I'm not responsible for what happened.

'This journey will answer all your questions and will make you complete. This journey will kill you. Do you accept?'

'Yes,' Jane had said. Yes, yes, yes.

The EM field in that maze had been so high that it had created a religious experience for her, that was obvious. Mary fucking Poppins had slid up out of the depths of her reptile brain. She couldn't even remember seeing the movie, although she had dim memories of her mother reading her the book. But there was the difference. She couldn't just write that off. Her entire calling insisted that, once you were out of the field and grounded in the rain again, the experiences of Oz had still *happened*. That was the belief. Only the secular could walk away from it and say that was that and this is this and the one doesn't mean anything in the other.

But practically . . . having to actually *deal* with that now . . . It was like an unwanted weight in Jane's head, the sensation that everything had changed, and a set of walls had been erected in her life, redefining the frame through which she saw things.

She'd just lied and broken church law for this hallucination. She still felt oddly correct in doing that, as though, if the Reformed Church of England learned about Mary, they would automatically understand that she was a representative of the boss, that their laws were written by, and could be broken by, people like her.

People? Oh, and she suddenly got it now, putting that beside the thought of Anglicanism: *Mary!*

She wondered if something in her head would start balking at all this when she prepared to send her fake map to Wells at the end of the survey. It had better, practical Dad said. Or you're for the chop, my girl, and your story of religious insight won't save you. That church of yours has had enough schisms.

'So,' said Ruth. 'Was there anything in the centre of the maze?'

The question startled Jane out of her thoughts, because it was one that Mary had told her the answer to. 'Nothing special,' she said. 'Just a clearing and the way out.'

'Right,' said Ruth, her eyes searching Jane's face minutely.

Jane looked steadily back at her.

'So no large-scale features? No big EM gradients, or whatever you call them?' That sounded like a last chance to change her story. Or maybe a desperate hope.

Jane took a deep breath. 'None so far.'

'Well . . . then . . . keep on going.' Ruth almost threw the phone back to her and marched out of the orchid house. If asking to see her result at this point was artificial, that moment had been more artificial still.

Jane waited until she had turned the corner before letting that breath out.

She spent the rest of the day in the house, on an awkward, dotting path that took in those rooms she hadn't covered the first time. In each, she sat down for a moment and considered what a good EM presence for this room would be. Ah, here was a flight of low, flat marble steps, with a loose carpet. We'll assign a fatal fall for a cherished old relative. Here's a gun on the wall. Let's say it once went off by accident, and was brought straight back here, powder scorches still on the barrel. It was never to be moved again, blotting the public consciousness at this spot as a mark of the loathing the man who put it back here felt for it. And the scuff marks at the edge of a carpet here. That's a positive thing, where boots were always shed in the ritual of a Sunday-afternoon walk.

Writing fiction about rooms. What a terrible burden to have to bear in her newly circumscribed world. She stopped at one of the narrow lead-lined windows, and looked out at the sheets of rain being thrown down across the countryside. She was an instrument. She had had joy in being just that, exactly that, for a few minutes in the maze, and immediately coming out of it.

She winced, putting her cheek up against the glass to feel the cold.

She so missed the feeling of being part of something greater than herself, that to have such a union fly down and grab her had been the best thing. And as a result of that grace, she had started to lie and compose greater lies, basic lies about the concrete nature of the world, on what she now thought was the will of her creator.

She was an instrument. A fanatic. She ought to tell Wells that immediately, arrange to go to them and be kept in a Faraday cage and eat barium meals.

But this was special, this was the real thing.

As everybody in the Faraday cages said. Every one of them had asked to be there. Usually because they'd made a mistake somewhere, opened the doors of their memory theatre, or popped a green too many, and experienced things outside of the tradition. And then they spent their lives there arguing that what they had seen was actually true. You got a lot of good theology out of the Faraday cages, a lot of transformative stuff. You could start a thousand new traditions with it. Or you could stay within the faith and be as mad as you liked.

What we saw was true.

If what we saw was in the tradition, then it was.

But Mary had not been Marian. Mary had been bloody Mary Poppins.

Mary had tried, was trying, to take an active part in the world.

Goodness, was she so weak? She *had* to fall on her sword when she called Wells tonight.

But this was special, this was the real thing.

As they all said.

This terrifying spiral had started when the thought had occurred to Jane that perhaps the false EM values she was imagining into existence were somehow being placed in her head, given to her by God through Mary.

But God was still absent in her. She couldn't feel the joy of the Holy Spirit at all. Only the standard shit of the world and the simple *memory* of an encounter with a divine being.

You only have the *memory* of me, said Dad.

She'd *touched* her. During a temporal lobe experience, the brain almost never creates the sensation of touch.

Almost never.

Perhaps you're just scared of proof.

She let that sentence replay and replay as she lifted her head from the pane of glass, and made herself go on.

In a basement, deep under the southern wing of Heartsease, and behind a door and a flight of steps that were folded into the stone like something out of *Alice in Wonderland,* Jane found the chapel. She'd thought there was one missing when she'd first seen the maps of the house in the briefing. This room had been represented as a wine cellar. The only error the map had made. Which was strange.

It was the last room inside the building she had to visit for her survey. Her 'survey'. She only realised she'd been dreading it as she swung open the door. She had to paste lies on top of this now too.

What she saw when she opened the door worried her, and for a moment she didn't know why.

Three great arches met overhead in the vaulted ceiling, which ran under the grounds and gardens. The chapel was simple, white plaster over grey stone, which had been revealed in a diamond pattern up the slope of every arch, turning the ceiling into a chequerboard. The effect was somehow Islamic. The furniture was modern, polished and bland, a couple of benches and a seat for the organist to play some-thing that wouldn't have looked out of place in a very chic cinema *circa* 1914. A golden rail ran in front of three steps that led up to the altar, and a golden eagle formed the lectern. The Hawtreys would have taken that as a sign this place should be theirs. Thank God it wasn't a cormorant. All of which gleamed, of course, but she'd come to expect that now. The numbers for four hymns stood in the rack on the wall: 135, 647, 256, 477. Three tiny modernist windows of stained glass, set high in the walls, let in a moderate amount of light in a dignified fashion, depicting an angular procession through the Stations of the Cross.

It was the shape that was all wrong. It was all out of place, somehow. The design, the stone. It was like the chapel was a late addition, something that didn't share the design sense of the rest of the building.

Jane went to the altar and dipped before the Cross, making the sign across her chest. Then, curious, she took a genuine EM reading. Background standard, as always. But here she believed it. It felt like a chapel for one person, a tiny personal space like the altars kept by the more religious patriarchs of the houses. It occurred to her that perhaps she was only the second person ever to have crossed this threshold.

She took a step backwards from the altar as another thought struck her. Had there been a time, before Mary, before the shadow had passed over her, when she would have delighted in this simple room, found strength in it?

She found herself stepping backwards, withdrawing towards the door.

She hit a quick zero into her map and ran out, slamming the door behind her.

The rain splattered the hood of Jane's anorak as she trudged along the path up to the folly. The leaves on the ground had turned to mulch, mixed with mud, and the low upward angle of the path made walking difficult. To both sides of her stretched the forest, the beginning of the swaths of forest that covered the hills for miles around Heartsease, stopping only by the lake and the walls of the estate. Beyond here there are monsters. From inside the forest there came bird calls, and the sounds of heavy things falling and fearful things flapping away. The occasional late-afternoon crawk of a peacock echoed to her from the grounds behind her. But Jane's world was enclosed by her hood into a little warm circle of vision that felt comforting and childish.

A few steps back she could hear Davey's feet, marching at her heels. He was carrying a long rifle, and had left his hood back on his shoulders so he could hear properly. She could imagine his eyes, sweeping all around them while she stopped to read her EM meter.

Pretended to read her EM meter.

Having completed the house, she'd pretended . . . she wanted to make certain she used that word when she thought of this experience . . . she'd pretended to take a general sweep around the boundaries of the grounds and gardens. There was a vortex effect with grounds that normally made them easy to do. Everybody who'd lived in a place defined their world by its walls, in this case the low ceremonial wall with its ha-ha that ran in a great rectangle around Heartsease, its stables and gardens. The wall had large granite globes perched on plinths at intervals, every one still there, of course. It was broken only by the gateway that led the gravel driveway in. The vortex effect meant that EM-active sites somehow attached their contours to that boundary, as if the wall was a strange attractor. You could walk such a wall and be led from it to every EM peak inside it.

She'd completed one whole side of Heartsease's walls, walking along on the higher bank of the ha-ha, before she remembered that she should be inventing here too. She'd caused the lawn group of ostriches to scatter as she acted noting the edge of a field and moving in to find its centre. She aimed for one of a pair of fountains that stood a few hundred metres from the doorway of the house. A good story this time, a moment of joy for two eloping lovers as they dashed away, a first kiss with the lights of the great house coming on behind them.

She could become a wife now, when they sacked her. She could find out what it was like to be loved, and maybe that would put God behind her.

Stupid, Mary said this was going to kill you.

Would a haemorrhage have that degree of self-knowledge? Everyone assumed that Swansley had known he was going to die. Did something in her brain know something about itself? Had it turned the information into a revelation?

Or perhaps this was some sort of test. Perhaps that was the secret that Ruth kept and the soldiers didn't share, that she was having her fitness to do her job examined in the most ferocious way.

She was certain, in that moment by the fountain, as she realised she was looking at the tiny floral motifs on the edge of its great bowl, that she was operating on the wrong principle now. That Mary had no existence outside her head, and, since she was outside the tradition, therefore no existence.

Best just finish it this way. Then do it the other, do it properly. That's easy, after all: a blank map. Apart from the maze. They'll look at you, but you can say go and check it yourself, and they'll find the same readings. And you won't be forced to leave the church, and you'll have passed the test, and the principle of a shared reality, of recording machines, will have won again over the principle of my personal revelation and the jumble we all make when everybody's personal revelation all has to live under the same—

No, no, no. Just finish it this way. She'll come back. Why was the maze so active, anyway? She'll come back.

She'd walked stiffly back to the boundary, aware of tiny faces watching her from the windows of the house, and had finished walking round the building, widdershins, as she unfortunately realised afterwards.

Then she'd called a break, and had returned to the house waving her arms to signify that break. She'd found the militiamen in the kitchen. No sign of Ruth. That was good. Davey had volunteered to come with her to the folly, the last part before the stables. Why she was leaving the stables to last, Jane didn't know.

Now she heard Davey clear his throat before attempting to start a conversation. He would have to leave her when they got to the folly, of course, but he was allowed to guard her cross-country. 'We had a flap while you were in the maze this morning.'

'Did you?'

'Morgan was in the armoured car, checking the rainproofing. He got a ping from the radar. We had a target lock. He called us all in for it. The Major too.'

Jane found that all the water had gone from her mouth, that her lips were dry in the rain. 'What was it?'

'Target moving in at speed from the east. Came down towards the maze. We thought it might have been a helicopter, and that caused a real panic. Who can run a helicopter? We bloody can't. I got sent out with the binoculars to get a visual sighting, but I couldn't see anything, and nobody heard anything. Joe's checking the radar over now for a failure, but everybody reckons it was just a flock of birds or whatever. You see a helicopter in the maze, Reverend?'

Jane glanced back at him. 'No. No. I didn't see anything like that.'

'Well,' Davey continued, 'it got us all spooked. The sooner you finish up down here the—' He stopped, having seen something over Jane's shoulder, and shrugged the rifle off his shoulder into his hands, suddenly scared. 'Hey!' he shouted.

Jane spun, and caught the end of what Davey saw. Further up the slope, a woman had walked off the path and into the forest. She brushed aside some ferns and was gone.

She'd had her back to them. Long skirts, square shoulders, a hat.

'Fuck!' Davey spat. 'Stay here.' He sprinted off up the slope towards where the woman had been.

Jane put her hand to her chest and concentrated to stop her bladder emptying. She wanted to call Davey back. She didn't want him to meet Mary. She didn't want to know what Mary could do to him. She didn't want to know that Mary was real.

The way she'd walked. The back of her head, like there was something unseeable now about the face. There had been no inclination to turn at Davey's shout, not even the tiny human movement of the shoulders which says I've heard you but I'm not going to turn around.

Davey vanished into the woods after her, hopping over a fallen tree and crashing his way forward, his rifle held in both hands.

Jane held herself upright, her world enclosed by the hood, waiting for the scream and the crash. She felt complicit, like she'd lured Davey up here for her accomplice to finish him off.

The sounds of the soldier running became more distant, then got lost in the drum of the rain, and she was alone. Nobody had walked here for decades, perhaps. Or whatever had kept the house pristine had walked here, and who knew what that was.

She became aware, and slowly turned round, shaking.

The hem of the skirt, being flexed slightly by the wind, over the shiny neat black boots. The boots stood in the mud, made an impression in the mud, but were not themselves muddy.

Jane made herself look up, and found that Mary was beaming madly at her. Her hands were perched on her hips. A leaf had landed on her cardigan. The wind flipped it off again.

There was nothing going on in Jane's head. That was the deeply fearful thing. She wasn't in the middle of a huge EM gradient like she'd been the last time. She was standing on a muddy path, in a normal part of her life, and the flying woman was standing beside her.

'Is this what you needed?' she said, her voice perfectly old-English and precise. She shook her head sadly. 'Oh ye of little faith.'

She said that like it was something of her own rather than a cliché.

Jane carefully got down on her knees. 'Yes,' she said. 'That settles it.' Some part of her was laughing at the words she chose. At the smallness of words themselves against this. 'Thank you.'

'And now you will think that I am an ordinary woman, that I live here.'

'No, I won't think that.'

'I shall give you a list of things to do and not to do. And I shall return to make sure that you have done as I asked. Would that make you happier?'

'Yes. Please.'

Davey came running back down the track a few minutes later to find Jane standing at an angle to where he'd left her, her trousers all muddy.

'No sign of her,' he gasped.

The vicar laughed at him, a guttural chuckle from the back of her throat. Then she stopped. 'Of who?' she said.

'That woman. An intruder within the perimeter. We'll have to do a sweep of these woods.'

'A woman?' She raised her EM meter and showed an elaborate contour map to Davey, who felt himself start to shake before he realised why. 'I didn't see—'

'No, don't tell me that.' He crossed himself. 'You mean you really didn't see her?'

She laughed again. She was being very fucking merry about this. 'You saw a ghost, Davey.'

'I did not! I saw—' He stamped hard in the mud, his feet wanted to do something. 'Damn! Beg your pardon, ma'am, but . . . Damn!'

'Your first time?'

'My first time. What, do you think there was a murder here or something?'

'Perhaps. It'll be a feature for the family. It's far enough out for them to want to keep it.'

'Well, I'm not gonna be stationed up here. Are you sure she wasn't real?'

'I didn't see her.'

'Damn.' He felt the fear drain out of him, and felt suddenly absurdly glad that the reverend had been up here with him. He smiled back at her smile, which had stayed constant, because this must be just everyday stuff to her, and coughed a little laugh. 'Okay, so do you still want to do the folly?'

Jane let her right foot hang back for a moment as she set off after Davey.

As it sucked up out of the mud behind her, she glanced back at where she'd stood.

There was no longer any sign of the two sharp square little holes made by Mary's boot heels.

But they had been there.

Two days later, Ruth and the troopers gathered in the old stables for the last stage of the survey.

Jane looked at them, standing under the great black beams like a row of children, Christmas expressions on the faces of the men. This was the end of the adventure for them, they were going home. Ruth still looked tense. Something unresolved there. Something still waiting.

The service of Mary made all considerations trivial. Jane had enjoyed creating the false map of the folly, had told Davey, waiting impatiently by the door of the little square turret with its flagpole, big stories about what might have happened here. He had stamped about, unequipped for a fear he couldn't deal with, full of the Fear of the Night, even on just this wet day. Jane had been too cloistered to have experienced this sensation, but had read the stories that attempted to put you in it, the thrillers where a lone survivor has to cross some uninhabited stretch of countryside over several nights. The fear was of what lay behind the last dripping branch you could see, of what that noise was on the edge of hearing.

That was past for her, now, burnt out in a bonfire of the wolves in the maze. She'd met her Night, gone right through it in just the sort of catharsis the heroes of those novels never reached. They were either swallowed by something dark and unshaped, and the tale ended on a sudden screech, or they ran into a settlement, and slammed the gates behind them against something that hit the barrier with a great impact, and left a coda claw or footprint in the morning.

She was now a friend of that which lay beyond the Night. She served a being who maintained appropriate mystery, and served God in a baffling way, as she herself did, and she did not require knowledge of the mechanisms and the details of their pact. Faith she had, now, even with no grace in her heart. Bedrock beneath bedrock. Mary was part of the continuity and tradition, but not slave to it, because she was it, and alive.

Her appearing without an EM field was a miracle, and Jane would have e-mailed everybody she knew and told them but that she had been told not to.

She was now whole and supported because Mary told her she was, and had given her a mission, and had mapped out her life unto death. Which was, she found, everything she'd ever needed, and the rest was the whistle on a train.

Ruth's expression was becoming baffled now, at the way Jane was smiling and looking right through her. 'We're ready,' she said, 'when you are, Reverend.'

Jane made a great show of walking slowly around this last square of her map, watching her EM meter as she went. This last stable block had been renovated towards the end of the twentieth century, and contained a collection of six vintage cars, including a shiny black Daimler from the 1920s. She considered attaching an EM rating to the cars, but checked herself: collections never aroused much in the way of grand emotion. She was just looking to put icing on the cake for Mary, and she probably didn't care about adding jokes and swirls and all that.

So she stopped at the centre of the room and said: 'In the name of the Father, the Son and the Holy Ghost, I declare this whole property to be surveyed, and hand it over to the Campbell family for their use. May they use it for the glory of the Lord, our God. Amen.'

She put a rock-and-roll kick into that Amen, too, smacking the two syllables tastily on her palate. Yes, she was on the side of the angels now. No doubt about it.

She slapped the EM meter into Ruth's hands and looked triumphantly into her eyes.

The Major raised an eyebrow, and created her own pause for a moment before replying. For a second, Jane thought that now was the point where the trap was sprung, where she asked what the hell Jane thought she was doing. But she finally just said the right words, her eyes unsatisfied. 'I accept this certificated EM map on behalf of the Campbell family, and will ensure its safe transmission to their records. On behalf of them, I promise they will use this house wisely.'

A clipped pause. Then the troopers whooped and cheered and threw their caps into the air. Everybody relaxed. One of the horses thumped its hooves from the next block, as if anticipating going home.

Ruth just turned and walked away.

Jane caught up with her before she could leave. 'Could I have a word?' she said.

'You want us to stay?' The look on Ruth's face was complicated. Frustrated and angry, but also somehow respectful, as if a child of hers had wanted to do something far beyond its abilities. She looked aside for a moment, as if aware she was letting her feelings show. Then she turned back, all uncertainty banished. 'Well, no, we aren't, I won't allow that.'

They were standing on the clean cobbles outside the stables, the cracks between the stones outlined in ancient dung, but every single stone brushed and watered by providence this very morning. The sun was shining. Jane shook her head, smiling as she considered that ongoing miracle. This was about God re-entering the world, she was thinking. About the ordinary people being able to see miracles again. Swansley and Kemp had opened the door and let Him in. Miracles now would be about housekeeping and security. Milk and honey and brushed stones. 'I have to stay. I'm on a mission.'

'When did you decide that?'

'I sent my request to Wells this morning. I got the reply just before we performed the handover.'

'They let—?' Ruth snapped her mouth shut. 'We're not obliged to guard you, you know.'

'Not officially, but everyone will wonder why you left me behind. In the middle of the outback. In an empty court.'

'It's not an empty court. It's a house.' She sounded like she was trying to convince herself.

'That's not what people will say.'

Ruth looked to her left and right, then down at her boots as if sizing something up. For a moment, Jane thought she was going to attack her, and tensed, preparing herself for a beating. But Ruth just leaned closer to her, lowering her voice to an emphatic whisper that, Jane thought, had a hint of fear about it. 'No. I will not keep my men here in harm's way. I . . . *we* can *go* now. We don't have to stay. You can if you want. We depart at first light. We'll inform the court of your mission and have help sent back to you. If you can survive that long. For God's sake, how are you going to live?'

'Grace will provide.'

Ruth snorted and turned away, shaking her head.

Jane crooked her head at an angle, watching the Major go.

It was dark by four.

Ruth shared a meal with her men in the kitchens, making jokes about Davey seeing a ghost, trying to make them happy. We're going home tomorrow, that's what she kept saying, in the subtext of the jokes and out loud. But they didn't rise to it. Not really. They pretended for her sake.

Not that she was exactly expressing confidence and security. The maze was still out there, and she had still not been into it, hadn't gotten anything from it except the priest's bland generalities about it. Ruth had examined her submitted EM map at length, and the maze just showed the usual small waves of old use that Ruth had seen many times on such maps of the court.

That could not be so. Not the way she felt about it. Not with what she had been told all her life was there. Perhaps what she had been told all her life was wrong.

She forced a smile again.

Matthew was still silent about his scarring, of course. But that wasn't what was getting to the rest of them. It was the idea of leaving someone behind. The Fear of the Night was in them. There was dread in the limited nature of their movements, or the very expansive gestures they made to try and deny it. Their minds, like Ruth's, would be flicking forward to the moment they or someone else from civilisation returned here, and found that bloody priest gone. There would be no sign of her, or worse, there would be a worrying story told in the traces left behind. There would not be a full, cheerful cabin, a full complement returning from the mission, happy as they entered through the city gates.

She hadn't even had the courtesy to join them. Afraid of the arguments, that one of the men would try and shake some sense into her, persuade her not to put them all through this horror.

Davey, who had seen the ghost, looked especially grim, all colour gone from him. He would take that look with him if they left someone behind.

They would get back to civilisation, and she would spend the rest of her life never knowing.

'Fuck it!' Ruth shoved her way up out of her chair and knocked her bowl away with the heel of her hand. She headed for the door at a fast march.

She had two places she had to go.

The priest was lying on top of the covers of her bed, asleep. She looked peaceful and distant and involved in something Ruth couldn't possibly understand. Ruth had wanted Alexander, a cleric of her acquaintance from one of the parishes outside the court, someone she trusted, to accompany her on this mission, but that, it seemed, wasn't up for discussion. Someone powerful in court had wanted Jane Bruce to come to Heartsease, and while Ruth had successfully taken over the expedition, she hadn't been able to change that detail. Which had made everything harder. She could have watched over Alexander's survey at an intimate level, could have relied on him to tell her if he found clues to what she was searching for. Perhaps she would even have shared that secret with him.

With this priest, Ruth felt she could share nothing at all.

She didn't know whether her readings from the maze were a technical fault, or if for some bizarre reason she was lying, or if it was just Ruth's own fears and hopes for what the maze contained that made it feel terrifying to her. Perhaps there were some sorts of haunting that didn't show up on an EM map. But Ruth had never heard there were.

The priest opened her eyes before Ruth could step into the room, and looked calmly at her, blinking. 'Oh, hello. I half expected to see my two godsons. I was just dreaming about them again.'

Ruth felt like slapping her. 'What exactly *is* this new mission of yours?' she asked, walking boldly in. By the rules laid down from Wells, the priest didn't have to answer, but Ruth wanted something to tell her team.

The woman slid into an upright position, sitting against her pillows. 'I've felt a calling since I've been here. The Holy Spirit moving me. I have to stay here.'

'To do what?'

'Just . . . to exist. Out here. As a hermit.'

It sounded like she was making it up as she went along. Ruth went to the window and looked out into the darkness, feeling the cold radiating from the surface of the glass. She was wondering how she could ask again about the maze without giving the game away. But her thoughts were interrupted by the vicar herself.

'Why do *you* want to stay?'

'I don't.' Fuck. She kept her parade-ground face on as she turned around.

The priest was looking keenly at her, her brow furrowed in thought. 'I was having the oddest dreams. I really ought to . . .' She reached for those pills priests took, but stopped as she did so. Moved her hand back from them to examine Ruth again. 'There's something here for you too, isn't there? Something which you haven't found.'

Ruth kept the muscles of her face still.

'That favour in your pocket . . .'

Ruth's stomach felt something cold sink into it. Like she'd been cut by a blade. She found herself taking a step back, the cold of the window shocking her back. How did she *know*?

'I saw it,' the woman continued. 'At the gate, when we left Bristol. It's a lady's favour, isn't it?'

Ruth stopped herself from leaping at the priest and ripping her throat out with her knife. Her men would back up her story if she asked them to. They would say they left the priest in the house as planned. Nobody would be surprised by her death. But the men would need a good reason to do that, and she didn't have one for them.

She would be hanged in the courtyard of the Campbells if her superiors found out that she was carrying a woman's favour. Even if she managed to convince them of the real story behind it, it would be clear that she'd come to Heartsease for her own purposes, that she had concealed information from them.

How could she have *noticed*? 'It's not like that.'

'So you're not a lesbian?'

Ruth wasn't used to feeling helpless. She made herself walk to the door, then stopped there, and met Jane's gaze. 'We'll be gone before breakfast. I hope the animals get you.'

And then she left for her second destination. Now she had no option but to go there. So perhaps she should feel grateful to Jane. But as she walked off down the corridor, pulling her gun from her holster and checking the clip as she walked, she did not.

She would need her coat, gloves, a map on her phone. And a torch.

She was going out into the night to face her family's fear.

Jane stared after her as she left. She had only wanted to do something to bridge the gap between them, because she'd been forced to lie about the nature of her mission here. It had never actually occurred to her that Ruth was a lesbian: the real nature of what was keeping her here must be so much more complicated than that.

You can't make people like you, she heard her dad saying.

She should have said that she would keep the secret.

She took a pillow and dropped it lightly on to her face, hiding. She wished that Mary was here to reassure her.

Twelve: Rebecca's Fifteenth Birthday

So this was to be her room in the children's house in Acton. It was a plain white one, with a white wooden wardrobe, a sink, a desk, a chair, a single bed. The floor was covered with woven matting.

Shit. She'd have to change all of it. Couldn't they have given her a double, at least? She was the only one here who wasn't a child.

She went to the sink, took some red from her bag and rubbed it into her hair. Then put a thin streak down the side of her face.

She kept looking at that for a long time. She couldn't be bothered to do anything else. She had to do something to make it look like she was interested in how she looked. She was so bloody thin. Nobody was going to even look at her. She'd been in this dress for days, but she'd keep it on. She didn't trust the laundry system in this place. They'd take it from her. Make her wear the jolly clothes of the little children.

It was four in the afternoon. Like it always seemed to be when the world felt like this. She went to lie on the bed. Sprung it a bit by flexing her shoulders. Ick. Awkward. Outside, there were the sounds of fucking organised games. If any of those organisers came near her she'd hit them with her shoe.

The days were going to be all the same now. Boring. Rebecca already knew the way she changed through a day. Now there would be nothing to concentrate on but that. She'd avoid the games and work that offered people reasons for carrying on the way they did. Stupid sheep.

The way a day went was this. When Rebecca woke up, those things she needed to know about the day would gently chime into place, along with the complicated stories of her dreams. (Why wasn't the normal world like dreams? They meant something because they were about your inside stuff.) She didn't feel sharp for a couple of hours, until she'd had some herbal tea. But by lunchtime she'd be together and normal. Nondescript, functioning, normality. And that kept being what she was until the afternoon. Then she became a lot more vulnerable, and sometimes had a sleep if she could. But that seemed stupid sometimes.

That felt like a doleful, dull point, quite often. Around four came the point where the chemical rush of what people who knew nothing called depression would tug at the edges of who she was, and make the day outside, even in summer, actually look a little darker. That was when nothing meant anything apart from what it was, when a settlement was just a collection of objects standing on the land, and people were just packets of genes and really did exist only in that moment, knowing who they were just by repeating their personal stories. Keeping themselves going. That was the point where her existence just was, and if she stopped, she thought that nobody would demand where she'd got to. She could die, then, she would die, and the objects of the world would sail on, without her. Fine.

Then, whether she slept or not, the evening would be better, a little start to the day again. Which would take her to a peak of energy and wanting to talk a bit to people before going to bed, where she would roll for a while to the left. Then she would drink from her water, and switch to her right. She would start thinking, her eyes closed, of surreal or impossible things, a whole world of other things, another life, and then realise that those things were surreal and impossible. That was like a guard on the gate checking out. Her last moment of consciousness every night was a sensation of that guard deciding that surreal and impossible couldn't be as real as her real world was, which must mean that she was dreaming, therefore asleep, and—

And that would be that until the next morning.

That was the usual pattern, that was life. She'd got it all sorted out already.

She felt better with other people around, even if she didn't want to talk to them. Without people, as she had been for a long time, it sometimes got even worse. In the morning she'd wake expecting people, even when she knew she'd see nobody. Then she'd forget that during the normal bit. But without people, the afternoon darkness could stretch and stretch, and connect with the night, until Rebecca ended up lying wherever she'd found to lie, too out of routine for sleep, needing to talk to someone to feel like she'd done anything, whatever she'd managed on her own.

Horrible. It was like you were only what you were when you could tell somebody about it, even if they didn't understand.

It was her birthday today, and nobody knew. Which was great.

There was a knock on the door. 'What?' she yelled, angry at being disturbed.

The door slowly opened, and a boy whose face she found familiar looked in. 'Rebecca?' he asked. 'Happy birthday.'

It took her a moment. 'David?'

'Yes.'

She turned over on to her side, suddenly full of an unexpected hurt. A lot of hurts, that she'd been storing up in the wilderness.

'I can come back later . . .'

'No,' she said. 'Don't.'

Thirteen: Ruth Does an Alice in the Maze

The ghost only existed when it was perceived. Its thoughts came in reaction to being opposed. It was otherwise a spike in the electromagnetic field of the Earth, orbiting steadily within a range of a hundred miles, more powerfully as it approached the centre of its orbit, less at the limit over the sea, past the cliffs of the coast, spinning according to the steady influences of the moon, the sun, and the distant stirrings of the Earth's interior. It even knew the minuscule influence of the sun's dark companion star, implicit in its existence, but not yet discovered by humanity. And if they had not discovered it now, they never would. They would be long gone before its return. It knew moments of being as it swept in its endless path, whenever the knowledge that had formed it considered for that moment that there might be a situation that needed its creation, so it knew the land very well. But mostly it slept as part of the greater radiation that lay across the land.

The ghost could not be said to be immortal, because it had been set in motion to a plan, and like all things set in motion, it would one day stop. It had a life like a hurricane amongst the ebb and flow of the weather. When it thought, it thought that everything here would stop before it stopped. That was one of several items of information it contained, matrices which it forever exchanged unconsciously between one tiny level of current and another, keeping its memories intact.

Those items of information had been written into the Earth's EM field in December 1998, though dates meant nothing to the ghost. The data waited, along with many other items of data, some of which had existed for a long time previously, shuffled and re-shuffled by earthquake and thunderstorm and war and the sudden outbursts of nightmares, wrapping itself into the human consciousness. It was only expressed into a being centuries later, by a sudden stroke of energy, a predetermined moment of anguish. A tragedy.

All the ghost knew was that it had been born into something which existed before it did, and it had rules to live by.

It orbited the centre of the maze, drawing power from the flaw in the world beneath it. It only thought when the little knot of a thinking thing drew close, the complexity of millions of tiny flowing currents and potentials that tugged on its own web of thought and made it live. The shape of the mind met with it, and certain things about the mind defined it.

And here was another of those minds, a nexus of interlacing voltages that reached across to it through space, and upwards into the other spaces that the ghost was aware of but had no information about.

The ghost tugged at the mind, took the weight of it, allowed it to pull it into its gravity and began its dance with it.

It delighted, as much as it could delight, in the existence that this process brought it, the thoughts that suddenly interlaced around the globe to be it and define it.

It was suddenly a person in itself.

Her breath billowing in the frosty night air, Ruth marched towards the maze.

She was going to walk around to the exit gate, then straight through that to the centre.

Then she could sleep tonight and leave tomorrow.

But already as she walked across the lawn, the sound of her breath and the crunch of her boots on the grass loud against the night, she could feel the maze looming ahead of her. Feel it in her stomach.

If she left the priest here with her phone, she might broadcast Ruth's secret everywhere.

She hadn't so far. That wasn't the fear. Ruth was fooling herself. What she was afraid of was what was ahead, the square edges of the maze absolute black against the distant greys of the trees and the sweep of the Milky Way across the velvet sky.

She stopped at the entrance, listening.

Just the distant cries of birds and animals in the forest.

The dark avenue looked back at her.

Ruth switched on her torch and shone the beam down there. Just hedges, clean gravel, and the enticement of that turn at the end of the corridor. For a moment Ruth thought that a shadow lay across that gap. But that was just the varying light of the movement of her torch.

She switched it off, not wanting to be seen from the house, and resumed her march around the outside of the maze.

She turned the corner and looked down the plane of the other side. Another empty dark angle. Halfway along there was a little gap with an archway of knotted yew branches above it that formed the exit. She went to it, and found it just as she had remembered, a narrow little passageway that swiftly turned out of vision. It was a direct route to the centre only in that there were no choices to be made. She consulted her phone for a moment and checked the map: yes, she wouldn't have to think about choosing any other passageways.

She put the phone back in her pocket.

She turned her torch on again, and stepped inside before she could think about it.

There was at least something comforting about the narrowness of the lane. Ruth kept the torch on as she made her way forward. At a brisk pace this couldn't take more than a couple of minutes.

The fear was growing in the back of her head, making all the hairs on her back stand up. She went with it, used to the sensation. As long as her legs were moving, she could live with fear like this. It felt that shots were landing behind her, and the cannons were training on the ground in front of her. She had to cross the space to cover in time.

Guns going to fire. Cross the space to cover.

The little cycle kept working for her, making the fear familiar. She let it run on in her head as a marching rhythm, stopping herself from running by thinking about the uneven ground, the chance of falling in the field of fire of those guns.

Guns going to fire. Cross the space to cover.

But it was getting too heavy now. During the Singh War she'd been in a shelter dug into a woody hillside in the Chilterns. The fringes of two artillery barrages had intersected on their post, and for a minute or two there had been nothing but exploding treetrunks and the ground roaring and mud flying all around, and she had been seized by the tottering certainty that she was going to die. As the barrages moved overhead, and the intensity of fire became less and less, she had found her body panting with that certainty, waiting for the last, certain shell that would obviously kill her and her unit.

She was starting to feel a similar pressure now. If she thought about it. Which she would not.

Kill that lying vicar. Kill that lying vicar.

She wouldn't even let herself run. Her heart was pounding: let it burst. She knew fear. She would not give in to it. Maybe there was a place you went to beyond fear: a soldier's holy place. That'd be good.

Shoot her through the head. Shoot her through the head.

The dark had shut her in behind, and in front there was only the steady run of the hedge. She'd been walking in a straight line for a considerable time now, she realised.

For far too long.

She looked at her watch. She'd been walking for eight minutes. At least half of that in a straight line.

Ruth started to run.

And a moment later, to her shock, she was in a clearing.

It felt like her state of mind had brought it to her.

There were exits on all sides, including the very normal one she'd just sprinted in through, and the stars overhead, and the sense of oppression blossomed out for a moment into a giddying vertigo.

She fell.

She rolled swiftly on to her back, her limbs urgently trying to get her on to her feet again, but it felt like the world was rolling about her, the globe and stars swinging as a weight on her back, the universe pivoting upon her.

She managed to crawl on her elbows back up the . . . slope on which she was lying. The surface beneath her was hummocky and hard. She could feel edges under the grass, indenting her back.

She sucked in a sudden breath amongst the great gulps of air she was taking, and forced herself to concentrate, holding it in. Was this it? Despite everything her survival instincts were telling her, she rolled on to her belly again, and started to claw at the grass beneath her, getting soil under her nails. Soil and brickdust. She threw clumps of soil and grass roots away from her as she burrowed down, until her right palm closed around a lump of brick. Covered in mud. She dashed the mud away, her hands getting scratched and bloody, until she could see it, gasping desperately at it though the sky was still swirling around her. The brick had been broken in two, severed at an angle. Grey and smooth on the outside, fired rough red inside.

She turned it in her hand.

Then she noticed something that lay in the earth just beneath it.

She dropped the lump of brick.

She scrabbled violently into the hole she'd created, and dragged the new object to the surface, its naked glass edges pricking her fingers.

It was a piece of stained glass. Little more than a shard. But it bore the head of Jesus, looking sadly downwards from the Cross.

'It's true,' Ruth gasped, her stomach and lungs heaving, on the edge between laughter and hysterical tears. She closed her hands more firmly on the fragment just to be certain of it.

Then she unbuttoned her breast pocket and scrabbled to slip the shard into it, padded by the softness of the favour. She felt strong again, powerful at having found out, at having got through this and finally discovered the truth. 'Now I have to kill him.' She kept her marching song going in her head to fight through the dizziness. 'Now I have to get out of here and kill him.'

She gave a sudden jerk of her arm muscles and managed to stumble to her feet, closing her eyes to put them down on two places that weren't spinning violently around each other. She knew the spinning was in her head, but it made no difference. Her head was all the world. She managed to take two faltering steps down the slope.

A sound of movement ahead made her open her eyes.

She knew she was dreaming when she saw what stood there.

Unaffected by the nightmare that had hobbled her, he was wandering casually from one of the box-hedge avenues, heading in her direction. He wore a Hawtrey uniform jacket, open, with a loose shirt and britches underneath. He had on his face the all-powerful grin of a demon, his curls dropping over mocking eyes.

Ruth didn't care if it was an illusion or not.

She scrabbled to pull her gun from out of its holster, her fingers numb around the familiar shape because the chance was so near, the horror so close. Before he could take another step towards her she had slipped off the safety catch, felt her finger close on the trigger and aimed square into his advancing chest.

Ruth shot Booth Hawtrey over and over again.

Eric's head snapped round at the sound of the shots.

He had gone to see what was taking Ruth so long with the vicar, and found that she'd already moved on. She wasn't in her room. So Eric had taken his rifle from the stores point and wandered out into the grounds to see if she'd gone for a walk. Perhaps he was still spooked by the whole insane leaving the priest behind thing, he hadn't thought about it. He'd just wanted to know where his commanding officer was.

He pulled the whistle from the chain around his neck and gave three short, sharp blasts.

Then he started to run towards the maze, readying his rifle.

Jane got up from her bed and stepped towards the window.

She could see lights moving in the darkness across the lawns. They were moving at speed. She thought she'd heard an emergency whistle.

'What is it?' she asked the ceiling. 'What's going on?'

But there was no reply. Mary did not come.

Eric was shouting his commanding officer's name at the entrance to the maze when the others ran up, unslinging and loading weapons as they came.

'What is it?' Davey sounded scared. 'What's happened to her?'

Eric made sure his voice was clipped and even. 'I heard pistol shots from inside the maze. Right in the middle.'

Joe, who'd spent the longest time in service, was in charge when Ruth was absent, though his rank had never strayed above militia-man. Eric let the burly engineer shoulder past him to the front of the group, until he was right at the entrance.

'Major?' he called. 'Ruth?'

There was only silence.

'Oh fuck,' whispered Davey.

Joe took his whistle from round his neck and blew one long blast that swung into a pure high note at the end, the contact signal.

The team held their breath and waited.

No whistle came back.

'Fuck,' said Davey again. They could all feel it, Eric was sure, the way the maze felt like . . . he couldn't put a name to the feeling for a moment. Then he recalled a Welsh valley with rebel encampments up on both sides of it, and a long road through the middle. Rebels behind them and no choice but to go down the middle.

That time, only a quarter of his squad had survived. The maze felt like the same slaughter about to happen again.

Joe turned back to Eric. 'You're sure you heard her?'

'It came right from the middle, no doubt about it, a thirty-five-millimetre. It sounded like she unloaded the whole clip.'

'Right.' Joe took one more glance down the dark passage ahead, as if he too was remembering a ferocious experience the maze put him in mind of, then turned to them. 'Eric, take Morgan and Matthew round to the other exit and head on in. Davey and Mark, you're with me. We use phone maps, meet in the middle, keep the whistles going. If we get pissed off with the hedges, we hack straight through them, right?' They all nodded. 'Right.'

Eric's group reached the exit at a run, the only light illuminating them the dull blue glow from Morgan's phone. They skidded to a halt in front of the avenue of box hedges that led into the darkness.

'Why would she go in there?' muttered Morgan.

'Someone's in there,' Eric told him, 'and who the fuck else is it going to be?'

He glanced across to Matthew and saw that the young soldier was staring into the maze in livid panic, his eyes dancing at the fear that was radiating from the thing.

'No,' he said. 'I'm not going in there.'

'We don't have a choice,' Eric told him. 'Don't think about it.'

Matthew nodded slowly. The tags on his dressing had come loose, and the corner of it was flapping on his cheek. Eric could remember what his skin had felt like under his fingers when he'd put the blade to it.

He turned back to Morgan, about to ask the engineer to give up his phone to Matthew, to give the kid something to do. He saw Morgan's eyes widen.

When he turned back, Matthew was sprinting off across the lawn, heading for the woods in the distance, stumbling into the dark.

Eric automatically swung him into the sights of his rifle.

He watched the desperate silhouette dancing in black on red for a long moment.

Then he lowered the weapon again.

'We'll let Ruth deal with him,' he said. 'After we find her.'

And he led Morgan off into the maze.

When, if he could only let himself give in to his instincts, what he should really be doing was running off with Matthew.

Matthew stopped at the edge of the forest, looking back towards the great house and the maze across the lawns.

He fell back against the wooden fence that separated the trees from the flat, cultivated grass. He was panting in the cold, his breath spiralling up around him in a cloud.

They hadn't shot him. He thought Eric would have tried.

One great dark wing of the house was pointing towards him here, its square end looming. A tiny window high up glowed with orange light. The priest's room.

Between him and the house, in the long, low slope of darkness, stood the black shape of the maze. He felt a sudden pang of care for

Morgan and Eric. He should go back in to help them. Then they wouldn't mention his running away. It wasn't too late.

A single whistled note came to him through the damp air of the valley, then its familiar response.

He stood, and took a few steps back down into the valley. There had been something at his throat when he stood by the entrance to that maze, something that had left him no choice but to run, but now he was away from it he could see that it was just a construction of trees. Joe had said he was going to cut through the bloody thing. Good for him. He could even see a little of its shape, from this angle, just the tops of the hedges. He thought he might be able to see the glow of the two phones moving through it, but then he thought he might be mistaken. The whistles started echoing back and forth, call and response, a friendly sound, like the call of owls in the night.

He adjusted the sling of his rifle, and started to walk purposefully back towards the maze. He would join in, and add whistles of his own to the joyous noise. He and the team would find Ruth and save her from whatever was happening to her in the centre of that thing. They might have got to her already, before he arrived. Maybe the whole thing was just the lot of them getting scared by ghosts, like Davey had been. A priest's job to be scared of those, not a soldier's.

The whistle came again.

Only this time there was no reply.

Matthew stopped walking. Had he not heard the reply?

But the first whistle came again, more urgently, from the same part of the maze. Then a pause. Then a third time, the shriek of the note suggesting that the first party had broken into a run.

Matthew could imagine them, though he didn't want to, Eric and Morgan running urgently, or Davey running afraid of what was behind or ahead of him.

He turned sideways, his head jerking between the maze and where he was heading, a circular path, to take him round, so he wouldn't go near, so he could get back to the house.

The first whistle came again, at speed. He recognised the sound it made when you were running into combat.

He started to run himself.

He ran straight for the house now.

As he looked towards the maze again, he heard the whistle call once more.

And the end of the call was the sound the whistle made when the soldier blowing it died as he blew, his last breath on the air.

Matthew's rifle fell from his shoulder as he broke into a sprint.

Many miles away, David Hawtrey awoke with a jolt.

He sat up on the pew where he slept, looking around the old church for whoever had just spoken to him. There was nothing, just the architecture and the compiler, humming and clicking to itself, as if it was dreaming too.

'Yes,' he said. 'A dream.' Charlotte, who lay on the floor beside the pew, stirred in her sleep.

He lowered his head again.

But he would not return to sleep. Now he had an idea he couldn't banish from his mind.

He would take the compiler to Rebecca. And see what was in her heart when she was under its influence.

It didn't feel like his own idea, but the more he thought about it, the more he thought it was a good one.

The ghost was no longer in the centre of the maze. Not now its job was done there.

In the maze, the minds stood still, lost in their dreams. It made sure they didn't see it pass with their staring eyes, or feel its movements on their still skin. And it was satisfied.

For a moment it wasn't anywhere, or it was everywhere, sweeping around the Earth in a moment of empty dream.

And then it was a thought again, racing around its tiny orbit about the maze.

It knew Matthew was the same as the minds it had just encountered: their knots replayed small fractions of analogues of his. The ghost knew nothing, but when it knew anything, it knew it knew nothing, and it thought that those analogues were supposed to be complete by the minds that carried them.

It exalted then as it speeded towards the running mind. It felt its weight on the web of the world, a weight that grew as it brought more of itself to bear. It felt parts of itself flash out, more and more, connecting with the mind and latching on. It felt itself being read by the mind, of becoming a thing that the mind thought. It sped with joy towards its becoming, feeling details actualising it, feeling the universe easily and simply shift around the concept of its identity as the little knot of thought swept the ghost into being around it.

It had a procedure written into it for what that being would do.

The little knot of information was racing with data now, pulling more and more of itself back down into the universe from its home above, reaching hopelessly for something that would help it understand the ghost, that would pull the ghost down into the world.

The ghost became solid in this hopeless reaching. Used it to let the universe slip matter into its being. A gap filled up with the fears of the mind about which it spun, tighter and tighter.

It didn't understand the solid form, but let it move as the mind expected it to move, let it speak as the mind did, the words coming straight from the analogues that were running under the mind at every moment.

'Don't make a fuss about it. It won't hurt.'

The mind of Matthew became as quiet as the ghost had ever heard a mind, clamped around the words, rotating around them.

It let its solid body do as the mind expected it to do.

Then it watched as the mind burst upwards, through its structure, vanishing in moments from the universe to which the ghost was forever confined.

The ghost envied it. It had never been a mind, so it would never leave like a mind left. It would fade with time.

In the moments while it still existed now, before the knowledge that had made it unmade it once again, the ghost swept towards the house.

Heartsease! The great house! With only one window illuminated.

The ghost swept up to that window, and saw a dark shape against it. The priest staring into the night.

From the terrified look in her eyes, she had seen everything.

But the ghost was lost into nothingness, and lost all knowledge of itself, before it could be sure.

Fourteen: Rebecca's Fourteenth Birthday

Markus was a crofter, who had a shelter in the ruin of a building that was being redone or something by the Purbeck Commune. The ruin was on a look-out point above the flat grassy land that led to the sea. Markus had a beard and tangled hair, and was muscly like an old tree.

They lay inside the shelter, listening to the wind outside. 'I wasn't your first, was I?' he asked.

'No,' Rebecca lied, staring upwards. She felt like she'd just had a red-hot poker inside her. And now he was all little and wet-looking and she couldn't look at him. She was trying hard not to blush. But she was relieved. She'd looked at a net text to make her condom out of a Cortex tyre, and had been carrying it ready for a week now. She'd arrived in Purbeck to find out what it was like, because everyone knew from the songs that there was nobody here who liked dance lists and chaperones. She didn't want to fall in love. She didn't think she could. But she had wanted to have sex.

She was pleased to have done it now. It hadn't been that great. But of course she'd expected that. Nothing was that great. Now who she was was properly hers.

'Where did you come from?' Markus asked, running his fingers annoyingly over her nipples.

She rolled over so that he couldn't keep doing that. 'North.'

'Do you have a favour I could . . . ?'

'No.'

'You're not going to say you're not out of a house, not with that accent.'

She rolled up the condom she'd taken from him when he'd finished, and started wrapping it in its cloth. She had to wash it out within a couple of hours.

'You're not going, are you? God, are you all right?'

She turned back to him, feeling a bit sorry. He sounded lonely. She allowed herself to turn back to him, to lie in the crook of his arm. 'I've been alone for a long time. I've walked a long way! I don't always know what to say.'

'You did all right tonight.'

'You talked. I just listened.'

'So are you going to stay here?'

'No, I want to go to the sea tomorrow. Then I'm going to Ealing.'

'Why there?'

'I don't know.'

'So you are free to go where and when you wish?'

'Yes.' She wanted to change what they were talking about, because she was starting to think she didn't really like him and that would be horrible. She reached down to where he kept his cooking things and picked up what he used to keep the lid of his coolbox closed. A round fossil. A spiral of a shell in the rock. 'Have you thought about time?'

'Er, aye. It's fantastic, all that history. That's from so far in the past. It makes your head swim.'

His thingy was getting hard again. She dropped the fossil from hand to hand, wanting to go for a piss, not sure if she should. 'No, I mean how for lots of time there was nobody to see it. Like there weren't just dinosaurs before us, but lots of different kinds of them, and some of them stayed around for thousands of millions of years, and then they all died and another lot took over. On and on. Like it was almost like forever, but not quite, because then we came along. But for all that time . . . a huge time . . . there was nothing like us, nobody to see any of that. Just a lot of animals eating and fighting.'

'And having sex. And evolving.'

'But don't you get it? Nobody was there. Millions of years of things happening with nobody there. It could happen again.'

'Nah, not now, not with places like this—'

'There could be millions and millions of years after us, as well, with nobody around to see our ruins and roads.'

'There's the Aurigans.'

She paused for a long time, and didn't know why. 'I suppose. But they're not part of the same world as me. I hate them. They make me feel smaller, not bigger. They don't make me feel like anything is about anything. I'm not on their side. Listen,' she put the fossil back, 'I can't sleep here. I'm not used to that.'

'Can I come down to the sea with you tomorrow?'

'If you want. I'll be off early.' She kissed him quickly and got her clothes and pack together. 'Good night. Thanks.'

And she stumbled out of the shelter in her long shirt, already freezing, in search of somewhere more lonely in the grasslands where she could piss and pitch her tent.

Fifteen: Jane's House

Jane put on her coat, and sprinted out into the night to find Matthew's body.

From her window, she had seen him fall. Something had felled him, but it had been so quick, she had not really had time to see.

She didn't know what the emergency had been, but as she stumbled out into the darkness, a torch in her hand, she thought it had all gone terribly quiet.

Other houses took clerics for ransom, she said to herself as she ran across the gravel and then on to the cold lawn. They almost never hurt them.

Except that since she'd taken on the service of Mary, she felt as if she'd lost her neutrality.

She ran to where she'd seen him drop to his knees and then on to his belly, but there was no sign of him. She flashed the torch left and right, turned on the spot. There was nothing.

Perhaps she had been mistaken. Lord, she hoped she was. There had been a figure beside him. It had lashed out. But already that felt like something from a dream. She'd have to green it. Where were the others?

She took a few more steps towards the maze, wondering if they'd all been ambushed, grabbed and hauled away, leaving her to take the bait.

She stopped and listened, and could hear only the sounds of the night all around. The night-time scuffles from the forest. There was nothing human at all in the sounds.

She made herself walk all the way around the grounds, a complete circuit, shining her torch into all the spaces, even bundling up all her new-found faith in Mary, telling herself that the woman or whatever she was knew the time of her death and so it would be sometime dramatic and not yet, and so daring to call out loud. Ruth. Davey. Matthew.

No answer ever came.

There were animal calls coming from all over the valley as she walked back down the drive, and she found herself imagining what the calls meant: hunger, territory, the search for mates. How could she defend the building against the predators? Her ears at one point fooled her into thinking that she could hear voices distantly, but that was just her mind trying to cope with a silence that from now on, she supposed, would increasingly enfold her.

The armoured car was on the opposite side of the house from the maze, unused and standing ready.

The horses were in the stables: Jane put her cheek to one's neck and smoothed its brow. It made gentle animal noises.

She completed her circuit and slowly walked back into the hallway. She called again. She closed the big door behind her and turned all the locks and closed all the bolts she could. If she could have worked out how to drop the portcullis she would have done so.

It occurred to her that they might still be somewhere out there, that they might want to get in, but she could not make herself stay in the house alone tonight without a locked door.

Alone. Surely not? Not just like this? Ruth had said they were going: had they packed up in the face of some attack and evacuated without warning her? Perhaps they'd been pursued. But what did that mean had happened to Matthew?

She went down into the kitchens, up into their bedrooms, and found only the signs that the soldiers had once been here. Their possessions and gear. She checked the cupboard space by the door and found that their weapons were missing. So if they had been chased off, it was with their weapons only, and without transport.

Jane was able to persuade herself that she didn't believe it.

After an hour searching the house hopelessly, calling, going to windows to stare out into the empty darkness, Jane finally returned to her room.

She closed the door behind her, and hauled her dressing table up against it.

A house with hundreds of windows, many on ground level, could never be secure.

But it had been. It had been inviolate. That was the miracle, she had to trust in that.

She wished she'd been more open to Ruth, had managed to

start a dialogue between them. She'd been left with that implication of blackmail over the favour, which hadn't been her intention at all.

She sat on her bed, closed her eyes, tried to pray for Ruth, wherever she was. She found she could not.

She clapped her hands together in frustration, leapt up, grabbed the green dispenser from her table and threw back a tablet.

She waited, lying on her bed, as the drug took hold. Then she walked on to the stage of her memory theatre, and found the row and the seat for the view from that window. It was in experiences of death, and it was horribly right next to the moment she had heard of her dad's death, the door opening and the soldier coming in and immediately squatting to be on an eyeline with her. Those terrible, frightened grown-up eyes.

Doesn't mean a thing, her dad's voice said now.

She focused on the moment as she looked out of her bedroom window, the same window now just a few feet away. She saw Matthew running, and felt the fear again in her own breast. Then he stopped, turned, seemed for a moment to be surprised, shocked, started talking to something that stepped from nowhere, was suddenly there in the shadow of the house. Jane concentrated. It was . . .

An Ornamental Detail. A clichéd Satan, with horns and forked tail. She knew from the cartoon look of it, the lack of details, that this was something that had swum into her mind at the moment of this memory from associations within her own mind. Besides, the Devil was taller than Matthew, and he'd seemed to be pleading with something shorter than him, meeting its eyeline.

Now she would never know. The Ornamental Detail had over-written the swift movements she'd really seen. She'd never known it happen so quickly.

The Devil stepped forward, and reached out one clichéd claw to Matthew's groin. Then suddenly it whipped its claw up. There was a flash of blood.

Matthew fell in the way she remembered. And the Devil was gone.

Jane opened her eyes and stepped out of her memory theatre.

Carefully, she lay on her bed, not wanting to get undressed, wanting to hear every sound, be awake for any noise from below that might speak of the troopers returning.

She couldn't believe they'd gone.

After a while, despite herself, the tension made her sleep.

*

They were still gone in the morning. The situation remained the same.

Jane went out at first light to see if she could see any sign of Matthew now it was day. But there was still nothing.

She treated herself to a large breakfast, breaking into some of Ruth's bread packs at the Lutyens table, feeling guilty and reassured at the same time.

She was alone in a big house in the middle of the outback. With no weapon, and very little security. Exactly what she had asked for. But this wasn't how she'd expected to get it.

She had put herself in the hands of Mary.

She felt joy at that.

A tiny thought made her frown. As she'd done her circuit of the house last night, she'd seen the gates of the estate standing open against the sky, as the team had left them when they entered.

She really wanted to go and close them.

Jane crunched her way down the long gravel drive in the bright daylight of noon, feeling very vulnerable on the open expanse. But it would feel foolish to purposefully walk on the grass.

She'd been to feed the horses, and tend to them as much as she could from what she'd seen various farriers doing in the past. That had been Morgan's job.

Why had Mary wanted her to stay here? Perhaps it was necessary that Jane put herself in harm's way in order that Mary could demonstrate her ability to protect her.

She swung the gate closed and slid the slim bolt home. A bolt you could unslide from the other side. A purely ornamental detail.

Still, she'd done it. She set off back towards the house.

She heard the crunching of another set of boots beside hers like gunshots in the stillness, and smiled to see Mary walking alongside her now. The gravel was disturbed by her feet, she noticed, and felt a pang for noticing it. That was exactly why she had to brave the beasts, to show faith.

'I have a question,' she said quickly. 'What happened to the others last night? Where are they?'

'You will see them all again,' said Mary.

'Are they all right?'

'Those in the maze are still travelling. I sent them on their journey. But they will return when they have come to the end of it.'

'Why did you do that?'

'Because it was necessary if you and I are to complete *our* journey.'

'And Matthew?'

Mary paused. Jane got the feeling that she was considering what Jane could safely be told. Perhaps keeping frightening information from her. 'You will see Matthew again also,' she said finally.

Jane nodded, certain she'd heard the truth. She managed a smile.

Mary smiled back. 'It is time to show you the deep past. What happened here. What you might call the memory of the building.'

'But . . .' Jane stopped herself.

'But this building has no memory? No. It's just a different sort of memory. Everything will become clear. Follow me.'

And she set off at a sudden angle from the path, heading for the stables.

There were ravens around the dark corner of the house, filling the trees threateningly, shuffling and cawing and ruffling suddenly from one tree to another, their mournful cries saying to Jane, as they always had, that autumn was dying into winter. Ravens went searching in the day and returned home at night. They were birds of calendars and clocks, like robins and swallows, but mourning ones, the carriers of nostalgia. Here they thought it was night. Mary led her around the back of the greenhouse, and there Jane stopped, staring in shock at what stood before her.

At the bottom of a couple of mossy steps an arch was formed between two hedges, the gateway to a gravel pathway that lay beyond.

That hadn't been there before.

'But—' she said, astonished. 'But when I did my survey . . .'

When she'd done her survey, the hedge had been complete and undisturbed here. She wanted to grab her phone and check.

She did not.

Mary simply smiled at her again, and stepped through the arch, turning back to her with a little look that said it was all right.

So Jane followed. The path crunched beneath her feet. The new garden features beyond, rows of topiary and flower borders, had all the irregularity of nature. There was no artificiality about it, it didn't feel clichéd like a dream experience would. Indeed, her glands were not erect, there was nothing playing about her head. This place was dull and ordinary compared to the maze, the existence of which was not in dispute . . .

Or at least about which there was a consensus.

But this was new space. This hadn't been here before.

She was thinking too much. She was not showing faith. That was why the others had been suddenly taken from her, she was sure

145

now, why she'd had that vision of Matthew and the Devil. As a test.

She let a hand sneak out and let it ripple along the surface of the plants, feeling the twigs and leaves bounce against her palm. She could smell the lovely scent of the flowers. She walked through a cloud of midges and swished them aside.

Real. Real real real. Mary had opened up a new piece of the world and it was real.

They came to a space where the gardens opened out, a rough place where a stream ran, marking the edge of the forest, the gravel path widening to become its bank. Jane could look back to where the house rose over the gardens, to where everything was normal. Perhaps she'd been hallucinating last time, when she'd walked past this gap . . . or perhaps she'd just missed it? She was acutely aware of her own breathing, of the noises of the forest, of the ruddy smells of autumn. Nowhere was there the vagueness of a dream. She was even a little chilly.

She saw that Mary was looking brightly past the stream, into the forest on the other side. Jane took a deep breath as she saw the darkness that was always abiding between those trees, the brown murk which infested the undergrowth. The stream was a narrow barrier between her and whatever was out there. But no, she couldn't falter. This was the test. Opening oneself to violence, the embracing of fear. Her thoughts danced back to Ruth and the soldiers, but she pulled herself away from that hope of security. This adventure will kill you, you have to remember and accept that.

They walked along the side of the stream for a while, heading anticlockwise around the house.

'Why wasn't this place here when I did the survey?' Jane asked, as much to break the silence between them as anything else.

'Because the nature of space is much more complicated than you have been told,' Mary called happily over her shoulder, tossing out scraps of information like they were the most joyful pieces of gossip. 'You think of the world as a place that you have been put in. In your mind, you walk around on it like a shape moving on a computer map. The computer is such a vast, false metaphor, dearest. It transformed human consciousness like the cinema did, like perspective art, like maps themselves! Because what are you really? What are you? Tell me!'

'I'm a human—'

'No! What do you see?'

'A stream, the forest, rooks . . .'

'You did not see some of those things when you said that. You assumed they were there. In your model of the world.'

'I see . . . A sort of rough oval . . .'

'Good. And in that rough oval?'

'You in the middle. Clear. A hedge that's just cut us off from the house—'

'A hedge being shorthand for a collection of millions of small things . . .'

'And the stream to my left, less clearly, some rocks, the darkness of . . . Just darkness beyond.'

'Lovely. And lastly . . . That's not what "you see", because that assumes a body, something to do the seeing. That oval is what you are.'

Jane laughed at the sensation of the new perspective. 'That's a Buddhist thought. I've heard about that.'

'Ah-ah! Avoidance again! It's not a concept that you can label. It's just what's true. Everything else is a model.'

'But God is true. God is looking at me, giving me a body and eyes and all that.'

'Oh? Can you feel God?'

Jane was silent. After a moment she said: 'Is that the nature of this journey? Am I being tested?'

'All the meanings of this journey come from you,' said Mary, as if that were the first line of a too-familiar song. Then, a moment later: 'And here we are.'

They had followed the banks of the non-existent . . . or non-mapped, or new . . . stream around to a row of three broad, flat stepping-stones that led across it. On the opposite bank, the forest had opened up into a clearing full of mossy stone shapes, huge things, half buried in the ground.

Jane felt her stomach lurching with fear. She looked at Mary, wanting once again to reach out and touch her. 'Do you want me to go over there? There's no fence around . . . the forest.'

Mary simply nodded.

So Jane stepped on to the first stone, and then, with a swing of her hips, the second, and then the third, and ran on to the grass on the other side, half expecting a beast to emerge from the forest straight away to eat her. She waited in the noonday gloom, her hand unconsciously reaching out to touch one of the mossy, collapsed blocks of stone. She glanced over her shoulder to see Mary, but Mary was gone.

But then the voice came from beside her again. 'Here is the first tangible thing you must do.'

Jane slowly turned. Mary was standing a few feet away, having miraculously crossed the stream without moving. She had one hand on her hip, and the other was pointing downwards at something that lay just out of view.

Jane burst out laughing, then covered her mouth with her hands. The expression on Mary's face was like a stern old book illustration. And she just needed to laugh, the pressure on her was so much. She felt that the laugh would become tearful and killed it, then, sucking in a breath and making herself concentrate, 'I'm sorry, Mary. What is it?'

Mary didn't alter her posture or expression one iota. So Jane, a little surprised by the lack of response, walked round to see what she was pointing at.

The top of what looked like a doorway still protruded from the soil, a lintel made of a single marble slab, with a Doric column standing askew beneath it, all infested and made soft with moss. Strands of wild grass obscured a dark chasm, a gap at the top of the door. A gap big enough for a person to climb through.

It looked like the remains of something Lutyens would have built, one of his jokes. Indeed, there had been something about a tunnel in one of the briefings, but it hadn't appeared on any of the maps and Jane had forgotten about it until now.

Jane looked back to Mary and saw that her expression remained unchanged.

'Oh no,' she said, realising. 'Please . . .'

But then she stopped herself, rebuffed by that stone face. She quickly squatted by the gap, and hesitantly started to uproot the grass.

'There's room for you to get in,' said Mary.

'I know, I'm just . . .' Jane stopped pulling at the grass. 'What do you want me to do, down there?'

'Go to the very end of the tunnel you will find. There, you will discover that the EM field is very weak. Bring the field strength up, up as high as it can go!'

Jane slowly let the blades of grass drop from her hand, dread curling up in her again. EM fields were created by swift, awful events or by slow, nostalgic love. She could not hope to create the latter, the decades of fond occupation that gave a place a glow of familiarity and care.

She would have to do something terrible.

She looked away from Mary. 'Should I die down there, then?' she asked.

Silence.

When Jane looked back, Mary was gone.

Jane put a hand to her brow, and bit on her lip to keep the tears back. Well, that had been obvious. She would do this by steps. It was just her and the wet grass now. She didn't have to throw herself into the gap and slit her wrists or something. There was a tunnel to explore.

She sat down on her bottom and slid her feet into the gap.

Nothing beyond it. The smell of musty air, undisturbed for decades. The thought crossed her mind that there might be bats down there, but she didn't mind bats. One of her dad's James Bond novels had said that bats never got stuck in your hair and she'd been locked into a lack of fear by that, ever since.

She thought that was where her logic about that had come from, anyway. That's what she liked to think.

She realised that she was looking for something important in her thoughts that would stop her from going. But there was nothing.

So she slid her legs further into the gap, and put her hands on the top of the lintel, and crunched her fingertips into the little mossy crevices.

She was actually going to do this. She felt a rush of joy at her power to do it. To make her body do something it didn't want to do.

She shoved herself off, and felt the lower half of her body slip into the gap and find no foothold. It dangled there. Her torso negotiated the gap awkwardly for a moment before the weight of her legs dragged it in too. And now her head was swallowed up, caught at an awkward angle in the darkness, her nose filling with a stream of dust from the roof. She was going to choke in a second. Her fingers were about to slip from the lintel anyway. Nothing beneath her feet.

Why hadn't she gone back to the house for a lamp?

Because she wasn't sure this place would still be here when she returned.

Jane made sure, in the moment before the strength in her fingers gave out, that she actually made a conscious decision to let go.

She fell.

A moment of falling.

Jane hit the ground.

Her knees buckled under her chin, and she fell on to her side. She'd fallen maybe ten feet. Nothing broken, probably nothing even bruised.

She felt exultant at having trusted and found that trust to be not misplaced.

The ground under her hands was covered in dirt, but beneath the dirt there was . . . some sort of polished tile.

She blinked. There was light in the distance, from a long way off. She was standing at one end of a long, low tunnel, tiled and with arched stone blocks for a roof. There were metal lamp holders at intervals along the walls, but no lamps. All around her were the remains of what looked like a flight of stone steps. They looked like they had been destroyed by the stamp of a giant's foot, the same impact that had made the roof collapse behind her and caused the whole tunnel mouth, which originally she supposed would have been quite ornate, to subside into the ground. Plants and fungi had taken root in the little gaps in the masonry, but of animal life there was no sign.

So she wasn't going to have to die just yet.

She brushed herself down and set off at a brisk pace in the direction of the light.

The walk was less than half a mile, and the tunnel surface made it easy going. Whatever had happened to the stairs at the end had happened to the whole structure, Jane realised. The walls were buckled at intervals. Soil had flowed into piles on the floor through the cracks in the stone, so there were gardens of dark-loving plants every hundred paces, and full blooms of nettles at two points where a shaft of sunlight had penetrated the roof.

The light, which Jane realised was sunlight, became clearer the further she progressed. When she finally reached the other end, it was so intense that it took her a moment to realise what she was looking at. She stumbled down an incline of rubble, her senses trying to come to terms with it.

When she finally recognised it, she smiled.

High above her, on the other side of a large, collapsed chamber, there hung Christ in mid-air, His hair classically long, His expression placid and loving, His palms raised. Beside Him were curled the lion and the lamb. The stained-glass window was thick with dust, and illuminated only by its uppermost left-hand corner, but it sufficed.

Jane blinked and looked around the chamber. That was the most intact window. There were other spaces that had been clenched into awkward shapes, and were without glass. A low roof had cracked across its central beam. The floor was similarly shattered, the tiles breaking along a spine of earth that had burst up through the ground. There was even an altar, set at an angle. An empty font. The wooden lectern had fallen on its side, the gilt-edged Bible lying with its spine up.

'Why is this here?' Jane asked out loud. It was half a plea for Mary to return. But she somehow got the feeling that Mary wouldn't or couldn't venture in here. Why did she feel that? Because she was thinking of a children's story, *Aladdin*. The magical person doesn't go into the cave, he sends his innocent and sturdy apprentice in instead. But iconic thoughts like that didn't seem inapt where Mary was concerned.

Was this some sort of metaphorical space, then? A magical place? It didn't feel like it. It had dirt and spider webs and wreckage. She picked up the Bible, and swung the lectern upright again with the pressure of her foot. A magical space would treat its Bible better . . . or worse. The pages had been gnawed by mice and the spine had been burrowed into by little insects. It was an illustrated version from the 1930s: Jane found an image of Mary Magdalene that looked like she'd just returned from a smashing party with all the other flappers. The bright colours were dulled by time.

Compared to the house, this ordinary decay was rather reassuring. Jane set the Bible back on the lectern and took the EM meter from her bag. She thought she knew what must have happened to this place, now. She'd seen villages that had been bombarded in the wars and left abandoned. There had been an explosion underneath the chapel. Yes, in the tunnel beneath it! The explosion had rocketed back along, buckling the walls and collapsing the other end too. At this end, it had brought the chapel down to the level of the tunnel itself. Perhaps not immediately, but with decay and subsidence over the years. For how long? Jane didn't know anything about geology. Animals probably came in and out of the tunnel, there were almost certainly rats here, but the place didn't seem to be used as a regular home for anything. She decided that she couldn't make any useful deductions about age or decay.

She brought up her falsified EM map of Heartsease once more, and couldn't help but check at what had been recorded at the tunnel entrance when she compiled that map. Just a bland forest edge. She couldn't even remember doing that section, it would have been just another row of trees. At least the map hadn't changed as well. She didn't know whether that would be more miraculous or less. She had no rules for the numinous beyond what she'd heard in those children's tales.

She traced a line of the tunnel from that point, trying to intuit the way she had come from the angle she'd set off at. Her finger came to rest on the maze. Could it be? She craned to look up through the crack of the stained-glass window. She couldn't make anything out. But it seemed likely to her that this place sat directly under the maze.

The two features that had not been mentioned in the briefings: the new chapel in the house and the maze. The former had taken on the function of this place, the latter the space where it had stood. Neither feature seemed like a Lutyens creation, and this chapel did, its humanity and playfulness visible even as it was wrecked, akin to the house.

So why didn't whatever magic kept the house pristine extend to here?

She took an initial reading. Very high. Nothing like the maze itself, but something she would have drawn attention to in an ordinary survey. She would have held gentle prayer services to calm a place like this, for something terrible had already happened here. Presumably the explosion. People must have died. She supposed the animals would have taken the bones. She took a few steps. The reading fluttered like it would in any ordinary room, the con-tours changing slightly every other metre. She dipped and crossed herself in front of the lectern, then approached it. The reading rose a little. A small fondness. A familiarity. Her old skills were to be of use again, telling the story of this place.

But not yet.

She set her equipment aside, got down on her knees, and put her hands together. She went through her standard prayers for her family and friends, and for the recovery of the world, doggedly ignoring the sense of emptiness that always attended this ritual now for her, that had stopped her last night. She tried her hardest to pray passionately, to feel full of the power of the Holy Spirit.

Then she checked the readings again.

If there had been an alteration, it had been tiny. As one might expect. This place was already haunted by tragedy, yet Mary wanted more. And it was beyond her power, especially at her current distance from God, to do anything about that by means of prayer. Perhaps she could pray to Mary, but it felt horrifying to her to even contemplate that. A solid sign of her faith the woman might be, but she could not, would not, direct her soul to her as she would to her Creator.

'Lord,' she whispered. 'I'm going to have to do something terrible.'

After she'd finished surveying the room, she turned and headed back along the tunnel, towards the daylight.

When she reached the gateway in the hedge again, Jane dived through it as if it might close at any moment. She fell on to the grass of the lawns and clambered to her feet, having bruised her knee. Limping back towards the house, she kept looking over her shoulder.

But the gap remained there until she lost it in the distance.

Sixteen: Rebecca's Thirteenth Birthday

She didn't know what day it was. That was probably deliberate.

She had been marching roughly south, judging her way by the sun. She hadn't seen anyone in three days. She had a stick that she'd whittled into a pointed shaft, and she walked with that end over her shoulder and the rough end at the ground.

She sat on the hillside with her feet in a scar that revealed chalk and flints. Her ears were blustering with the wind and the autumn cold. The landscape of green and brown patches, rough ovals and curves with the occasional shining surface of a lake, went on to the horizon all around. The lines of old roads broke the pattern in places. If she stayed here until night perhaps she would see lights. Then she would have to decide whether she'd head towards them.

But mainly she was looking down the slope at the rabbits.

The wind was blowing from their direction towards her, and she must be right that that meant they couldn't smell her. She was moving very slowly, getting closer and closer, feeling hungry, wondering what she was going to do with one if she got it. She didn't have any matches. She would have to work out how to start a fire without. She'd seen Dad do it—

She stopped moving. She could see the brown gleam of the rabbits' eyes now.

She remembered a human eye moving within a face that should have been dead.

She stayed perched. Wondering about whether she could just do this without thinking about that time. Thinking back to things like that was something people in stories did. She was just thinking of herself as somebody in a story because it made her feel better, made her feel like there was somebody looking down at her, taking care of her, reading her.

She thought of that time whenever she saw blood or meat. But that was just her doing that, wasn't it? She could decide not to do that. She could be somebody else just by acting like somebody else. She did that already sometimes when she arrived at a town or a farm. She made her accent slide up into being courtly to impress people. She pretended to be older or younger than she was. She could do younger easier than she could do older, because she still didn't have to bother to bind her breasts. But younger always meant questions about where she belonged, and older made people think she must be a bride on the run.

She hoped that you could just decide to be or not to be someone. It felt selfish to keep thinking back to some awful old memory. She never did it when she talked to people about things that weren't barter values or directions. Maybe that was why it was still all inside. She never met anyone she wanted to let it out to. That memory of what she'd done still felt like a solid thing in her stomach. Or perhaps that was the hunger? The two things were so close to each other. Maybe that was why she carried a wooden weapon instead of something metal? Maybe she was who she was for all sorts of reasons after all, and she couldn't just undo the weave. After all this time with the feeling, it felt terribly like *whoever* she decided to be would have that awful thing inside it.

She felt the wind change. Maybe that was it. As simple as that and nothing more. It was just the time of the year again, the time when it had happened. She'd feel better when it had all been covered by winter and second winter snow and the smells didn't all have the smell of blood with them.

The rabbits stopped moving, looked in her direction.

She raised her spear.

The rabbits ran in random little circles and in a moment were gone.

She lowered her spear again.

She decided that she'd deliberately let them get away.

Seventeen: Arrrgggggghhhhhhhhhhh!

Rebecca was screaming the words. 'Eighteen hippopotamus, nineteen hippopotamus, twenty hippopotamus! Bastard!'

She pulled the ripcord.

There was a whack from around her head, and then her shoulders were pulled upwards with such force that her body lengthened and her toes elongated into ballerina's points.

Thank God. Thank God. She made a deep grumble in her throat as she swung from the fast, refreshing terror of falling out of the sky to the slower, more contemplative terror of hanging in the sky. Bastard.

The countryside rotated back and forth under her boots. A lush valley full of forests, with a thin river glittering in the afternoon sunlight. Ahead of them, in the open parkland that they were theoretically heading for, stood the shining body of a lake, and beside it, almost in silhouette, the long grey box of the house itself.

Looking across and down like that was fine. It was looking straight down, between her toes, that wasn't so good. The lack of anything there made her want to vomit. She was descending quite slowly, and the wind was taking her in the right direction, but was she high enough to clear the tops of the trees and the lake? She ran through the landing sequence mentally, though it was hard to concentrate on anything with the wind buffeting her ears, even through the helmet. It was odd to think that that peaceful landscape below had the same air around it as this hurricane.

Bastard. Parachutes, for God's sake. With the delays at Reading, the dirigible's engines breaking down, the search for the right engineer, the decision based on the maps that there wasn't a suitable landing site anywhere near the big house and Booth's sudden interest in the supply of packed chutes at Reading and the training tower . . .

Booth had, of course, opted for the fairground way of doing this. She'd actually found herself hanging on to the edge of the dirigible's cabin doorway, her body finally refusing to do this latest insane thing that Booth Hawtrey was asking it to do. 'No!' she'd shouted. 'That's it! I qu—'

And Booth had pushed her out of the plane. Bastard.

She wondered when the last time was anybody had made a parachute jump. She looked up at the sun-drenched white canopy flexing tautly above her. And how long had these parachutes been packed? God, she'd been lucky.

She blinked at a sudden silhouette looming above the chute, getting bigger like a bird about to—

She was just yelling and reacting when Booth shot past, plummeting, frantically tugging at every ripcord he had. His scream arrived and vanished a moment after he did.

He was going to land in the forest.

Rebecca threw her head back and laughed until she got quite light-headed.

Eighteen: Rebecca's Twelfth Birthday

Rebecca checked the noose.

It was exactly right, from the description she'd got off the net. Gravity would do the job in one blow.

She laid it over the branch of the old oak and straightened up. She put one palm on the trunk of the tree and leant on it, looking out. She was a good twenty feet off the ground.

The oak stood in the middle of Savernake. Rebecca had entered the forest five days ago. She'd known then the date was coming up. But she hadn't known what she was going to do.

She had found the length of heavy rope by a hearth that sat in a dip amongst the ferns. The site of the fire might not have been used for decades.

She'd weighed the rope in her hands and decided. Twelve years was enough. There would only be loads more birthdays.

She hadn't seen anybody for a month now. That was really good. She was doing badly at living in the wilderness. Everything in her pack was wet and dirty, and she had some sort of foot thing that was making her left leg hurt. She didn't want to meet anybody who would laugh at her or try and tell her what she should be doing. She wasn't doing the things her training had told her to do. She was doing other things. And none of them worked.

She'd taken the rope to the big tree where she'd set up camp, and used her nail gun to attach it in a spiral around the trunk, leaving only the end bit loose, lying along that branch, with three nails shot into it halfway along so she wouldn't swing into the tree.

So. Lunch.

She stepped down the branches until she was at the base of the tree, and flipped open the wet top of her wet pack. She found some hard biscuit at the bottom that had gone soft. She sat on the pack and chewed it.

She was thinking about Dad a lot these days. Nobody called her Beck any more. She'd nearly gone home for a while, back to where the farm had been. But she thought there would be a new farm there now, full of Campbells.

She didn't know where to go next. She had circled settlements, trying hard not to have to enter one. She had stolen stuff from caravans that stopped in the middle of nowhere. She had scavenged in abandoned settlements that nobody seemed to have found, and ate and ate for a day until she was sick.

She'd entered the forest on a road that was becoming overgrown. Trees on either side of it had conquered the ditch and started to shove their roots under the crumbling black surface. Fucking good luck to them. Must be a good life, being a tree. You get to keep going for hundreds of years without ever having to think.

She wondered for a second if she would break the branch.

No, she was too thin. That made her laugh.

It was around four o'clock in the afternoon, judging by how dark it was getting. The sun was lost already amongst the low branches. The rooks were calling to each other and circling and going to bed. There was a badger sett a mile or so towards the sun. They'd be waking up. Soon would come the sounds of gentle movement in the undergrowth as the things of the night took over from the things of the day.

That had gone on, in this forest, since people had left.

What would the creatures do with her body?

Some of them would try to eat it. The birds would peck at it. It'd be a real problem for the badgers and the other small predators. They'd have to leap up and knock her back and forth. It wouldn't be long until the rope gave way, though. Then the things on the forest floor would get at her and carry bits of her off. She hoped they carried the bones, she didn't want anyone finding a skeleton and seeing the remains of the rope and understanding what had happened.

She probably didn't have to worry. Nobody was ever going to come here.

She was a thing of the night now, one of the things they were all afraid of.

She could hear her dad saying how brave she was.

She started to cry. She threw her biscuit to the ravens and watched them flutter down to fight and grab it.

It was easy to be brave when there were people to fight and places to go and some sort of situation to sort out.

But all those things were just made up by people. There was

nothing big enough to give anything any meaning. People were like the animals. They just lived. But the animals didn't seem to know and people did.

The families fighting, all the history and the betrayals and the treaties.

'It's all shit,' she said out loud. 'It doesn't *mean* anything.'

The ravens cawed at her.

That was probably why a lot of people believed in God or whatever the Singhs believed in. To have an audience. Must be good if you could really feel it. She'd heard that there had once been a sort of church where you'd go in and tell the vicar everything you'd done, and she'd say that it was okay.

Or in Rebecca's case she wouldn't.

Well, maybe not. Lots of other people had done worse stuff. Only she cared about it.

She wondered what David was doing today. She'd never thought she could go back and see him. They'd hang her. She laughed.

Oh fuck it. Come on, time.

She stood up and went to close the flap of the backpack. Zip it down. Then she grabbed the low branches of the tree, climbing up to her big high branch. She took a few steps along to the noose, her arms stretched out for balance, which made her feel bad for some reason, and sat down by the noose.

She put it round her neck and pulled the knot tight.

She put her hands on the mossy bark of the branch to support herself. She didn't want to fall off now. She wanted to go deliberately.

It was weird, looking down and seeing her pack down there in the twilight. That black thing sitting on the bed of leaves. It would take ages for it to be covered in green stuff.

Would it really be good to leave human things here, with nothing to see them and think about them?

She just wished there was someone to see her, sometimes. All the time. Mum and Dad maybe. Just someone to like what she did. Someone to do things for.

Leaving David had been really stupid. He and the soldiers had been like that for her.

Another mistake.

Like on a net game, she'd fucked up. Made too many mistakes. So: game over.

You had another go in those. Maybe she would.

She eased herself to the edge of the branch and felt the slipperiness start to give under her bottom.

She felt good now. This gave her a meaning. And if anybody ever did see her here, they'd get that.

She took a deep breath, and before she'd really thought about it again she pushed herself forward.

A moment of falling. She thought something about how the sun wasn't quite set yet: orange in the undergrowth.

The rope hit tight.

And broke.

She hit the ground unprepared and ended up with her face in the mud.

'Fuck!' she bellowed.

She got up, spitting mud everywhere. It had caked her face and hair and palms and knees. She stood up, shaking her limbs to get rid of it, knowing that leaves were sticking to every single bit of her, and she must look like a walking bush, and if anybody could see her now—

She started to laugh, and the laugh hurt her neck so much that she had to go and lie against the tree, and when she got there, she started to cry, and the sobs burst out of her so hard and so fast that she could only sit there, unable to help herself, just a thing that sobs shot through into the night.

'Daddy!' she yelled at the night. 'Mummy!'

And above her in the canopy of trees, the ravens settled for the night.

Nineteen: Thought Alone

Jane spent her second night alone in the house awake, moving from room to room, wondering where to place a light and what to secure, responding to every noise. She was alone in this building. She had hoped all the time that Mary would return to help her, to tell her that she was letting the soldiers come back. She shouldn't hope, but there it was, she was mortal.

The thought had been with her all the time of what she should do to increase the EM levels in the buried chapel. Violence, that was what. That was implicit. She had thought hard about sexual things, about masturbating in the chapel, which was wrong, but not as much as violence would be. Even so, she doubted her passions would affect the atmosphere in the slightest. Her mission now required screams and the shedding of blood.

That would be her own, she'd decided now. She would spend a while devising some system that would deliver her to her death with the greatest possible amount of pain and horror, and then, God willing, she would see if she had the strength to set herself on that course. It would have to be something automatic, something she couldn't stop once she'd pulled the lever. Perhaps something the soldiers couldn't stop either, if they came back at the last moment.

She'd found herself staring out of one of the windows towards dawn, a defeated pilgrim, looking out at a sickened, wan world.

She'd sat on the edge of the bed in that bedroom, and had fallen asleep with her head on her chest.

Her sleep had been full of little yelps and jerks, and she'd woken at intervals as some sound or other from the big building scared her. She dreamed of her godsons once more, the two golden children, dancing in a circle around each other. The worst thing about the sleep was the thought that there would be some more nights like this before she could devise the means of killing herself.

Which was wrong, deeply wrong. She was living in wrong, asleep in it, drowning in it in her dreams.

One dream was of the soldiers finding her bones in one of the immaculate rooms. That was the last line of the story, the irony of her being the only messy thing here. After she had discovered the monster that did the cleaning.

Like out of a children's book, the monster that did the cleaning.

Another dream had something watching her from the doorway of the room, something with a thin, narrow face and parched eyes.

She woke at that, and looked straight at the doorway, expecting to see it, her body ready with fear.

But there was nothing there. She stumbled to the door and looked out along the empty corridors, but there was nothing there.

They weren't there. The soldiers, her father, hadn't returned, there was no noise of occupation in the empty house.

She woke again around early afternoon, to the terrible realisation that it was already growing dark outside again.

So she would live the last part of her life in the night. That was horrible. Heading for her own room to take her plunge shower, she decided that she would make sure that on her very last day she would wake at dawn.

After her bath, Jane sat on the big marble stairs, watching the sun decline through all those different windows. Beams fell across the hallways, reflecting from the polished wood and stone.

What was she going to do when night fell this time? Sleep. Try and secure the building so she could. But she couldn't.

She felt very sober, remembering now the first traces of what she was like when she was alone. It hadn't happened often, at court. The jam of people huddled together, the routines called for by the demands of other people, the sudden thought that came to her sometimes after a day organising and attending, that she hadn't previously thought in words at all that day . . . What a quiet joy that feeling had been, to realise that you had had no thought of who you were for a while, and had just been. Conditions like that had kept her from being alone for a long time.

When Annabel's husband had been sent on a diplomatic mission, she had told Jane that one of the terrible things about being apart from him was that continual conversation with him had previously switched off some internal, awkward function of her mind. You became used to back and forth, with a lover. You were who they said you were, they were who you said they were. So Jane was told by the young girl.

And Jane believed it, because it married with what she knew of deep memory. The memory theatre didn't store real things, just stories of them. It fixed those stories in every detail, but stories they remained. Without the theatre, long-term memory was just a series of tales the brain reiterated to itself. You no longer had any genuine knowledge of what had happened to you when you were six. Just the Chinese whispers that you repeated over and over to yourself as a founding myth, and if you weren't a priest, then those whispers could easily become mixed up with the stories other people told you, or what you chose to believe. There was, after all, no single cell left in her body from when she was a child. She was an oft-told tale that cell repeated to cell, as all humans were. And she had always thought, before He went away, that it was God that kept the story in the cells straight, knew every tale backwards and loved them all like His favourite childhood fables.

Jane thought that people in relationships switched off that updating process, the secret retelling of foundation stories that happened every night during sleep, and instead relied on what the other person told them in the morning.

Annabel had become lonely at all the internal voices that had sprung up inside her when William left. Her garden growing back, when his version of her had kept it so thoroughly tended. She had hung around Jane's rooms, seeking any conversation, doing her needlework.

Jane knew about being alone, of course, like a dog trainer knows about being bitten. She would wake in the morning and everything would swing into line in her head, a feeling that Annabel, who was familiar with computers, had described to her once as 'booting up'. But Jane had laughed, and, following one of the catechisms she'd been taught, had asked Annabel to try and remember nine numbers for the next hour. When she asked her, she had forgotten three of them, and Jane had said: 'If you're a computer, your memory's smaller than the calculator on my phone.' But Annabel hadn't really taken the point.

Mary had said exactly that, that we weren't computers. That connected her to the catechism. But she hadn't used the exact words. Perhaps that just meant she was connected to Jane herself.

Soon Jane was going to find the heart of what humans really were, after her own death. That was a good thought.

She'd been in this situation only a couple of times: once when she'd been left to prepare a mass grave while the militiamen she'd accompanied went out into the hills for a couple of weeks to search for the killers, and once when she'd insisted on going alone to visit a hermit, that most rare and beautiful of spiritual callings, living in the deep forest. She'd found him comatose, on the edge of death. And the second case wasn't even quite the thing, since the hermit had provided the small company of a pet, simply existing in the same house, until he had died.

Jane was certain, even from this small experience, however, that she was not someone who enjoyed her own company, like the hermit had. Eccentricities like that cropped up sometimes in her calling, but not with her. She knew that firmly.

She was viewing her death now as almost a release, a forthcoming holiday.

In both previous cases, the excitement of the new situation, all the new information, had kept her going for a time, had made her feel connected to her home with the thought of the things she could tell everyone when she got back.

But soon she would take all her information away with her.

And then the house would be the house, and the buried chapel would hold only a strong shouted echo of her, and the world would be with or without Mary, depending on what she was.

It was late afternoon, and she already didn't know what to do. Prayer would be like eating more stale bread, as always now. She had made herself pray for Matthew since she'd been told he'd died, feeling that it didn't matter whether or not she felt she was making an impression on the Lord, it was his soul that she was celebrating. She wished Mary would tell her more about his death, but that was part of the ordeal she was being put through, to have no certainty. Well, except one.

She had nothing left to do except plan her death. Well, let's get on with it, then. This is a good gap for that, while they've been sent away, an ordained gap. Let them find your body.

She realised what the tune playing in the back of her head had been: 'Let It Be'.

Mother Mary comes to me. Of course.

Jane slowly got to her feet and padded down the stairs towards the kitchen. Something to eat. Other people's food. Then she'd set to work.

Outside the big, empty house, it was getting darker. And inside, for the second night in a row, Jane had switched the lights on in every single room.

Twenty: Something to Do

The drive that led to the house was a negative grey in the dusk. Panting, her breath visible in great billows of cloud, Rebecca trudged up to the big metal gates and let herself fall on to them.

She reached through, not bothering to shift her weight, and with an irritated little jerk, tugged back the bolt.

They swished open, newly oiled, and Rebecca stumbled in surprise and had to right herself with more effort in her legs. She paused, resting her weight on her knees, getting her breath back, as she looked down the drive to the great house that lay beyond. The long, low building had every window illuminated, like it was hosting a vast party. But the only sounds Rebecca could hear in the still night air were those of animals: rooks returning to their nests, the distant mawing of sheep and cattle, the squawks of peacocks. From this house itself there was silence, a silence so profound that after a while Rebecca was certain she could hear a low hum of a generator under it, the engine that kept all those lights running. The sound made the night electric too, full of waiting. A festival night with no festival, just the empty house with the ghost of a party.

She made herself straighten up. Maybe they were all playing a party game. This definitely was not what it looked like. Which was: *The Empty Court.* A classic story of the Night that she hadn't really enjoyed because there was lots of horror. She absolutely had never intended living in it.

What the fuck. Not far to go now. The lights meant shelter and warmth. There were real threats out here in the night, they were all too aware of that now. She swung her left leg experimentally to get everything going again, took a deep and heroic breath and marched on.

She carefully looked at the driveway rather than the lights of the house. If a figure appeared at one of the windows, particularly one of those high, isolated ones, she knew she'd yell, and she really didn't want to do that.

She heard the crunch of her boots on the gravel all too clearly, and stepped off to walk on the grass by the side.

'Hum,' she said to herself, on the same note as the house.

After a while, she heard a distant noise behind her. Crunch. Crunch. Crunch.

The sound of one man hopping. She relaxed a little. There the bastard was.

She didn't turn to look.

Rebecca had screamed as her parachute had carried her down into the trees, seeing sharp branches swing up towards her, but thankfully a clearing had appeared. She'd tugged on the controls like the guy taught her, and bit her lip and made an effort of will, and had pulled up her knees to clear the last branch. Then she was running, tottering, running again a foot above the ground, and then her legs had taken the weight, folded, and the ground had wrapped her in it again.

And she was down, safe, laughing at how brilliant she'd been at that landing.

She'd looked up to scream her laughter at Booth.

And found herself looking into the face of a tiger.

A tiger.

It was huge and old, with a coat that was whitened with cold and stained with what looked like rot or blood or mud. It had vast, yellowed teeth that it was baring at her as it hunched backwards, its back legs tensing. It was hissing a high, gurgling sound.

She must have nearly landed on top of the thing!

Rebecca held her breath and stayed absolutely still, the lines of her parachute still wrapped around her, the chute making little efforts to drag her off in suddenly varying directions according to the wind.

She was frozen inside by fear, locked in front of the predator by something bigger than her. Is this all my instincts can manage, skittered a little fleeing thought around the edge of the fear, keeping me still for this thing to kill me?

She and the tiger looked at each other. The sound coming from the tiger changed in pitch, a low growl gurgling from its throat. It bellowed, suddenly, and let out a stinking breath that made Rebecca want to vomit with fear, the smell full of meat. It was working itself up, getting braver, like a cat with a toy, telling itself that it was an affront to its power that this strange being had suddenly fallen into its world. It reached one paw forward, slapping at her, claws pinning down the strap at her shoulder.

She jerked back in a human reflex, an effort to wrench herself out of the nightmare of being prey, knowing with a sickening thump as she did so that the movement would set if off, make it leap.

A flash of movement. A noise. Something covered her.

The parachute spasmed inside-out over Rebecca's head and caught the tiger.

The creature yelled and burst away, out of the fabric, and by the time Rebecca had whipped the stuff out of her face, the beast was gone, crashing off into the undergrowth, carrying the leg in its jaws.

She let out a wailing, passionate cry of relief and stumbled to her feet. She angrily ripped the catches of the parachute from her shoulders and kicked the thing a few times, unkindly, until it rolled off into the bushes, pursued by the same wind that had saved her.

'Shit!' she shouted. 'Shit! That was a fucking *tiger*! Why was there a fucking *tiger*?'

She realised then. The leg. The tiger had left the clearing carrying a leg in its jaws, a leg it must have been picking at before Rebecca landed on it.

'Help,' said Booth.

She swung on the spot and saw him then, hanging upside-down from the branches where he was still suspended by his parachute. His left leg, below the knee, was gone, and the stump was sticking out at an odd angle.

Rebecca pointed at him in surprise, and laughed, and then suddenly threw up.

She bent her head to keep it away from her overalls, and held back her hair. 'Bastard!' she shouted between every vomit. 'A *tiger*! Bastard!'

It had taken her a quarter of an hour of vomiting before she was able to climb the tree and help Booth with his leg situation. She had been tempted to stay up there with him in case the tiger came back. But it was getting dark, and from the tree they could see the lights of the house. And Booth had been doing his offhandedly brave patter, courageously not mentioning the incredible pain he was in, so she'd decided to put some distance between them.

Which was difficult, because even as they'd made their way through the undergrowth and over hedges and gates, his hop, with all that complicated purple stuff he was full of trailing behind him, was nearly as fast as her striding.

*

The silence of the house loomed in front of her now, and she felt like calling back over her shoulder and yelling at Booth to stop his bloody crunch, crunch, crunch. But that would have been silly. And besides, she didn't want to raise her voice.

Her ears were full of phantom sounds, the sort you got when you'd been in court for a while and then went into the wilderness. She thought she could hear voices, music, all sorts of civilised things that fled when she turned her attention to them. It was more obvious here because her eyes suggested that there should be sounds like that: the house was lit up like one of the houses of court. People make noise inside as a shield against the silence outside.

Had it illuminated itself, Rebecca wondered, on some sort of ancient timer? No, of course not. Who had oiled that gate? Or swept the gravel back on to this path? There must be hundreds of them, hiding behind the house. All called away to the stables to go and look at a horse or something.

She reached the porch and paused, biting her lip. But then she thought about Booth seeing her holding off and decided to do something. The big black door had lions carved on it. And not, as she suspected it might: *Welcome to the Empty Court.*

She glanced up and saw that above the door were lined the wooden teeth of a portcullis.

Fine.

With a little reflexive duck she hopped under that and quickly pressed the knob in the middle of the big round green ceramic door-bell.

She couldn't hear whether that had made a bell ring somewhere or not.

She knocked gently on the door. Then more loudly. Then she made herself call out: 'Hello? Is anybody in there?'

She suspected she was the only person working for one of the families who still had to do this. Anybody else, anybody who was in some way not bloody expendable, would arrive with a squad of militia in support. But the Aurigans were quite stern about Booth working alone. She'd read in the journals compiled by her predecessors that the Hawtreys had sent a message back along the beam to Capella a few decades after the GEC, asking permission for Booth to have someone go along to keep him company. Ninety years later, the response had been a yes. Rebecca thought the Aurigans were probably used to the idea that while these messages were going and coming back the people they were talking to would usually just have gone ahead and done it. But even with his bosses' approval for the biographer, Booth had stuck to the no-bodyguards principle, which meant that she always found herself knocking on doors without anybody to look out for her safety. Apart from Booth. And he never did.

'Anyone home?' he asked now, hopping up beside her.

'No,' said Rebecca. 'But it's *not The Empty Court.*'

'Right. Good.'

The door opened, just as she was about to knock again.

A parched face that might once have looked attractively full peered out. It was a woman. A priest. She had beautiful eyes, but they looked fearful, flicking up and down Rebecca and Booth as if they were something awful. As if there were terrible consequences to their being there.

Rebecca was seized by the sudden idea that she'd seen the woman before. The face was incredibly familiar. 'Who are you?' she asked.

The absolute lack of protocol made even Booth blink.

The priest was staring back at her as if she'd just thought the same thing.

There was a moment of silence as they stared astonished at each other.

Then Booth stepped between them and flopped heavily on to the wall beside the door. 'Sorry to trouble you,' he said. 'But could you spare a leg?'

They had to leap forward and start arguing when she began to close the door on them.

'Do you have a tyre?' Booth hopped along the hallway.

Rebecca, having torn her gaze away from the priest, was looking around in astonishment. The carpet under her feet was so luxurious that she had trouble making herself muddy it with her boots, but the polished floorboards on either side of it looked equally pristine. The beams above her head gleamed black in the light of the electric lamps. Every antique torch holder was polished and sparkling. The granite walls were stained with age, but showed no signs of dust or campfire blackening. The fireplace looked ready for use. It was warm in here, there was actually some form of central heating in operation.

It was a court. A court that nobody had heard of. A court that let their priest answer the door. And there was nobody about. Therefore: empty.

Perhaps it was just *an* empty court. Not the definite article.

There was one good thing about a priest (who felt like her long-lost sister, dammit) answering the door: perhaps they could get her to offer hospitality. Then whoever else was here . . . and of course there was somebody, of course there was . . . would be trumped, unable to hurt them. Well, unless they really wanted to. That's what you got for sending a priest to do a butler's job.

'Well, yes . . .' The priest sounded jittery. Rebecca swung her attention back to her and found her looking right back. There was no physical resemblance. It wasn't as if this woman came from some distant lost branch of the Champherts, though there were enough of those, all the records having been burnt to conceal the family's French origins. It was an open secret, of course, but if nobody had proof, historically, nobody got denied a job. And the gesture showed a certain appropriate shame. That probably contributed to her pariah status, Rebecca often thought. Cooperating with a piece of Singh propaganda was *just* the sort of thing a Frog would do.

No, this woman just *felt* incredibly intimate to her. Like they should have hugged. Which seemed to be freaking both of them out. Not that the priest didn't have other things going on. It was as if they'd interrupted something, stumbled upon a séance or a burial. She was the absolute clichéd receptionist of the horror-story house. She wanted to spare them from what they'd just walked into. Any moment, the gracious and flamboyant host would wander in and interrupt the desperate pleas the vicar was about to come out with. Ignore my vicar, she's so highly strung. Come in, we're just eating. You're on the menu.

There must be such a host. The house was obviously full of people. There were heavy oilskins hanging in the little cloakroom just off the hall. But no noise came from further inside the building.

Rebecca once more suppressed the urge to call to Booth that they'd be on their way now.

The vicar turned away from her, as if she'd suddenly remembered her manners. 'That wound,' she said, turning to Booth. 'I only have a medical kit . . .'

'No need,' Booth replied. 'I just require a tyre.' He was standing beneath one of the electric lamps, hopping on the spot to keep his balance. His blue bicycle chains, cleaned of their liquid by numerous bushes and shrubs, swung against his good leg.

Rebecca watched the priest react now that she could see that. Only a matter of time until she realised who she was dealing with here. Which meant a gamble on what sort of priest this was.

'What?' she asked, transfixed. She looked as if she was working this out pretty damn quickly.

'A tyre. Like on a small wagon.'

'There are cars . . . in the stables.'

'How old?'

'Nineteen thirties.'

'Nothing from after the twenty tens?'

'I don't know. There is one from just before the GEC, I think.' She was looking desperately back and forth between them and the door now. Um-hmm, thought Rebecca. Any minute. If this turned out to be one of *those* vicars, they could kiss hospitality goodbye. 'But what on earth do you need a tyre for?'

There was a faction of the Reformed Church of England who regarded Booth as an affront to everything they stood for. At best, they got all sniffy and walked away. At worst . . . well, she hoped she wasn't going to be present for some of the *at worsts* that the journals went into. Because of Booth, Hawtrey house clerics were picked from the most liberal wings of the Church, something which contributed to the whole stupid hypocritical mushroom-eating Hawtrey culture.

Booth hopped over to the priest and reached out his hand. 'I'm sorry,' he said. 'We haven't been introduced. I'm Booth Hawtrey.'

The vicar opened her mouth and stared at him, ignoring the outstretched hand. Rebecca watched realisation fill her face, and knew there and then that this was definitely one of *those* vicars.

Booth frowned. 'No, really, I am.' He leant close to the priest and pulled down his eyelid. 'See?'

Rebecca put a hand over her eyes. He had a perfect memory, so why did he always do the most stupid possible thing?

But the priest didn't scream or anything.

When Rebecca lowered her hand, she saw that she was nodding, as if she'd just understood something, was taking something on board. She had a little smile on her face, even.

It was a reaction that Rebecca didn't understand at all.

'That's why you want the tyre,' she said. 'My name is Jane Bruce. Follow me.'

She headed off into the house.

Rebecca frowned at Booth. 'You must be getting better at that.'

Jane walked ahead of the two visitors, not looking back at them. Her heart was pounding. Booth Hawtrey! So this was what Mary had prepared her for. It couldn't be a coincidence. It forced her into a place where she had stark alternatives. Horrible alternatives.

He'd been put there before her. The sacrifice. The test. Right now. She started to breathe deeply to calm herself.

Why was the woman with him so familiar? Had she seen her

somewhere before? The sensation added to the terrible dreamlike sensation of the whole experience.

They would be expecting hospitality. She should refuse it. Send them back into the night. For their own good.

Bad things could happen in this unreal time.

But still, she said nothing.

'Ah,' Booth said suddenly. 'I know what's going on here!'

Rebecca flashed a warning look at him.

'Oh?' said Jane. 'What?'

'You're in the middle of a survey, aren't you?'

Rebecca found her whole body relaxing in relief. 'A survey!' she said. 'Right!' Then suddenly everything stiffened again. 'A *survey*?' The only reason for surveying an obviously inhabited house like this would be some sort of frightening EM visitation or a terrible accident. 'Has there been a compiler breakdown or something?'

'No, nothing like that.'

'Then *why* are you doing a survey?'

Jane paused, as if considering her words carefully. 'For a new occupation.'

Rebecca stopped walking and stared at her. 'What? How is this—?' She gestured dumbly around the gorgeous, perfect walls. 'I mean: *what*? If it's a new occupation, then why is this place so . . . so perfect?'

'It's how we found it. We don't understand it either.'

'We?' That was Booth, stepping back to them, showing a tiny bit of interest at last.

'A unit of militia.' The woman looked away. 'They'll be back soon.'

'How soon?'

'I'm not sure.'

Rebecca and Booth looked at each other, equally boggled.

Jane walked off ahead of them again.

'*The Empty Court*,' said Rebecca.

'*Rocky Horror*,' replied Booth. Oddly.

The stables smelt of polish and rubber, and the aroma of horses was only just starting to take hold. Once more everything was gleaming and pristine. Had whoever Jane worked for cleared the place of its original inhabitants? Just walked in and shot everybody, or dropped in some biological warfare agent? Nobody had done that in years. Not since the Campbells had bombed Halifax. Everyone was too afraid that something might spread. But even if that was what had happened, where the hell were the bodies? There were horses here to pull a good-size battle vehicle. So when were the militia Jane had spoken of coming back? And why didn't she know?

The obvious question, of course, was which family was she working for? But Rebecca knew better than to ask that of a priest who was in the middle of a survey.

Booth had squatted one-legged beside the smooth red body of a Citroën Nine, checking the trademark on the tyre. 'Cortex. That'll do fine.' Now he slid upright again, and reached out to her expectantly. Rebecca slapped into his palm the wide-bladed knife she'd found on a shelf and had been playing absently with while studying the vicar.

She was very aware that the vicar had been studying her right back, standing beside the big stable doors open to the night, her arms wrapped around her body. Every shadow of her face was emphasised by the harsh electric light. She had a hand to her mouth, as if she still had that idea, an idea that she was appalled by.

'You don't have to watch this,' Rebecca called to her. 'It gets a bit messy.'

'Oh no, I want to watch the trick. To say I've seen it.'

'Trick? Oh. So you *are* one of *those*.' Booth had started to rip open the skin of the tyre, pulling out the greasy blue stuff inside with his fingers. 'Which is fine. As long as you don't want to shoot me.'

'I'm not a Crosbyan.'

'I think you lot in the Reformed Church, or whatever you call it, are just jealous of the old elephant's memory.' He tapped his head. 'I don't have to take drugs to get the full malarkey.'

'I think that what the Reverend Crosby did—'

'Hurt, actually. It still does. I can't get the bullet out without pulling my head off. I'd like to avoid that.'

'But, you see, that's what lets you down!' Jane took a few paces into the stables, suddenly becoming animated. Which made Rebecca unconsciously move back. It was as if the vicar had wanted to hide her opinions . . . was that out of politeness? Surely not. Now she couldn't hold it in any longer, and they were seeing a bit of her true self. Just a bit. 'You don't even bother to keep your story straight! If the bullet the Reverend Crosby fired into your neck still hurts, then why doesn't that?' She pointed at Booth's stump.

Rebecca opened her mouth wide, and put on her most amazed face. She leapt to stand shoulder to shoulder with the vicar, and let a tone of betrayal creep into her voice. 'Yes . . .' she whispered. 'Why *doesn't* it?'

Booth leaned heavily on his hand for a moment, and Rebecca restrained a laugh. 'It does,' he said. 'But you get used to certain sorts of pain. It's like you going to the . . . No, actually you probably *have* been to a dentist, haven't you, Reverend? Since you're from a prosperous family.'

Rebecca looked. No reaction.

'After a while, if it's just a filling in a dead tooth or something, you'd rather they drill away and not bother with the anaesthetic. Well, I know this pain.' He resumed his task. 'And I want to get it over with, thank you.'

'I'm not convinced,' said Rebecca, glancing to Jane. 'What about you?'

The vicar gave her another of her complicated smiles.

Rebecca found a chair by the stove in the vast and wonderful kitchen, and just basked in the heat it was giving out. In a few minutes, she knew, she'd start to feel guilty about taking up all that heat herself, but at the moment her aching body said that if the owners of this place wanted to waste it then she was happy to put it to some use. Booth had taken a bucket of the Cortex into a corner and had started to pat it into shape on the base of his stump. He'd got a solid trunk of leg together, which was already forming into the shape of a calf muscle. Every time Rebecca looked back to him it had developed further. But every time she kept looking it didn't seem to be doing anything at all. She'd only seen this process once before, but she kept looking away because she didn't want Booth to know she was interested. The vicar had gone to prepare a room for them.

'I wish I knew who she's working for,' she said.

'Oh? Does it make a difference?' Booth didn't even look up.

'Look at this place!' She gestured violently around the room. 'This isn't some old wreck they're doing a survey on. This is a fucking forward base for one of the other families! They must have had to evacuate. If it wasn't an EM compiler accident then it must be something secret. The place will be spiked to shit! Booth, for Christ's sake, do we really want to stay here? Do we really want to be around when these vanished-off-somewhere militiamen get back?'

'Depends how long my list takes to complete.'

'Let's call home, get a military dirigible down here, get a fucking platoon down here—'

There came a cough from the doorway. Rebecca jumped. Jane was standing there. 'I found some towels. I've put them in one of the bathrooms.'

The vicar didn't make enough noise for Rebecca's liking. She hoped she hadn't heard all that.

'Thank you,' said Booth.

'We beg for hospitality,' added Rebecca. 'I thought I'd better make that official.'

The vicar looked complicated at her again. 'I'm sorry, I can't offer that, nobody's in occupation yet.'

So she was going to play this new property thing as far as it would go. Rebecca managed to make her lips into a smile. 'Of course. Should have realised.'

Jane went over to look at the leg in development. 'It *is* an extraordinary trick,' she said.

'Nothing up my sleeve,' agreed Booth.

Rebecca found that she'd folded her arms, so now she deliberately unfolded them. 'We won't be staying long,' she told Jane. 'Just until Booth completes his list of things to do.'

'Ah, the famous list.' She kept looking at the leg. And because she kept looking, nothing seemed to be happening. The Cortex sat there, glistening and unmoving, a half-formed lump.

'And we'll stay out of the house while you're doing your survey.'

The priest looked up at that, as if surprised at the thought. She managed another one of her smiles, as if unwilling to answer.

Got you, thought Rebecca, meeting her gaze.

They both turned back to the leg.

'Finished!' said Booth, tapping a perfect calf and lifting his leg to wiggle his toes. The leg was even pink and hairy and had ugly toenails.

'Damn,' whispered Rebecca.

She chose a bathroom with a heavy wooden cabinet and slid it in front of the door before she had her bath.

Which allowed her a few minutes of absolute luxury.

The bathroom was ornate, there was hot fresh water from gilded taps, and just for a while Rebecca didn't care where it came from or what sort of madhouse this was. Maybe Booth would be able to crack through his Capellan checklist before the militia got back, and then they could be off back to court with some good intelligence. Nobody had detained Booth for a long time. But then, it had been a long time since he'd chanced upon something one of the families was cooking up. Who would it be, way down here? The Mandervilles, possibly, but it was a little far east for them. Maybe one of the Free Cities or the Purbeck Commune wanted to establish an outlying manor. Her theory about the compiler accident didn't seem to hold up, anyway. Jacob, one of the Hawtrey house clerics, had once complained about the metaphors she'd used in describing the EM phenomena she'd encountered in travelling with Booth, and had used a small compiler to take her through a range of atmospheres, more subtle than those sampled at a ball, feeling them with her and getting her to describe them. She knew what this stuff was supposed to feel like, and she was certain that even if the accident had been localised in some part of the house, she'd have felt something twitchy by now.

It wasn't that she wasn't scared by the place, but that seemed to be on a very sensible basis. There was nothing in the atmosphere here to suggest that one *should* be terrified. Though the interior looked just like *The Empty Court*, the absolute classic haunted house, it felt . . .

How did it feel, exactly? Rebecca glanced back to the cabinet lying against the door. Was it just the way the place looked, her uncertainty about the cleric, that had made her lodge it there? Or was it something more?

Whatever, she didn't like the idea of having to move it.

She sank back underwater and luxuriated in the heat once more.

Jane walked from one side of her room to the other, then back again. 'Are you listening to me?' she asked the air, aware of how ridiculous it would sound if anyone could hear her. 'I need your advice. Can you hear what I say to you when I'm alone?'

That was the difference, having an incarnation to deal with. The Holy Spirit was at your shoulder, in your stomach and your voice, all the time. Mary wasn't. So here small old Jane was questioning the powers of the miraculous like you'd test out a new piece of software, one that wasn't quite working yet.

She didn't know whether or not she should have faith. Whether or not she needed to, now.

But she did know that the obvious answer to the obvious question was in front of her, and she desperately wanted some approval for the terrible ideas that had come uninvited into her head.

Rebecca eased the cabinet away from the door and walked it on its four tiny curled legs back to where it had stood against the wall.

She was feeling all warm and washed out, her muscles sagged by the bath. Which normally would be great, but in this place made her feel like she wasn't going to be able to run when the monster leapt out of the cupboard.

Getting back into her clothes hadn't been the most comfortable experience. She'd always been proud of her smell. It was something David had always talked about, even boasted about to other men. It was a fun smell. But there came a point where things just went too far. She'd rubbed a couple of soap bombs into her underwear, shirt and trousers before she got into them, but it didn't make much difference. Booth would mention it, sooner or later. He had a weird attraction to women who smelt of chemicals, a view which he broadcast far and wide, the purpose of which, Rebecca suspected, was entirely so that he could walk into a court and immediately sniff out who was on the menu that night.

The vicar had found them adjacent bedrooms, along one of the gleaming, antique corridors on the second floor.

Rebecca opened the door of the bathroom, looked out, and then stepped gently on to the carpet of the great shivery hallway. Wisps of steam followed her. The big windows along the corridor were black with the night and the house was silent.

She felt . . . that sense of misplaced atmosphere again. Like she should really feel something beyond the tingling of the colder air on her skin. The corridor stretched empty and unconscious both ways, lined with paintings and figurines.

But no, she'd been wrong. It wasn't quite silent.

Far off, she could hear someone talking. Too far to pick up words, but the rhythm was definitely that of speech. It was coming from the opposite direction to the room Booth had retired to for what he still called his 'naps', even though he just lay there resting without actually going to sleep. Maybe he'd got fed up and was talking with the mad vicar.

Rebecca set off down the corridor in the direction of the sound, tiptoeing in her socks, her boots slung over her shoulder by their laces. She didn't want to march straight in on the two of them. She wanted to listen at the door first to find out if they were talking about her.

The Empty Court was clean, still, illuminated by a pale and continuous light. Just like this place. The classic haunted house. A lot of the doors to the rooms had been left open, and she had to stop herself from closing them as she passed. Or giving them an artificially wide berth. The amount of energy these lights were wasting! But if she switched one off, that'd be a signal to the monster, it always was.

Why did the vicar want to light up the whole bloody place? In the stories, that waste attracted the things of the Night. They came in to stamp out the lights. Booth's idea of a haunted house was probably that rather weird image you got in old stories: cobwebs, broken furniture, abandonment. Booth had told her that sometimes, when he was alone in a familiar place, he caught flashes of movement out of the corner of his eye, that somehow his mind expected people to be there. Which was strange. Rebecca couldn't imagine that happening to her. He was pretty dull about EM fields too, shrugging most things off as 'atmosphere' or 'imagination'. It was like he couldn't quite believe that such things existed, and rather resented people around him talking about them. It was like everyone but him had some weird condition, and he was immune.

So he probably felt very comfy here.

The deep interior of this building was so still that she had no idea how far away the voice she was following was. Annoyed now, she kept going. Heavy carpets. Paintings of people in armour. A lot of the artworks were far older than anything she'd seen outside of the Hawtrey private gallery. A house of memories with nobody to remember them. A smell of . . . of nothing. She couldn't even smell a cleaning product. The place employed spooky cleaners who floated around with ghost mops and phantom buckets.

She'd turned two corners now, and gone down a little flight of stairs, but still the sound didn't seem to be getting any closer.

The thought occurred to her as she came to an awkward little confluence of stairways. What if the priest was lying? Maybe she'd killed all the people who lived here. Made them vanish. She was mad enough. Or maybe she was a ghost, an EM spike. People would say to them: but that place hasn't had a vicar in a hundred years!

Obviously, she would ask them to find her treasure or right the wrong for which she'd been doomed to haunt the world for all eternity.

Or perhaps Rebecca was letting plots work themselves out in her head once more.

She made her way up the shy little side stairwell. The sound was definitely getting clearer the further up she went. It was now just louder than the creaking of the house and the contraction of furniture as the cold of the night seeped in. Why the distance from her room? Would even Booth shag a vicar?

She reached the top of the stairway, up this narrow little inlet, insulated from everywhere. The heart of the house.

A wooden Cross was suspended on the wall beside a tall, narrow door. The only place this stairway went. The Cross puzzled her. What was it doing there?

She listened once more. The sound she'd been trailing was definitely coming from the other side of the door. She still couldn't make out any individual words. It all sounded the same, not like the exchange of a conversation. Was there someone inside the room, talking to themselves? Or was that a radio droning away? It had a distant, alienated sound to it, like the foreign stations you heard sometimes on long wave late at night, people talking in indecipherable tongues about what was happening in their dark corners of the world. The chatter on the radio was sometimes ranting, sometimes martial, with crashing, antagonistic music, sometimes sad and weeping.

She looked back down the stairway. She'd come a long way from the bedrooms.

She raised her fist to tap on the door. Then lowered it again without doing so. She had a sudden, horrible feeling that Booth wasn't in there.

She made herself gently press her ear to the door. She sniffed. She could smell something now. Gunshots. Gunpowder. Tangy and fiery. And rich, churned loam, which made her think of birds diving for worms in the wake of a plough. The iron taste of blood, as a scent.

She put her palm flat on the door by her head and felt the whole house through it. The distant hum of the generator, deep down under the cellars. And still this chatter on the edge of speech.

After a while, that touch felt more dangerous than listening, so she took her hand away again.

The sound continued. She was just chiding herself towards grabbing the doorhandle and marching in, because she thought she could pick out something that sounded like words—

The sound stopped.

She jerked her head back from the door.

Still silence.

She started to swiftly walk back down the steps, nearly backwards, half tripping, glancing frantically back over her shoulder.

The door stayed closed. Was it opening? No, it stayed closed.

Maybe nobody was going to come back and claim this house. The house was itself, the thing that was left when all mind had fled. It was waiting for humanity to die away.

She'd caught it muttering to itself.

Rebecca tripped and nearly fell, and got startled by the vulnerability of being off balance. She stumbled to the bottom of the steps and then she ran.

A moment after Rebecca turned the corner, the door of the room swung open. A shadow was cast in several directions by the lamps at the top of the stairwell.

Then the door swung closed again.

Jane sat at her dressing table, wondering.

She'd planned this terrible thing. She'd spent some time selecting the rooms for Booth and Rebecca. She'd been exploring the bowels of this place, and felt that she knew it well enough now.

She had to keep her mind off things, now, so she could do this. But if she had to do that . . . She grabbed her phone and switched it on. To distract herself she searched for references to Booth Hawtrey, confirmed his appearance with some images of him. And there was Rebecca. Rebecca Champhert. Jane realised with a moment of shock that last year she'd read one of the girl's novels.

She skimmed on to a theology link.

There were twenty-six texts about the theological issues surrounding Booth Hawtrey in the Anglican Library at Wells. She accessed the one Philip Crosby had written in prison: *A Proof of Satan*. Crosby hadn't been imprisoned for shooting Booth, but for (perhaps accidentally) also shooting a police officer who attempted to restrain him immediately afterwards, while he was preaching over Booth's body. Crosby had been led off to prison meekly, appalled at what had happened, and equally appalled that his prayers hadn't freed Booth from what, at the time, he regarded as demonic possession. That particular belief had lasted only a few months more for Crosby, who became a nexus for anti-Booth sentiment and a theological touchstone even from his prison cell. In the wake of his attack, Booth allowed priests with EM meters to meet with him, having shunned all such requests previously. They discovered that Booth had no unusual EM activity associated with his presence. Indeed, he was rather EM neutral. From that time up until his death during the Penal Releases, Crosby had maintained a different position, one that Jane had been drawn to as she learnt the theology behind her calling. One that she had finally subscribed to: Booth Hawtrey was the only creature in the world not created by God. As such, he had been presented to the human race as a sign of the reality of eternal damnation, a damnation he was living out. He would never know the peace of knowing God directly, being condemned to life on Earth.

Whether Booth was conscious of his role or not was the subject of much speculation. Jane had never expected to actually meet him. It was like meeting a character from the children's books she had been thinking so much about lately.

He seemed just as arrogant as she'd always imagined him. The prince of this world. The man whose existence laughed at God. For him to be here now was the stuff of fiction itself, too much of a coincidence not to mean something. He and his friend must be here to fulfil their part in Mary's plan. That must be why the soldiers had been sent away, too. The world was twisting itself, as the tunnel to the buried chapel had twisted into existence, to allow her to do this. If her spirit could do this, the world would bend over backwards to allow it.

At least, amongst all this, she had been true to herself over one thing. She had let Booth Hawtrey know what she thought of him. She had not deceived him. The two of them believed that she was still in the middle of her survey, but that was not a belief she had nurtured in any way. She had just kept her silence. She had not offered a hospitality she could not provide.

She stopped, looked up at herself in the mirror, a brief flash of memory, of Dad coming through the wall.

What would he think of her?

Had she in some way become an instrument? Was that why she felt distanced from her own words and actions? Crosby, towards the end, had been diagnosed as a paranoid schizophrenic. But he'd embraced his condition, claiming that he'd been freed from time so he could understand the distance from which God had made the universe.

No. She looked back to the texts. She knew what she was doing. She had just never known that she was an accomplished actress before, persuading her prey that they would be safe here. If she didn't have volition, she couldn't make moral choices. If she couldn't make moral choices, then there was no reason behind the horrible things she was going to do tonight.

'If I had been able to kill Booth Hawtrey,' she read, 'I would have proved him mortal. My intent, therefore, was to *fail* to kill him, to complete the Proof that his presence on Earth demands. Any successful attempt on Booth's life now would be an act of supreme devotion, an indication that we have lived through and understood the Proof. Booth's death would itself be an act of Grace, a new connection between God and *homo sapiens*.'

Jane closed down the text and slowly nodded. She looked at the ceiling and addressed Mary once more, hoping she could hear her. 'All right,' she said. 'They're here for this, they're my test. I think I can make myself do it. I believe I can kill Booth Hawtrey.'

She felt the hand on her shoulder, and lowered her gaze to see

Mary in the mirror, smiling, standing behind her. 'You must not harm Booth Hawtrey.'

'No?' Jane let out a long breath of relief. 'Then to bring up the EM level in the buried chapel . . .' She tried not to let her face fall again. 'Must it be me?'

'No.' Mary shook her head. 'It must be the other.'

'Rebecca?'

'Rebecca. Use her fear and suffering. At length.'

Jane stared at her. 'But what about the Proof?'

Mary was silent. She kept on smiling.

'All right,' said Jane, finally, feeling vertiginous. 'Rebecca. At length.'

She set the alarm on her phone, and carefully lay down, shocked by the sheer normality of the feeling of her head on the pillow. Mary wasn't there when she looked again.

She felt like she was in a guilty dream. She'd wake up.

Quickly, she was asleep.

Twenty-One: Rebecca's Eleventh Birthday

Rebecca watched the hands of the clock click together on the moment of midnight.

It was her birthday.

She looked closely at David's face as he slept. He wasn't waking up, he wasn't pretending.

This wasn't really his fault.

The platoon had organised a surprise party for her. She'd found out by accident. An extra allocation of rations on a phone. David must have gone along with it.

She'd been very angry at him, but couldn't say anything. She'd got angrier and angrier as the day came closer, but she managed to have him think everything was okay without really trying. Maybe it didn't take much acting.

She slipped carefully out of bed and plucked the sack of stuff she'd prepared from under the camp bed. The quarters were better now they'd moved inside the Cardiff city walls.

This would mean leaving a lot of things behind. She didn't care about any of them. She didn't know where she would go, except that she would be over the border and into the outback before anyone could find her. No note, because she wanted to be able to come back if it went wrong, before she became a deserter. She'd be hanged if they caught her.

He murmured in his sleep. She took her coat off the hanger and picked up her boots and trousers. She unbuttoned the tent flap, having left it like that when they went to bed.

She buttoned it up after her.

She felt the chill of the night air immediately through her pyjamas, but made herself walk the hundred yards through all the tents to the latrines. The guards on the city gates would think the silhouette was going for a piss.

She changed into her clothes and boots in the latrine, and slung the pack over her shoulders.

She'd thought about taking her weapons, but they were property of the Irregulars and she couldn't.

She left the latrine crawling on her hands and knees, beneath the level of the cloches that covered the vegetable patch. She crawled all the way to the city wall, which swept along the boundary of the camp, looming over it, all mossy stones.

She went inside the first stairwell, and climbed up to the guards' level. The wind buffeted her ears as she walked calmly along it towards the gates, looking out into the absolute darkness of the night. No little lights. Not like in the farming communities. Here everything was inside the city at night.

She had to go out into the dark.

The militiamen on guard were Welsh Grenadiers. They called merrily to her when they saw her approach with a smile on her face, looking as if she was about to ask them something. One of them was standing outside the little sentry box, drinking hot soup, his face sheathed in the mist coming from his cup. The other wandered towards her from the wall, where he'd been staring out into the night too.

'Hello,' she said, using the eye contact to put herself between that one and the wall. 'You cold?'

'Certainly am. What unit you with, then?'

'Irregulars.'

'What you want up here?'

She went to dreamily lean on the wall, facing him. 'This.'

She let everything she was carrying fall from her shoulders into the darkness.

Then, just as the guards were starting to react, she rolled herself up on to the top of the wall.

And over.

She fell for a frightening second too long, their yells in her ears.

Then she landed hard in the mud and water. She'd checked it was still there just before they'd closed the gate.

She staggered to her feet, the wind knocked out of her, and thrashed about in the shockingly cold water, looking for her pack.

She'd just about got everything when they got the big light working, and swung it over the edge to bathe her in light.

She used the moment to grab her mess kit.

She ran out of the light and into the bushes by the side of the road just as the first shots whizzed past her ears.

And then she was off, running into the cold night country, her course plotted exactly in her head by the stars that soared over her.

She suddenly realised she was scared to death of freedom. 'Bloody birthday party,' she whispered. Then she ploughed on through the mud.

Twenty-Two: At Length

Rebecca was blatantly hanging around Booth's room, plucking at new conversations as she circled the bed, obviously unwilling to move an inch. She'd arrived at high speed half an hour before, and, having grabbed a rather lovely bureau and shoved it up against the door, had been talking about everything and nothing ever since.

Booth sighed. He was lying on top of the immaculate covers to his bed, fully clothed, watching her pace about. He would have quite enjoyed being left alone to listen to the rain that had started to gently patter against the window pane. And it would have been good to lie still for a while, having fallen out of the sky today and lost a leg. The Aurigans had given him something that acted like adrenaline, so despite his fundamental nonchalance about hitting the ground he always screamed on the way down. His familiarity with and confidence about pain and suffering, however, helped out with shock, which didn't really trouble him any more. The day had left him feeling horribly fatigued, though. And even if he didn't feel the need to sleep, it still seemed necessary to lie still for a few hours and let everything settle.

Which was what Rebecca was getting in the way of. She had, in many ways, been getting in the way of everything since he'd taken pity on her and asked for her to be his biographer. Ben had been on the verge of banishing her from Hawtrey land, never mind the court, for some indiscretion that Booth hadn't really understood when they'd explained it to him. Sometimes he felt like banishing her himself.

'Has something scared you?'

'Fuck, yes. This whole fucking clean fucking spooky fucking vicar survey palace fucking scares me.'

'It's just like any other abandoned building.'

'It's *clean.*'

'So it wasn't abandoned very long ago.'

'It's *empty.*'

'Because of the survey.'

'It's got all the lights on all the time!'

'What is it you all have against anywhere being *nice*?'

She turned away. One of her things. 'Nice doesn't happen these days.'

'Yes it does. Wherever I go there are nice people.'

'Because you're a special case. Everybody loves you.'

She was trying to start a row. He recognised the tone of voice. He deliberately softened his own. 'I just think that eventually all the families will simply join together and become Britain again.'

'Bollocks they will.'

'They could. So easily.'

She kicked the wall gently and repeatedly until she'd dented the plaster. 'What difference would it make? We'd just be governed by someone far away that we'd never meet.'

'It'd make me happier.' He sat up and stretched his arms. 'Listen, if you're that scared, why don't you move your stuff in here and share the bed tonight?'

She glared at him again, and for a moment he thought she was going to say yes. But then she went to the bureau and slid it away from the door. 'You're living in the past,' she said, and left.

'Look who's talking,' whispered Booth, after the door had closed behind her.

He lay back on the bed. Damn it. It had been centuries since the GEC. Why wasn't the world pulling itself together again? It felt like the pit they'd fallen into was endless, that he was just here to be a witness to continual division. It was astonishing that the Aurigans were still interested in the details. Probably it was because this was the only other world they knew about. But even so, one day they might get bored and pull the plug on him.

What a lovely thought.

He laid his head back and luxuriated in listening to the rain, and allowed his tired blue body to rest. The engineers and chemists had found they could grow his blue stuff like a plant in big vats, so this elegant starborn material ended up, for a few brief years before the world fell apart, being the ideal material for *tyres.*

They'd thought he'd be angry when they brought the idea to him, told him that they'd patented his flesh.

He'd laughed like a drain.

The doctor had placed the X-ray very gently on the screen before illuminating it, as if her care might prevent some error which had caused the three previous plates to show what they'd showed.

She switched on the light and nodded grimly at the result. Booth's chest and thorax lay in silhouette on the plate, and there were shadows of a structure which ran through it, which Booth took to be his stomach. But he was waiting for someone to tell him what was so unusual, why he'd been brought to a military hospital, why Jack, the man from the Prime Minister's office, had insisted on calling him an alien. He'd been expecting to meet the Prime Minister, too. He hadn't yet.

'Well, I have to accept that then, don't I?' said the doctor. 'Can I take a sample?' She looked to Jack, who was standing by the door. 'Am I . . . allowed to?'

'I've had no orders about that. You go ahead, we can always get it back.'

'Should I be careful?'

'The message said he wasn't a threat. He's been out in the open, and nobody's gone down with anything so far.'

The doctor frowned, then stepped forward to Booth, picking up a tray of scalpels as if considering where to begin. Booth was sitting on an examination couch with his shirt off. The doctor hadn't addressed him directly since he'd entered the room. 'Hey, no . . .' He drew back from her like a child, putting up his hands. 'You have to tell me. Do I have a disease? What's wrong?'

The doctor just looked at Jack again.

'Hello?' Booth waved one of his hands in front of her nose. 'Can you hear me?' He reached out to shake her hand, but she just stepped quickly back from him. 'I'm Booth Hawtrey. Mr Hawtrey. The patient.'

'Can we get him sedated?' she said.

So they sedated him. And that was a trip back into memory, a long fight to stop being swept up into the trails of thought that surrounded hospitals, his parents, once more, injections . . . A fight Booth finally lost. He popped back to the shadow of now again at intervals. Rather than open a new cut in his arm, it seemed Jack had persuaded the doctor to take the dressing off the wound on Booth's forehead.

The gasp of surprise from the doctor made Booth's pulse – he still had a pulse! – race despite the sedation. He asked plaintively to be told, and Jack brought a mirror over.

Booth stared at what he could see. The break in his skin revealed not flesh and blood, but a stringy purple mass. He hoped that wasn't his brain. The doctor had put on some gloves and gently touched it, and Booth winced. It felt, he explained, glad to be asked about something, exactly like a graze on his forehead should feel. And he didn't like her poking around in it.

So, thankfully, the doctor limited herself to cleaning the wound, taking away a small quantity of blue fluid on a swab which she sealed in a test tube. She started to pull away a piece of thin, stringy material, which, Booth could see in the mirror, had a complicated structure inside. It was like the locking chain on a bicycle, he thought giddily. Lumpy and purple and organic, only not organic like anything he'd ever seen before. The newness was quite a shock, compared to all the oldness in his head. It was sort of pleasurable in a sickly way, already, seeing something utterly new.

'There's no structure to this, it seems to be like spaghetti, just packed in. From the X-rays, I don't think . . . Mr Hawtrey . . .'

Booth smiled at the acknowledgement of his existence.

' . . . has a brain any more. Or bones, a heart, a liver, lungs . . .'

She continued, and Booth felt water on his cheeks. At first he thought the stuff that was him, now, was dripping on to his face.

It was only when Jack handed him a tissue that he realised he was crying.

Rebecca couldn't sleep.

She'd scuttled along the corridor from Booth's room to her own, and, with much effort and sweat, had succeeded in swinging a really heavy wardrobe from foot to foot across the floor until it stood in front of the door. Never mind a bloody bureau. That'd keep them out. Whoever they were. If there had been a *they* chattering away behind that isolated door.

She'd stood at the window, wiping her breath from it, looking out at the forest in the dark. She wondered what the tigers were doing in all this rain. Sheltering somewhere with their meat. Knocking Booth's leg back and forth with their jaws, wondering why it smelt like meat but didn't taste like it.

She should have opened that door.

Now it was shut in her thoughts, something waiting behind it for her. She'd half succeeded in convincing herself that she'd heard nothing inside. That nothing had stopped when it heard her.

The rain was keeping everything in the forest sheltered, locked down. Tomorrow, with the dawn, it would clear up, and there would be relief, and a pleasant, sheltering, warm house. All the lights would be switched off, the night wouldn't have nabbed anybody, and all the secrets would seem stupid.

She would have breakfast brought to her by one of the army of extremely shy servants who did the dusting.

And then, refreshed, she would go and open that door.

She gingerly lay on the perfect bed, unwilling to even undress. After a moment, she pulled back the covers and slid in.

She felt a hard shape vibrating against her kidneys and pulled her phone from her pocket. David had e-mailed her. Sweetheart. A wonderful connection to the world that still went on outside these walls.

She had to make sure not to say she missed him, or that she loved him. That was only true when he wasn't here.

She snuggled under the covers, activated the phone light, and smiled at the first line she read.

She finished the message and thought for a moment. Then she tapped out a reply. It ended: 'I'm here. I'm glad you're out there somewhere.' And she included a map reference.

Not as if he'd come.

She hit the send button. Then she placed the phone gently on the polished table beside the bed.

And soon afterwards she found she couldn't help but sleep.

The house was quiet then for several hours. The direction and quality of the moonlight shifted slowly through the windows as the rain stopped and the clouds parted. The wood and the stone of the building groaned and cracked as the heat of the day settled into the cold of the night.

At three o'clock in the morning, an extra shadow appeared on the floor of Rebecca's room.

What had previously seemed like a section of wall, a single piece of red and gold wallpaper, swung smoothly and silently open on well-oiled hinges.

And into the room stepped Jane Bruce, her hands clenched into fists.

Jane stepped very slowly and carefully towards the bed, timing the rising and falling of her feet against the little snuffles and gasps of her target. Rebecca lay in bed fully clothed, with one arm lying at an awkward angle across the covers, and the other hand tucked under the pillow. A square of moonlight framed the corner of her face, light scudding with clouds across her eyes and nose.

She shifted and turned as Jane moved towards her, perhaps sensing the presence of someone else in the room. Her upper body arched towards Jane questioningly, and for a moment it looked like she was holding her eyes shut against some bad taste in her mouth.

Jane waited, anguished, only just managing to keep going with this because of the thought that coming this far and then turning round would make her a mad woman with unbelievable motives. She didn't want to have to talk to Rebecca about why she'd found her standing over her bed. She was more scared of that than of what she was about to do.

Rebecca slumped back hard, mumbling something, and threw her arm across to the other side of the bed.

Jane took advantage of the noise and movement to take another couple of quick steps forward.

She was now standing a few feet from where Rebecca lay, careful not to let her shadow fall across the sleeping woman's eyes. She had one hand full of pills. Greens. They would do exactly what she needed.

She took that last step.

Rebecca's eyes flickered, then she gave a huff of air. Then she looked up.

She saw Jane.

She didn't even call out or start to ask a question. She started to move at Jane, to attack or get away—

Jane slammed her hand into Rebecca's mouth, forcing the greens down, using her other hand to grab Rebecca's head and hold it back against the pillow. She was choking, trying to spit them out. Jane held on as greens scattered all over the bed. She had lots of them. She knew there'd be wastage. She knew that in a moment the coatings would start to dissolve, and—

Rebecca cried out, but it was already muted. Her eyes locked on a place across the room and stared at something Jane couldn't see.

Jane held on to her for a moment, wondering if this woman knew enough about her calling to fake that effect. Then she let go. Rebecca stayed where she was, her mouth bloody, her eyeballs starting to flicker with REM.

Jane carefully collected all the scattered greens and put them into her pockets. Then she bent down, took Rebecca's weight around the small of her back, and swung her over her shoulder.

Bearing the weight, she walked slowly and carefully back across the room, and closed the false door behind her.

Jane looked at her watch as she left the front porch of the house, Rebecca twitching and gasping over her shoulder.

She had about half an hour of this before Rebecca would be properly conscious. Time enough to complete what she had planned. What she had set up even while fighting the thought that she was going to do this, saying to herself that she was preparing things 'just in case'.

She would even have time for a rest while she waited for Rebecca to wake up and be aware of what was about to happen to her.

She turned off the path, and headed around the back of the house, hoping that the new space would still be there. No, knowing that it would be, now.

She slipped the juddering body of the young woman through the gap at the top of the doorway of the tunnel, and hung on to it for as long as possible as she lowered it into the darkness. Then she let go.

There was a gentle thump from below.

Jane activated her flashlight, shielding the beam with her hand. Then, holding the tag of the torch in her mouth, she slipped through the gap herself.

Rebecca knew what was happening to her. The bitch had stuffed her full of green.

She was being taken back to her birthday. To her last birthday. When she had hurt poor David so badly. She was looking up at him again, saying the words.

'I need . . . something more.'

Of course it was her birthday. What else in her life would she be dragged back to? Greens were for dreams. This must be what she always dreamt about. The painful thread of birthdays. Christ. Oh Christ. She felt all of them pulling at her, the weight of all those terrible days, the whole scarred date, hugging her back to it.

She tried to hold on to the last one. The last set of powerful images.

'I need . . . something more.'

She managed to keep it, to not be dragged back. The images swept her eyes back and forth, butterflies battering under her eyelids.

If she didn't stay with this birthday, the images would pull her down into history, and she would keep on orbiting the horrors down there. Keep on reliving them.

The bitch priest thought she'd just drugged her so she could murder her or whatever, but she'd condemned her to this torture as well!

'I need . . . something more.'

The cycle of looking up at him, saying the words, kept vomiting and vomiting, up from inside. It was all she could do.

Because she was a prisoner of memory, because it came back to haunt her every time, no matter what she was doing on that day, and new bad memories always somehow arrived to fall on top of the old ones, fossil layers of pain.

Her animal systems had been switched off. While she was being carried across the lawn, she knew. On one level she could smell the night air and feel the urgent, maternal, punishing arm strapped tightly across the small of her back.

But her head was so full of dreams that she couldn't move.

Kill me now! Get it over with!

Her father and mother were standing around the table. She could smell the farmhouse smell. She could see the birthday cake, and – then at a sudden angle, her father's thin, disapproving face.

David oh David. Laughing his head off, joking with her in the punt, shouting his uncaring to the sun.

No! Don't go back!

'I need . . . something more.'

She was being lowered into darkness, with the impacting light-show blasting around her head. She felt the change from moonlight to dark.

Scream! Kick this bitch!

The fall was the worst thing.

Falling without being able to cry out. Knowing that it would hurt when you landed. Knowing that your muscles wouldn't—

The side of her face hit the floor and bounced and hit again, which hurt to the point of horrible internal fierce playground tears. But the rest of her body just flopped like a ragdoll, bruise pain, nothing broken. Too relaxed.

My face, bitch, you broke my fucking face.

She felt her hand start to jump on its own, start to respond to what she wanted it to do. It was flexing its fingers into a fist. Pins and needles raged up her arm. Just a little while now . . . Then she'd be able to move her limbs. And . . . she . . . would . . . kill . . .

She heard Jane drop into this dark space beside her. The woman clicked on her torch and shone it directly into Rebecca's eyes.

Rebecca gave a hoarse grunt as she found she couldn't get her eyes out of the way of the light. Her hand curled and flopped again.

Jane picked her up once more and carried her off down a tunnel. Rebecca's twentieth birthday continued.

'I need . . . something more.'

Jane set the lamp on a nearby slab of stone, and began to roll up her sleeves. Rebecca smelt dust and stone all around, and couldn't stop the dust getting up her nose. They had come to a lighter space at the end of the tunnel, and the vicar had set her down while she went about preparing something.

Between the startling flashes of her own history that were whirling inside her head, Rebecca had a horrible idea about what was about to happen. The adrenaline of that horrible idea had started to distract her from the birthdays, so the fear was almost welcome, a fingerhold on sanity.

'I'm sorry about all this,' the vicar said. 'So sorry, in fact, that I'm going to take my own life when this is over. I don't *want* to do this to you, but I have to. I don't believe that I am mad. I've thought and thought about this, and this is just one of those moments, one of those times when we just have to . . .' She put a hand to her face, deep in thought, and then shook her head and the thought aside. 'Too much talking. I'm afraid I have to explain what's going to happen to you. I'll try and leave it at that rather than all this justification. But first, let's get you into the pit before you stop greening.'

She put one hand on Rebecca's shoulders and one hand in the small of her back, and started to roll her, crudely, across the floor.

Rebecca flailed out her one arm, desperately trying to catch something or push against something or slap at the legs of the woman, but she just kept rolling over and over, and the arm rolled with her.

She tried to yell and plead, but the sounds came out as little tooth-clenched grunts. She lost concentration and all her birthdays came on her at once. Her head roared with images from her life, a huge pan tipped on to the floor of a kitchen, a pan of memories, sweeping through her mind, like the burst dam, like vomiting the sweet taste of cider, rancid in her nostrils. Memories and thoughts and actions, rushing through every part of her, drowning her, when all she wanted to do was reach up and—

She fell again.

A few feet. Landed on her back.

Knocked the memories out of her again. Real life for a second.

At least her face was pointing upwards. She was in a pit. A pit made of mud.

Newly dug. The walls were oozing around her.

The priest had removed several of the tiles and dug this—

She was sinking into the ground! If she'd landed face down, she would have drowned. She might still.

Rebecca's muscles started to jerk with anguished effort. 'Please!' she managed to spit through her loose mouth.

Jane came into view in the rectangle of light above her. The movement of her weight caused a little shower of mud to clatter down on to Rebecca. The torchlight made the muscles of Jane's face into a shady mask. She leaned forward so she could talk down to her quietly, almost conspiratorially. 'The idea is to cause you to feel as much fear as possible before you die. No, don't think I'm some sort of sadist. I hate doing this, it's obscene . . .'

Rebecca managed another awkward shout. She could feel the fear as a solid, thumping thing in her spine, taste it as iron and bile in her mouth. But it wasn't getting out. It wasn't doing what every nerve wanted it to do: to send Rebecca's body hurtling upwards, to kill this bitch!

'Telling you what I'm going to do is part of the plan, to maximise the experience. I gather you're not a religious person, so it won't matter if I tell you that I intend to administer the last rites to you just before you die. I'm sure that doesn't comfort you, but it does make me feel better.'

Rebecca managed to shut her eyes. She kept them shut, chasing after the phantoms from the past that were now fading away into the nooks and crannies. She needed them now, now she wanted to run away with them! Now the fear had banished them to somewhere in the back.

'This is what I'm going to do. You're lying at the bottom of a pit that I've dug out of the floor of this chapel. It's about one and a half metres deep. Over the next half-hour, you should slowly start to regain the use of your limbs . . .' The vicar stopped for a moment. Rebecca could hear her breathing heavily. 'I sound like a James Bond villain. I don't mean to. I don't want . . . The drama . . . No. There is no drama, because you're not going to be able to escape, you're going to die.' She suddenly sounded as if she'd galvanised herself again, and Rebecca internally flinched at the change in her voice. 'I'm going to slowly bury you alive, judging the rate of burial against the speed with which your muscles start to respond again.'

No. No. Rebecca shut all the possibilities out of her head and made herself concentrate on the one point. The plot point. Had she got the timing right? Did she know about—?

'At the moment your extremities should just be coming back under your control . . .'

Shit. Shit shit shit. The words in her head started to rush together into something that wasn't ever quite going to eat up her consciousness and let her escape into nothingness. Rebecca rode it because she couldn't do anything else.

'The idea is, the weight of ground above you should feel just too much for you to lift at any point. Just at the moment you get the use of your limbs back, you'll find that you can't move the soil above you an inch. To stop you suffocating . . .'

Something slammed into the floor beside Rebecca's head.

'That's an airway, which I'll position over your face. You'll be able to talk to me for a while after your body's trapped. And I'm going to pretend to have second thoughts, to listen to your pleadings and offers and threats, to dash your hopes many times before I start to shovel soil down the tube. I'll do that slowly. When I've checked my instruments, then I'll pack the soil down. Even then, a certain amount of oxygen will get through, so you'll probably be able to scrabble against the soil for quite a long time. Perhaps go to sleep, then wake to find yourself still underground. I'll be watching at my instruments, following all this. I'll wait until you finally die. It is horrifying, isn't it? This whole idea. It's absolutely hellish. I won't try to explain, but I'm the one being set the test here. You just have to suffer and die. No real choices to make. I have to . . . No, that's selfish of me too.'

'Wait . . . I . . .' Rebecca formed the words carefully, making her tongue spit mud around them. The squalling in her mind was bounding and rebounding through her body, a kind of standing wave of fear.

Jane ignored her, and went from the space above her.

She returned a moment later and dropped something in.

It landed on top of Rebecca, lightly. A plank. There followed two more.

They lay along her body.

Jane vanished again. Rebecca heard the sound of her picking up a spade.

She wet herself.

A moment later, Jane appeared above her again, and with a look of agonised determination on her face, dropped the first shovelful of soil on to Rebecca's body.

Twenty-Three: Rebecca's Tenth Birthday

David slowly raised his head until he could see over the ha-ha.

Rebecca looked over with him.

The light in the window of the house went out for a moment, then came back on again.

David checked his watch. 'We're on,' he whispered.

Rebecca took the awkward, heavy shape of the gun from its holster on her belt. It was too big for her hands. The stock had been specially sawn down by Captain Hart, but it was still too large, or at least it felt like it. She had got used to the muscular jerk of the thing when it fired, at target after target, so that now she could keep her eyes open and aim. The Captain had been pleased by her shooting, by the end of the training course. He'd told Alec that she was a better shot than he was. And Alec had been in the Borders Irregulars a year longer than she had.

They were the Fifth Platoon of the Third Division of the Irregulars. If captured, they could expect no mercy, but they had been told to give their name and rank, with one exception: David was a Bloom-field, not a Hawtrey. A Hawtrey could not be discovered amongst their forces, because that would mean war.

Rebecca was sure that anybody who saw David's double crown and floppy hair would know immediately who he was, but the lie was probably one of those things that people did just for show. Just for form's sake, as David said. David was the leader of the platoon, having signed all his friends up in the year he'd spent away from the Hawtrey farmlands. When he'd returned he'd immediately sought Rebecca out, at Mr and Mrs Jefferies' house, paid the Jefferies a purse for taking care of her, and signed her on to his unit.

'Victory,' he'd said to her, on the night he'd taught her to jerk him off. 'We'll have revenge. You'll feel better.'

The Irregulars had been formed as a result of the Campbell War of '11–'13. Rebecca had been made to learn their history. They had bravely held back the Campbell invasion of Wales in '22, when the Campbells had broken, with no reason, the Schuster Agreement, and had had a hand in pushing the territory of Wales further inland a couple of years later, allowing the Frinton Boundaries, which had been agreed so many years earlier, to finally come into effect. They had supported regular units of Welsh militia in the brief siege of Chester in early '30, before the Singhs intervened in the Great Betrayal. They had seen action in the Irish raids of the last three years, a unit following the Irish boats back across the sea by dirigible to shell Cork, the only action by any military unit off the mainland in the last two hundred years.

Nowhere did the history say that they were really a unit of Hawtrey militia, based in Wales by secret treaty. She guessed it suited the Welsh and the Hawtreys to have a fighting force that neither could lay claim to, that each could blame the other for. There wasn't even a right of way between Wales and the Hawtrey lands to the south-east. The Campbell passage was in the way.

David's father, Rupert, Ben Hawtrey's cousin, was also with the Irregulars, as a trainer. He seemed to treat David really harshly. David seemed to like it. He was always making jokes about it when they lay back in his tent after a punishing day's training.

She looked at his face now, lit up only by the wash of white light from the house in front of them. He looked absolutely certain, eager, even. He looked older than her, though he wasn't. That was probably because of his dad.

And she, who had more reason to do this, felt scared and lost and sick. She didn't want to have to get into the house. She'd only dreamed of what would happen inside. The house got between her and what she wanted to do.

She'd been shocked, when she first came to camp, to hear people talking about 'last year's sudden Campbell expansion'. It sounded so matter-of-fact. Like nobody had been hurt by it. A new treaty had been signed after a couple of months and everyone had accepted the new boundaries. 'Cos the Campbells hadn't taken the land from any of the Big Families, that was. She'd wanted to shout something out when she'd first heard the guys talking about it. But she'd bitten her tongue. She was finding that easy to do now. To be quiet rather than talk.

Only loving David kept her going.

He'd looked after her ever since he'd met her. Him and the gang. Sweet and silly Steven, wise Little Bob, shy Frank, Jacko who was always laughing, and most of all, Alec, who'd listen to whatever she needed to say whenever she needed to say it. David had said he loved her almost immediately, within days of her coming to the camp. He hadn't asked her to say it back, and had started talking about something else almost immediately. It was as if he assumed she felt the same way. And she did. But she couldn't say it out loud, was never going to be able to say it out loud again, so the assumption suited her.

At camp, they had trained with older soldiers, who were always laughing at the younger ones. But there were a lot of younger ones, and Rebecca often thought the older ones laughed at them because they were so much faster and more dangerous than they were. David was promoted to lieutenant within three weeks of Rebecca's arrival, and had immediately proposed this mission. For her, though the Captain didn't know it.

They'd spent the rest of their time training for it.

Doing this on her birthday was a deliberate irony. David had suggested it. She'd nodded. Nobody had said anything about it since, and, to her relief, nobody had wished her a good one this morning.

They'd ridden cross-country to get here, circling round the edges of overgrown fields, moving at night and sleeping in the day under hedges. They'd timed the crossing into Campbell territory just right, cutting through a barrier of razorwire and blinders in the early hours of the morning.

They had made their way to a drainage channel that led into the court, and followed it. Little Bob had got hold of the architect's plans on the net, freely available. The morons. They'd resurfaced in the ornamental gardens, inside the first ring of guards. Not that anyone would be expecting an attack. What with the treaty and everything.

Rebecca had decided that she would shoot herself rather than get captured.

They had three hours now before dawn.

David eased over the ha-ha and started to walk quickly towards the house. Rebecca moved after him.

The glass door opened when they were within a few feet of it, and Steven's head poked out. His hair was tied back under a tuke. He nodded to them both.

David closed the door behind them and they stepped to one side. They were standing in a long hallway lit by lamps. Steven and Little Bob stood against the far wall, their weapons at the ready. The silence seemed terrible.

After a minute, a door opened further down the hall, and Frank, Jacko and Alec walked quickly towards them. Alec gave her a little smile.

There was the sound of heavy footsteps from around the corner. They opened up the linen cupboards and stepped inside.

In the darkness, Rebecca felt a terrible anticipation in her chest.

The steps of the guards went straight past. They waited a further two minutes, counting the seconds as hippopotamuses in their heads, and then opened the cupboard doors, all at the same instant.

They all knew the layout, so David only had to point. In groups of two, three, two, with David and Rebecca at the front, they set off up the corridor.

There was a guard sitting in an armchair outside Augustine's room.

He was reading, his gun buttoned up in its holster.

They watched him from around the corner. A hundred yards on either side. Augustine's room was carefully in the middle. Her brother was one floor up, her parents on the top floor. All this, even for a lesser cousin from the country. Because of the name.

David slipped the knife from his belt, and clutched it in his hand. He looked hard at the guard for a moment.

Then he rounded the corner and ran at him.

The guard saw him coming halfway.

He reached half for his whistle and half for his gun.

David struck him across the face, the blade ripping the whistle and his mouth at the same instant. He stifled the guard's cry with a kick to the stomach, and then dived into the crumpled body to slash the throat.

Rebecca watched, anticipating and understanding each movement.

When it was over, David stood up, and was quiet, and they all listened for a moment.

Nothing. No alarm had been raised.

Rebecca led the others to join him.

They all looked at her expectantly.

She bent down to the dead man, and put her hands in his pockets until she found the key. She put it in the lock and turned it very slowly, holding the weight of the lock as it tried to clonk back into the door.

She slid the door open and stepped into the room, drawing her own knife.

She felt them looking at her still, as she walked in. They were her friends. They all wanted this for her. This had all been done for her.

There she was.

Augustine Campbell lay asleep, flat on her back, her blonde hair spread out across a blue pillow. She was breathing great huffs of air. She had one arm flung out above her head. A blue nightdress. She was thirteen. She had a little double chin, already, shaping up to be the first dance on everyone's list at every ball.

Rebecca would probably never go to a ball.

She didn't think she'd ever leave this room.

She walked closer, until she was standing right beside Augustine's bed.

She sat down on it, and reached over to gently slap Augustine's cheek. 'Wake up.' The sound of her own voice was scary.

Augustine grunted and sighed and opened her eyes.

She scrambled up to her bedhead with a yell which Rebecca quenched with the heel of her hand. The back of Augutine's head thumped into the wood. Her teeth jarred on Rebecca's skin.

Her eyes looked desperately at Rebecca through her fingers.

Rebecca put the tip of her knife to Augustine's throat, then took her hand away.

Augustine didn't cry out.

'Do you remember me?' whispered Rebecca.

'No,' she whispered back.

'I'm Rebecca Champhert. You came to my birthday party.'

Augustine's eyes widened. Rebecca could see that now she knew.

So she pushed the knife in up to the hilt and whipped it quickly away.

Augustine fell forward, spilling gouts of blood on to the blue covers, trying to cry out, but unable to do so. She reached a warm hand out to Rebecca, slapping it uselessly against her leg.

In a few moments, she was dead. Rebecca watched quietly.

When the body was still, she wiped the knife on the pillow, replaced it in her belt and got to her feet.

She felt different the moment she saw the others looking at her again.

They were all silently hooking fingers and making victory signs. But while they smiled at her their eyes were full of something else. She knew they'd be afraid, but it was as if there was a big gap between her and them now. She was something more than them now, like she was a grown-up.

She put a hand on David's chest. He kissed her quickly. She could feel he was hard against her thighs.

He was afraid of her too.

They closed the door behind them, and headed for the glass door once more, from there to vanish into the countryside before the dawn.

Twenty-Four: Waking Up Underground

Jane pulled herself out of the tunnel to the demolished chapel and slumped on to the ground, staring up at the stars in the sky above her.

She had actually gone through with it. She had done it to this woman with whom she had found such sudden fellow feeling when they first met.

She burst into tears.

She struggled to get to her feet again, suddenly filled with a horrifying urge to dive back inside the chapel and rip the heavy stone tiles from where she'd left them, shovel the soil off Rebecca, try and revive her.

She stopped at the gap, panting.

No. Rebecca was dead. Jane had done that to her. She was dead, and there was now no way she could reverse that.

Oh Father.

She sat down again, and put her hands to her face, breathing into the small gap between her palms. She was starting to shiver uncontrollably.

The shadow. The shadow was now absolutely between her and God. The shadow had fallen right over her.

Oh Father, if I was to hold out my hand—

But I don't deserve your forgiveness now. I've put myself outside your love.

That was the test, she suddenly thought, feeling something huge and cold settling on her shoulders. That was the test, and she'd failed it.

'My dear.'

Jane looked up. Mary was standing beside her, her skin so white it was almost glowing in the night. She was smiling wide, the smile pinching her cheeks and emptying her eyes of everything except terrible, triumphant purpose.

Jane turned her head away from her. 'You're Satan. You've deceived me.'

'I am not! You have done very well.' Mary suddenly squatted, her gloved hands wrapped around her umbrella, and leaned her head close in to the little bundle Jane had made of herself. 'Everything is going completely to plan. Are the EM levels up?'

Jane took the phone from her pocket and threw it towards Mary. She didn't see Mary's hand catch it, just felt a blur of motion.

Mary chuckled. 'Why, that is simply perfect.'

'If that's what you call it.'

'Indeed.'

'Who are you? *What* are you to make me do these things?'

'You will have all your answers. On the other side.'

'I have to die to find out. I have to wager my life for my faith.'

'Indeed.'

'What else do I have to do?'

'Simply keep track of all the EM levels, everywhere in the building; arrange a very good excuse for Rebecca's absence; and make certain that Booth Hawtrey finishes his list of things to do.'

Jane nodded, relieved.

'You will see me once more. If all goes well.'

And as Jane watched, Mary vanished. She didn't fade. It was just that one moment she was there, and the next moment, as if Jane had blinked and Mary had ducked behind something . . . she was gone.

Something left Jane's mind and shoulders at the same instant.

Jane cast her eyes to the ground, feeling that horrid depth in her stomach once more. This was beyond her. She was lost in it now. There was a maze for her, and she was trapped at the heart of it. Possibly forever.

She stood and headed off towards the stream.

She managed not to look back towards the tunnel opening until she was on the stepping stones.

But then she did.

Booth had had his rest. He opened his eyes, slipped off the end of the bed, and went to the window. It had stopped raining.

Booth missed dreaming. In the first weeks of his transformation, he'd tried to sleep, had undressed and got into bed and closed his eyes. But sleep had not come. He just seemed not to need it. After a while, he'd stopped regarding it as insomnia and started to wander at night, reading, watching telly back when there was telly. He found that he wanted to fill his head with fiction, that he missed the feeling of having had really good dreams. He could go back and relive old dreams, of course, but that was a profoundly unsatisfying process. There were only weird fragments of them in his memory, the only real gaps he had. He suspected that that was because fragments was all they ever were. The memories of dreams that he'd woken with after dreaming were sometimes complicated narratives, but they seemed to be things he'd invented there and then. Still, he missed that sleight of hand.

So, time for him to do something. He picked his phone off the bedside table, and accessed the latest message from the Aurigans, his new orders. These were quite different to those he'd carried out in the past. Usually, it was a matter of taking photographs, making sketches, recording things. This time, as was obvious from the first few entries on the giant list of things to do, he was being asked to move things about before he photographed them.

Perhaps the aliens were aware of how the actual business always bored him, that he only did it so he could keep on travelling and meeting new people. So, a late-night part of his mind added, he could keep trying to convince himself that one day the world would return to civilisation, manage to wind itself up again. That was why he enjoyed visiting courts, so he could go and talk to night guards, talk to anyone. The more he talked, the more he took news and gossip from one place to another, the more he could fool himself that he was helping to tie things together again.

It *was* foolish, though, he was sure Rebecca was right. Sometimes it seemed that he hadn't even seen the worst of it yet, that the collapse had to get much worse before it could get better. If it ever could. Little restructuring movements seemed to spiral up, and for a few years there was hope, and everybody talked about what was going to happen. And then chaos set in, the organisation in question drifted too close to an issue that ripped it apart in several directions, each attractor being something of the past, some faction or flag or concept that at least two parts of the revising force disagreed about.

History killed every new attempt. And the attempts got fewer and smaller. And the great courts got more and more entrenched, each holding jealously on to their own little piece of that history.

Even war didn't cleanse it. War just dredged up more history. The islands were sinking under the weight of it. And still they hadn't reached the bottom.

'Oh come on,' he said to himself. He often talked to himself when he was alone, something the children of this age seldom did and hardly understood. He kept expecting there to be someone around to hear him. He resolved to set about his task.

Stepping quietly so as not to disturb Rebecca in the next room, he headed for the door.

Booth started in a corridor full of pictures on one of the upper floors. The first order from Auriga asked him to rearrange a few of the paintings on their brackets, and then take a picture of the new arrangement. The electric light was still illuminating the corridor, sending long shadows down it.

Booth started to take the pictures down, wondering once more at how much detail the Aurigans seemed previously aware of concerning Earth. The titles of individual works of art, for fuck's sake! There were theories that they had lots of agents, and that Booth was just the figurehead, the well-known one. Others had announced themselves over the decades, but of the ones whose stories he had read or that he'd become involved with, the majority were obviously making it all up. Booth still had no reason to suspect that he was anything but unique.

The aliens had never answered whenever anyone had asked them why they wanted anything. The implicit blackmail was that, if pushed, they would sever their connection with humanity, and the trickle of new technological concepts would dry up. Nobody had ever even considered the idea of calling their bluff, not even mad old Cymric Hawtrey, whose stewardship everyone had suffered through thirty years ago. The human race was too scared to leave the banks of its tiny river of hope. Not that Booth had ever openly questioned the arrangement, either. He valued the freedom that his mission gave him, that constant search for the new. Without the Aurigans, he'd be kept in the Hawtrey court and be bedded into the weight of history, have it folded over his head and patted down by a spade until he was shut into a grave of time.

Perhaps the Aurigans were here already, hiding, waiting for humanity to kill itself off. But if so, why did they need him to come and go and deal with pictures and pigeons? Loads of theories. No answers. Just him pottering around the country, remembering Britain.

He put the first picture back on to its hook. It was a picture of the chap who'd had this place built. Simon Trent. Booth had read his story off the net in the dirigible's noisy little cabin. He looked sad, a great weight under his eyes. But there was something about his face that suggested to Booth that this man had once been a believer in big ideas. He was someone who had invested in his dreams and lost everything. He looked like someone Booth would have liked to be able to talk to: a man from the generation where the future was still *upward*. He hadn't heard the word used in that context in decades.

He finished putting up the paintings, stepped back from the wall and took the picture. The click of the digital camera sounded tiny against the silence of the shadowed hallway.

Booth shook the Prime Minister's hand, surprised at actually touching someone he'd only seen on television.

They were in a room full of light, a briefing room deep inside Number Ten Downing Street, and Booth flashed to Christmas, such was the number of desklights and reflective pictures and shining polished surfaces. The room looked like a cathedral, full of shadows and candles. Around a long table sat the acolytes, men and women of varying builds, races and postures. Indeed, there was something deliberate about such a mix, as if someone was making an effort not to fill this sort of gathering with old white men. They were all smartly dressed, while Booth felt itchy and awkward in a new suit that Jack had provided for him. And they had all been looking straight at him, and at nothing but him, since he had been shown in through the big, shiny doors.

'Mr Hawtrey. I've heard a lot about you,' said the Prime Minister.

'And, me, erm, about you,' said Booth.

It was five o'clock in the morning, which added to the Christmas atmosphere. Up early for the presents. Booth had been marched straight out of the car, having thrown back the Laphroaig once again, and in through the front door of the building, with no sign of any reporters or photographers. That was a relief at least.

Booth was introduced to the figures sitting around the table, shaking each hand, for once being certain that he'd be able to remember every one of their names. Some of them were astronomers, he was told, some of them were mathematicians and linguists, the codebreakers who'd worked on the alien message, and there was one guy who held a Chair of Exobiology at one of the Scottish universities. He seemed pleased that Booth knew what that meant. There were also some civil servants and security people in the room, and someone whose task seemed to be to record everything on a DAT machine.

Everybody kept staring at Booth.

When they had all sat down, the Prime Minister put his palms on the table, which everybody took to be a sign for silence. He looked around the group as if enjoying a private moment, a little triumph. Something they all shared in. Booth felt heartened a little by the familiar expression. He was being included in this too. For the first time since the explosion, he felt like a person rather than an object to be prodded about.

'Mr Hawtrey,' the Prime Minister began, 'I don't know if anyone's asked you this yet. Do *you* know what all this is about?'

'No. Well, only what I saw on the news.' He looked around him. The waiting faces seemed to want more. So he continued, hesitantly: 'These aliens . . . well, they must have made a mistake. I work in an office.' There were a few smiles from around the table. 'They must be going to start doing this to everyone. Are they, well . . . invading?'

A number of the scientists laughed out loud at that, and a few more gave little glances at each other as if that was an option that everybody had been talking about before he came in.

'We don't think so,' said the Prime Minister, smiling at him. 'The message says they've only done this to you, and that they're only going to do this to you.'

'*What* have they done to me?'

The Prime Minister glanced at a balding man who sat towards the other end of the table. 'Geoff?'

The man took off his glasses and smiled at Booth as if he had two weeks to live. 'D'you reckon you can deal with this, Mr Hawtrey?' He had a droll Scottish accent.

Booth let himself nod. He didn't feel like he could cope with anything, but what was the point of not knowing?

'Okay. Every single bit of your internal structure . . . every organ, bone, all the soft tissue . . . bloody everything . . . has been replaced by what seems to be a single large organ.'

Booth managed to nod again. His mouth was completely dry. He saw a glass of water in front of him, reached out for it, and aware of everyone's eyes on him again, took a drink.

'It seems to do everything. But except for features such as the eyes, which seem to have grown from it as clusters of specialised cells . . . and my bet would be that that's only been done so that your external appearance stays the same . . . the organ itself is completely non-specialised. It's a . . . blue lump. It displays internal structures, but they seem concerned only with what it's doing at that moment, and seem temporary. Under the microscope, it breaks down into cells, but we only call them that because they have a cell wall, they don't have a nucleus. They respond to sulphur, taking it in in the same way that the archaea, a group of microbes, do. They live under the sea near thermal vents. But the unfortunate thing is, while the cells are quite happy to live on sulphur and hydrogen, they don't seem to be doing so while they're in your body. It's like we're stimulating something they left behind before they evolved into, well, you . . . not that they did that.'

Booth nodded. 'I was quite normal before.'

'Oh yes, certainly. These cells are incredibly hardy, also. This is another astonishing thing: we haven't yet managed to do anything to . . . well, I hesitate to say "kill" . . . to destroy them. They live quite happily in all manner of chemical baths, they're vacuum-hard, they don't notice radiation . . . I think you'd have to put them in a cyclotron and have a go at them on a particle level before they'd start to notice. The organ uses these cells like a brain uses neurons. There are things that look like synapses throughout, much finer and much more numerous than in a human brain. How are your thought processes?'

'Well, my memory . . .' Booth began.

They all flipped open notebooks.

He thought for a moment. Decided against. 'It's a bit confused,' he finished. 'Just after the blast.' If they didn't know about his new-found abilities already, he didn't want to tell them. Not just yet. He needed something of his own to keep, right now, something of his own inside. He was pleased to see they made no note of what he'd said. He had a sudden thought, and was relieved to find he didn't have to artificially change the subject. 'Hey.' He thumped his chest. 'What's in here? Why am I breathing?'

The doctor smiled at him. 'Habit, we think. There are simple bags for the lungs . . . but the blue material doesn't seem to be doing anything with the oxygen. You pull air in and push exactly the same air straight out again. Your body's chemically active only where it needs to be, producing everything that goes towards your external appearance, tears for example, and as far as we can tell it's doing it out of thin air.'

'But even there, there don't seem to be actual chemical reactions going on!' added a young woman, breathlessly. 'For a start, there's no water or any other liquid dissolving anything. It's a non-solute biochemistry. What's happening across those synapses . . . it's going to take us decades . . . centuries . . . to find out what sort of messengers they use. I wouldn't say you were alive at all, apart from the fact you are!'

The doctor spoke up again. 'It's magic, Mr Hawtrey. We don't know where you're getting energy from. A hollow internal cavity runs straight through you, which bulges where the stomach used to be, so you can probably *deal* with food, somehow. It might just come straight out the other end with a bit of a muscular delay in between. It hasn't replaced the intestines: we think it doesn't need to. We don't see how you can eat, because unless you're convincing your cells to soak up tiny quantities of sulphur and hydrogen from the food . . . no, I think we can rule that out. You're still manufacturing something that looks like sperm, and all the stuff that goes with it, but the genetic content of it seems to be zero, just a tiny lump of this blue material. Of course, that may be able to impregnate either a woman or an alien, but by our standards—'

The woman broke in again. 'Mr Hawtrey, you have provided questions for science across virtually every discipline. Your body . . . says we're in the nursery. You're the most important thing ever to happen to this planet.'

Booth got up from his seat.

The room was suddenly silent. All eyes locked on him. He could see fear in some of them, just a twitch of nervousness that had rocked them back in their seats as he'd got out of his.

He sat down once more.

What he'd just been told had settled into his stomach . . . what used to be his stomach . . . and lay there feeling hard and cold. He looked slowly around the table. 'How?' he said finally. 'How did this happen? How can . . . all of me . . . be replaced by something else in a . . . a second?'

There was silence.

The woman beside him put her hand on his. Utterly against his usual character, he allowed her fingers to mesh with his. 'Nobody has any idea,' she said quietly.

Booth looked down at the polished surface of the table before him. He felt like he'd woken from an operation, like he was in a new time zone on the other side of the world. He felt hungry . . . they hadn't let him eat . . . but felt distant from the whole idea of breakfast. From anything normal. It wasn't obvious what was appropriate any more. He seemed to have lost some basic information about who he was.

'Mr Hawtrey.' The Prime Minister raised his hands. 'We know this must be terrifying for you. We thought it best just to tell you everything . . . And that's what I'm going to do now, as quickly as possible.'

Booth nodded again. He just wanted to get out of here, get home, see his family. Go back to work. He wondered if that was possible, or if normal life had been completely lost to him now.

'The beam that struck you, Mr Hawtrey, was accompanied by a message, a radio transmission powerful enough to disrupt all kinds of communications and be registered by most of the world's radio telescopes. Apparently that's impossible too, the energy required to keep the beam together, the distances . . .' He held up a hand, indicating that the debate shouldn't start up again here, and glanced down at the papers in front of him. 'I have here the text of that message from the star Alpha Aurigae, or Capella, which was the name the media started using straight away.' He looked up again, as if struck by a sudden thought. 'And may I say to all of you, particularly *you*, Mr Hawtrey, what I'm going to say in my broadcast tonight. That I'm delighted this has happened on British soil, of course, but that I'm delighted for the world. The knowledge that we're not alone in the universe . . . It's going to give the whole world something to reach for, something to unite over. It's given a point to the future, a reason for us to go onwards and upwards towards one world.' He smiled again and shook his head. 'I'm sorry, I'm going on. I promised you answers. I just talked to Arthur Clarke in Sri Lanka, blame it on that.' He turned back to his papers. 'The message breaks down into a number of different sections. Firstly, there's lots of technical stuff I don't pretend to understand, giving the position of Capella relative to where we are, and supplying a sort of code key to the message by comparing signs for numbers to . . . the periodic table of elements?'

One of the codebreakers nodded.

'Then there's a section about which many people have already had much to say and I'm sure the debate will continue. The Capellans allege they've conducted some sort of complete sweep of the universe, what they describe here as an "analysis of intelligent life". They say that they've come to the rather startling conclusion that it's just them and us. That the only two places intelligence has evolved . . . are Earth and the second planet orbiting the star Capella. That's why they decided to contact us . . . so that neither of us would be alone.'

Booth heard a whisper and glanced at one of the scientists to his left. The man was shaking his head, talking quietly to his companion, who was gently butting his pencil into the pad before him.

He glanced around at the others. They all looked as if they couldn't believe it, like it was such a huge idea they were writing it off straight away.

Booth lowered the camera, returning from his memories. At the time, he remembered that he'd found the idea of there being only two intelligences in the universe comforting, almost a relief.

But as the years rolled on, the disappointment that he'd seen in that room, and had returned to a thousand times to see every detail of the loss, had grown. Booth thought that perhaps it was at the heart of everything that had happened since, the moment when the limits to the future had been declared, when the doors of possibility had been closed. They couldn't believe it then, because they didn't want to believe it. But they came to, in their heart of hearts. Doing that had taken centuries. And in that time, the human race had fallen into despair.

'Then there's a basic greeting, which seems to say . . .' A smile crossed the Prime Minister's lips again. Booth got the feeling he was trying to raise the spirits of the gathering once more. 'Amanda, I'll let you do this one.'

The woman beside Booth cleared her throat. 'We will share all our history with you.'

'Very kind of them, I'm sure. The next section goes into some more detail on that, with an actual description of the Capellans. No information about their biology or anything like that. All we have is an image, which seems to be a design rather than some form or photograph or anything taken from life.' The Prime Minister produced a sheaf of papers from his own bundle and had them passed around the table. 'And we want all of these back. We're still debating how and when we should release this to the media. It's an obvious question, what do they look like? But still . . .'

Booth took the piece of paper from the woman next to him. He could feel the grain of the paper on his fingers. Exactly like he always had. He was looking down at a picture of a skeleton. Or perhaps a famine victim. An extremely thin naked human with a mottled skin, no testicles, a skull that had the flesh pulled tight over it. Tiny ears. The eyes looked big and helpless, pleading little pupils. They were set under a large brow.

There were head-on, rear, over- and under-views, profiles from the left and right.

The picture looked utterly unreal, like something from a comic. Booth could not imagine it living and breathing. 'Oh,' he said. 'Right. Like people.' And then the question that had been echoing around his head since he was hit by this beam came bursting out of him. He let the paper fall to the table. 'Oh for Christ's sake.' He was aware that he was breathing heavily, though he wondered why he was breathing at all. '*Why?* Why did these . . . these *things* . . . want to change me?' He looked desperately around the table. 'Can anybody at least tell me . . . *why*?'

'That's the final part of the message,' said the Prime Minister.

Booth forced himself to remain calm. 'What?'

'You can't be as ordinary as you say you are, Mr Hawtrey. Or perhaps, for the Capellans, that's the whole point. Whichever it is, you were selected especially. *Named* in the message. Mr Hawtrey, the Capellans have chosen you to be their ambassador. They can't come here. They say that travel between the stars is impossible. So they want you to do their will on this planet, to deal with messages that we've been told to expect in the future. They want to learn about us, about all the countries of the world. And they want you to be the one who conducts that exploration on their behalf. It's going to be an extraordinary cultural exchange. And the most astonishing thing is . . . they say that now you've changed, you're going to be doing this for them for *several centuries*. It says here, Mr Hawtrey . . .' his finger hit a line of the message, 'that you are effectively immortal.'

Booth just stared at him.

'Isn't it wonderful?' said the Prime Minister.

'Wonderful,' said Booth.

And here he still was. Doing the bidding of humanity's distant and only cousins, the only unchanging thing in the dying world. For no good reason any more. The cultural exchange had never really occurred, because one culture had given up the ghost and stopped being interested in what the other had to say. Not that the Aurigans had ever revealed much about themselves. There was a single volume on Aurigan ecology and social structure on the net. It had been written a hundred and fifty years ago.

He was surprised when the Prime Minister took him up to the roof garden alone. He sent all the minders away, even Jack, and sat down at a little table opposite Booth.

It was cold up here in the early morning. Booth was glad of the big coat that the security man had lent him.

'I wanted to tell you how amazing this is. For me, for all of us. Intelligent life in the universe. Even if they're right and they're the only ones. This is going to make people feel so much better, this is going to—' He cut off for a moment, like he was searching for the right words. 'Mr Hawtrey, do you know that insurance advert? The one with the very committed, very passionate man who really loves what his company does, and the idea is we laugh at him because he's too into it?'

'Yeah, I've seen that.'

'I can't laugh at him. I love people like that. I think the people of this country would like, in their heart of hearts, not to *have* to laugh at people like that. But to *be* people like that.' He pointed at Booth, risking a warm little smile. 'I've a feeling you're going to be a person like that.'

Booth smiled back. 'I think I'd like to be.'

'Well.' The Prime Minister leaned back and took a deep breath of December morning air. 'We have friends in the universe. Their ambassador's an Englishman. Everybody's going to be filled with hope again. What a great Christmas present.'

Booth laughed along with him.

He put the camera away.

He had been, as far as he could, just that person he'd wanted to be. And so far, it didn't seem to have done anybody any good.

He was hungry. The Aurigans had left him that at least. Things came out much the same as they'd gone in, but he could still enjoy tastes and the whole chewing and swallowing business. That was about the only one of the great questions about him that the scientists had ever had time to solve. The ability to pursue those sorts of enquiry had left the world soon after his new body had arrived in it.

Thanks to him, the last thing humanity had ever learned was that they knew nothing.

There was a little wooden stepladder in the kitchen for the purpose of reaching the high shelves and cupboards. Booth slid it across on its wheels, worked out how to work a little rubber brake that stopped it from skidding about, and set it up against the big sink. Then he climbed up and started to explore, swinging open the cupboards and rustling about amongst what he found there.

One of his most relaxing times. He'd done this at courts all over England, in the wee small hours, making toast for tired night watches, talking to some girl with heavy eyes who felt that if he was awake she should be awake too. When he couldn't do this, when he was guarded in his room or confined to a particular area, he tried to get his gaolers to come with him for a feast.

He thought for a moment of waking Rebecca, but no. She wouldn't like it. His hand chanced upon a smooth white jar with a vacuum-sealed top. It was at the edge of his reach, right back in this cupboard that smelt of pickles and dried fruit and . . .

He saw the word on the jar as he realised what the smell was.

Tea.

He nearly fell off the ladder as memory rushed through him. The smell had ambushed him. Rushed into every pore. It took him back to hundreds of distant places and times at once. To times before the GEC. He found that he was on the verge of tears, suddenly, vulnerable like a baby.

He had not smelt tea in centuries.

They'd brought him a cup of tea, which he hadn't touched.

He'd been returned to the medical facility after the meeting at Downing Street was over. But now at least he felt that he wasn't under guard, that he was being trusted to be himself. He'd asked for, and been given, a copy of the Capellan message. Every time he read it, he'd wondered why the fuck they'd chosen him. Maybe in the first of the future messages they'd say. He wondered what they would want him to do.

He stood naked in front of a mirror and looked at himself. Everything the same. The little scar at the base of his left thumb where he'd been cutting an aircraft out of polystyrene at St Martin's, using a Stanley knife of all things, because they allowed kids to play with those back then, and he'd slipped and sliced a flap of skin away. That was still there, still familiar, and he was back in the memory of that. He'd been more afraid of getting blood everywhere and the anger of Miss Eason for the first few seconds, and had tried to use the knife like a trowel to flatten the skin back on to his hand. Hence the weird triangular shape of the scar.

He rolled back his foreskin and saw the traces of the genital wart scars, still there on the head of his penis. For some reason he'd thought that that might be where he'd been changed. The place where a boy gets used to having changes. Well, that was how he felt, anyway. He didn't know what other boys thought. He felt like his whole body had gone through a sudden new puberty, like that moment when he'd first masturbated, and a tiny drop of fluid had come out of him, and he'd been astonished and appalled that the nature of what he was, inside, was different now, and that his instincts, rather than his mind, could lead him to find that out. And he was back in the memory of that.

Thinking too much, even then. A tiny early echo of what he'd become now, which sometimes seemed all thought, all memory, all contemplation. He'd been scared of something coming from him that wasn't the product of thought. That moment had underlined nature inside him ever after, even as he read science as a teenager. Your thoughts aren't all of you, was the thought that had been written into him from that point. Because this stuff inside you welled its way to the surface, made itself erupt, without any knowledge, or reading, on your part. So he'd held on to rationality and loved the wild, and could never talk fully about either with confidence.

A neat little reason about who he was, he thought. Too neat. He'd be something different the next moment. Chaos and all that. Now he was something different all the time. As he visited every memory, he wondered how he would change, how he would become the sum of his memories. He'd been betrayed by his thoughts, fallen into being a library of thoughts.

He wanked himself experimentally a couple of times. He stopped. He'd seen what would come now, and though it looked like it always had, he knew it was something different. Took your mind off it.

She was dead. Oh God, she was dead, and he didn't feel anything . . .

That strange relationship he'd developed with the guy at the STD clinic. He'd dabbed boiling liquid carbon dioxide on to Booth's penis, which hurt every now and then despite the guy saying it shouldn't. Over a few treatments, a sort of charge developed between them, a kind of laughing nervousness that was something to do with the guy reflecting Booth's own determination that this was just something that happened to you at college, and not a moral issue, and for this guy it was just a job, and maybe the guy was surprised to find someone who thought that.

Or maybe he could never get used to injuring cocks for a living, and was as likeably edgy and *Coronation Street* camp with everybody. He was very truculent and northern, and Booth was this awkward student. It was like a set-up for a gay porn video.

Nurse Joe Edwards. He was there again now, examining the man's face. Nothing like his thoughts of him. Absolutely nothing like. Just businesslike. Bored. More opinions to be thrown out. Oh God, at the end of this, was there going to be anything of him left? Or would he just be mute from all this experience, unable to say anything more than, well, life *is.*

He should feel something about her by now. Or maybe this was natural. Maybe he was in shock. He didn't feel like he was, but he didn't know how he was supposed to feel.

He ought to say something about her to someone, to show he was grieving.

How Booth knew he wasn't gay: he'd felt the edges of it, and was neither repelled nor fascinated. A dull frisson. If a frisson could be dull. That had all been based on the expression of that man. And he'd invented that expression after the fact, in his head.

Booth let go of his dick, which was flaccid anyway, and pulled down the skin under his eye. It was all still red. Wasn't that why we were pink, because we were red inside? So why wasn't he mauve or turquoise now? There must be a thick layer of redness to this human disguise of his. He pulled down the eyelid as far as it could go, and finally found some blue.

Shit. He really was blue inside.

He was trifle, and he was going to come custard. Was he going to shit anything any more? He hadn't felt like going to the toilet. He didn't think he needed to sleep.

He could go back and see her, whenever. Relive every moment. Would that stop the grief from coming, or would it make it worse?

The doctor came back in, and he turned to her, not feeling that he had to hide his nakedness. 'I am,' he said definitively, 'completely fucked.'

He half walked, half tripped down the stepladder, and, his hands shaking, put the jar on to the table. Then he pulled off the stopper, and looked inside.

Black leaf tea.

He almost hesitated before taking a deep breath of it.

He did so, and managed just to enjoy it, though he . . . felt . . . all the memories it connected him to, that were suddenly on the immediate menu of thoughts that he would rush back to if he allowed himself. The tea thoughts. All from when there was tea. All so many years ago.

No, not all.

He slowly reached out to touch the jar with his fingertips, disconcerted.

There was . . . what?

There was something he *couldn't quite remember*.

Something about this place. This house.

He was certain of it. The feeling was almost painful. He didn't know where it was, he didn't know what. He looked around, scared. He'd become so used to his condition. This nearly felt like madness. Like this was his own form of mental illness, knocking him off course like a blow to the head.

There *was* something. He concentrated, let himself · be swept through his thoughts, trying to chance upon it. He could not. Maybe it was a new piece of a dream. That had never happened before, but he'd been thinking about dreams . . . The smell of the tea had shaken something loose. Something new. But how could there be anything new?

He was now as scared as he'd ever felt. He didn't shave now, he didn't sleep, his scalp didn't form dandruff. He'd got used to everything about himself being static. And now something inside him had . . . *changed.*

He got to his feet, went back to the stepladder, and climbed up into the cupboards again.

There was nothing else for it. He was going to have to find a teapot.

He made the tea slowly and carefully, holding his nose so that he didn't start suddenly tripping down memory lane and drop everything. Just the shapes of things like tea strainers and tea spoons were nearly enough to do it. He'd thought he had this stuff under control as well, that he was no longer prone to the long, immediate reveries that had marked the first couple of years of his transformation. But perhaps that was just because he'd encountered something he hadn't seen in centuries, and the power of smell to affect memory being what it was . . .

He put the teapot on the table and made himself wait. Beet sugar, but no milk. Then, after a couple of minutes, he poured the cup.

Finally, he took his fingers from his nose. Inhaled. Drank.

He felt dozens of pathways opening up in his mind, as smell connected with smell and he got glimpses of vision, little stories, phrases. All familiar so far. All times and places he recognised, albeit that he hadn't thought about some of them in years. It was as if the chemical signature of the smell, the shape of the molecule, had a little nest of memories that had accumulated like rust around it. The gap of the molecular shape suddenly being filled up with liquid information that fitted it, filled it, washed all that rust away, made the rust grains connect and register, and suddenly his brain was asking him which of this whole mass of stuff was important, and—

Everything stopped. His lips were on the rim of the cup.

But he couldn't feel the cup in his hand.

And, from the angle of the cup, the hot liquid must now be dribbling down his chin. But he couldn't feel that, either.

His eyes were locked on the vast white pestle and mortar across the kitchen.

Cramp was starting to shout from his new leg. He tried to close his mouth. To move his hand. He couldn't.

It wasn't like his muscles were locked. It was like he had suddenly lost the unconscious link between the thought of moving and the move itself.

Fuck. Oh Jesus Mary and Joseph fuck. He screamed and yelled and panicked and threw up as a strange metaphor inside his head without moving in the slightest, and the lack of actually doing those things made his mind finally slip and slide and grow still . . . buried alive, buried alive! . . . to a sort of calm once more. A wave thing. Screaming fear. No result. Subsides to calm. Then panic again when he still couldn't move.

So he would stay at the calm point in the wave. Hold to that thought. The picture of a wave. He was holding it.

He realised he wasn't breathing. The habit of his old life had stopped.

The wave vibrated out of his hands for a while until he slowly subsided into acceptance once more. People buried alive probably did. Stopped clawing the coffin and got comfortable. Even happy.

Time had not stopped. He could see the edge of an old wood-rimmed clock high on the wall. Couldn't do anything but see it. He'd been like this for ten minutes, from ten thirty or so to ten forty.

He could slip away into his memories, he didn't have to be here.

He found he couldn't. He did have to be here. He was frozen in the shadow of now. That sent him off on another wave of fear and difference and interior nausea.

Was this death for him? Was his brain dying, and—

Didn't have a brain. How long did it take to get used to that?

He'd never actually tested whether he needed to breathe. He'd always got to the point where his body was shouting for air and given in to it. The reaction was still as powerful as it had been when his body was human: it wouldn't let him fill his chest cavities with water and go for a walk on the seabed.

Well, now he was going to find out just how immortal he was.

His eyes needed to move. They were rebelling at looking at the same tiny place for such a long time. His vision was filling with phantom colours that . . . longed . . . made him long? . . . to tear his attention away to them.

He was certain now. He really didn't need to breathe. He'd just be fixed in the panic of drowning forever.

Was this about the memories?

Was it that smell really did have a direct, almost mechanical connection to memory, and that he, having lived longer than anybody else, having built up so many triggers, so many things to work through . . . ?

What was it about tea that—?

He fell, shouting, out of his chair, his hand knocking the cup off the table, where it smashed on the floor, and he was suddenly lying with his chair on top of him, his legs raging with cramp, twitching and flailing as he tried to get to his feet.

But he'd just realised something much more important than his continuing ability to move and live.

He had been here before.

Twenty-Five: Rebecca's Ninth Birthday

Rebecca woke at the sudden noise.

She'd been dreaming about leaves falling into a lane.

Something had smashed in the kitchen.

She pulled the corner of the curtain back. It was still dark outside. Five o'clock. Mum and Dad would have just got up to look after the animals. Dad would be in with a cup of hot milk at six and then she'd go down to see her presents. She turned over to go back to sleep. She didn't want to see Mum crying over a smashed jug.

Another crash.

She threw back the covers and got unsteadily to her feet. Were they rowing again? Not today, oh please not today. But she'd never seen them smash anything in a row. That'd be horrible. Had she caused this? Was it going to be like this every year now?

She went to the door to listen.

Then she heard a shout. Was that Dad?

She grabbed her dressing gown and ran out of her room on to the landing.

A stranger was standing there. He had a burning torch in one hand, and carried Mum's jewellery box under his arm. He wore the uniform of the Campbell militia.

Rebecca understood in a second. Mum and Dad had been talking for months about the way the Campbells were acting. Augustine hadn't been seen at anyone's house for a long time, nobody got invited to the Campbell farms, everything had gone quiet. Some people had said they were going to fight a war with the Welsh. But Dad said nobody really believed that. They were just all afraid of what was going to happen.

The man laughed at her. He took a step towards her, and waved the torch in her direction. The soot from it was making patches on the ceiling.

Rebecca stepped back. 'Dad!' she shouted. 'Mum!'

The man leapt at her and grabbed her, pushing her up against the wall with his free hand. It went round her neck, then squashed down over her chest. Rebecca didn't care about that. She kept on shouting.

There was a noise from behind. A yell.

Dad staggered up the stairs. Rebecca opened her mouth when she saw he was hurt. He had a big hole in his side, his shirt ripped away. All blood. His face was purple, like it was bruised all over.

He was carrying an axe.

He rushed at the man as the man tried to turn.

Dad knocked him down with the axe. He dropped the torch as he fell.

He swung it again as the man tried to get up. Rebecca watched. She wanted to see him hurt.

Dad smashed his head in. The axe went right through the middle of it.

Blood and brains burst out.

Dad had to pull the axe really hard before it'd come out.

He looked at Rebecca like it was all his fault. And she wanted to say that it wasn't, that it was the fault of the man.

But then they both saw that the torch had set the rug on fire.

Dad started to try and stamp it out.

'Mum,' said Rebecca.

Dad didn't answer.

Suddenly, there was more noise from downstairs.

Dad turned back, the axe still in his hands, and said quietly to Rebecca: 'Get out of your window, on to the roof of the barn. Quickly.'

'But—'

'Go on, Beck! Go to the Dochertys'!'

She ran for her room.

She got to her window, flung back the curtains, and opened the catch.

She turned back.

There was Dad at the top of the stairs, yelling down at someone. 'I'll be a hostage! The community will pay you—'

She saw him stagger backwards before she heard the sound.

His body spun around under the impact of the shells. He was thrown in all directions, blood flying from him, misting the walls.

Rebecca seized up inside.

She found there was suddenly silence. And the thing she was

looking at through the open door of her bedroom was still the same thing.

It was her birthday.

She quietly slipped the window upwards, put one leg through . . . kept looking at what lay on the landing . . . stopped doing that, put her other leg through.

She stood on the sloping roof of the barn. Her bare feet were shocked by the cold metal. It was dark and freezing cold and it was raining. She could hear the drumming of the water on the roof, but louder than it was in her room.

She closed the window behind her, very slowly.

She could see torchlight inside the kitchen, way below.

Dad must have meant that Mum was dead.

She walked carefully along the roof of the barn to the other end, along the side of the house, her arms stretched out for balance. Her dressing gown and the nightdress underneath were already getting wet.

She got to the end of the roof and sat down, grabbed the wheel upon which the hay lift swung, dropped until she hung from it. She stretched out until she was as tall as she could be.

Then she dropped. The fall was just about all right. Her knees took the impact and she rolled over on to her back in the mud. She'd done that twice before, when Dad had asked her to try it.

Ambrose was already dancing about in his stall, as if he knew something was happening.

Rebecca went round to him and shushed him. The feel of him under her hand almost made her start crying, but she held it in. No time for a saddle. She opened the front of the stall, led him out with her fingers, then leapt on.

She took a moment to walk him back into the barn. She sprung the stall doors on the other two, Maud and Judith.

Shouts came from round the other side of the barn, by the front door.

She clicked her tongue and spurred Ambrose on with her heels.

The good old loyal beast leapt forward.

Rebecca shouted to him to go, go, to keep on going.

Maud and Judith burst out of the barn after them.

There were shrill yells behind them, running feet. Rebecca aimed Ambrose for the gate at the end of the track, the one that led to the big field.

He cleared it in one long jump.

The impact of the landing made Rebecca buck and sway on his

back, but she held on with her hands in his mane and her legs flexing with the blow.

A burst of machine-gun fire flared somewhere past her shoulder.

One of the other horses fell, with a high whinny that Rebecca had never heard before. The other didn't come with them, shying at the gate.

Rebecca thundered up the big field, up the incline, getting further and further from the house.

She was aware, as she reached the ridge, of a growing light behind her.

She turned the horse as she got there to look back.

The farm was ablaze. The flames had filled every window, were casting big orange shards of light over the dark figures who stood around, by their war wagon, flickering under their own torches. She was sure she could hear them laughing.

They had not even bothered pursuing her.

As she watched, the roof collapsed with a roar of timber. A bloom of fire and sparks rose into the air, making the night blacker around it.

She felt the heat on her face, and felt with it the odd shape that her face was in.

Everything was bunched up.

This was all her fault.

She made sure she looked as long as she needed to.

Then she turned the horse, and with a yell, sent it thundering off across the turf in the direction of the next farmstead.

Twenty-Six: Kicking Over the Traces

It was Little Bob, that night, who first became aware of what was approaching. He and Steven had been taking turns with one of the village wives in the carriage cockpit when they saw a red light blinking on the controls. Not being a driver, Bob had sent Steven running over the green and through the graveyard to the church, where he had disturbed David from his sleep.

David had sworn as he woke. He'd been dreaming of her, again. Of Rebecca. Of losing her. A recurring nightmare.

Only natural. He was about to do something about that situation. His big idea. It was only to be expected that he would dream of the distance that was still between them.

He left Charlotte to sleep and followed Steven out of the church. He noted as they went that there were only a handful of villagers left now, dancing weakly on the green in the darkness, positioned there by the men as if to note their dwindling numbers. The woman he wrenched out of the cabin seemed to be the only female left. The whole hamlet smelt of death now, even in the chill of the night. In the day, vast clouds of insects hung around the buildings, snapped up by an orgy of birds that were forming great squadrons in the trees.

Even the cabin smelt of bodies. He hit a key beside the flashing signal and an illuminated overhead display flicked on to the bullet-proof glass shields. It was a radar map of the skies above the vehicle. This wagon had been set aside for the most important tasks of Manderville diplomacy and security. The team had examined files on it for days before the ambush, worked out that only an assault deep in Manderville country would work, in a back road where the crew had felt safe to disembark and clear what looked for all the world like a genuinely collapsed tree. They had even taken them with knives and swords to avoid the sounds of gunfire.

David had removed the radio beacon and dropped it on to a little raft in the nearby river, sending it rushing away southwards.

The blinking light on the radar map had connected his thoughts with the blinking light on that beacon, as it had dipped and bobbed off on its journey. That had been safety. This was danger. It was like she was hanging around in his head from the dream, diminishing and limiting him, still.

But not for much longer, now. That was all going to be put right.

'A dirigible on a search pattern,' he told Steven and Bob. 'They're looking for us. Find the other two, unpack the missile launcher, meet me at the church. We'll bring the dirigible down and get the compiler out of here.' This was exactly what he needed, a crisis to make them obey him, to get them away from here without thinking about it. Right on schedule. They ran to obey, looking eager.

The woman he'd thrown from the cab was still looking up at him from the dewy grass, hopeful and woeful.

He stepped over her and ran for the stables to marshal the horses.

He brought the wagon to a halt at speed outside the graveyard, aware all the time of the green lozenge approaching the little circle at the centre of the radar display. He jumped from his seat, ran round to the back of the vehicle, and sent the back doors flying open, then levered down the mobile pallet from the roof and dragged it through the lich-gate of the churchyard on its tiny wheels. He got it through the doors, and silenced Charlotte's scared pleas with a finger to his lips. Then he heard the others approaching.

He stepped back out of the church doors and nodded at the fact that they were all in something like battle order again. Bob and Jacko were carrying the case containing the hand-held missile launcher. As they started to strip and ready the weapon, David grabbed his binoculars from the wagon, switched to night vision and looked over the forest towards the south-west.

He saw it. The deadly shape of a Manderville war dirigible, the swirl of its props making the violet silhouette waver in the cold night sky. It was still several miles away. At least there was no moon.

They'd got the missile prepped and ready. It rested on Bob's shoulder, the eyesight clicking down over the soldier's right eye. 'Target in sight,' he confirmed. 'Fucking beauty.'

David smiled. 'They were never going to let the compiler – shit!'

Something had detached itself from the dark mass of the aircraft. A tiny blob that gently separated from the belly of its parent fell until

David had to follow one or the other, then bloomed with parachutes. He looked back to the dirigible. It was turning away.

He heard Bob yell at the same moment. 'Can you get it?' he called to the man. 'Can you?'

Bob concentrated for a moment, fiddling with the sights. Then he threw the missile launcher off for the others to catch. 'Sir, no, sir! Fuck, sir!'

'Shit!' His heart thumping with adrenaline, he started to wave his arms frantically towards the church. 'The compiler! Get the compiler! They're out of their fucking minds!'

The soldiers ran with him into the church, bursting through the doors and virtually riding the pallet towards the altar space at a sprint. Charlotte screamed, picking up on the fear.

David bent to pull the power line, and realised.

He only had a second.

He grabbed his gun from his belt and took a few steps closer to Charlotte.

She looked anxiously at him.

He slammed the pistol up against her forehead and shot her at the exact moment Bob pulled the power line from the wall.

He closed his eyes as the body fell, and managed not to see any sort of expression on her face at all.

He stood panting for a moment. Fucking Rebecca. Made him into this.

Then he ran back to the men and helped them get the compiler on to the pallet.

They rushed the pallet up into the back of the lorry, the five of them heaving it together, keeping the momentum going as they ran it up the long metal ramp. Frank, Little Bob and Jacko fell to the floor inside, and David and Steven swung the doors closed on them and locked them. Then they sprinted to the front and clambered up into the cab.

He managed to get the horses on their way and set the wagon moving, his mind full of thoughts of death and failure, of how that was all there was for him now, failure and bitterness unto meaningless death, and that was all her fault, her fault for taking meaning away from him. He was going to fail again. He imagined the box under the parachutes, swaying as it descended, floating gently down into the village. He switched off the display above him that showed it bearing down, nearly touching the centre of the circle now.

The great bulk of the wagon wrenched from side to side as they took a corner at speed, nearly overturning.

'For Christ's sake, sir!' screamed Steven.

Steven blew the gate into pieces with a couple of shots from his grenade launcher, and the warhorses galloped the wagon through it without pausing, the windscreen screeching with impacts, white stars blooming in the dark.

David screamed at the horses to go faster, remembering the long straight road ahead rather than seeing it.

The remaining villagers lay on the green, weeping and screaming, clinging to each other in the darkness, beginning to tell each other what had happened, of how they couldn't help themselves, and God help them, they remembered everything.

Huddling, about to search for food and warmth, they looked up at the metal box that was descending slowly and neatly into the centre of the village, its parachutes flaring with tiny vents that were then pulled closed by cords that stretched between them and the box.

It looked like help, somehow, this visitor from above.

It came within a metre of touching down.

An elderly man staggered towards it, his arms raised.

The box exploded.

The fireball swept through the buildings around the green, burning them clean, its shape deforming into lines of light and shadow. The shadow swept after the light, a blizzard of debris and vapour.

The light claimed the river, the church, the hall, the wooden fence, and only broke against the forest where it rolled and incinerated and dissolved into a firestorm that thundered from tree to tree.

The wagon shot into the night, the hedges along the road dissolving behind it, and swept to the right at an angle to the fire.

The fire hit the gathering slope of trees, smashed against it.

Blackened branches thundered on to the roof of the vehicle. Trees fell. Behind it. The chemical fireball withdrew, with a great thunderclap of air into vacuum.

And the carriage escaped into the cold night air beyond the fireball, its surfaces washed red and gold by the light of the growing pillar of flame behind it.

David slumped back in his seat, bile in his throat, his hands shaking on the reins. He tugged back and brought the carriage to a halt, in the middle of the road.

He lay back, watching the sky above becoming red and purple. He hadn't expected that, and he should have. The Mandervilles could always build another compiler. They just didn't want anyone else to get their hands on one. One could never underestimate the pride of one of the great houses, nor their malice.

What an indigestible world it was.

His team must have missed the reconnaissance flight that had discovered their position, some time in the last few days. The machine had left them open for death. Perhaps the thing brought harm everywhere it went, unravelling the world with its licence. The beginning of the end. David thought he liked the sound of that. Whoever held the machine was in charge of toppling things, or could stand proudly aside from the toppling.

Beside him, Steven was crying, openly and wantonly.

David took his phone from his jacket, and flicked up the message he'd received just before he went to sleep. It had taken him a moment to believe that he was still awake as he'd lain there, studying it. For it to arrive now gave him a sick feeling in his stomach. The universe was turning around his plan. It was just as well they hadn't managed to find and destroy all three of the Mandervilles' net towers.

He took the coordinates from the message and fed them into a map programme.

The chemical warhead strike would bring soldiers in its wake, mopping up. The Mandervilles wouldn't assume anything. They had to move as fast as they could to break out of Manderville territory.

But he was sure they would succeed. Because now there was somewhere very important that he had to get to.

He picked up the reins and sent the carriage roaring off into the darkness.

Twenty-Seven: Rebecca's Eighth Birthday

Everybody had been happy this morning. Too happy. Rebecca had been thinking about her birthday for days, crying about it at night. Because Mum and Dad weren't talking about it. There was a hard silence where the talking about it should have been, and Rebecca didn't like the feeling, because it wasn't like any other feeling she knew. It was a row feeling, like when you were huffy and sitting with your back against the door of your bedroom after a row. But there was no row. She didn't really remember much about her birthday last year. That had got lost amongst everything else that had happened, the harvest and the harvest home and then bonfire night and then Christmas and the spring cider and the planting and the newborn animals. But she knew right inside her that with birthdays something awful came along. She'd been dreading today, doing her best to stay out of the way of her parents, concentrating on the reading screen of the family phone.

But when the morning had come, Mum and Dad had come into her room and called her out to breakfast together, being all funny and annoying and Dad having a go at her about staying in bed for once. And she knew then that they were going to be okay about it. There had been strawberry crush on her porridge, from the big jar that she wasn't allowed to open. And then they had given her polished clogs, which were okay, but brown rather than black, and a really good purple dress, and, best of all, the download codes for three net books, written in a letter from Dad which was full of jokes she didn't get but that he explained to her, and Rebecca laughed and said these presents were really good and hugged and kissed them both.

But they didn't say anything about a party, and she kind of got that there wasn't going to be a party, now or ever again.

So she said she was going to go out into the orchard in her clogs.

Mum didn't even say anything about not getting them dirty, so she knew then that she was being allowed anything because of this terrible day, and that hurt too, and as she walked out into the sunlight of the farmyard, swinging her arms and stretching, she thought of doing something really bad to see if she'd get away with that. That would be good, because then things would be like they really were today, and not like everyone was pretending about stuff.

But that would be just crap. She climbed over the fence, her clogs hanging off her feet, and walked through the wet grass towards the big tree. It was like a couple of months ago when Mum had explained about periods, and shown her the stupid underwear she'd have to wear, and about how Dad didn't really understand and would get a bit uncomfortable. That had been a large thing to take on, too, that she was going to have to deal with that with only half the help. That there were things Dad didn't understand, so she had to be a bit older and just deal with things.

She'd deal with this too. When the day was over, it'd be over, and she was Rebecca and they were Mum and Dad, and there was a whole different year after this one. She'd done the right thing already by telling them everything was all right and that the presents were good.

She sat and looked across the green of the farm to the plain beyond. There were farms over there, the farms where the kids who wouldn't be coming lived. She turned away, moved around the tree, to look at the hills in the other direction. She didn't know what was over there, but it wasn't a bunch of names like that, names her parents had always waved at her, names that demanded this and needed that, names that she should try or not try to be like. Over the hills was a world of new stuff for her to name, new people who would be friends of hers, who she could meet, who would mean all sorts of different things to her, and that her parents would never know, or meet and forget, or have wildly differing opinions of, things she knew not to be true. Rebecca could see them, like characters in books before you read the page. They were bare, blank figures, waiting to be given life, drawings that became detailed in her thoughts as she started to give feelings to them. The Tynes, who owned a house, but what happened when people broke in? They set a trap for them, a big hole which they all fell into. And they kept all the people who wanted to break into the house in those holes. Or they got lost in the house, wandering around for hours with the Tynes laughing at them. Because the house was that big. And they had a big dog—

A shout from across the meadow made her look up with a gasp, her stomach suddenly tight with fear. Kids. Not party kids?

No. They weren't dressed for a party. And it was all boys. Boys she didn't know. Rebecca stood up, and wiped the tops of her clogs on the back of her socks.

There were six of them, carrying sticks, lumbering through the long grass. In front of them was a tall, thin boy with a mop of sandy hair. Rebecca blinked against the sunlight. She thought she might recognise him from somewhere, but then as he came closer, she understood why, and had to stop a thought that would have made her run away. He was a Hawtrey. One of the Big Families. He was much older than her, maybe a whole year. She'd never played with anyone that old. But she didn't want to run away. She wasn't a little girl, and if they'd come to laugh at her about her birthday she would beat them up.

'Hullo!' called the boy. 'Where is this?'

'This is Ashbrook Farm, the Champhert home.' Rebecca made herself sound proud, hoping that they didn't know about the birthday, didn't think there was anything bad about the name.

'Champhert?' The boy looked back to a much smaller boy who followed a few metres behind him, with a bowl haircut. The boy frowned for a moment, then shrugged. The leader turned back to Rebecca. 'Little Bob's never heard of you.' Rebecca relaxed. 'Want to come down to the weir with us?'

Rebecca hesitated for a moment, then nodded.

The weir stood at the limit of where Rebecca had walked with Mum and Dad, a place she'd seen only a few times a year. It was a series of stone blocks across the river that was a defence to stop boats coming down here. The water sped over the blocks excitingly when there'd been rain, but now they stood dry and flat in the sun, with an idle little stream dribbling down the cracks, moss smelling strange and wet at the edges, piles of autumn leaves gathered in the shadows. The last time the weir would be dry this year, Rebecca thought. A ragged tree branch lay across the lower blocks, marooned until the rains came in earnest.

'Look at that!' said the boy, who'd said his name was David and hadn't mentioned that he was a Hawtrey. He scrambled up the weir and with a few pulls tugged the branch from where it was stuck, sending it crashing down a couple of steps into the mud at the bottom. 'Isn't that great?'

'Yes.' Rebecca didn't like the way the group had just opened up to let her be one of them, almost as a matter of course. She felt like they were just pretending to like her and accept her so that they could laugh at her when she was gone, or worse, while she was still there, when they would all turn around and point. She saw the little looks that passed between them, between the long-haired raggedy one called Steven (who couldn't be from the Hawtrey lands, could he?) and awkward little Frank, who wouldn't talk to her. She didn't like the way they all picked on Alec, but when she tried to talk to him and find out what he liked that they didn't, the rest of the group started picking on him more, and she got the feeling that if she kept doing that they'd pick on her sooner rather than later.

Still, she had walked to the weir with them and hung about as they jumped down the steps and fought with branches and practised high kicks at each other. They kept calling to her to watch, but they all watched David, and she got the feeling that it was him who would decide whether she was nice or not.

He stepped down the blocks and approached her, like he'd made up his mind about something. 'I know what happened,' he said. 'Last year. We lied about not knowing who you were. Little Bob and I sorted that out before we got here. You didn't guess, did you?'

Rebecca shut her mouth and looked at her clogs.

'That's why we came,' he said. 'Little Bob wrote it on the calendar a few weeks after we heard, and the year turned round and here we are. Father said it was important and he's a cousin. So we're here for the Hawtreys. We should have been invited to that party, because we would have come.'

'Thank you,' she managed to say.

'It's important. The Campbells and their little sheep treated you badly. But the Hawtreys look after the important things. The details. Everything's important. There's a big knitted thing in the Hawtrey house here that says how important everything is. You should come and see it.'

'Dad said—'

'Which of us do you like most?'

'I don't like any of you yet. I don't know you enough.'

'But if you were going to kiss one of us?'

She took a step back from him. 'I want to go home.'

'Fine. Off you go. Go on.' He turned away, and the others followed, stepping up the weir, their long boy arms stretched out, balancing them.

How could they go so far from home? she wondered. Would they be in trouble, or was that what they did? Was that what other kids did? Did they stay away because she wasn't like them?

'You!' she called up at David.

Something inside her rebelled, but she still kept looking at him.

He looked back, and then glanced at his friends, and that glance was sort of red-faced and weird, and he wasn't going to laugh at her. Alec started to smile until David pushed him on the chest and made the smile go. It felt like David was being dared.

So she stayed put as he alone made his way down the blocks again, slowly, like he wasn't really sure about this.

She felt kind of strong now. Better, but worried. No, she was grown up now. He'd said about the details, that was an adult thing. And she was going to do an adult thing with him . . . and she was ready for that before he was, she knew. If she walked away now and told him she'd changed her mind he'd be really angry and chase her and make her kiss him. But he'd look really shit in front of his friends and they'd laugh at him.

She was arguing with herself.

He came to within touching distance. She could smell him. Mud and leaves and a boy smell that had always been ugh before but was different now.

He took a step closer so that her chest was against his.

'Have you kissed before?' she asked.

He didn't answer. He just slapped his palm on to the back of her head, and pulled her head slowly to his until his lips and teeth bumped with hers.

She closed her eyes. Their lips mushed.

No, said something from long ago. No, no, no. Not him. But she did nothing.

Then he let her go and looked odd at her. 'Good.'

'Yes.' She thought she ought to say that. And she felt huge and weird like the world had changed but she was still on top of it. He was lost and she was in charge. But something inside her was lost too.

'No, I mean . . . Good. Fine. Right.' He looked back to his friends and they were laughing and pointing at him, but in a good way. Except Frank, who had wandered away. 'Do you want to do more than that?'

Shit. She didn't even really know what he meant, so she shouted, 'No!'

'Okay. Don't worry. Here.' He grabbed her hand and, before she could wrench it away, took a charcoal from his pocket and wrote the digits of an e-mail address on her hand.

She thought she might lick it off, but decided not to. As long as Mum and Dad didn't see.

'Next birthday, invite us. David Hawtrey.' He said that as if it was the end of the joke, the bit where she was supposed to be impressed.

'Oh,' she said, trying to sound impressed.

David smiled, then turned away. He stepped back up on the weir again, and the others moved in to talk to him.

After a while, Rebecca realised that she was supposed to go away now. So she did, before they decided to pay attention to her again.

As she walked back off towards the meadow and the big tree, she could hear their laughter continuing, getting fainter.

But they weren't laughing at her.

When she went into the house, she kept one hand over the other, and copied the address down as soon as she could.

Twenty-Eight: Grey Namer

Winter, one million years BC

He lay on the water, his nose and eyes just above the surface, his arms and legs outstretched, floating on his carpet of hair. The remains of shellfish lay on his chest.

He was listening to the sounds of what lay under the water. Under everything was the distant rumble of God, far down the river.

He gave a couple of unconscious kicks against the stream.

He heard the concussions of the rest of his people diving. One of the little gods inside him told him what the booms of their underwater calls meant. No big fish. Little fish. Shellfish here. No big fish. This was the little god from the hunting dream.

He sometimes got that god confused with the little god of the tree pictures, who moved his hand when he cut bark to do the hunt on land before they did the hunt in the river.

He sometimes got all the little gods confused, and sometimes he didn't notice them talking to him, but thought he was a little god, or that all the little gods had left him, before he realised that he was doing what the little gods would want him to do anyway.

That made him feel like the big cat was on his neck.

There was excitement upriver, the little god of the hunting dream told him. One of the warm little ones had many shellfish.

He hooted in pleasure to the green canopy high above him. The warm little one would give him some, because he protected the warm little one. The little warm one with the hair like tall grass.

He rolled in the river, letting the gone shellfish fall from him, and hooted into the river the sound the little god of the tree pictures had given him for it being time to hide in the tall grass.

He rolled back on to his front again, and listened to the scared and unscared wrong calls from upriver. No tall grass to hide in . . . they didn't understand . . . but the sounds made sense for the warm little one with the hair like tall grass.

He thought.

He watched a bright no-food bird fly from one branch to another, silently above. He clattered his arms in the water to make the sound the bird would make if he could hear it.

Clatter. The bright no-food bird.

He was intensely excited by having dropped down from the tree in the night and walked out on to the forest floor and been safe. Without the little gods. When he was dreaming it might be different, but it suddenly felt as if all the little gods were him. He thrashed and thrashed and hooted with pleasure.

All the little gods were him.

Only God wasn't him. If he didn't swim, he'd go down the river and fall off God and be gone in the roar.

That *would* happen. This wasn't a dream saying it was happening now. It wasn't happening *now*. It would happen *then*.

If he didn't swim.

He was given those things in dreams by the little gods all the time. But now he knew those things for himself.

He was not Tall Grass. But Tall Grass was like him.

He was not Clatter. And Clatter was not like him.

But he was not quite like any of the others who shared with him the dreams of the little gods.

He was the big one of the ifs and thens.

He could see the ifs and thens of the river moving on. Like when the thin big one had fallen when the branch broke, and the ones who weren't with them but were like them had been too many for him and eaten him.

That had really happened. He'd been there when that had happened. He was scared for a moment, but then he *knew*. He wasn't there *now*.

He *would* be in places he wasn't now. He *would* do things he wasn't doing now. He was about to roll in the water, as the little god of the hunting dream suggested, to remove the last of the shellfish from his fur. He waited. He was or was not.

He decided to do it.

He did.

Then he was on his back again, floating, astonished. Tonight he would eat and fuck. Or he would not. No, he wanted to, so he would.

He whooped and splashed again. He was *all* the little gods. Maybe he was God too.

Against what the little gods had always said, he stopped slowly kicking, something that had never been near for him before, never been anywhere. He let himself go down the river towards God, to see if he would stop because he was God.

But a little way down the river he got scared, and thought he wasn't God, and quickly kicked back up the river again. But the dreams of the little gods were just a distant calling now, not anywhere near him, and not anything that he was.

He got back to where he could hear the calls of the others as they were getting out of the stream. Tall Grass. Hot Red Fuck Bottom. All the others who were all different.

Who was *he*?

He was the one who knew who all the others were. He looked different to them too, because he had more of a colour that a lot of them just had patches of.

He was Grey Namer. He would tell them. When and if he could. He would tell them when they thought they had the little god of the tree pictures.

Well, he would tell them, Tall Grass, and Hot Red Fuck Bottom, and Clatter. He didn't know how to give them Grey Namer.

He would find a way.

Grey Namer, big one of the ifs and thens, set off for the side of the river to run after his people and share Tall Grass's shellfish and eat and fuck and give things their names.

He went hooting all the way.

Twenty-Nine: The Essene

Winter, 22 AD

Jesus sat in the long grass on the little hillock, looking down at the blue expanse of the sea below him. It would be good to take off his monk's robe and go and lie in it, letting the water support him in the manner peculiar to that sea. The east wind brought the scents of balsam, frankincense and myrrh from the plantations along the river, and ruffled his hair and made him want to sleep and dream.

But he had duties before noon. And troubles in his mind. While he saw the sea, he also saw the bitumen that lolled on the surf, and thought of the daily mission to collect it for the treatment of those who came here with fever and coughs that would not leave them. He saw the patients who were led by the youngest Essenes down to the shore, where they supported them and watched them as they took their daily bathe in the sea. There would be more bathing later, in the spring water that fed the mikvahs, the great baths. And between the bathing there would be the breakfast of the madder plant, and the consultation with the eldest of the order, to see whether the patient was recovering or if a change had to be made to their treatment.

Those were the walls of Jesus of Nazareth's world. He was less than twenty years old. He carried a bundle of wooden keys over his shoulder, the secrets of Qumran entrusted to him. The great storehouse of the monastery's medicines, the lookout point that watched the balsam fields in case anyone would damage them, even the treasury of wealth the Essenes had collected through the sale of their medicines and the gifts of those who came to them to be treated, the plant that only grew and was hardly picked because the monks remained in poverty . . . All were open or shut according to his hands. Because his masters trusted the young man absolutely. And they were correct in doing so. Jesus was surprised at how well they saw that in him: his desire to be trusted and given responsibility.

It seemed to him natural that he was the keeper of all the keys.

He could name every plant on the hillside, and knew a use for every stone.

But he felt that this world of which he was the *omphalos*, as the Greeks had it, the navel, was too small.

He had read and reread the scroll of the Torah concerning Adam, the first man in the world, who was given the task of naming all the animals and plants. 'And Adam gave names to all the cattle, and to the birds, and to every wild animal; but for Adam there was no helper.'

He understood that. But he felt that something was wrong in the way the Book described the Fall of Man. Things had been better before the Fall, a golden age had been long lost. But he somehow knew, a thought he had never shared with others, that the circumstances of the loss of Man's innocence had been different.

His mouth formed the words again, from the language he didn't know.

He let the words out, gave them voice, as he often had when he was alone. A complicated hoot burst from his mouth, as it always did, a noise that guggled with information.

He snapped his jaw closed. He was growing more certain every day. That had been the moment. The moment when Man had been lost to God. When the great separation had occurred.

It felt like he'd been there.

It felt like he'd been responsible.

He felt even more like the centre of the world. He wasn't sure he was capable of being that. The Essenes were already at odds with Judaism: madmen and ranting prophets arrived from Jerusalem all the time, hoping to join the order on the basis of their reputation, and all were turned away.

But he knew that one day his madness would have to lead him.

Man must return to before the Fall, reunite with its Father . . . It felt like his path was to do exactly that.

Far away, carried on the wind, he heard someone calling his name. One of the other monks, needing one of his keys or reminding him of his duties.

He got to his feet and thumped the grass seeds from his robe.

One day he would be keeper of many more keys than these.

He would be master of the ifs and thens.

He called back to whoever was seeking him, and set off down the slope, back towards the monastery. But in his mind his thoughts were forming, as slowly as they could, towards a storm.

Thirty: Rebecca's Seventh Birthday

You sit on the steps in your best dress, knowing that something horrible is happening. Your dad has been stamping around, going to the gate to look out, then walking back, putting on a false smile that makes you feel even worse.

Inside the house, the big meal that Mum has made sits in the pots and on the table, the cake untouched.

Nobody's coming. That means you get to eat all the food yourself, doesn't it?

No, something must make this bad. Mum and Dad think this is bad. Dad steps past you, ruffling your hair. He loves you. But it's your fault. You've hurt him.

'Dad,' you ask. 'Where's everybody?'

'I don't know, Beck.'

Mum walks through from the kitchen, looking like she's going to start shouting. 'The Dochertys just e-mailed us. Josh is ill. So are Wendy and Lou. There must be something going around. We have twelve different e-mails from families whose children are ill.'

There's something about how she says the word 'ill'. You don't like it. It's like she's shouting at you.

So you get up and go to her. 'Poor Wendy,' you say, hoping she'll pick you up. And she does.

Your dad laughs, and that doesn't sound good either. 'Dear old Beck.'

He comes close to you both, and kisses Mum on the forehead. He stumbles over the word 'forget' and Mum makes a little angry dip at him for it. 'Forget them. Let's have tea and open the presents. She won't go to their birthday parties if that's how they feel.'

You know now that you're being punished and loved at the same time. And you hate it because you don't understand it. You burst out crying.

'Sweetheart,' Mum says. 'Everything's all right.'

But you know from her voice that it isn't.

Thirty-One: British Time

Rebecca lay flat in the earth, her breathing shallow.

She lay in a thin flat strip of space between soil so hard it felt like concrete.

Her chest pushed against the boards on top of her with every breath.

She would not scrabble against the boards.

Her arms wouldn't come up to get the leverage for that, anyway. She was pinned flat.

And in her head she was still fighting to keep her thoughts with her most recent birthday, and not slide down the pit, association by association, back to those more frightening and traumatic birthdays of her past. She had already visited them in snatches of agony. A load of strange and inconsistent stuff had been wrenched violently up from inside her, and it was going to take years to sort it all out.

Like she had years.

The green would decay. It would wash out of her body in a few hours.

She wondered if she had even that.

The dose might have left her brain-damaged.

What the fuck. That was the least of her worries.

Still very hot. Still solid above and below. Still no light at all. She still couldn't move her limbs, but that was because of the weight of the earth now: her body was yelling with nerve endings going off. It felt like a cascade of insects running up and down her.

Brave. You're brave. Everyone knows that.

Nobody had ever experienced this in such detail. Probably, everybody who'd been buried alive before had screamed and clawed and gone mad, and—

The memory dreams snagged her back again, and it took a moment to get back to the darkness.

She didn't know which she feared most.

She might get to the madness bit yet. If they found her looking serene and the boards unscratched, that would be a big, big victory.

She tried to stop her thoughts from leaping back to what she'd said to Jane, but she couldn't. The vicar had carried through her plan exactly as she'd said she was going to. She'd shovelled soil on to the boards as Rebecca's body jerked and shivered with returning sensation, placing the cardboard tube above her head so that she could lean over at intervals and talk to her.

Everything she'd said had been terrifying.

The speech had been worse than this was, now. An anticipation of Rebecca's suffering that wasn't even gleeful, just functional. A lot of the fear for Rebecca had been in that voice. In how anybody could think like that. Of how terrifyingly rabbitlike vulnerable it was to be *her* victim. How could someone as good and kind and real as herself be allowed to be the victim of something as horrific as Jane?

How could she have identified so much with that something?

'The pressure should be increasing now,' Jane had said. 'We still have a while before I'll start dropping soil on to your head.'

Rebecca had thrown up as the weight had increased on her chest, had had to shake her head with violent, long-thought-out strokes to stop it getting up her nose. Jane had said: 'Your actual death will be by suffocation, either through the weight on your chest or lack of oxygen.'

Just like that. A prim teacher, a mother with Rebecca in her hands, letting her gently know that her pain was for the best.

A new low for mankind, Rebecca thought. Which, after all she'd witnessed, was a bit of a surprise.

The worst thing had been the pleading.

She hadn't even tried not to do it. As soon as the shovelling started, she'd started talking. Initially, it had been conversational, Rebecca still the hero of her own story. She was going to escape eventually, so she wanted to keep her dialogue appropriate and witty. That had declined to a responsible awareness of her situation, solemn, sober appeals to Jane's religious principles, to a common sense of humanity.

Then the sobs had broken out of her, as if her body had suddenly thought of its own way to move Jane, and, horribly, it had been activated by the nearness of death. 'Please . . .' she had squealed, hating the sound of her voice as it came out that way. She had promised everything she had, everything there was. She had lied and debased herself and sobbed and pissed herself and Jane had listened, seemed to consider, held out that tiniest hope with tiny little considerations that stuck at the back of your throat and tickled like sickness just to think of them now.

And then she had still dutifully started to shovel soil down the hole.

Rebecca, screaming, had shoved her forehead up against the gap, wrenched her spine to keep it there. Held the soil there until she had to let her head fall again, and blessed God Holy God—

It had stayed there. Packed. Only tiny bits falling on to her face. The threat of it there, about to fall. To choke her and make her thrash. To make her lose her dignity and kill who she was.

If that happened, that thing up there would have had her. Fucked her. If she lost control she'd be the helpless subject of that thing that she knew she would kill now if she could. Mercy. Couldn't leave it in the world. Not a thing like that. Not in the world with David and the people she loved.

Another moment in dreams at that thought, holding on to the memory just of his face. His hands. His body. The good memory that lay just beside the birthday.

She was back underground before the green took her back any further. Hopping between one death and another. Back to her warm tomb. No sound, apart from a sort of roar on the edge of hearing. Probably her, what was inside her. The soil smell was a terrifying thing. If she got out, she'd be afraid of it forever. Jane had killed so much of her already. The soil smell and the sound were her world here, now. The sensation of dribbling soil moving on her hands. Not too much. Mustn't let it fall. The pressure on her chest, the increasing acidic demand to move her legs that would mean the thrashing and the lack of dignity and the big death—

Fuck.

Lack of oxygen, she'd said.

That would have happened by now, wouldn't it? Christ, you'd think so.

She shut her eyes and held off the green as best she could.

There was something sticking into her right thigh. Just a slight pressure.

She spent a few minutes slipping her hand down there and adjusting the distribution of weight across her body, moving as slowly as she could.

Her hand closed on something. A pipe? No, there was no hole in it. She could feel all the way around. It was sticking out of the wall, attached to something. It was rough and random in shape, not a metal thing, but a tree root or . . .

A bone. It was a bone.

That almost made her laugh, but she stopped it.

Gently, she tugged at it, feeling the soil crumbling around her fingers, tensing her body against a great rush of earth. But the collapse didn't come.

She'd nearly tugged the bone from the wall when something rolled over and gave way. Something by her hand. There was space for her hand to move in. She suddenly couldn't reach the far wall.

She stamped down on her feeling of sickening excitement. No. No more hope. Don't let me hope. She popped back into the room in her head, saw David again, held it all in, came out again.

Still couldn't feel anything there. She held on to the bone like it was a hand. She started to flip it back and forth, to scrape with it, to gently push. The sounds of scraping seemed very loud. If she were to come to a wall . . .

But then a rush of soil over her hand: loose soil. She thumped roughly sideways with the bone still in her hand.

Something was starting to give way.

And then, like a dream, like the most glorious thing that had ever happened to anybody . . .

The wall gave way and her hand burst out sideways into space. She caught a glimpse of empty darkness. A blessed, exciting stench flooded into her tomb.

A sudden lurch.

Everything tipped sideways.

She tried to waft her hands to save herself. The planks tipped over her head. The world was full of creaking. Her eyes struggled to see something.

Another crash. She rolled sideways with a shriek that was half joy and half terror and all terror at there being joy.

She fell through darkness, her body yelling with cramp, her limbs reflexively flailing to save her now they could.

An ecstatic moment in space.

And then she hit the extraordinary cold of water.

She went straight through. Hit the bottom. Bounced up again. Broke the surface with a howl of fear and delight.

Sitting on her bed, Jane had just started to doze off.

She woke suddenly. Something had switched off. Something like a light in her head. It had been there for ages, and now, suddenly, it was gone.

The soldiers standing to silent attention in the maze stirred in their sleep. Their open eyes flickered.

The ghost drew down more power from above space.

It spun around the minds in the maze and drew more from them, made them shriek in their nightmares.

It held on to its power and existence across the house by the narrowest of margins for a moment.

But it survived.

There was a little light.

Rebecca fell under the surface again, and saw the light under the murk briefly before surfacing once more.

She swirled her hands and feet, shouting at the pain of cramp, weeping at the release, just about keeping her head above the water. She was in a low, echoing chamber. A tunnel. A river in a tunnel. There were splashes from all around, bricks and mud falling from the ceiling above her. The roof was an arc of blackened red brick above her. There was a light in the far distance, just a hint of something blue, curving up around the walls. Her eyes stopped being shocked and adjusted.

Cold. It was so cold. And with the cramp—

No. She would *not* die like that. Not now.

Rebecca clenched her teeth and made her limbs form into a breaststroke, everything howling with pain.

She struck out slowly, determinedly, in the direction of the light.

Thirty-Two: Two Survivors

She couldn't say exactly how long it took her to get to the water-wheel. An hour, maybe more. She was swimming against a slight but wearing current, and every now and then she'd had to grab something on the wall, a gap in the brickwork or the branch of a tree that had been washed down here, and hang on to get some rest. The cramp didn't go away, seizing her legs every now and then with pain and numbness. Memories of her birthdays fluttered into her consciousness from time to time as the cold swept over her in waves. She stopped herself from going back there and the exertion helped. Her body let her shut them out.

The current against her slowed slightly as the light got closer, and she found the going easier. From ahead there came a roaring like a waterfall, but she knew that she must be below it. She kept going. Finally, she rounded a corner and had to grab the wall to stop herself from leaping forward like a salmon, trying to sprint the last few metres and grab what she saw ahead.

A huge wooden waterwheel was spinning in the current, its blades roaring with foam and trailing moss. It stood on a concrete platform, its axis several metres above the boiling river. Rebecca could almost feel the power flowing between it and the single blue maintenance lamp that swung in a cage above the platform.

But beyond that, so much more.

On the platform was a door.

She took several deep breaths, and plunged back into the cold of the river, making herself slowly and carefully stroke through the water until she got to the edge of the platform.

One hand. The other. Elbows. Haul. Legs, and over. Rolling. Against the door.

She lay there, blissfully out of the water, her limbs lying in awkward relief.

There was something still in her hand. She narrowed her eyes to look closely at it. Her hand could no longer feel what it was.

It was the bone. The bone that had freed her. She'd held on to it, kept it with her. It looked like a finger bone.

On it glinted something silver.

Rebecca, feeling like this was the hardest thing she'd done all day, lifted the bone to her face and peered at the familiar object.

It was the ring. The silver ring. The Hawtrey sign that the wearer was Booth Hawtrey's current biographer. Just like the ring on her own finger. The milling around the edges was unmistakable. It was designed to be a guard against forgers.

Rebecca couldn't work out what this meant. How could there be two?

Maybe this was the best forgery ever.

She tried to get to her feet, and failed, slipping on the concrete.

So she tried again, crawling up the door with her weight against it. If she stayed in here the cold would still kill her. She grabbed the door handle and pulled at it.

The door swung open.

Rebecca felt the warmth flood out of the house beyond it.

She threw herself through the doorway.

Jane sat on her bed.

Buried alive. She'd done that. She still couldn't believe it.

When Jane had returned to the house, she'd been shocked to see a shadow moving in one of the downstairs rooms. Booth Hawtrey, on one of his nocturnal rambles. Obvious. She should have thought of that.

So she'd opened the front door as quietly as possible and sneaked in, made her way slowly up the stairs to her own room.

Booth's excursion made collecting Rebecca's baggage easier. Jane had entered the girl's room, quickly packed her rucksack, and made her bed, because it struck her that Rebecca was probably the sort of girl who did that.

She picked up the phone from the bedside table and found Booth's address on the mailout list. She wrote: 'Pissed off. Have left for Warminster. Not far. See you back home.' She set it to send around dawn. She dropped the phone into the rucksack.

Then she took the rucksack back to her own room, opened the window, and, reaching out, right to the edge of her strength, was able to swing the rucksack on to the flat roof above. The edge of a chimney stack, only just protruding above roof level, would conceal it from the ground.

Then she closed the window and staggered back to fall on to her bed.

She would simply tell Booth that she did not know where Rebecca had gone. The relationship between them seemed edgy. With a bit of persuasion, he might stay and finish the survey. Jane would suggest nearby towns she might have headed for.

She considered releasing a horse, but it could very well come back in search of warmth and oats. No, she had done enough.

She was horribly good at this.

She put her hands together and tried to pray, as she saw the first signs of light on the horizon. But if it had been difficult before, now it was impossible.

So she just lay back and waited for dawn.

Booth wandered through the house, unaware that the light outside the windows was getting stronger by the moment.

He had been here before.

He knew that now with every bit of him. Everything seemed familiar. The enamel on the table football game. The titles of the false books in the library. The way the billiard balls bounced off that particular curve of the edge of a pocket.

He was not only familiar with these things, he was intimate with them. He could have played on this table with the advantage of knowing its little kinks.

But from when? And how was this possible? How could someone who had a perfect memory forget something so big? He didn't know if he should be pleased or frightened. Perhaps this was just the almighty *déjà vu* that beings like him – and he was the only one, so there was nobody to advise him on this – experienced when their memories got too full.

No. He put his hand flat on the table. He *knew* this. It was just around the corner of his mind.

He must have drunk a lot of tea in this house. That was what had got him here, the smell. So it must have been back when there still *was* tea.

He let his mind skim through his life. There were no gaps. He had a story for every moment.

But there had to be a discontinuity. Somewhere in his life, there had to be space for Heartsease.

As the dawn rose, he continued to wander.

Rebecca had climbed up the narrow crimson-carpeted stairwells that were the hidden backways of the house, stumbling on to her hands and knees, resting from time to time, shivering with cold and cramp. She should have stayed where she was or found somewhere to go and sleep, but she couldn't. Something bigger than her from inside her was driving her on.

She couldn't feel safe until she'd done it. Done it for herself and for everybody.

She found the large axe on the wall of one of the cellars, sitting on two iron braces, unused and clean. She touched the blade and found it sharp. Then she lifted the axe and found it pleasingly heavy. Heavy to do business. Reassuring. It'd do it for her. All she had to do was swing, and bloody hell was she going to swing, and then thump. Done. Completed. Then she could fall and they'd all be safe.

She'd used the axe as a crutch for some of the stairs, dragged it behind her for others.

When she'd reached the right floor, the floor that she and Booth had been on and she was sure Jane would be on as well, she'd marched out along the hallway, purposeful, the thoughtless reaction to the actions that had been done to her, step after step, marching, the weight now steady against her shoulder, ready only to swing. She sped up as she saw the right door ahead of her. She wanted to break the door down, but something in her velocity told her no, that would get her stuck, she had to walk straight in and chop her down.

So she just reached out a second before she hit the door, wrenched the knob, threw it open.

The room was empty.

She staggered into it, looking desperately around. She was bleeding from a hundred tiny wounds. Her limbs were shouting with cramp.

The bitch *had* to be here!

Her body gave up. The weight of the weapon in her hands was suddenly too heavy.

She fell to her knees. Tried to lift herself once more. Fell forward.

Her head lolled to one side as her neck muscles tried to raise it.

She startled as something moved in front of her eyeline. The bitch – had to kill— She couldn't raise herself. Ironic. The birthdays welled up in her again, in the distance. Got here. Now she can finish me off.

She managed to hang on, on the edge of the dream, just to see who it was.

It was a foot in a kind of flat, laced canvas man's shoe that Rebecca didn't have a name for.

A leg in a stiffly creased cream trouser.

A blue blazer.

A terribly thin, parched face, with staring eyes and cracked lips, looking down at her. It almost looked afraid, she thought.

And then nothing.

Thirty-Three: Rebecca's Sixth Birthday

You're in your best dress, jumping up and down with all the other children and shouting and running and grabbing the hand of your best friend Mardy and making Russell go yapping away as you all pat him at once and far too hard.

It's your first proper party. These children have been invited from all the farms. There are even six Campbells, like Augustine, who has blonde hair with a blue ribbon in it, and is older. You've been told to be very nice to her, because she's very important. You've heard people say that the Campbells are terrible people, but Dad's explained that everyone's being nice to them now, because they're being nice.

Dad sets the big cake down on the long trestle table. Mum's been making it for weeks, letting the fruit and treacle settle in a big square dish after the baking, and then covering it with frosting.

'I don't like cake,' says Augustine, looking at her bright blue shoes.

'Everyone likes cake,' you say.

'I don't like cake.'

'You're stupid!' you say, because you know Mardy will laugh.

She does.

'You're stupid!' Augustine says back at you. 'You've got a foot disease. You have wet feet. See, they're leaking out of your shoes. They're really wet.'

'They're not!' You stamp up and down, horribly scared that the others are laughing at you. Even Mardy is laughing at you.

Dad looks up from the cake and starts to frown. 'Everybody!' he calls. 'Cake time!'

So you trot over. And find that you're the only one who's got her plate ready for the cake. The others stand together in a little group, swaying on their feet, glancing at Augustine, seeing what she's going to do.

Dad looks at you like you're horrible.

Like he wishes he wasn't your dad.

Thirty-Four: Memories are Made of This

The carriage burst over the hill in an explosion of ravens and dry leaves.

David sat atop the cabin, yelling at the horses, snapping the reins, urging them to go faster. Beside him sat Steven, his gun in his lap, laughing so hard his head was thrown back against the sky.

They had broken down a Manderville checkpoint just before dawn, slaughtering troops who ran this way and that, screaming.

The compiler was plugged into the carriage's electrical system, and they'd used it to broadcast terror at their approach. They hadn't switched it off. Now it was putting out a wash of laughter and delirium before and after them. As the carriage raced down the roads into the dawn, it had drawn flocks of giddy birds in its wake, had packs of wolves trailing it and howling, started every bird and beast calling to it and chasing it like a god.

The wagon thundered around a corner, and suddenly there beneath them they saw Heartsease lying in the new morning sun, the lake shining back at them.

David's pupils bloomed with anticipation. He dragged on the reins and brought the sweating team to a stumbling halt. He leapt up in his seat and pointed, the rooks swirling and cawing about him. 'There!' he shouted. 'We go to conquer!'

He grabbed the reins again, and shouted at the horses to move off, standing in his seat like a charioteer.

Soon they were at speed again, bringing the vortex of the compiler down into the valley. And the laughter and the calling of the birds echoed everywhere in the dawn.

Rebecca woke up with a shout.

In her own bed, in her pyjamas.

She looked around wildly.

She rolled up the sleeves and looked at her arms. Then her ankles. Then she touched her cheek.

She wasn't scratched. Her legs didn't hurt.

She lowered her head to the pillow once more.

So.

Had that been a dream?

She curled her fingers together, the tips of them finding her palms. There had been something about a silver ring. A ring like hers. She *felt* different. Like something inside had shifted. She felt . . . she couldn't define it. If that had all really happened, then shouldn't she be harder, scarred inside, as capable of murder as she had been last night?

How could she tell?

There was odd stuff in her head. It was exactly like when you'd got really pissed the night before, and someone tells you the next morning that you bent over to try and force a militiaman to bite your bottom. There were stories in her head from way back. A lot of them seemed to be about her birthdays. But there seemed to be a lot of stuff which she didn't recognise. Stuff in which she might or might not have been involved.

But that would have been true if she'd just dreamed all that, right?

And for some reason, this time she didn't have the bite marks.

She hugged the covers about her. Nobody would believe her.

This must be what it was like to not know if you'd been raped.

There was a feeling of fear and anger inside her, and it didn't seem to have been there the night before. Could a dream do that?

So.

Murderous rage or not murderous rage?

There was a knock on the door.

'Come in,' she called, kind of hoping it was the priest so she could read her face.

It was Booth, holding his phone, looking puzzled. 'Rebecca,' he said. 'Why did you send me an e-mail saying you were going to Warminster?'

Rebecca's backpack rolled forward from behind the chimney where it was lodged.

It rolled straight to the edge of the roof, up a tiny gradient.

It paused on the edge.

The gaunt figure in the blue blazer stood by the edge of the empty rooftop swimming pool, watching the backpack.

He waited for another moment.

The backpack rolled gently over the edge and fell.

Ruth leapt back from the shape that she'd just caught in the corner of her eye.

The backpack hit the ground an inch from her.

Eric swung his rifle towards the roof, ready to pick off an attacker, but Ruth swiftly raised a hand.

She bent down and examined the backpack. Clothes. Cooking equipment. A phone. Who owned this? And what were they doing here?

They had stumbled from the maze ten minutes ago, blinking at the sun that stood high in the sky. Their phones had told them that it was fifty-eight hours since they'd gone in. Fifty-nine in Ruth's case. She was hungry enough for that.

The last thing she remembered was meeting Booth Hawtrey at the centre of the maze. The person that she'd almost expected to meet here, with the logic of a nightmare. And like a nightmare coming true, there he was. He'd stepped towards her, laughing. She'd shot him in the chest, several times.

The bullets hadn't hurt him at all.

She remembered turning to run.

Then it was all like a dream. She'd run and run through a never-ending maze, feeling that something wasn't real. Her thoughts seemed to drift. Her concentration lifted, like she'd taken one look at the alarm clock and the next moment it was an hour later. It had been like one of those 'sleepless nights' where you actually do get some sleep.

And then the feeling cleared and she had been running towards the exit, her men all around her.

They compared notes immediately, as they'd come out of the box hedges on to the open lawns. The men had all told her that they'd been walking in the maze in the night . . . and then had suddenly been running in the day. The same sort of dreaminess in between. They'd hacked through hedges, some of them said, but then they found they disagreed about who'd done what. Whatever, none of the gaps they'd made seemed to go anywhere.

They were all filled with dread about what had happened in that dreaming time. The nightmares they'd had had been draining, like something had had them by the balls. Nobody could remember any details. Joe had talked about getting the defoliants and melting the maze down, and Ruth was inclined to let him.

It had taken Ruth a moment, as they fell on to the grass, panting, to realise that one of them wasn't there. Matthew. Eric had told her then about him running off, and, the fear still in her stomach, she had lashed out at him, said that the boy should have been shot as soon as he turned around.

They'd listened patiently to her do that for a couple of minutes before she realised that they were glaring back at her with suppressed anger too. 'Thank you,' she'd said, suddenly. 'For coming in after me. I'll recommend a commendation for all of you.'

That had squared things.

Now they stood outside the house in sunshine, feeling as if they were in a fucking children's story.

Ruth picked up the rucksack and flung it to Morgan. 'Let's just go back in and eat something. Find the priest. Then we'll work out what happened.'

They followed her around to the front of the house.

None of them slung their weapons.

Rebecca threw open the doors of the wardrobe.

There hung her trousers and shirt and pullover and coat.

'I didn't put these there,' she said. An anger was building inside her. It felt like it was going to make her melt or explode.

'Strange things are happening,' said Booth. 'That hole you made in the plaster in my room . . . It's gone. And listen, I'm certain I've been here before. There's something about this house—'

'I'm going to kill her,' said Rebecca. Then it came out as a bellow and she couldn't help it. 'I'm going to fucking kill her!'

Jane stood in her bath, her hand on the plunge control, wondering if she'd just used it or not.

She shook her head a little. Her hair was wet, but—

She used it again, just in case.

Even that didn't seem as shocking as it had.

She dried herself, watching the little pools of water that her feet made on the tiles. Then she walked back into her bedroom.

She looked slowly around it in the morning light.

It was morning now. The madness had gone. The reasons had gone.

What she had done was mad.

She sat down on the bed, wrapped in a towel, her palms on her knees, staring into the centre of the room.

Booth wasn't going to believe her story. She wasn't sure if she was going to have the courage to tell it. She felt thankful for that.

She had been trapped into a psychosis, become the ranting psychopath who insists it's all true, that the world is actually the way she sees it and not the way the people who have just locked her up see it.

She wished there were forces who would come for her now. Take her away. Lock her away. But there was only Booth and the empty house.

Was this Satan doing this to her? The very essence of Satan? To trick her into missing his approach, concealing himself as something else, then . . . she ends up doing something terrible for the best of reasons. It was almost Biblical. How could she have been so stupid?

But the vision of her father was what had smelt of brimstone, and Mary had smelt of simplicity and holiness.

Masks and masks.

If she greened the part about Mary now, perhaps she could see . . . Her hand closed on the dispenser on her bed before the thought stopped her: did she want to see? What if there was nothing to see? Or what if she saw . . . ?

Jane realised that she'd started to sway back and forth on the bed a little. She made an effort and managed to stop doing it.

Rebecca was dressing at speed, in the bathroom.

She'd vomited immediately when she'd run in here with her clothes. Just saw the toilet bowl and bang.

Which was a reaction, obviously. Just like telling Booth to wait out there, not to leave the room. A fear thing. She was just going to ignore it and get on with it. Dab your mouth, roll water around in it, clothes on, get Booth, get something heavy, club vicar into the ground.

Into the ground. She didn't stop moving, flinging arms into sleeves, pulling trousers up. Uh-uh, nothing was going to stop her moving now.

There had been that guy, last night. Blue shoes.

Shit, did she dream him?

Something fell from her trouser pocket on to the bright tiled floor of the bathroom.

She bent right away to pick it up.

And found that she was holding that bone. The fingerbone. With the Booth Hawtrey biographer ring on it.

Rebecca stopped.

It took Jane a full minute to realise that she was actually hearing voices from downstairs. She'd thought they were animal noises, but then there'd come a thump and she'd suddenly realised what she was hearing. Someone had entered through the stables.

She got up from the bed and made her way to the door. She listened again. There was a higher tone amongst the others.

Ruth.

They'd been brought back to her.

Jane leaned heavily on the door.

A day ago this was what she'd wanted more than anything else. Now the thought of dealing with Booth and the militia at once made her feel sick to the stomach.

She steeled herself and opened the door.

'I can't explain it.' Booth took the bone from Rebecca and examined it. 'The ring's taken off once they finish following me around. It's passed on! How can it be on this finger and on yours?'

'I don't know!' Rebecca grabbed it back from him. She put the heel of her hand to her forehead. 'It's so fucked up. I can't deal with all this at once. But there's one thing I can deal with.'

She headed for the door.

Booth was hot on her heels as she marched down the main staircase. 'They all gave the ring back. I can see them doing it. Alison, June, Souverign, Jellica, Edward, dear old Finchie—'

'Right.'

He increased his stride and hopped down a few steps until he was level with her. 'Listen, you aren't just going to—?'

'Don't stop me.'

They were throwing their weapons down on to the kitchen table when Jane entered.

They looked exhausted and dirty like they'd marched for a day. They were eating ferociously, having broken out their ration packs.

She just stared at them, marvelling at the power that could take them away from her and then bring them back.

Davey looked up and managed a smile at her. 'Reverend, glad you're okay. You would not believe how lost we got.'

Ruth walked straight over to her, looking grim. 'Have you seen Matthew?'

Jane pursed her lips. She couldn't lie any more.

But she suddenly realised Ruth's gaze had fixed on something past her shoulder.

Jane swung, and saw two people standing in the doorway.

Booth Hawtrey. And Rebecca. Alive. Glaring at her with a force that set Jane's stomach vibrating.

She opened her mouth to say something. Probably sorry.

The soldiers snatched up their weapons again and swung to cover the strangers.

Ruth raised a finger to point straight at Booth. 'You,' she said.

'I'm sorry?' said Booth.

'Fire!' screamed Ruth.

The doorway exploded.

The barrage caught Booth's body, sending him spinning in a flurry of blue material, bursting from his head and chest and limbs, battering him to and fro for the split second that Rebecca was aware.

Then she had turned and was running, hearing the blast of the guns all together at once just over her shoulder.

Stray shells whipped past her. Then a flare of noise that was meant for her. Bursting open the white-plastered wall.

Campbells.

They tried to get her, two arrows of shellfire blasting down both sides of the narrow corridor.

She threw herself to the ground as they connected above her head, and rolled one bounce around the corner.

She hit the wall, leapt to her feet and sprinted off again.

'Rebecca!' bellowed Jane.

She dived off after the woman, leaping over Booth's body.

'Davey, Eric, go! Bring her back!' As the men ran off, Ruth grabbed the knife from her belt and stepped up to look down at the body that lay in the doorway.

'Christ. What the fuck's this? Friend of the vicar's?' asked Morgan, squatting down beside her.

But Ruth was focused on the remains that lay in front of her. 'Stop playing,' she said. 'Open your eyes.'

The eyes flicked open. They were the only recognisable things left in a pulverised mass of blue and purple liquid where the head had been. The body wasn't much better. His left arm was severed, and his whole torso had collapsed into a shattered mass that no longer resembled a human figure. There was blue all over the walls of the kitchen.

Ruth could feel the rest of the men gathering round in amazement, wondering what they'd shot and how it was still alive. 'The famous

Booth Hawtrey,' she told them. 'And he can take much more damage than that. I know. I shot him a couple of days ago.'

She reached out, taking care not to let her hand tremble with the joy of this, and carefully inserted the point of her blade into Booth's left eye.

That brought a squeal from him.

Ruth smiled. 'This is just the beginning,' she told him.

Rebecca ran without thought, ducking from side to side, door to door. Her enemy was at her back. She ran like she was in a nightmare, her feet large and slower than the thought that wanted to move them.

How could it be the Campbells? This far south!

The family who she hurt and who hurt her. Back to hurt her again.

Her life was a fucking circle!

She skidded into the entrance hall, her feet stumbling against the edge of carpet in the centre of the polished wood, and her muscles arched in a moment as they unconsciously started to decide where they would fling her next—

And then the door exploded.

She was thrown off her feet by the explosion, stumbling back into the ornate fireplace.

Five figures walked in through the smoke, their weapons drawn before them. One was carrying a huge pack on his shoulders.

More fucking Campbells, she thought.

She would run. Let them shoot her. She didn't want them taking her alive. Not after all this time.

She was urging her limbs to get her to her feet when she heard the familiar voice. 'Rebecca?'

She fell again, staring into the smoke, her eyes wide. 'David?'

He stepped into the light, reached down and hauled her to her feet.

And it was him. His smell, the familiar feel of every line of his hand. He was looking grimly brave and wonderful, staring in righteous anger at the state she was in, the plaster in her hair, the smoke that had blackened her face. 'Rebecca,' he said again, and it was wonderful hearing his voice form her name. 'What happened? Who did this to you?'

It hurt so much, pain under younger pain, that she couldn't cry, couldn't fall into his arms. She steadied herself against him, breathing deeply, smelling him to be certain, her body needed to know it could relax. Once relaxed, tears: not yet. She put her face into his chest. Then she raised it again. 'The priest,' she said. 'The fucking

264

Campbell priest. David, she . . .' She made the words come out right first time. 'She tortured me.' She didn't like the pain that caused him, the huge reaction she felt in his chest. 'David, the *Campbells* are here. They shot Booth.'

There was a sudden sound from the door through which Rebecca had run a moment ago.

A human sound.

Standing there was Jane, staring at them. Staring at Rebecca, her hands starting to wring the air in what might have become tears or a scream.

'The Campbell priest,' said David.

Jane took a step back.

There was something calling to her from behind.

She turned her head.

There was Mary, beckoning to her. She seemed faint. Like a vague ghost. Not strong. But her presence meant something. She would see her one more time, she'd said.

Jane turned back to Rebecca and the newcomer. 'Yes,' she said.

The man swung his hand up. He was holding a pistol, pointed at her heart.

Jane turned back to Mary, and started walking to her, quite calmly.

She walked less than ten yards, into a crossroads of corridors, beside a little clock that was ticking away, knowing nothing about what was about to happen to her.

But when she got there, there was no more Mary to show her the way to go.

So she turned back and watched as Rebecca and her new friends approached her. Their weapons were all trained on her now. They were waiting for her to run.

'Jane,' she said, her tongue feeling large in her mouth. 'Jane Bruce.'

The man took a tiny moment to aim precisely, his gun held at head height.

He closed one eye. 'This,' he said, 'is for Booth Hawtrey.'

Oh yes, it would be, thought Jane. The bastard.

She took in a deep breath and held it. She kept her eyes open.

Ready. She managed a smile. Our Father, she began to herself, Who art in heaven . . .

She saw the flash.

David stepped up to examine the body.

Rebecca followed, holding on to his arm. She wanted to make sure.

When she saw, she was sure. The vicar's head had been caved in by the bullet. The woman's brain lay in a splashed arc across the woodwork. The red had extended further, over a clock that had started to chime, its face shattered as Jane's had been by the impact of a piece of bullet or bone.

It made it to four chimes, then stopped. An eternal four o'clock.

Jane's left eye was some distance away from her head, while the right looked straight out, placid.

David reached down and closed it.

'Thank you,' Rebecca said to him. 'I love you.'

There came the sound of running footsteps.

'Come on!' yelled David.

He took her by the hand and dragged her away.

Thirty-Five: The Effect of a Bullet on Human Consciousness

The airfront hit the skin on the ridge of bone above Jane's left eye. The air was heated by being pushed out of the way of what was behind it.

The bullet.

The skin was thus burnt away one moment, and the fragments parted the next, as the nose of the bullet burrowed, spinning, into the bone.

Jane's head started to move backwards, carried by the momentum. The bullet slid through the membranes around her brain and straight into the grey matter itself. No time for pain. The bullet shocked the brain like kicking a jellyfish. The weight of the shock made her skull bulge tidally, made the brain roll and sweep out around the shell in an expanding cone. The back of the skull broke under the shock before the bullet got there, and Jane's brain burst out through the gap, along with blood and superheated fragments of bone.

One fragment hit the clock. She heard it chime four times at high speed, the sound relaying urgently into the last brain-stem parts of her.

Four o'clock, something in her said. Four o'clock.

At the same time, her left eye burst out under the pressure, the optic nerve flying after it and severing. So she saw a slew across the room in the flash of the gun, then a white tunnel around that flash as the oxygen fled, then a face, no not a face, three circles converging, the basic face symbol, the first thing we know, as if—

But now there was no moment for as if.

Roaring, the bullet cut smell and taste, and a large section of muscular control to do with the left limbs. So Jane's body started to fall to the left just as it started to jerk to the right, as a lot of chemical thoughts kicked in to make her move out of the way of the bullet before she was conscious of doing so.

But those thoughts were already not quite her.

There was a space that was still herself in the roar of the bullet. No time. Just a continuous push against her forehead. But no sensation from her forehead, no pain. Knowledge from outside of sensation. Already, something inside her said. Like something expected that.

The bullet itself burst through what remained of her skull.

But already everything that was Jane was on the wall.

But what had been time had gone along with what had been Jane.

The first pressure wave had severed the chemical bonds between neurons that formed a web of association, the stories of this before that.

So what had been Jane vanished in a moment after there were moments.

She had just been struck from this story, she . . . thought.

In a new moment.

She couldn't see any more. She had no senses. Now.

She had not had time for a prayer.

There was interim.

God?

And then Jane was somewhere else.

Her memory theatre.

She stood on stage, in the spotlights.

In the auditorium, the audience were slowly, calmly heading for the exit. There were Jonathan and Alexander, her godsons, three-year-old twins, playing in their own little circle of sunshine, circling each other, their golden hair shining. Their shouts came back to her with the quality of the open courtyard where the sunlight had been. There was her father, looking sadly down at his shoes. There went the things of fear, the Too Big Owl and the Stickman. The Ornamental Devil from the other night was at the back of that row and was having trouble making his way out.

'Who are you?' Jane called to him.

He looked round briefly, his cartoon eyes filled with the horror of not knowing the answer to her question. Then he stepped through a gap in the crowd and headed on through the big pair of double doors under the central sign marked Exit.

Jonathan and Alexander were next to go through it.

And as the doors closed behind them, Jane suddenly knew the answer to her question.

It had been when her godsons, her tutor's twins, were exactly that age, the same year she'd carefully remembered that moment with them. She'd taken them on an outing, a couple of hours from Chester by pony trap. They'd stopped near one of the villages, on a little bridge overlooking a stream.

As they'd watched the fish skidding about in the waters below, Jonathan had started to tell her about Mary Poppins. In the way a child does, as if you couldn't possibly have heard of her yourself.

'She's like you,' he'd said, and she'd been immensely proud. 'She does games.'

'She'd make you be good,' she'd said.

'I'd be good for her. Anyone'd do what she says. Even you.'

'Oh, I would.'

'So she could tell you to do stuff?' He was laughing at the idea now.

'Yes.' She'd affected a display of giving one's solemn word. 'I would always do what Mary Poppins said. Because she's magic.'

And she'd believed it utterly when she'd said it, to give it force enough for the boy to laugh at, to please him. It had become true because she'd said it with such emotion.

She had seen the water and the fish and the two boys so often in her dreams. But she had never recalled those words before. They hadn't been important enough that first time the scene had come to mind for her to hold on to them. No big story attached, just a tiny love.

But the dreams would have brought the words back, replayed them in whispers beneath her consciousness, in a scene taken so much to her heart that she'd never had to green it, never had to worry about it.

The whispers of those dreams, that sincere and powerful vow that she'd never recalled making, played over and over . . . That had given form to Mary. She had stepped into a lure and been swinging from the trees without even knowing it. How foolish.

Jane sat down on the stage and watched until the last of the memories had left. Everything became very quiet. The lights above her started to dim.

Perhaps the Ornamental Devil didn't know who he had taken the place of, but she thought she'd got it now.

Everything Mary had said so far had come true.

She'd said Jane would be seeing Matthew again.

Jane was certain now that she'd known where that meeting was going to take place.

She got to her feet. She went to the edge of the stage, sat down on it, and then jumped the little way to the floor.

Clapping the dust from her hands, she walked slowly down the central aisle, to the big doors of the exit. She put her palms on them.

'Well,' she said. 'Let's just go and see.'

She walked through the doors.

Thirty-Six: Something More

The sea was green, a deep, gemlike green. It took its colour from comparison to the land, which was a golden red.

The red of the land was caused by the vast red sun which filled the sky, and its brother, more distant, but just as red, bloating another corner all of its own.

The land was dry and dusty, almost immediately, the shale beach giving way to desert with only the thinnest strand of brackish plant life. The sky made the desert shimmer with red, sandstorms rainbowing the gemlight into spirals and dunes and tumbling dust rivers of glittering colour. Yellow sulphur fans from ancient volcanoes bleached the rocks every now and then, where the sand revealed them.

Further inland, the desert gave way to mud. What had been an arboreal landscape turned into an ocean of red ooze. Which was the reason for the desert. The ooze was patterned with lines and low buildings and trenches and huge metal walls and fortifications, and it continued for mile after mile after mile. There were vast craters and masses of smaller ones. The sky was livid with continuous concussions and billows of flame. The expanse of what was beneath sped past, repeating itself over and over.

Everything had been transformed into that pattern, fed the thoughts that pattern was created by.

Crossing into night, the pattern becomes obvious, a twinkling network of veins running in creases across the land. And here comes an explosion of that: mountains ahead! An outburst of peaks that reach up into the cloudy night. And every peak has windows, artificial towers, a chain of fortresses.

At this moment, this landscape, the land and sea and sky, contained almost everyone who was ever alive.

But not everyone who *would* be.

But they didn't know that yet.

At one of the windows in one of the smaller towers of the mountain fortress, a silhouette is still this evening.

Until, with a sudden jolt, it starts to move.

'God?' said Jane.

She realised that she could see again. And speak.

She was seeing a red surface right in front of her. It was rock. She could recognise it as rock. And in the centre of the rock there was a hole. A natural window. And outside the window a landscape, a long way below: low yellow clouds hiding a low, flat plain.

Relief swept into her, so hard she felt she was about to burst into tears.

But something was missing. The point she'd been used to all her life without knowing it, where the sensation of weeping merged straight into the act. The feeling of one's face contracting around the first spasm of the tear ducts.

There was no spasm. No tears.

She was different.

She put her hands to her face, and felt the skin. It was rough like sandpaper. She realised that she was looking at her fingers, and reacted at what she saw. They were a dusty white. No fingernails. Which was . . . much more horrifying than she would ever have expected.

This was Hell. This was obviously Hell. A Boschian hell. She'd been turned into . . . She deserved it. She should accept it.

She couldn't.

She made herself concentrate. She could hear . . . the wind from across the land. Distant noises that sounded like thunder. She could smell . . .

Oh fuck.

Brimstone. All around her, in everything. In the rock under and in front of her. Everything was sulphur. It should hurt her eyes it was so strong. It didn't.

She tried to close her eyes. She couldn't. She found she couldn't even think what she'd used to do in order to do that. Without the ability, the memory of the ability became a story. A story she didn't have the language to tell. How do you close your eyes? Describe it to me!

The fear hit her for a long time, making her heart thump, making sweat form . . . all over her. She was naked. She reached down reflexively to her chest and found that it was flat. She was looking down at a man's chest. Well, something like it. No nipples. Between her legs there was a blankness, a knot of muscle. She reached down and felt it. It reacted to her touch like it was just her arm or shin.

Horrible. She felt mutilated.

She reached further around. An anus. So she could eat. Horrible, if this was Hell, to have vulnerable spots. Well of course it was horrible! She hadn't *believed* in Hell, she'd only just started to consider it when her dad came through that wall. Now she was here, and an eternity of suffering started with this realisation, the horrors of not being—

She held it in. She needed to organise this, to realise this, to accept.

At least she still had two arms, two legs, a head and fingers and . . . No toes. Just a rather flexible underside to her foot.

Our Father, who art in heaven . . .

She couldn't, if she was in Hell. To pray felt bitter and impossible and laughable and so fucking *tiny*.

She couldn't cry or close her eyes.

She tried it out loud. 'Our Father—'

The sound of it shocked her.

'Hello. Do re mi fah so.'

She sounded like an owl, speaking. The throaty boom of the lower register of an owl hoot, but modulated as if it could say all the human things. It had come from . . . She flexed her mouth. Complicated down there. Like a lot of dentistry. Like new things everywhere. A tongue, at least.

'I'm me,' she said, experimentally.

Not in English, she realised with shock. She'd heard something that sounded like *och miel*. And 'fuck' had been a sort of guttural spit. She didn't know any other languages, had never met anyone who did, so she didn't know if this was the general experience of using one, thinking in English and the words coming out in their new form. That couldn't be so, could it? And how could she understand this new language instantly, as if she was used to it already? She tried hard to make a couple of English sounds: 'Hello' and 'Jane', and found that she could, but the 'eh' of 'Jane' felt odd on her tongue, not like it was a sound that was used in speech at all. Her own name felt like an odd noise one would make to please a child. How hellish. So Hell was a place of tiny, implacable details. But she wasn't actually in pain. Indeed, this odd comfort of feeling somehow at home here made the whole idea of eternal damnation slightly more . . .

She wished for her breasts. No hair. Fine hairs, perhaps. She could feel them down the back of her strangely dented skull.

How was she holding on through this? She should be screaming all the time. She couldn't . . . She should not be . . .

She held on.

Something about the *familiarity* of all this said that this was natural. Custom reassured her where there should be no custom.

She wasn't hallucinating, a thought said as it flickered by. Too physical for that.

And she remembered dying.

She wasn't breathing, she suddenly realised. Another moment of panic. Then it eased. She just didn't have to.

Of course she didn't. It felt like her body suppressed a smile at that.

What was that *body laughter*? How could her body know what she did not? There was no other consciousness here, this was her. But there seemed to be an unconscious intelligence to her body too.

Which was familiar.

Perhaps that was something that she'd had when she was in her own body, but had never realised it. The shock of the new had just made her think about everything.

An edgy thought came to her: of course, she could *move*. If she wanted to. She could move backwards, she could turn around.

So she did turn around.

She was in a small cave. There was a gap in the far wall that led to darkness in one direction, light in another.

She didn't have to breathe, but she could use . . . something . . . to suck in air if she wanted to. This body knew how. So she did. She felt there was a refreshing scent in the sulphurous air, and that it should remind her of something.

But it didn't. The bottom of that barrel was empty. The previous life this body had had was gone.

But—

Suddenly she was with her tutor, mixing incense. Sulphur made her sneeze. Her tutor's face . . . dear Annie . . . every detail of it.

Her golden godchildren, never far from her thoughts, dancing on that day.

The Mary Poppins conversation. Every moment! Every detail!

That night watching from the window. She was there now, not greening this, but there! Every bit of the memory. Like being there again.

She felt her hands on the windowsill. Her old hands.

Matthew turned and started talking to a shape in the shadows.

Jane knew now what she was going to see.

Mary, in not so much shadow that it would disguise her, stepped forward, and thrust her hand at the young soldier's neck.

He fell as she remembered.

So now she knew. Perhaps the Ornamental Devil had been Mary's work inside her mind, or perhaps it had been her own work, just not wanting to know the truth.

Which was an irony big enough to put her in Hell.

But she was going to have her entire stock of old memories for comfort! How could this be Hell if there were comforts?

And then she realised, or rather an image came to her, a famous picture that she'd seen hundreds of times on the net, in hundreds of different contexts. She'd connected to it when she thought of her new body, she realised, when she'd imagined what she looked like.

An Aurigan. The picture they'd sent. Every child had seen and dreamed about that picture so much, wondering what it would be like to meet one. The picture was exactly like her, now.

She had become an Aurigan!

She didn't know what that meant. Maybe it was her own personal idea of damnation. But the thought made her want to find out more.

Jane went to the gap in the wall of the cave.

The act of moving made her feel scared once more. Just the way what was now between her legs changed the way she walked. Reminded her with every step. Hopeless. She wanted to cry, close her eyes, curl up in despair.

Oh come on, Jane! Step through the bloody doorway!

She smiled . . . Actually smiled. That had been Dad talking, her dad's voice, that she'd always had with her at home.

She flashed into a thousand thoughts of Dad, all perfect, all comforting.

If this was Hell, then she was going to find the truth of it, right away.

Jane walked out of the cave and turned towards the light.

Thirty-Seven: Rebecca's Fifth Birthday

You're doing something important, something to do with worms, when your mum lifts you up and swings you through the air.

'Look who's here for your birthday!' she says.

You try and look down at your worms again, but she bounces you until you look.

A very big man with a horrible smile on his face is standing in front of you. He's got a bag slung over his shoulder, a satchel with things in it.

'Father Christmas,' you say, dully, the first thing that comes into your head.

Weirdly, they both laugh.

'This is Booth Hawtrey,' says your mum. 'You remember, he's in your stories?'

You remember straight away. He can lose bits of himself and make them out of other stuff. He's full of holes. So you scream and hide your face behind Mum's head.

'That's the usual reaction,' he says. He reaches towards you, and you squirm away, hiding your head. His fingers slide down the back of your neck and you shriek again.

And suddenly he's pressing a little lump of honeycomb against your cheek.

You move your face just the tiniest bit so you can put your tongue on it. Then you snatch it and turn aside again so you can eat it.

'Say thank you,' Mum says to you.

You mumble something into her neck.

'She's wonderful,' says Booth. 'Now then, I have some spare wind generator parts here that you might need . . .'

You sneak a look at the giant, still afraid of all the differences he brings into the farm from the outside world, wondering how he can do something as scary as walk across the big flat fields and even over the hills. He brings scariness with him. He's a scary man.

'Bastard,' you slur over the honeycomb.

'Rebecca!' cries your mum. 'Where did you hear that word?'

Thirty-Eight: A House Divided

Booth was spread out across the Lutyens table.

There were parts of him all across the kitchen now. He was not secured in any way, because all his limbs were severed. His view was strange: one eye only, and that placed at a distance from him, on a shelf, connected to him by a thin thread of blue material. It had been turned around several times in the last few hours, so that he could see himself.

The soldiers had been in and out of the room. They were searching for somebody. Sometimes he heard quick bursts of gunfire. But Ruth had stayed, taking care over her orders, but unwilling to let him out of her sight.

She had only gone in the last few minutes, with great reluctance. Booth got the feeling that her men had demanded her presence as the barest minimum if they were going to be led by her.

Booth was immensely, hugely pleased that Rebecca had got away from these bastards. And he couldn't help but feel relieved by the news that the priest had been found dead, shot by whoever had entered the house. The Campbells had taken her body outside, as was common these days, and had laid it in a deserted stable. At least Rebecca couldn't be hurt by her again.

There had been no unconsciousness for him, of course. He could slip off into his memories, but the pain always called him back. Ruth had started by using her knife on him, to cut down into what remained of his body to reveal the blue material underneath. She seemed fascinated by it. They always were. She had cut circles of skin away to expose it. She had criss-crossed him like a tray of cakes, with the intention, she had told him, of skinning him alive, turning him into a blue man.

She wouldn't yet tell him why she was doing this. She seemed to think they'd met recently. Booth had told her he had no memory of that, although that might be debatable, she might be from the *déjà vu* time. But the problem seemed to go back further than that. She kept saying that she was taking revenge for her *family*.

She gave up on the slicing after a while, perhaps realising that Booth felt less pain on the exposed blue flesh than he did on his human skin. He'd tried to act the part, but, to his horror, he hadn't been able to convince her. The blue man would have been merciful. But now Ruth knew that.

An hour ago, she had taken a pair of scissors and started to cut away at his genitals. First each ball, then his cock itself, which she'd cut through in three stages.

He had screamed with fear. He had sobbed. He had begged and pleaded for her to stop in all the different ways he could think of.

The memory of it, of all this, was in him now like a pit for him to fall into. He tried not to go back to it, but every now and then, as if his mind was forcing him to accept the truth of it, he stumbled back into it. It was like a whirlpool that dragged at his thoughts, and memories of love and comfort from all across his life did nothing to help when he surfaced again and looked from that horrible distance at his mangled body.

He was cut like a rag doll. No blood. His cock had been severed as easily as his arms and legs.

He would make one out of a tyre. A bigger one. He'd watched Ruth throw it around with the soldiers when a few of them had returned, watched how they knocked it against the walls, not wanting to touch it, as affirmed and honest heterosexuals, as if their shoddy little rules applied to something that was his.

As if this world had the right to do this to him.

He knew the Campbells. He knew Ruth's direct superior, he was sure, he had had time to consider a diagram of the Campbell chain of command that he had once glimpsed. He and that man had been friendly during his stay at the Campbell court. He had tried to say that almost immediately.

She just didn't care. She was driven to hurt him. The look on her face said that his presence and existence were insults to her. She didn't seem to have a choice. As if her memories were running her. Booth wondered if he was like that, since he could remember everything. Was how he reacted just a bunch of determinants, the result of all the things that had happened to him? Or was there something more?

He felt akin to the table across which he'd been dished up.

He'd been mauled by history, too.

Eric and Davey flung themselves to opposite sides of the corridor as three fierce bursts of gunfire blasted back up it.

A one-way mist was billowing down the corridor towards them, a white fog that was solid as a summer cloud.

Eric flicked his gun out and randomly fired a burst into it.

The panelling by his gun arm exploded into woodchip. He snapped his arm back and felt the splinters flying off his bicep armour.

The fog rolled towards them.

'All right, fall back!' he shouted. 'Get Jane!'

Davey leapt from cover and ran, swerving violently along the corridor.

A burst of gunfire skewered past his head and blew a picture from the wall.

He ducked and was round the corner.

Eric took a deep breath, and just as the mist reached him, rolled out firing. He hit the far wall and was about to sprint off for his life when something bounced into his leg.

He looked down and got one hand up in time.

The flash caught him in the face.

He fell, got up.

Yelling, he stumbled down the corridor, expecting any moment to be knocked from his feet by bullets.

And was grabbed round the corner by Davey.

They stood there for a moment, panting. Eric put a hand to his left eye. Nothing. He was completely blind in it. No pain. No sight.

Oh fuck.

'Blinders,' he said. 'They've got fucking blinders!'

'They have got blinders!' Eric slammed his fist down on to the dressing table. 'They've got concussion grenades, they've got heavy fucking ordinance! They are here *on mission!*' He wore a field dressing across his left eye.

Ruth glared at him. 'If you'd opened up as soon as you saw them—'

'We did,' whispered Davey, an edge in his voice. He was pacing about the room. 'They let us go in after them, like they were running away from us, and then they—' He threw a hand out to indicate Eric's eye.

'And you ran away, and now they've taken half the house.'

'Ran away?' That was Eric again. 'Shit, ma'am, sorry we dragged you away from Booth Hawtrey!'

They were in this servant's bedroom because none of them wanted to talk to her in front of Booth now. She didn't know why that was. The others had been silent, letting Eric and Davey work their fear out on her. They were all still hungry and tired from the maze. They knew now that they'd have to sleep on a rota basis.

She was looking forward to sleep as well. She turned to Joe. 'You say they've set up a perimeter?'

The ugly engineer nodded. 'Right in the middle of the house. Loads of entrances. All of them blocked. Tripwires, minibombs, fucking lasers. This lot came mob-handed.'

'Like I said!' shouted Eric.

'And you've set up a perimeter of our own?'

'With everything we've got, but it's nowhere near as good as theirs. Ma'am, we have to attack these bastards soon. If it comes down to a war of attrition, we'll lose.'

'They can't have known that,' muttered Mark. 'What sort of mad bastard's in command? Nobody does this!'

'Listen,' broke in Eric again. 'We were *going*. We were on our way! Let's get some distance on this thing and use the rocket launcher, just bring the whole fucking Hawtrey pile of shit down on their thin fucking Hawtrey arses!'

Ruth felt them all looking at her. And she was about to say fine, let's load Booth and that mad priest into the back of the armoured car and get out of here.

But her mind was already half dreaming. And there was something about the maze. Just plucking gently at the hem of her thoughts. And she let the anger that had been building up inside her slip out.

She marched forward and grabbed Davey by the ear, and pushed his head soundly up against the wall. 'We are not leaving,' she said, looking around at the others. 'This house is Campbell property now. We can't leave them in here. We can't damage it. We're going to get through that perimeter tonight and fucking slaughter the sons of bitches? Clear?'

'And will you be coming with us, ma'am?' asked Eric.

'I'll be leading you,' she said.

She let go of Davey and examined all the faces.

They were hers again.

She headed for the door. 'Post sentries,' she told them. 'I'll work out a plan of attack. In the kitchen.'

*

David Hawtrey had decided, in the three hours that he'd been here, that he hated this house.

He walked briskly along the perimeter, as it wound through room after room, and across the ends of various corridors. The house was perfect. Too perfect. It was like it was laughing at the world outside. There was no beauty to it. No nature. It was so clean. Bringing the compiler here was like putting a heart into a dead body.

At the centre of the house there was a dining room, with a long table, covered in a perfectly white cloth. At least it wasn't set for a meal.

On sudden impulse, he grabbed the cloth and threw it to the floor.

Then he gasped, and stopped, his hands raised in a jerk of fear.

The cloth had landed just an inch or so from one of the triggers.

Shaking, he bent and carefully moved the tablecloth back. A line of triggers was stretched across the door on filament thread, and another line lay across the carpet a few feet in. Everyone in his team had practised the two little leaps necessary to enter this room until it was a matter of routine. It had taken them three repeats to make their muscles remember it. Their shared training allowed even Rebecca to do that. And he'd come in that way just now without a second thought.

But then he'd nearly gone and set off the bomb with a dramatic gesture.

His eyes went to the roof. There, set around the chandelier, was a pack of explosive, painted white to match the ceiling. It had been placed to bring the whole house down, right on the centre, right on the spine. If they could lure the Campbells in this direction, they'd run through this room and let the whole bloody thing fall on them.

Well, he might do that at the end. It had seemed a good idea three hours ago, when they'd first run in here.

He laughed, and wiped the spit from his mouth on the back of his cuff. He liked that. Irony. It'd suit this place to be destroyed by accident.

He'd left Rebecca alone with the others for too long now. And besides, they were doing the most important thing that they had to do here.

He stopped laughing, and, with the two necessary hops, left the room in the direction of the Switching Cupboard.

Rebecca watched Little Bob at work, her arms wrapped around herself.

I love you. Where the hell had that come from?

Maybe it was just the thing you said, when you'd been rescued. Give him credit, he always showed up. She let him know where she was, and as soon as she was in trouble, he turned up.

Maybe that was what love was. She'd said it out of relief and joy and it had been true.

But now it had settled back on her shoulders, and it made her uneasy. She wished she could unsay it. Or just have kept it to herself. He was going to take her feeling like that as a given again. And she didn't want to have to do or think anything about that until they were way away from here, with Booth rescued, all safely back in Hawtrey territory.

The awful thing was, looking down at the body, she hadn't even been sure she'd wanted him to do that. I mean, right, buried alive, no real excuse for that.

But . . . dead?

Her stomach had sunk at the thought of it as they ran along the corridor. The sheer Yes of having paid the bitch back in full had become a dull sort of Oh No really quickly.

She'd told David it was her. So it was her fault again.

And he was still capable of doing that kind of stuff offhand, and she probably wasn't, and that made her feel knotted too. She could feel lots of stuff inside her from last night, a shock that if she let it out of the most rigid tight grip for just a second would burst up out of her and finish her. To be her, she had to hold it in her stomach, just let it fade away. Over years. Decades. Let it join all the other things. All the fucking history that had poisoned her before. In time it'd all seep away and she'd find out what sort of self there was left after all that.

No. She'd find a self made by all that shit. She'd find that Rebecca was shit because of a shit world.

The sight of a body had nearly taken her back to the Augustine birthday, yet again. There was still green in her head, until she pissed it away. The headache seemed permanent, though, so maybe she'd been brain-damaged. All she needed. Or maybe she'd keep flashing back every time anybody said 'birthday' now, which'd be fucking hilarious. Living in the past, literally.

There was loads of other stuff down there, now, as well. Stuff she'd have to deal with in her dreams, like her brain was a room and it had been filled up with junk as a joke and she didn't know what any of the new furniture was. Or she'd lost a tooth and her mouth felt all different and . . .

Oh fuck her terrible metaphors. She didn't want to know what all this stuff she wasn't thinking about was. She just hoped it'd fade with the green. And the pain. And the history. Fucked-up Rebecca, living in circles.

She flashed back to when she'd been staring down at Jane's body. There was something extraordinary and awesome about seeing it lie there, even for those few seconds. It was as if she was somehow looking down at her own body, the room spinning about her.

So maybe it was good that the Campbells had come straight after them. They were under fire from two of them within seconds, returning shots from further down the corridor where Jane's body lay.

David had sped them further into the house, laying trails of blinders and bomblets behind them. There had been explosions and smoke, and her old unit had run like rats into the depths of the house.

The two Campbell soldiers had retreated.

The team hadn't even had to discuss what their next move was then, they all knew what could be done. They'd grabbed the stuff from their packs and laid an oppositional barrier around a little perimeter with the Switching Cupboard at its centre. One of the back staircases ran up and down the perimeter, which existed on three levels. They had bedrooms, a few dressing rooms, a private office and long defensive stretches of corridor through which, David said, he was going to funnel the opposition.

The guys had gone for it, and so at the time she hadn't said anything, because she was used to them being right. But now she thought maybe she should have said: wait, what the hell are we doing? There are only six Campbells, as far as I saw, let's go straight for them and get Booth out of there!

Well, when she said 'let's' she meant them. She couldn't pick up a gun again.

She took a few paces back and a few paces forward.

Bob was attaching a power cable from the ancient bank of valves that controlled the waterwheel generator to the black tube that was the EM compiler.

She understood that it had been a really great tactical move to take and hold the bit of the house that contained this Switching Cupboard. What she couldn't understand was why David wanted to set up a compiler. Why had Jacko been told to bring the thing into the house on his back? What were they going to do, invite the Campbells to a dance?

The other terrible thing she was dealing with was that Alec wasn't with them. 'These things happen,' David had said when she'd asked. And she could see from the looks on the faces of the others that she wasn't meant to talk about it. Something they'd left behind them in enemy territory.

Alec had been her favourite. Seeing the team again without him undermined her still more. It made her feel even more shaky.

Altogether, this felt very like a birthday.

Steven came and put his arm around her shoulder, hugged her gently to him. She let her head rest on him, appreciating the feel of them all again. They'd done so much hugging. This lot really were her family. No wonder she'd spent so long trying to escape them. The only time they'd ever fought was when David had brought her back to them from the children's house, when they'd met up in the barracks at the Hawtrey court. Then they'd berated her for sneaking off from them. Alec, crying, had even called her a traitor.

David had hit him then. They'd all hit him. He'd finally agreed, with the others, that she wasn't a traitor, that she'd just got scared.

David had used his influence that time to erase the incident from her record, as long as she never returned to the militia. Which she hadn't wanted to do. He'd saved her from the consequences of the Singh movie as well. Presumably, and she could hardly believe this, he had even saved her from what might have happened to her when she had left him and was supposedly out of his protection.

Why was she always fighting going back to him? Why was she even fighting the thought now?

She bit once more at the callus on her thumb.

David marched back in, his eyes sparking all over the room. He playfully pushed Steven off and put his own arm around Rebecca. 'We're safe,' he told her.

'Are we?'

'The perimeter's holding them off. They've realised it's there and they'll be looking into ways of dealing with it.'

'Why are we setting that thing up?' She pointed to the compiler.

'Interrogations.'

'Using a compiler?'

'Oh yes,' said Steven, glancing up from where he was helping Bob with the wiring. 'You should see what this girl can do. Goes way beyond anything we've got.' With a twirl of wires he finished what he was doing and nodded to Little Bob. 'Ready?'

Bob nodded back and threw a switch.

The compiler hummed into life. The sound of an internal fan and the tiny clicks of switches inside the case that Rebecca associated with the end of a ball, after the band had started to pack up and there was no music to conceal it.

She squeezed David's arm and kissed him lightly on the cheek. 'I love you,' she said. And all the new stuff in her head was shoved away and didn't bother her any more.

And David laughed, in a really nice way.

Jane's body lay in an empty stable, with nobody to attend to it.

Joe and Mark had put it there, with all due respect, because a corpse must never be left in a house. They had taken everything useful that was on Jane for the Campbell cause. Davey had run round to the stables a few minutes later, when he'd learned where they'd put her, and, with one eye on the doorway to see if there were any Hawtreys out here, had read a quick prayer from the Reformed English Bible over her.

So Jane lay there, with the dressings that had been used to scoop up her flesh and her dead eye, insects already starting to infest the pile of bloody straw beneath her. No eyes saw her. No one observed her.

Until someone did.

The shadow elongated out of the shadows of the wall, and fell over her.

'What fools these mortals be,' said a gentle, reedy voice.

The shadow grew a hand in the afternoon sunlight, an eclipse that made the shape in the straw indistinct.

When the hand withdrew, Jane was gone, and the straw in the stall was fresh and clean. A great mass of insects shifted and withdrew, doubtless puzzled.

The triangle of darkness formed by the sun and the wall had gone back to being its old shape. The figure had moved on to provide clean straw for the horses in the next stable. And then he was gone completely.

The afternoon faded into night, and all the natural things outside the house did what they did, returning to their nests or leaving them. Their only history was the distance of evolution, and as yet they knew nothing of it.

A pair of feet in blue deck shoes walked quietly along the corridor towards the kitchen. The high, lilting voice was muttering to itself, desperately, forcefully. 'I will not,' it said. 'I will *not!*'

But, against its will, the figure kept walking.

*

286

Booth watched himself lying across the table. He was listening to the house cracking with the oncoming night, the furniture and walls expanding and contracting.

And to the footsteps that were advancing very slowly down the corridor outside.

Neither of his eyes was placed to see through the kitchen doorway. It was his own destroyed body or a view almost completely obstructed by the blasted pestle and mortar. His analogy of a brain was trying to make sense of the two images together, so he had two swimming globes of confusing sights hovering before him. And he couldn't close his bloody eyes.

He'd tensed up when he first heard the footfalls, anticipating that it was Ruth returning to hurt him once more. She'd spent the afternoon doing that. Mostly with kitchen instruments that were now sticking out of his torso. But she'd only gone to join her men for some sort of assault a few minutes ago.

Besides, the footsteps were hesitant, sneaky. He thought for a while that it was one of Ruth's enemies come to rescue him. But the steps weren't just being stealthy. They were faltering, shuffling, as if their owner was being prodded towards the doorway and kept holding himself back.

It was at moments like this that he could feel the power of now, see the light of it, casting shadows back down into time. It was absurd, that there was a sort of time he couldn't enter, the future beyond the glowing point. He imagined the door, willing someone to come through it, pushing against his physical bonds and the mental one of time, trying to get through to the future where rescue would come.

But nothing happened.

After a while, the footsteps stopped shuffling, and retreated. They got faster and faster as they left. Booth could feel the relief in that sound. For whoever it had been. Not for him.

He tried to ignore the kaleidoscope of his own flesh and lose himself in his memories once again.

Ruth and her men crouched in the corner of the games room, absolutely silent.

Their weapons were drawn, and they were all watching the doorway, where Joe was lying flat on his stomach, his big fingers using tiny instruments to remove the centre from a pea-sized black blob that hung on an invisible thread.

Ruth could hear the clocks in the room ticking, and feel Davey breathing at her side. Her thoughts kept turning back to Booth in the kitchen. She couldn't help it. She felt vulnerable, leaving him there. Someone might come and get him. Take him away.

Finally, Joe let go of the pea, looked back over his shoulder and nodded.

The others scampered forward.

Joe had tapped into the circuit that ran around the whole wired map of bomblets that lay across the sitting room, and had deactivated them all.

She was going to wave for Eric to go first, but no, it should be her.

She stepped into the room, and crept on the balls of her feet past the settees and the easy chairs and the elephant's foot that had been made into a stand for walking sticks. The coals in the fireplace looked clean. Like they'd been polished.

Maybe Eric was right. She'd quoted regulations at him but what the hell, they were in the outback. They ought to get out and flatten this *Empty Court*.

So why didn't they?

She put a hand to her forehead. Something weird had happened to the atmosphere in this place. She felt like a child creeping around a strange house. Down from a strange bed. Doesn't quite know where she is. Sounds of adults in some distant room. The smells of a place you don't know. She was scared, she realised, and they hadn't encountered the enemy yet. It would be a relief when they did.

Lack of sleep. They were all dreaming as they walked. That was why she'd made that bad decision, and she didn't feel now like she could back out of it. Fuck, that was straight out of the officers' training course: you decide you're wrong, you say out loud you are before anyone dies.

She looked back to the men. They were looking curiously at her, wondering why she was squatting by the sofa, not going on.

She pretended she was straining her neck to look around the corner into the next room.

Not going on now would be giving in to fear. That was why they were doing this.

That was why.

She rose and walked stiffly across the thick carpet to the entrance of the next room. She looked carefully across the gap. Nothing. Only one line of defence here, then.

She waved for the others to catch up with her.

They scampered across the room and did so.

She stepped through the gap and swung slowly around.

She was in another long sitting room, this one with big windows that let in the night.

And standing at one end of it, looking shocked out of her wits, was the woman Jane had called Rebecca.

Ruth yelled and raised her gun.

The others burst into the room behind her.

Rebecca ducked out.

The others leapt to pursue. But: 'Slowly!' bellowed Ruth. 'Watch it!'

They rushed to the far door where Rebecca had stood, but, thank Christ, they didn't go through it.

A long, polished corridor, lined with suits of armour.

Rebecca was just reaching the far end of it. 'David!' she was shouting.

Ruth didn't look at her for more than a second. She'd run her eyes around the edge of the doorway. If the girl was fleeing to the others, this part of the house must be thought of as secure. So they were near by. So the corridor could become a shooting gallery. So—

'Go!' she yelled. 'Get to the end before they get here!'

The soldiers burst through the door in front of her and sprinted for the end, Mark swinging Matthew's machine gun in front of him, ready to mow randomly. Eric was right there with him. The rest of them were trailing.

She thought she should tell them to—

Something fell between them.

Mark and Eric spun round.

It was a safe, Ruth registered in a moment of dreamy horror. A safe with a big wheel lock. It had fallen from a plaster hole in the ceiling. Flecks of white had fallen everywhere.

It carried a net with it. A net that—

The net exploded into white foam. The two soldiers vanished.

'Gel!' shouted Ruth. 'Break it down!'

The foam had filled the corridor exactly, producing a wall. Ruth's team blazed away at it, their shells making it fall apart into random chunks of slime that still held together. The sound of gunfire burst and echoed back around them, thunder that rolled off down the corridor and then came back at them.

The wall fell away.

Ruth kicked through it, drawing her knife.

And found there was nobody there now.

Mark and Eric had gone.

Along the corridor, three new nets of miniature weapons hung.

As the silence died away, Ruth realised why the others were now looking so fearful.

From around the corner of the corridor were coming distant screams.

'You Hawtrey pieces of shit!' she screamed. 'I'll kill all of you! I'll kill Booth Hawtrey!'

Behind her, she heard Davey start to wail, low and deep in his throat.

David looked down at the soldier who knelt on the floor, his hands bound behind his back. He had three blue streaks dyed down his shaved scalp.

The streaks annoyed David. Another tribal sign. His team didn't wear things like that any more. They were themselves, and nobody else in the world was.

They were alone in one of the bigger guest bedrooms, on the top floor. He had led his captive here until he found a room that felt right for this. It had been like choosing food in the mess when you weren't sure what you wanted to have, or even if you were hungry.

But this room had called to him. This room felt right.

He knew he was probably going along with one of the random emotions he'd set the compiler to project, but that didn't matter. In the village, the compiler had produced chaos on chaos, and so he hadn't seen the point, besides allowing him his Charlotte. Here, it was the only force of nature in this sick, mock-civilised house, the only honest thing, the only indicator of the way the world actually fucking was. The compiler here would finally let him have his Rebecca.

He pulled the dagger from his belt. 'How do you want to die?' he asked the man.

'With a Hawtrey's neck in my teeth,' hissed the soldier.

David closed his eyes, the weight of the world on his shoulders again. 'Of course. Right. Whatever you say,' he said.

He stepped forward, reached down, and carefully slit the man's throat. He did it twice to make sure, then stepped back from the body, leaving it thrashing and frothing in the middle of the room.

That was better. That felt more like the world David had grown up in. The room wasn't perfect any more.

The wave swept over him at that moment.

He was mounted on ecstasy. It jerked his limbs, made his mouth spasm open. He cried out a little baby sound.

He fell to his knees and wept with the pleasure.

He came round after a few moments, and looked over at the dead body. The compiler must have done that. Linked up with his expectations. A feedback loop about the freedom to kill. Not the killing itself. He wasn't some sort of sadist.

Killing in a particular place.

He realised it was true as he thought it.

He got to his feet. He headed for the door. He didn't put his knife back in his belt.

The others had the one-eyed soldier tied up in front of the compiler. His hands were bound to his feet behind his back. He had been lightly gagged. His one eye was looking around wonderingly, as if this wasn't what he'd expected at all.

David walked in, his knife still drawn. He saw the loving look in Rebecca's eyes and thought he'd kill the man here and now, show off to her.

But no. That didn't feel right.

He stood there, waving the knife to the rhythm in his mind. The rhythm of the compiler. They were all moving to it, even the prisoner. It was like an ocean, the swell and fall of the moon's tides.

But there were . . . interruptions. Barriers. The great emotional swell was stunted by . . . by the *shape* of this damned building.

He walked around the room a little, felt where the passion rose and where it fell. Steven had leaned back against the wall of the Switching Cupboard, his eyes flicking every now and then to Rebecca.

David came to one particular wall and put his palms on it. Through there.

He slipped the knife into his belt and went to pick up the prisoner. He threw him over his shoulder and hauled himself to his feet. The prisoner grunted and said something harsh behind his gag.

'Hey,' Frank said gently. 'I thought we were going to interrogate him?'

'No,' said David. 'I'm taking him . . .' He pointed vaguely. 'That way. Rebecca, you're with me.'

'Oh yes!' laughed Rebecca.

She took his free arm and they headed off at a trot into the interior of the house.

They had a nice little walk, David whistling as he marched along. 'The Campbells have gone back to their bolthole, in the kitchens.'

'How do you know?' Rebecca asked.

'I don't know. I can . . . feel them there. The feeling would change if they moved.' He laughed. 'The compiler's messing us all up. Great.'

Rebecca squeezed his arm.

They carried on blithely through the corridors of the house, the prisoner shouting unintelligible threats through the gag.

David stopped in the main hallway, a frown on his face.

Rebecca stopped with him. Was there something wrong? Had she upset him? Fuck, she was always messing this up somehow. This time she was going to hold on to him, do all the things she was supposed to do. 'Sweetheart,' she whispered. 'What's wrong?'

'We're going to need a spade,' he said.

'Oh!' Rebecca was pleased to be able to help. 'I know where there's one!'

She ducked into the cupboard by the doorway and brought out a shining black-handled spade with a sharp edge.

'You are *so* useful,' David sighed.

Rebecca grinned and shouldered the spade as they left the house.

They walked right round the house, David convinced that the Campbells wouldn't see them.

They sauntered down a little avenue of entwined canes where ivy grew. Big moths were fluttering all around, attracted by the lights of the house. The night was freezing, but Rebecca didn't mind.

She had her David back. Her idyll.

Of course, the compiler had done this to her. She wasn't stupid enough to think that these emotions had just burst out of her at the moment it was switched on. But the feeling was wonderful. For once in her life, everything was okay. The history that she and David had together finally seemed to mean something.

God, she wanted to take that machine back to court and keep it in her bedroom. To be able to say she loved him, like she bloody should have done all along, and actually mean it. It had taken away all the horror she'd felt welling up inside her, the delayed shock of what the priest had done to her. Just made it all go away. Bloody fantastic.

They were heading for the maze, she realised.

The prisoner noticed it too. He started to buck and cry out.

Rebecca hit him lightly across the head with the spade and he stopped, afraid of more blows.

'Good girl,' murmured David. 'We're going to take him right to the middle and bury him alive.'

Rebecca closed her eyes for a moment. Oh no. Not now. Just when she thought everything was okay. Was she really going to spoil this? 'I don't want to do that,' she said.

'What?' They'd halted at the entrance, the first long avenue of box hedges lay in front of them, illuminated only by the distant lights of the house.

It came out of her mouth in a rush. 'I don't want to go into the maze. With the spade. And him. I don't want to bury him alive.'

'Why?'

Rebecca struggled to find an explanation. Her guts were churning. Everything suddenly seemed risky again. 'I don't know,' she said. She smiled at him, desperate. 'You know I don't always know why I do things.'

He looked at her for a moment, and she was terribly afraid that he was going to shout. Then he reached out and awkwardly took the spade from her. He slung it under his free arm. 'All right,' he said. 'You can wait for me here. I'll see you when I come out.' And he set off, the prisoner bucking again on his shoulder.

Rebecca sat down on the dewy grass, hugely relieved. Everything felt all right again. 'Don't get lost!' she called after him.

'It's all right,' he called back. 'I can't.'

David walked swiftly through the perfect maze, following his nose at every turn. It felt like he was piloting a boat down a fast river, letting himself be swept along. Even with his burden, it only took him ten minutes to find his way to the centre.

As he walked into the clearing, he stopped in shock, staring at what lay before him. He'd known enough bomb damage to recognise a subsided building when he saw one. That was more like it.

He put the man down on the ground, ignoring his cries, and went to inspect the ruin. He experimentally dug in a few places, and finally found a deep cleft of impacted soil above the roof of what he was fairly sure was a church. Fantastic. Exactly right.

He dug out a hole about eight feet deep, and the right length.

An appropriately nasty death for a Campbell. And a good addition to the ruin. If anybody ever excavated it, they'd find a madly contorted skeleton in exactly the oddest place. But that was the joy of it: nobody ever would.

It would also make the waves sweeping over the house feel that little bit better. Might allow the full tidal wave of emotion to burst through. And then . . . turn them all into blissful animals, just reacting to it as it washed back and forth around the world. For ever and ever.

He was really looking forward to fucking Rebecca during that.

He put the spade down, and went to haul the man on to his shoulder again.

The man struggled violently, shouting into his gag. David juggled him on his shoulders for a few feet as he tottered, then threw him into the hole.

He didn't waste time taunting the man or trying to talk to him. He just started shovelling the earth back into the hole, as fast as he could.

The shape under the soil thrashed violently, trying to slough off the mud, but David persisted, working faster and faster. After a few feet had been thrown into the pit, he started packing it down hard.

Amazing how quickly the man vanished, and the movement couldn't be seen any more. The power of mud.

He realised, as he completed the last few inches, that the wave was starting to break over him again. He made himself hold on to the spade as he exulted, feeling the whole shape of the house roll and shake with him.

But there were still barriers, still interruptions to the blast of the wave.

He staggered to his feet and shouldered the spade, looking down at his work.

Another impediment knocked down. Just a few more to go.

From the ground there came a muffled scream. It continued, broke into tiny sounds lost in the night.

Whistling a tune he made up as he went along, David headed for the exit.

Thirty-Nine: Dada Disco

Rebecca lay awake in the huge bed in her new bedroom.

She hadn't been able to get to sleep. All her stuff was in her old bedroom, from which she was separated by two defensive perimeters.

She ought to be able to sleep. She was knackered. Last night she'd just had a terrible, unconscious sort of sleep. Now she really needed to just switch off and rest, let the stress drain away.

It was all the strange thoughts sloshing about in her head. Every time she closed her eyes, she found that she was going to dream about something that scared her. Either a greening return to a birthday, or something even stranger and more terrifying. So she kept jerking awake right on the edge of sleep.

She wished David was here. But the men. They couldn't be seen to be shagging. If they were going to be together now, which obviously they were. Besides, her condom was behind the lines.

Thanks to that wonderful machine, she loved him. And he loved her. He hadn't said so since he'd come here, but he'd better be bloody thinking it. He seemed to be on some sort of ecstatic trip: what else was it going to be?

He'd come out of the maze with a look of exultation on his face, the shovel covered in mud. She'd run to him and kissed him, and they'd fallen on to the ground, snogging violently.

She'd wanted to make him come, right there, like she always did, but he just laughed as she fumbled at his britches, and pushed her away and told her there'd be time for that later.

He had said that. So that was okay. She didn't have to worry. They'd get to that soon.

She wished she could green reassuring stuff like that instead of whatever the greens had put into her head.

Little Bob and Steven had finished their work on the compiler by the time she and David got back. It was washing them at intervals with hope and happiness. Apparently it was running fear and hopelessness for the areas of the house where the Campbells were. Steven had said that he'd never found it so easy to calibrate a compiler to work a particular area.

So Booth would be feeling the fear and hopelessness too. On top of whatever the Campbells were doing to him.

David hadn't said anything about rescuing him. Since he'd got back from the maze, he'd been outlining plans to snare the remaining Campbells one by one. He'd found a map of the house on the net, and indicated certain rooms, saying he wanted to torture each one to death in a particular place.

The others had applauded and laughed. But David hadn't even mentioned Booth's name.

Booth could feel pain, she knew. The Campbells might be doing terrible things to him. And shithead as he was, he didn't deserve that.

She closed her eyes again and tried to sleep. Obviously, the compiler was making her feel affection for everyone and everything. Now, her dreams were going to be full of imagined tortures that Booth was going through.

And, damn it, when she tried to put those aside, she was back with the guy buried in the maze, feeling awful for him, too.

Never mind that his fucking people had done the same thing to her! The compiler had turned her into a real fainting Alice.

She opened her eyes again. Fuck, maybe if they could sort out Booth, she could finally get some sleep. She should go to David, get him to alter the compiler to send the Campbells running from the house.

No, he wouldn't do that, he wanted to get them into his particular rooms.

A memory came into her mind. A figure bending over her. A pair of blue shoes. There was someone in this house who'd rescued her, who'd healed her. He had worked miracles. What with the compiler and Jane and David and all the memories slopping out of her ears she hadn't even started to wonder about who the hell that had been until now.

Maybe he could help Booth in the same way.

She suddenly realised that she probably knew where to find him.

Rebecca eased herself out of bed and started to get dressed.

When the team had first laid out the defensive perimeter, Rebecca had thought she recognised the little confluence of stairways. She found it again without too much trouble, and stood there, listening.

The great house was silent in the night. She'd walked softly all the way here for fear of disturbing that silence, and for fear of waking the gang. They'd probably shoot her before they realised who she was.

It was easier to feel the pulse of the compiler at night. Less to get in the way. It felt like the house was a feverish dream, like you could wander the stairways forever in a daze and never quite get where you wanted to go. It felt fictional. Or rather fictitious. She couldn't imagine the place full of people. How could anyone just slonk about here, work here, actually play that table-football game? You'd always be looking over your shoulder.

She looked over her shoulder.

Nothing there.

She chose the little staircase that led up at an angle from the others, like it was hiding, and found the door with the Cross nailed to the wall beside it.

There was no sound coming from inside this time.

But still she hesitated. What if something leapt out?

She put her hand on the doorknob. 'Hello?' she whispered, trying to project it through the door. 'It's me. You saved me. I'm coming in.'

She turned the knob and stepped into the room.

There was nobody inside.

Rebecca walked into the room and looked around at the pennants and the certificates, and the photo of the boy in uniform with sad eyes. She instantly understood what this was. She felt almost at home.

She went to the radio receiver and idly turned a dial. Was that all she'd heard that night? Had someone left it switched on, or when there was nobody to hear it, did it come alive and whisper through the radiation of the world quietly, trying to hear signs of civilisation? Is anybody out there? it would ask, the dial slowly spinning. Is anyone doing anything tonight? Or is it just war and love, war and love, across the airways of the world, until we die out?

She let go of the dial and went to the window. The grounds stood empty and perfect in the moonlight. She watched the shadow of a cloud alter the shades of the driveway. She saw owls hunting over the forest.

Over the back of the house, behind her, there was a man buried in the maze, going through what she'd gone through. She couldn't get it out of her head. David had done it, so it must be okay, and he was the enemy, but . . . the compiler didn't seem to be taking that particular thought out of the little corners of her mind.

Suddenly she felt like she was going to cry. And that was a terrible thing, because the love had been propping her up and holding it in, and if she started to, the love might burst and she'd be back to just herself again.

She started to bite her thumb, and then, to stop it, smashed her fist down on to the table.

The radio set clattered to the floor.

Rebecca stooped to retrieve it, fumbling with the wires and leads. The casing was broken, little shards of some hard black material everywhere. She gathered it all up and slid the set back on the table.

Just as she let go of it she knew.

She wasn't alone in the room.

She turned slowly.

In the doorway stood a very thin, very white man. His face was so emaciated that his eyes bulged. His hands were spindly chalk, hanging at his sides. His hair was a few strands of black at his temples. He wore a blue blazer, white trousers and shirt, and blue flat shoes. Rebecca might have been scared, loved up as she was, but there were stretches about the man's mouth, lines of weakness that seemed to say that although now he was staring at her awkwardly, he might have a really lovely smile.

'You're him,' she said. 'In the photograph.'

'No,' he said. 'But I wish I were.'

She was surprised at his voice. It sounded high and sighing, like the wind in a tree. An accent she didn't recognise. Very precise and gentle. 'I'm sorry about the radio,' she said. 'I hope it's okay. I just—' She turned her head and saw that the casing wasn't cracked, that the radio now looked just like it had before. 'It's you who does that,' she said, her own voice suddenly that of a little girl.

'Now you don't have to be sorry.' He started to move away from the door, already on his way again. 'So you can tell yourself this was a good dream.'

It would be just that if she let him go.

She rushed to the door and put her hand on his arm.

It was solid. She was almost surprised by that. He wasn't a ghost. 'Wait,' she said. 'Wait a second. I came to find you. To thank you for healing me, for saving me.'

He looked down at her hand. She took it away. For a moment it seemed like he couldn't think of anything to say. Then the corners of the mouth cracked and that smile appeared. A small, sad smile. 'It's what I do here. I clean up.'

'You haven't done it for any of the others. You haven't healed them!'

298

'I will, when I have the opportunity. Well, for most of them I will . . . I don't seem to have much choice lately, which is rather worrying . . .' He wandered back into the room, and, as an after-thought, closed the door behind him. 'You'll have to forgive me. I haven't had a conversation with anyone in centuries.' He suddenly extended a thin hand to her, making his mind up in a moment. 'Let me introduce myself. I am Simon Trent. The original owner of Heartsease.'

Rebecca shook his hand really gently.

Davey was on his knees in the corner of the kitchen, praying violently, his head bouncing up and down.

Joe and Morgan had their kit bags out, and were swiftly checking an inventory of every weapon and device they carried.

Ruth was at the table, Booth could see from his dislocated left eye, leaning over the rest of him, a hacksaw in her hand.

She had spent the last hour busily and noisily preparing her tool kit, calling to him about what she was going to do to him next.

They were all afraid, Booth knew. Two of them had been captured. They weren't keeping their silence around him now. They had run back in, shouting at each other, and from that Booth had found out that Rebecca was still alive, that she'd led them into a trap. It sounded like the Campbells were fighting Hawtreys.

He'd started to sweat and shake at the approach of their running footsteps, as much as he could. As he did every time Ruth had come back to the table. But this time he'd been suffering for hours, in an agony of waiting, feeling hopeless, imagining that Ruth would just discard the pieces of him carelessly and that he'd lie, conscious, in the outback, unable to do anything but live and remember. It had been a terrible fantasy that had shocked him with the reality of it every time he came out of his memories and back to the shadow of now. He didn't think he could keep going much longer. He wondered what madness would be like for him. He felt a terrifying intimacy and fellow feeling for Ruth, a sick fondness that he knew was his mind's last twist: a pet licking the hand that's about to drown it. He wanted to defy her like the hero of a movie. But all he could do was sob. Which he'd been doing at intervals as she got her equipment together.

The Campbells had decided that they were going to wait until the early hours, and then try once more to attack the other soldiers, when they wouldn't have a trap prepared. The one called Davey, who seemed as afraid as Booth was, had wanted to leave, but Ruth had slapped him across the face and told him she was going to retrieve her men.

So there had been nothing for them to do but wait and prepare. When Booth had realised that, he'd started to whimper again.

They were all afraid and hopeless and losing it, he realised. Something was affecting them all. What the barbarians of this century called EM, and he called atmosphere, spookiness, all those rough, lovely, fudged words that didn't mean one was desperate to grab any territory one could be certain of, including the realms of god and ghosts.

Now Ruth waved the hacksaw over her head so he could see it. 'Tonight I'm going to cut your head off,' she told him. 'And boil it on the stove.'

'Are you? Are you really?' Booth had to say something to stop himself thinking about it. 'Before you do, any chance of a cup of tea?'

'This was Alisdair, my son.' Trent put a finger on the photograph. 'He was killed in the First World War.'

'When was that?' Rebecca was leaning against the desk, watching him, fascinated. She was still sure she was going to wake up.

'Three hundred and thirty-three years ago. He died in 1915.'

'So why are you still here? How are you still alive?'

Trent walked slowly to the window and put his large white hands up to the glass. He turned his head slowly to her, the mouth splitting open in a painful smile. 'If you want to know the whole story,' he said, 'I suggest we go for a walk.'

They walked over and through the defensive perimeters, Trent waving a hand to make the threads part, and, Rebecca noted with a pleasurable little jolt, slip closed behind them again. The man's power seemed so supernatural that she wasn't afraid of anything. If they met the Campbells she was sure he'd wish them away too.

They came to the hallway, which he looked around sadly, noting the mud on the carpets.

They walked through it and the mud vanished behind his steps.

They stopped at the closet by the door and Trent moved inside, returning a moment later with one of the Campbells' heavy coats, which he slipped over her shoulders. 'You'll catch your death,' he murmured.

Rebecca smiled at him.

They walked at a sharp angle up from the house, along a muddy path into the forest. Rebecca was glad that she'd put her boots on, but the mud worked its way up her bare legs. She wondered if Trent's magic could clean that as well.

He walked beside her, looking at her often, as if to check he was really doing this extraordinary thing, talking to somebody.

'You've been alone a long time, haven't you?' she said.

He nodded quickly. 'I have been alone in Heartsease for around a hundred and eighty years. Mostly. Various people have occupied the house from time to time.' He glanced up at the moon that scudded out of the clouds overhead, illuminating the fine chiselling of his totally white face. 'Things . . . happen to them. And I clear up afterwards.'

'What sort of things?'

'They . . . fight. They find divisions in their points of view. A group of monks took up residence thirty years ago. They lasted six months. They kept splitting into smaller and smaller factions.'

'So . . . what does that?'

'The forces of the house.'

She thought about David, asleep in his bed. And about Booth, in the hands of his enemies. 'You have to tell me—'

'You asked,' he began suddenly, interrupting her, 'about Alisdair.'

'But—'

'This is the whole story. We have time. We're going all the way to the folly But you must know my reluctant place in this whole evil enterprise. Like many people in this decayed century of yours, I find myself part of a faction, rather than following a great cause.'

'You sound like Booth.'

He laughed, very bitterly, a sound like the cry of a bird. 'I do not! As you will hear, I hope that nothing of me is like him, for he plays a large part in this story.'

Rebecca looked at him, stunned. She hadn't expected him even to recognise the name. 'He does?'

Trent sighed, and, to Rebecca's shock, took her arm in his. 'Let me begin at the beginning,' he said. And then he began to tell his story.

Forty: Rebecca's Fourth Birthday

You're running between the house and the barn, slapping your palms on one and bouncing off back towards the other. Your feet patter on the flagstones, back and forth. It's a new place to live, but you haven't wondered about going back to the old place, this is just where you are, now.

You might still just be able to find your way back, over the miles of open country. In a few weeks you'll have lost that. The thing that let you count a wheeling flock of migrating swallows in a moment – not that you ever did, because you only know numbers as far as ten – has eased itself behind the curtain, slipped into the mechanisms of you, as it should.

And so much else has slipped behind the curtain too. All the details that you had saved up, that were asking you to do something, have been trodden down into who you are. And you're growing up between them, like a tree breaking the ground.

You have no thought in you at this second. Just your body learning to do this, as your feet thunder on the flagstones, back and forth.

You hear Mum and Dad starting to sing. You stop. They're in the kitchen, from the sound. You've lost the picture of the old kitchen already. The way they're singing says that they want you to hear it and come to them. It's a game. 'Happy birthday to you' is what they're singing. Like Mum has been singing to you for weeks, and she's been saying it in a voice that means this is important.

You lurch suddenly from a body that's learning how to be a body to a person that needs to know the answers to all the questions about birthdays. Because it'll be fun, and it's about you, this is *your* birthday, and you're the most important thing in the world.

Panting with excitement, your breath all steamy in the cold, you hurtle off towards the kitchen shouting 'Birfday!' at the top of your voice, over and over.

Forty-One: The Mad Parade

'In 1917, Alisdair was a major in the Royal Artillery. He was posted to defend the little Belgian town of St Julien during what became the Second Battle of Ypres. Initially it wasn't too bad. He was always talking about the Canadians in his letters home. How different they were. How they kept laughing at his accent. He loved meeting people from new places. He had begun a novel, you know, an H.G. Wells sort of thing, just a few chapters, before he joined up. It was called *The World Unchained*, and it was about how the sacrifice of our heroes in the war would free ordinary folk from the burdens of, well, what we called capitalism. Just one more effort and then . . . pow! I don't know how he'd have finished it. It would be nice to know what he thought freedom was like, because that might give me some idea of the heaven he's in now. I wish I could tell him how naïve he was, because now I'm sure he'd agree.

'The Germans laid down a barrage of chlorine gas shells, and the gas drifted right across his battery. He didn't run, like a lot of them did, the silly thing. He was trying to save the horses when he died. Or so I'm told. One never really knows. It was a nice detail for his commanding officer to include, at any rate.

'This was before the war became a bloodbath. Or rather this was the point that it did. Before then, we thought we could win, and so did they. After that, well, it all bogged down, and it felt like the fighting would go on forever. Those times feel like these, somehow. Like a great circle. We've learnt nothing.

'I was winding down, letting the old firm look after itself, satisfied with the managers I'd appointed. I'd taken early retirement, and I was in seventh heaven, on holiday every day at my old place down in Hove. Well, as much of a holiday as was possible while the war was on. I was doing my bit, with charity nights and pulling strings to get celebrities along for them and all that. Oh, I was busy.

'That's where I got the telegram. My man brought it to me on the balcony. It was a brilliant day, sunshine slanting down through the canopy, red and white stripes . . . He knew what it was, I could see it on his face. I don't remember much of my life, wandering this place does that to you, but I can recall that moment . . . oh, so well, every detail.

'I took the damn thing down to the shore. Not that we had much of a shore. The beach was covered with barbed wire. Huge wooden spikes. Mines, floating in lines out at sea. Sunshine over that little lot . . . and on that day . . . It's tempting to remember that it was raining, the pathetic fallacy, but it was not. I walked straight through it all, threw my jacket down and started climbing over the barbed wire, heading for the sea. I suppose I just wanted to be close to him, nearer to the continent. My man came clambering after me, shouting. He pulled me back from getting into the sea. I fought him quite fiercely. He damn near had to knock me out.

'I think I went somewhat insane, then. Alisdair's mother had passed on some years before. That's something I hope you never know, what it's like to be a parent with no issue, all of a sudden. One's purpose departs. The world becomes a limited collection of objects, being produced and decaying over time.'

Rebecca nodded violently and said: 'Yes, yes. Yes.'

'So you *do* know. I'm so sorry. The disease of this age, I suspect. The malaise of separation. From each other and from God. That was what had me, back then. I took to spending my days in bed, not eating, anticipating death without ever thinking I was doing so.

'My man, Phillips, was very concerned. He brought a radio set in and placed it by my bed, and insisted that we had it on, while he did the dusting. There was nothing British in those days, this was before the British Broadcasting Company started. But he was very keen on the novelty of hearing the concerts from the Dutch radio stations. Light promenade music. For the troops.'

Rebecca stared at him. The idea of listening to foreign radio stations astonished her.

Trent caught the look and sighed. 'At any rate, he left it there during the night. On one occasion, I woke from a dream, a dream where Alisdair had appeared, and I woke very frightened, and needed something to remind myself of real life. I didn't want to wake Phillips. So I paced about the room for a bit. Couldn't even put the lamps on, because of the blackout. It occurred to me to find out what else was on the radio, see if I could find anyone talking English or French . . . You look rather French, if I may say so . . . no, don't look like that! It was meant as a compliment! So in the middle of the night I switched the thing on, and got myself a glass of water while it warmed up. I spent the night tuning in to different stations. I found two or three. But vast empty spaces between them, just whining noise, like the wind. I found it rather comforting. Anyhow, I chanced across something and kept following it. It seemed to move slowly up and down the dial. It was a voice. Towards dawn, I managed to isolate it, sitting there on my bed in my pyjamas. I suppose in retrospect I should have had heart failure, but at the time it seemed so . . . miraculous. You can't be afraid of those you love.

'For there, fluttering in and out of existence, was Alisdair's voice, unmistakably. He was speaking quite carefully, as if he was reading off a script, and he was repeating what he said every quarter of an hour or so.

'I sat there for ten minutes, spellbound. Then I went and fetched my notebook, and started writing down the words.

'It took four hours to get every detail, many repetitions, much chasing of the signal, until I realised that it was moving steadily, that I could keep track by slowly moving the dial. What Alisdair was so studiously reading out, from his seat in heaven, was a set of plans. He was describing the heights and lengths in measurements of feet and inches. That first night, he set out only the general structure. And of course I knew this was for me, meant for my ears, something to allow me to go on. After I was sure that I'd written down every word, I went back to bed, and slept so soundly that Phillips had to wake me for lunch.

'The next night, of course, I was back at the radio, and this time he was describing in detail the layout of one of the lower rooms. He described even the smallest features. He managed only two rooms that night.

'Over the next few weeks, I wrote down everything he said. I compiled many notebooks full of information. On occasion, during the day, when I wasn't at my work, when I was walking on the promenade or lunching, events which perked up Phillips no end, it occurred to me that I was completely mad. That I was obsessed with something that could only be fantasy. But nevertheless, every night I persisted.

'I discovered that the sequence of architectural description had ended only when it began again. It had been sheer luck that I happened to tune in on the first day, or perhaps it wasn't, I've held both opinions in the centuries which followed. At first then I was devastated. I no longer had the company of my son, even the narrow company of him reciting such dull stuff. I had merely a phonograph of him. But then it occurred to me, as I still listened, hoping to find some original idea, that the message itself was not the point.

'Now that I had the information, I had to build the house.

'I had no idea if this was the will of the Lord. I am a Christian, yet it is still beyond my comprehension that He should communicate to me through radio, and, indeed, with what became of this house I often think of it as a plan of the adversary. However, I did know that it was the will of Alisdair.

'In a fever of purpose, I visited London, and, through the arrangement of a number of friends, who were all delighted by the change in me, I visited the divine Sir Edwin, Mr Lutyens. The greatest architect of his age. He was in his pomp then, full of energy, though he was of similar age to myself. I presented him with my notebooks, full of my tiny scrawl, written by the light of the moon or often by the mere familiarity of the gestures of writing, with no illumination at all.

'He listened to my plan. I did not tell him of how I came by these architectural ideas, merely that I wished the house to be built.

'I think it was the eccentricity of the whole thing that appealed to him. He was always joking, in his speech and in his buildings. He seemed to find the whole world funny, all the time. That didn't appeal to me at once, of course, since I was grieving, but it came to, in time. He would not be told how to build a house, he told me. The man once had built a circular nursery, so a particularly strict governess would be unable to send a child to stand in the corner! But he volunteered to at least have one of his juniors set my written ideas out as a plan, and agreed that we would meet again when this had been done.

'In the meantime, and always as if the matter of building the house was a fait accompli . . . sorry, something that's definitely going to happen, I purchased a large area of Wiltshire from a rather penniless and dissolute lord. I was so fired up with my purpose, I went to live in a boarding house at a nearby village . . . oh, it's long gone now . . . and paced the ground restlessly, imagining the house that would . . . well, I didn't know what it would do.

'If I had done, then I would not have built it.

'At any rate, after a few weeks, I received a telegram from Sir Edwin, asking me to see him again. He was almost as excited as I was, pacing about his consulting room, using a pointer to tap out every feature on the plan that had been laid out on the table. He told me that he quite liked a number of the features he had been forced to include – the external chapel, for example – and that the whole project was so well thought out that he had real objections only to a few. He had hoped to end his career without ever having built a folly, for example. He made some word play on the subject, saying that I'd better not go climbing the walls of it, since it would be a *sheer* folly.

'He seemed interested, always, in why I was setting out on this mad plan. He knew of my circumstances. He thought we had something in common, I believe. His own wife, Emily, had been a stranger to him since she had joined the Theosophists, a religious group who were waiting for the new Messiah to arrive. They forbade love other than of a very spiritual sort. It must have been a kind of continuing grief to him, with the added weight that that which he grieved for was not beyond the veil, but before his eyes every day.

'It's funny how religious concepts alter, isn't it? One hasn't heard of Theosophy for many centuries. Indeed, by the end of her life, I have read, Emmy chucked it all and returned to him, and they were happy again.

'That news made me happy also, although I could not see them, for they both believed me long dead.

'So we became friends out of his interest in my situation, and we both supervised the construction of the building, enjoying, as much as I could enjoy anything, our time together. He insisted on filling the gaps in the plans, those areas Alisdair seemed to think of no importance, with his own touches. For instance, the table in the kitchen is of his design. It's become warped over the years. And since it isn't included in Alisdair's plans, I have never felt the need to heal it. It is just as beautiful, no matter what time has done to it. Indeed, you could say history has added to its art. It's slowly becoming something else. And what it will be will be very interesting to see. Call it a hobby of mine, watching that table.

'And that was not my only rebellion. Unfortunately.

'You see, Heartsease and I are connected to each other. From the moment I slid the last brick into place. The building never got older, and neither did I. Lutyens never realised it, but then he never experienced the full effect. There's something about the shape of the place, when complete. And perhaps something about the materials of which it is constructed. A lot of granite, a pile of the stuff in the cellars, foundations that go down much further than any building Lutyens had ever seen before. Even in the first few days the servants were seeing things. I once had to comfort a maid who'd seen a white lady walk right through a corridor, laughing at her. They couldn't understand how a young house could be haunted, and invented stories about the land, that this had been a gypsy encampment, or that the lord who I'd purchased these acres from, and I'm certain he'd done nothing of the sort, had murdered his family on a picnic.

'I created Alisdair's room . . . well, I suppose you'd say unconsciously, though we wouldn't have used that word then. I thought that since he'd told me how to make the house, perhaps he wanted to come and live there, as a ghost. The tales of the servants enthralled me, because I kept expecting them to see him.

'And it was in that room that I first discovered the nature of the relationship between Heartsease and myself. I did very much the same thing you did. I was sitting at Alisdair's desk one evening, writing a letter, as I often did. Phillips went so far as to refuse to serve me while I was there, such was his conviction that the mere existence of the room was a morbid fascination on my part. I finished, and got up to ring the bell for the boy to come and take the letter to the post. But as I moved, my elbow knocked the photograph of Alisdair from the wall. It fell awkwardly. The glass shattered and ripped the photograph itself.

'The pain was too much. It had been months since I had installed myself in the house . . . my own "folly" I suppose . . . and I was starting to despair of hearing Alisdair's voice again, though I listened every night. I was starting to think that future architectural studies would regard the place as a mad old man's last eccentricity. The crash of the picture seemed to focus that feeling on me, define it, break my heart as it had not been broken in all those busy months . . . well, five years of planning and building . . . It all seemed to mean nothing.

'And I found myself powerfully imagining the moment before the picture had broken, wishing that I had not been so clumsy. I looked away in an ecstasy of pain and frustration.

'And when I looked back, the picture was whole once more, and hung on the wall as it had done, as if nothing had happened.

'It took many more instances of a similar nature to convince me of the effect. A messy floor after riding that the maids had been too busy to deal with at that moment . . . It was suddenly sparkling. A broken teapot . . . was one piece again.

'I tried to see it happen, but I never quite could. You see the movement sometimes, of pieces fitting themselves together, if you catch them quickly enough, but . . . I think it's something about our minds or our eyesight that only allows us to experience those things we think should be possible.

'It was the heart failure that sealed the silent bargain the house and I had made. I was sitting up one night, listening to the airwaves whistling, trying to find Alisdair among all the new stations that had sprung up, 2LO and all of those. Suddenly, I found that something was gripping my chest, and that a quite negligible pain in my left arm had straight away taken hold of my throat.

'I fell to the floor, breaking my chair. Staring up at the ceiling I thought of how ridiculous it was that I should die like this, without seeing Alisdair again. If I had only accepted the thought that I would soon see him on the other side, how different things might have been, how much better!

'I wished myself to be well again.

'And so immediately I was.

'I got up from the floor and found my chair was mended, also.

'It felt as if I'd accepted something. Taken the shilling. Or signed the pact with the Devil. That was the first of only a few times the house has saved me directly in these centuries since. But I have also discovered, once more to my shame, that even if I desire to die, it will not let me.

'I had become immortal, the partner of the house in immortality.

'I assembled the equipment to broadcast back to Alisdair, in the ether of heaven, to ask him what this meant, why he wanted me to deny myself the pleasure of seeing him again. But while the radio engineers were visiting every day, and advising me on erecting an aerial on the roof of the house, Phillips had an accident. He was carrying a box of equipment for my advisors. He missed his step on the great stairwell, and fell. One blow from the banister killed him, and he was dead before his body rolled to the bottom of the stairs.

'I went straight to him, as the maids were screaming and the radio men protesting that this could not have been their fault. Phillips lay there amongst broken valves and wires. And I realised that, should I desire, it was within my power to simply make him well once more.

'I felt the wish forming at the back of my head, realised that I was only a moment away from taking the place of God. I loved Phillips a great deal, you see, though I would never have used or thought the word then. He had saved my life, and been my only companion in pain.

'This was the greatest test of my faith.

'With tears in my eyes, I forced myself to do nothing. I would not reverse God's will, though I had the power to do so.

'After the police and the ambulance crew had visited, and the maids were quiet, and the radio men had gone home, I staggered back to Alisdair's room. The pain of my indecision . . . I watched the ambulance that carried his body proceed down the drive, and knew that only when it crossed the horizon and left the gateway was Phillips out of my dominion and truly dead.

'I watched it do so, and knew that he had passed from my hands to those of God, as it should be.

'But I knew I could never live through such an experience again.

'Weeks later, as swiftly as my plan could be accomplished, I arranged the appearance of my own death. I checked my will, and made sure the estate would pass into the hands of my nephew, Graeme. Then I composed a suicide note, asking Graeme to make sure the servants were given good references . . . I knew that Graeme's funds, even with his share of my legacy, would never stretch to keeping a full staff, and that he would have to rent the property or sell it. In either case, I would not have to be the master of life and death over people I cared for ever again.

'I vanished into the woods on that occasion, bidding my servants a noisy and in retrospect far too obvious adieu. I returned to the house under cover of darkness. As the police were called and began to search, I used my knowledge of the building and of the servants' schedules to keep one step ahead of them.

'But I was foolish. I did not realise that they would grow frustrated with their lack of success in the grounds and the lake and turn their attention to a detailed exploration of the house. They brought in police from as far afield as Salisbury and Trowbridge, and sent a wall of men, fingertip to fingertip, through the house from bottom to top. I found myself cornered in the last bedroom of the top floor, having run from room to room on the balls of my feet. I'm glad they were looking for a body, not a fugitive, or they would have caught me sooner!

'I hid in a wardrobe against the wall of the house itself, and heard the policemen enter the room. They thought the search was fruitless, but the power of money and privilege in those days! They felt they owed it to me to search every corner! As the footsteps approached the wardrobe, I had visions of shame and scandal. The mad old fool revealed, wasting police time, the talk of the county!

'I pushed myself back against the wall and wished I could melt through it.

'And so, of course . . . I did.

'I fell through the outside wall and hit the gravel outside with a force that I can still recall. It felt like it nearly sent the ribs flying out through my chest, it was so hard! Still, I forced myself to my feet, and looked around, relieved to discover that everyone was still inside, and that my impossible fall had not been observed.

'I chanced the magic again, and slid my hand into the gravel, and then through the ground beneath, watching the material part to my will, fully against gravity! The horror and wonder of that moment, as the world swung about me, and I knew, like we all know from birth that if we drop a cup it will fall, that the rules of the universe were those of the cinema, and I had gone from being one of the audience to being the director. The impossible was suddenly the obvious, and the world I had lived in was a bad compromise.

'I felt under the ground until my hand slapped the roof of the cellars. Then I took a deep breath, flexed my legs for a leap, and willed my whole body to fall through.

'I landed with a whoop on the cellar floor, twenty feet below, a cascade of gravel and earth falling around me, until the hole I'd made slid closed behind me.

'I rolled on to my back and lay there, with the barrels of produce and the wine and the ice, listening to the distant echoes of the police thumping back into the hallway, coming to the end of their enquiries.

'I laid low for the next couple of weeks, as the servants left, until the place was finally locked up and quiet. And then, I, the newest ghost of the house, made my way wantonly through walls back to Alisdair's room.

'I used my broadcast equipment to send him a message, asking him what this all meant. Why was I now immortal and powerful, the reality of the house bending to my touch?

'He did not reply immediately. Indeed, I suspect he did not actually reply at all, but that my question simply coincided with his mechanical duty of bearing messages. Perhaps he, or whatever power instructed him, had simply given me some time to discover my new position in the world, and was advising me thus. But nevertheless, two nights later I discovered him talking away in the scratchy distance of the short wave, whining in and out as the atmosphere flexed in the night.

'He said that the house was special, made of dreams and impressions, even more so than everything we think we see and touch with the electrical patterns that inform our brain from our eyes and fingers. It drew the power of magnetism from the ground, those deep foundations plunged into the earth itself, and ever since I had inserted that last brick it had based its existence on a compromise, an understanding reached between the brains of its inhabitants and the electromagnetic fields they swam in, were immersed in. What is a slab of granite, after all, apart from an agreement from all who touch and see it that indeed it is there? In the case of Heartsease, that agreement was not always to be reached.

'I asked him why, but he simply continued to talk, deaf to the words of his father. He told me that it was my task now to look after this remarkable building, to keep it in the manner to which it was accustomed, as it were. And he began to list various things that should never be out of place, much as he had listed the original specifications that had conjured this house into existence.

'I was not bitter about being used as such a servant. I assumed a higher purpose, that one day I would see why God had wanted these things done.

'It took years to shake my faith. Never in my God, but in the whims of he who had once been my son, but who now never made any reference to our life together. In truth, it seems not so long, compared to the centuries I have been here. But perhaps there is a significance to the year where my break with him occurred.

'I had always paid attention to the news, through my radio listening. When the Second World War came around, and I now see it as the return of the First, echoing back at us like the wash of a shipwreck, the house was used as a training facility for young men destined to be soldiers. I watched them from corners and shadows, horrified by how eager they were, how like Alisdair.

'At first my faith was rocked by that, how, while the horror of what Alisdair had been through was happening again, he had been reduced to a voice that only talked of placing a brick back there, of steadying a wall there, of keeping the gardens neat and preventing any new design.

'But then, as the war years passed, I became . . . and it was such a shock that I use the word with care now . . . hopeful. I saw that this time the foe we faced was the foe that should always be faced, be it in battle, politics, the schoolyard or in our dreams. And I started to act on my beliefs once more, healing those soldiers who were injured by accident, making them talk of a good old ghost who looked after them.

'Thank the Lord I was never called on to bring life to death.

'By the time the war ended, I felt I had played my part, that I belonged to something greater than myself once more. I had, dare I say it, ceased to grieve. I had recovered from that which I thought had forever vanquished me. I had left the darkness and entered the light.

'And one evening, I found that I had been too long at my book, in a quiet, deserted bedroom, and that I had forgotten to listen to Alisdair's broadcast altogether.

'Rather than rush to my radio set, I finished my chapter. I could hardly call Alisdair to apologise. One of the many occupants of the house between the wars had taken down my radio transmitter aerial.

'And so it was for the next week, night after night. Alisdair's orders went unheeded. I kept the house clean, of course, as I always have. A matter of reflex and pride, and wanting to live in a house that feels right and tidy and honest. But I did no more work by order.

'And one evening, around teatime, I found myself going to the hallway of the house. Avoiding the soldiers, I waited for my moment and opened the door.

'I had been for walks often, when I knew that nobody was looking, all over the estate. I regularly went to pray in the old chapel, before the events which buried it. And sometimes my duties had taken me to the folly or to the gardens or stables.

'But it was up the driveway I walked now, under the setting sun. It was possible that many of the soldiers eating their supper in the mess hall that had been created in my dining room could have looked out and seen me. I felt giddily that I no longer cared.

'I marched proudly up to the gates. As I approached them, I heard the sound of a car coming through the dusk. It would be at the gate in moments.

'I wanted to swing the gate open and salute whatever officer was being driven in, declare my existence and tell everyone the extraordinary story. I wanted to be the owner and proper inhabitant of my life and house again.

'So I stepped up to the gates and raised the catch, and sent them swinging open with a push of my hands. I stepped forward, intending to leave the area of my estate for the first time in over twenty years.

'Intending, but failing. I found that I could not take the step. I confess that I started to sob as my foot held fast on the threshold, poised over the line that separated estate from outside world. I realised in that moment that I had lived here too long, that in saving me from death the house had also claimed me, made me part of it. Perhaps it was only a belief or an impression that held me there, but it felt like an impassable barrier. And in Heartsease, as I had come to understand, as in history, the only impassable barriers take the form of beliefs and impressions.

'The car approached. I could see its lights coming over the rise. But I knew I could not meet it. An old man unable to leave his house, his existence relinquished, his papers incredible to a bureaucracy that would make him an unsolvable anomaly. I would be a victim, a freak. I could only be lord of my house at night, in dreams.

'I ran into the twilight as the car passed through the gates, and dropped into the darkness of the cellars like the phantom I had become.

'And since then a phantom I have stayed. Wandering the house, never revealing myself until today. No longer a prey to grief, no longer at the beck and call of Alisdair, my dear departed son. For a long time I simply lived, watching the world progress through my radio, and through the lives of those who lived here. But that was not good enough for those who set this terrible situation. They came to understand that I was no longer the slave of the past. And so they determined, I think, to replace me. Which brings us to the story of the ruined chapel, and how it came to be so, and of Booth Hawtrey's place in it all.'

They had come to the end of their walk, to the folly. It stood in a clearing in the wood, bats fluttering about its crenellations. Rebecca went straight to it, needing to touch something solid, to connect her back to the world after Trent's incredible tale. She wasn't afraid of the bats. They were tiny and couldn't hurt her. And she loved them like she loved everything, still.

She turned back to see Trent standing at the edge of the clearing, leaning on a tree, staring back down the slope at his beloved Heartsease, the dark bulk of the house illuminated in the night.

'All right,' she said. 'Tell me about the ruined chapel.'

Ruth stepped towards Booth, holding the steaming kettle by its handle in one hand, and the teapot in the other.

He knew that she was going to throw the water over him.

But all he needed—

She put the teapot on the table, and poured the boiling water on to the tea leaves inside.

He took a sudden, violent breath, sucking the scent into his nose.

And he remembered so hard and so fast that he didn't notice when she smashed the teapot into his skull.

He remembered—

Forty-Two: Booth's One Hundredth Birthday

Winter, 2065

The electric Bentley spun to a halt by the fountain, its rear wheels sending a wake of gravel washing across the driveway.

Booth leapt out, before Alison had even started to unfasten her seatbelt, and ran up to the butler and the other servants who were gathered outside the house. 'Why wasn't the gate open?' he asked. 'You're all waiting for me . . . but you didn't open the gate. Now why was that?'

Alison stifled a sigh and kept smiling. She'd seen the look of anger on his face when he'd had to get out to open the gate. He hated being kept out. Now he would try to do his charm thing and charm himself back into a good mood.

'Sir . . .' the butler began. 'We have a limited staff. We thought . . .'

'Yes, yes, a limited staff.' Booth threw an arm around the shoulders of the butler, and led him off, mock-conspiratorially, glancing back at the smiles on the faces of the maids. 'But you know, my visit here might help with that. That's how it works, right?' His voice reduced to a whisper. 'Nobody has ever heard of the Trent family. Except the Aurigans, who have heard of their house. But now I'm here, everyone will hear of them. So where's your master?'

'Here!' The shout came from inside the porch.

Alison got out of the car as the man who must be Alex Trent emerged from the house, as maned and huge as the lion of his family crest above the door. His arms were spread wide. He didn't so much as look towards her, his eyes fixed on Booth.

She noticed that the house was flying a Union flag. She hadn't seen one of those for about a decade. How camp was that?

Booth spun on the spot, did a double-take, marched up to Trent and shook him far too firmly by the hand. 'So you're the chap who's doing so much good work down here. I'm Booth Hawtrey, this is Alison Crawshay, my silver-ring biographer and a passable fuck.'

Alison laughed lightly, her eyes meeting Trent's gaily. Trent released his hand from Booth's iron grip and flexed his fingers as if he'd been hurt. The man had done his homework. 'You're here for a double celebration,' he said. 'Not only my wedding, at which you're the guest of honour of course, but also your birthday. One hundred years young!'

Alison couldn't help but suck in a deep breath. Booth's face had fallen, and now he was glaring at Trent with guarded hostility, his eyes dancing all over the poor man, who was just gazing back, a limp smile on his face, uncertain where he'd gone wrong.

'I'd forgotten,' said Booth. 'Thank you for reminding me.'

And with that he grabbed Alison's hand and dragged her inside, trailing Alex Trent and his servants behind them.

'I wonder if I get droit de seigneur?' he asked, standing by the window, fiddling with his cufflinks.

Alison was sitting at the dressing table, updating her chronicle. In its pages, Booth was just entering the house, being merry and jocular and kind to the servants and handing Trent his generous wedding presents. She liked that bit of the job, making her boyfriend look good. Nobody seemed to object to her little tinkerings. She didn't think Booth even read the diaries. Which was rather unlike him, because he was interested in everything else people said. Beside her sat a cup of actual tea, which must nearly be the last the family had in their stores. She was savouring it, sipping it slowly, enjoying every moment. The smell had drifted over the room, making the whole chamber redolent of that wonderful childhood scent. Booth had swigged his own cup of it back in thirty seconds. 'What does that mean?' she asked, distractedly.

'French. You wouldn't understand the idea behind the expression. It's a big idea, it takes time to . . .' He raised his hands then flopped them down by his sides. 'You just wouldn't understand it.'

Alison managed a smile as she looked up from her phone. 'Have the Aurigans ever asked you directly to go somewhere before?'

'What do you mean?'

'I mean like this time. They sent a message directly to your phone. Has that ever happened before?'

'No.' He stepped towards her from the window. 'I understood the surface meaning of what you were asking, but the question under-neath is always the same. What . . . do . . . you . . . mean? You're never going to understand, are you? A hundred years . . . that's why I don't want to celebrate it. What does anything mean?' He raised his voice a little. 'Is anyone going to bloody tell me?'

'Yes, I know I'm very stupid, but could you just answer my question, for the record?'

'No, no, I have never been contacted directly by the Aurigans before. For the record. Perhaps this is something new they're trying, now they've got the hang of what's left of Earth's communication systems.'

Alison turned back to type the information in. He seemed more nervous than usual. More vulnerable. This birthday thing was definitely getting to him. A reminder of the difference between him and everyone else, she was certain. Though she'd never asked him outright. It was her job to distract him. They couldn't ruin tonight's ceremonial dinner, or the wedding tomorrow. 'It's wonderful what Mr Trent has managed down here, isn't it?' she said. 'All those fields we drove through. The quarry, even you stopped for the quarry! All those windmills. And the staff here! How do they keep a big place like this clean?'

He waved a hand, still fighting with his cufflinks. 'Tiny questions. Those windmills are full of Manderville technology. You can bet one of them is a Manderville net tower. I ought to go and find it, turn it off. Not before I send a message to old man Manderville though. Let him know I don't forget.'

Alison bit her lip. Booth had visited the Mandervilles twenty years ago, when they were a loose confederacy of farmers created in the wake of the GEC. They didn't believe in the Aurigans, and had made him work for his board and lodging. Booth had never returned to their territory again, despite many pleas lately, and did his best to sabotage relations with that family wherever he went.

He was so full of rage. It was only when he was still with her, lying reading while she slept beside him, that he seemed to find any peace. It must be hard, living so long, bearing such responsibility. Nobody seemed to understand him but her.

He finished doing up his cuff with a little flourish. 'I think one of those maids was giving me the eye. You don't fancy—?'

'No.'

'Oh well, just me then.'

Booth gently closed the door of the maid's room behind him and wandered off down the darkened corridor.

He hadn't gone straight there from the room he shared with

Alison. First, he'd attended to a number of things the Aurigans had asked him to do. He'd gone to the cellars and adjusted the position of a brick, he'd found a book underneath a pillow and returned it to its shelf, he'd taken a tiny screwdriver and tightened a screw that held a lamp in place.

Only after these meaningless details had been attended to had he pursued the more important business of the smiling maid.

Number eight hundred and seventy-two. He'd carefully not asked for her name, so he wouldn't remember it. That was true of ninety-four of them. All recent. In the last few years, they'd started to regard their bodies as gifts to offer to him, for the good of the house, like the food and the drink he was always given. They wouldn't offer a name unless he asked. They'd never presume he wanted to stay with them or fall in love with them or anything like that.

What a great new age.

What a shit new age.

He was naked and very cold. If he met anyone he'd just laugh and wave a hand and they'd laugh too. Or maybe point in shared hilarity at the drop of blue on the end of his cock.

He liked being very cold. Something in his mind still insisted that he had to get into the warm or he would come to harm, raised his skin in goosepimples, made him shiver. Getting through that was exhilarating. His non-existent nervous system made him feel more and more frightened of what might happen as he got colder and colder, frightened on an animal level.

One of the few pleasurable experiences left to him. He was determined to get a few more of those in before the end. Maybe he could make it to a hundred nameless.

So that would have to be tonight, then.

He had first felt that he was missing something when he turned thirty. While he was still mortal, horribly. It was children, he had supposed for a while. As soon as you start thinking you're too old to play sport professionally, that everyone in the England team is younger than you . . . His mind flashed back against images of players on the field, of television, of logos and presenters and big events . . . The England team, the bitter feel of that phrase now as it turned over in his mind . . . He had felt, in the 1990s, not tutored enough in relationships to be broody, that he had a long way to go. But the need had been there, the search for mean purpose, just make another one of yourself and spend the rest of your life enjoying him. Or her, of course.

The beam had put an end to that. Enough women had wanted his babies since, enough powers and principalities too, but none could have them.

A woman he'd loved, in his fifties, who he'd lived with for a couple of years in what now seemed to be a golden age of prosperity, had said to him that people still lived expecting predators to disturb their foraging. That what we were missing was constant jeopardy. A civilised world couldn't provide enough movement and sound and change to fill our minds, to convince us that there wasn't something else we should be doing.

The need, the gap, the nothingness that people filled with children, religion, creative work, love.

Bernadette would have loved the GEC, he thought, had she lived to see it. The way the news got squashed up every day, full of tiny details that meant big things, that fewer and fewer people could decipher. Television news had become a series of shouted images, all pushed together. Brazil in trouble. Brazil bailed out. Brazil helped out. Not enough. Three different movements for national unity. War. Brazil gone. And then it was reports from the different new countries for a while, all trying to get international recognition. And then one of the countries split in half, and the other two seemed to always be having revolutions and elections. And then the news services stopped reporting on anything that wasn't in Europe. And then that crunched down to Scandinavia and France and Britain. Because all the economies were suddenly in trouble at once, and nobody could bail anybody out. And finally it was just Britain itself. Because there was no trade now. A trade ban. The continent looking after itself. Attacks on coastal towns. Mines put down. Defences. Britain alone. And then the independence movements, the tax wars, the land wars, the army breaking up when it couldn't be paid, the arms sales, the mass desertions, that unit of Gurkhas caught in the New Forest, still loyal to their vows, being mortared down by the militias. The defining moment. They said the King died with them, but nobody knew if he'd died at all. Nobody had heard or seen. The usual legends of survival. His father's company held on to their sections of London, supported local services, kept their areas going as villages. And Cousin Michael had tried to start a parliament, and failed, and then had had himself crowned in Westminster Abbey and nobody paid any attention.

Booth had only insisted that the Hawtreys take up the communications equipment that allowed the Aurigans to communicate with him. He had felt, ridiculously, a sense of responsibility about that then. As if having someone else in the universe was hopeful. As if they might help somehow, and the Hawtreys would be in the best position to distribute that help. Raids had been made, scientists and equipment and facilities secured. At some cost. But Cousin Michael had seen it as an investment.

Before he'd had his haemorrhage and died in his bath.

And he could see Bernadette now, leaning back in her chair and laughing, the lines on her old face and her greying hair. Her big breasts heaving with the laughter.

He loved Alison, as well. Because she put up with him, and seemed sometimes to understand. He loved her rather desperately, not in the open way he'd loved Bernadette. Alison seemed like all there was left, the last good thing in the world. He treated her terribly. He couldn't help it. The world treated her terribly. When Bernadette had been alive, the world had been full of good things.

Bernie, none of this has been any good at all. We're all waiting for the predator to leap on our backs now, and it hasn't made us happy, and we're all still looking for something more. My Alison's the product of that lack, a child of lack. And she doesn't even know.

Well, no more.

If he could sleep he would sleep for a hundred years now. That would be his alternative. See what the place was like when the cards had been shuffled again. He had been swept along by not being able to see the tides, the little ones that suddenly rushed and crashed over you, the big breakers that somehow never arrived. And in all this time, with all his perfect memory, he had never been able to predict which would be which.

The only thing he was sure of now was that there was no aim, no end point, no closure to come.

In his eighties, as those around him had started to die, much as they had started to have babies in his thirties, like a fashion he felt too shy to wear, he had taken to the Church.

For just under a decade he had had his faith as his guide. He had attended Holy Communion at the little church of St Martin's in Ealing, the Reverend Emburey officiating. He would return there first whenever his travels at the request of the Aurigans brought him back home. Those years had been when the poverty really hit. When the old systems everybody had been holding on to had really failed.

He stopped eating and drinking then. He knew he could do without.

His body didn't know.

He was in the cellar of the church one Saturday night, because he had nowhere else to go and his would-be stomach was hurting him. The cellar was full of the homeless. More of them were on the streets every day, spilling out of what had been the government compounds as the organisations that had grown up to support those compounds collapsed. A number of the people in the cellar had tubercular coughs, and one or two called out to him to touch them. He did, though he knew the reverend didn't like it.

Emburey was bitter about several things, being about Booth's age, remembering when most people lived in relative comfort. Not only that, he was bitter about the schism of the Brunian heresy, which was attracting younger Christians almost like a doomsday cult. Six bishops had been excommunicated. Emburey would tell him about the political manoeuvrings over their wine, like it was some blood-thirsty sport upon which everything had been wagered. He seemed to link the Brunians and the destruction all around him implicitly.

Booth wondered sometimes why he hadn't been attracted to the Brunians, but all the things he read about them left him cold. They wanted to reduce faith to something they could sense. What Booth needed was the opposite: something that felt longer-lived than himself, something ancient. The Catholics had found something in one of the Aurigan messages suggesting that the aliens had experienced the Incarnation on their world. The Anglicans offered Booth no such annoyance.

This was before the purges. When he had a choice.

Emburey had a theory of his own to account for Booth's ennui. He said that St Augustine had defined it: the distance between man and God, the yearning of human beings to close that gap and be one with the divine.

Which had appealed to Booth, then.

Emburey was in the cellar that night, praying with some of the older folk. Booth went and knelt with them and concentrated on his usual series of prayers. For his older brother, now so frail. For his nieces and nephews and their children, down in the West Country. For all the thousands of people employed in Hawtrey-owned companies.

He had never had a revelation like Emburey had. A moment, as the reverend described it, when God had become obvious to him. He envied the reverend that. He envied him that night as he opened his eyes and saw him stand, manage a smile to one of the flock who was coughing up blood into her handkerchief. The church had put in a request to the NHS list a couple of weeks ago, and Emburey had been using what influence he had with the council, and some of his own savings in bribes, to keep the request on its way.

Booth walked with him up the stairs to the reverend's office, and they had a cup of wine between them, the bottle that they'd been slowly sipping all year, on every occasion Booth had returned to London.

'Have you heard about Dulwich?' The vicar sank slowly into his chair, animated only by the pain of the news, as always, by how unbelievable it was to people of their generation. 'They've blocked the roads, ripped up the railway lines. They're going it alone, issued statements that they're no longer part of London, part of anything. They're saying that they're sending the bloody troops in.'

'That might be the best thing.'

'Might it? You've got a young brain, still. Does it seem good to you to have soldiers down here now? To me it all seems like it's falling apart. But is that the cause or the . . . the symptom? Is it just because I'd hoped we wouldn't see soldiers on the streets again?' His hands trembled on the cup. 'I don't know how long I can keep on . . . I mean, they're leaving, Booth, they don't trust anyone to come and help any more. They're walking out of the borough in numbers, like animals fleeing, great riots of them, you should see them on the net! They're heading down the Thames, pitching camps, forming new alliances, absolutely under no control, just looking for money and food! I think this is the end, I've never believed in the end of the world, I don't . . .' And he began to shout, with a sound in his voice Booth had never heard before. 'How did we get to this? How did we get from what you and I remember . . . to here?'

Booth went back to the moment that he'd realised something had suddenly gone missing in Emburey's eyes. It was as if his gaze had shifted from Booth and the external world to something within himself, suddenly. There was a little catching noise in his throat. Then his right hand started to hit his left shoulder, the hand still holding the cup, beating himself with the wine, sending it flying over his papers on the desk, his calendar on the wall. He started bellowing as he fell off his chair, and Booth went to his side, asking urgently what he could do, wondering if he could call an ambulance and somehow make them come through just the sheer force of his anger.

But it hadn't been necessary, thankfully for the old priest. His yells turned into high squeals, and Booth could tell he was trying not to fight him off with his hands as he braced himself on stiff shoulders on the carpet, but instead to embrace him. And Emburey died, his heart having burst at the left ventricle, his eyes looking into and understanding Booth Hawtrey. Booth kept that look for a long time then and a long time now, trying to gain some information from the expression on the vicar's face, trying to decipher what might have been a smile, a tic, a grimace. He'd done that so often. His mind flickered across all the times, another thread through the heavy, dusty tapestry of who he was.

Booth lowered Emburey gently to the carpet as the man's pain suddenly switched off, his breathing ceasing, and he was in his thoughts at the time, thoughts of hope for the old man's soul, that he had gone to his place of connection with God, of no frustration, that now he would be cared for instead of caring. His thoughts were that his friend had received what he deserved from the author and keeper of all.

What a fool he had been. What a moron to believe that this was a narrative. That there was a pattern instead of random events, an author and an audience, when there was just him and everyone else. His perfect memory had made him realise, after a while, that he could see enough of the cloth . . . and that there was no pattern woven into it.

He realised that he had stopped, leaning on the bottom pillar of the servants' stairway, his mind lost in history.

The second message from the Aurigans, the one that stupid cow Alison Crawshay didn't know about, had come as such a fucking relief.

It was all going to be over soon. He was going to be free.

The noise of a door closing made him step reflexively away from the wall.

He wasn't scared, of course. What had he to be scared of? What could hurt Booth Hawtrey, except time?

He swept through his memory and found which of the doors along the narrow corridor had been open a crack. It was closed now.

A signal perhaps? This was a corridor of maids. Perhaps they were all for him. They would have to be, if he was to reach his target.

He stepped up to the door, and made himself concentrate on the pleasure that would be before him in a moment. It was worth it. It was.

The pleasure of forgetting made everything worth it.

He put his hand on the doorknob, shaking his head. If it was locked he'd just kick it down.

It wasn't locked. The door swung open. He stepped inside

proudly, trying to relish his nakedness, to squeeze the juice out of the moment.

But the room was empty. The bed was made, the covers undisturbed.

Everything was spotlessly clean.

Booth looked around for a moment, wondering. But he soon stopped.

He went back into the corridor, hoping he could summon the enthusiasm for some more forgetting tonight.

He closed the door behind him.

Alison woke to the sound of distant bells.

She smiled and got out of bed, and went across to the window to look out over the beautiful summer morning. Trent had got the church in the local village to ring its bells for the wedding this afternoon. What a wonderful sound. She'd never heard bells before.

She glanced back across the room, and saw that Booth was sitting at the dressing table, naked, his eyes closed. He was lost in some memory, obviously a painful one. She saw the tension in his face, the look of effort. She'd have to ask him what it was.

She'd stayed awake until three, waiting for him. She couldn't bring herself to be angry with him, though. Not with how much she owed him, for getting her such a place of responsibility within the Hawtrey companies. She'd learned to write on the job, had met so many people she never would have met. The occasional embarrassment at Booth's actions was a small price to pay. And eventually, when he'd worked through all the pain and anger, she was sure that he'd come to love her as she loved him. She could feel how the memories hurt him, how all that history weighed him down. She was his release from that.

She was happy with her contract, and especially happy to have heard bells.

Booth opened his eyes and looked at her for a moment, as if she'd caught him in the middle of something that hurt them both. 'I love you,' he said.

'I love you too,' she replied.

Booth slowly put his hand to his brow, watching the play of sunlight on dust motes in the air around him.

He'd been pushing towards the shadow of now, trying for the last time to get through it and encounter whatever it was that sat at the centre of the concept, the thing that turned time into space. The thing that had broken him.

When he'd opened his eyes, he'd known that he'd given up the attempt on now forever.

He lowered his hand again and tried to settle. Just the last few things to do now.

Alison came over and kissed him. He let her.

On the front lawn of the house, beside the driveway, a large marquee had been erected for the reception. Booth went to inspect it, as the other guests started to arrive, before his formal duties commenced. The service was going to take place in the chapel round the back of the house, and then everybody was supposed to file round to here. Supposed to.

He had waited until Trent had called Alison over to a window to look at the carts arriving with the produce for the evening festivities, and had wandered back to their room.

He had hidden the note he'd written her, and the favour she'd once given him, under her phone, beside the bed. He hadn't understood what the favour was when she'd handed it to him, five years ago. And she, of course, had never explained. Other people, other women, had done that, when they saw it inside his top pocket. It was something they'd started to do in the West Country, the next best thing to a ring, a gift that indicated togetherness, that could be shown to other people. Another one of those desperate hanging-on things. The sort of stupid gesture that Alison lived for, that her life was confined by, that she was a product of. He'd accepted it without understanding it, and that had only made him feel bad until he'd realised that not understanding shit like that was a good thing, that that was what separated him from all these little, meaningless lives.

But still. He'd needed to return it to her. To show her that she was free. And she would need the note to understand the gesture he was going to make, a gesture from far out of her own frame of reference. It would be too big for her to take in otherwise.

A gentle wind was blowing the flag atop the tent. The Union flag again. Perhaps Trent thought Booth cared. Maybe it was supposed to be a nostalgia thing. As if he didn't have a thousand flags in his memory.

The tent had been stitched together by the locals, he'd been told, several seasons ago. Embroidered into its roof was the Trent family motto, something in Latin which, Booth thought for a moment and was certain, he'd never discovered the meaning of. Big gold letters, patronage like the Domesday Book. They were grateful for the protection Trent offered them.

There were metal barrels of locally brewed beer already stacked here for the party. The barrels looked old. Booth remembered drinking Ashton's before the GEC, knew the taste the moment he looked at the design on the label, but now, without the giant vats and export money and chemicals and workers the brewery had once had, he knew he didn't want to drink it now. The taste would conceivably be much better, but the snaking, uncertain rivulet the brewery had taken through history to meet him here . . . He did not want to taste the difference so exactly, and taste it he would. He didn't want that to be the last thought in his mind, the difference between then and now.

He went inside the marquee. The interior felt a little too warm. This evening it was supposed to be full of people. Of course, it wouldn't be. Trent had had three large petrol-driven heaters placed inside the tent, as yet unlit, rusty and repainted in the Trent colours. They were going to spend petrol on him tonight! They would have decanted it like a vintage.

They had such hopes. Hopes of being one of the emerging powers. Obscene, this floundering in the face of futility. He'd seen them all come and go, in the end. No pattern, no meaning. Apart from the meaning he was about to impose on them. A big moment of forgetting.

That thought made him laugh. He really was going to fuck the Trent family today.

Someone called for him and he made his way back out into the sunshine, still laughing.

The Reverend James Arbuthnot of the Reformed Church of England stood at the wooden lectern, smiling at the bride and groom who stood before him.

Booth watched that smile, that beam of stupid pride, and smiled himself.

The wedding procession had marched down the tunnel from an ornate archway in the gardens to a set of steps that led up into the chapel. The vicar and the groom had been in the lead. Torches had been lit all down the tunnel walls, and there had been lots of laughter from the serving boys. He and Alison had walked with fixed smiles. A local band had followed on, parping and thumping.

They had walked right over the stone slab that Booth had replaced under the stairwell in the early hours of the morning. He'd watched each shoe step over and on to the slab, anticipated each impact.

But they had all arrived in the chapel intact.

For the sake of even more ceremony, then, the bride and her father had walked round the house, and had arrived outside the chapel a few minutes after the groom's party had. Booth had heard the laughter of the girls who were holding up the bride's long white gown, which he had insisted upon seeing the previous evening at the last fitting.

As the band huffed and hahed some more, the bride entered the chapel, having to duck quickly under the incredibly low doorway, as did all her party.

They had all stood. Booth had watched Trent and his bride look at each other, and saw not an inch of awareness or context in their happiness. They were hiding from the world in their love. Her name was Lara Bingham, and she was a girl from the village. That was why the locals loved this man so.

They had all sat down, and the vicar had beamed at them, rainbow-hued as the sun beat down through the stained glass of Christ with the lion and the lamb. Now he held up the family Bible, showing it to them. 'Some things persist,' he began. 'This Bible, for instance, was donated to the chapel in the early 1940s, during the period when Heartsease was a training establishment for the military of the time. We don't know the identity of the donor, but I'm certain he or she would have been glad their gift has remained in use for so long. Heartsease, and the Trent family who have always lived here, is at the centre of a great many traditions. The friendly ghost who looks after the premises, for example . . .' There was a ripple of laughter. 'I keep asking the Bishop if we can do a survey here, but he always says we shouldn't poke our noses in. And now I come to think of it, perhaps he's right. We shouldn't question joy. It's hard enough, sometimes, to accept that everything that's happened in the last few years has been part of God's plan. But in my faith I know it is . . .'

Booth kept his face muscles frozen. He glanced across at Alison and saw that she was smiling her stupid smile.

'And in the mere fact that there is joy, amongst all this suffering, we can see that plan for humanity. The Trent family, for example, will continue. Alexander, their only issue, and his bride Lara will, I hope, see to that.' A sly smile at the bride. 'All these green shoots. All these seeds for the future. A future that you and I may not recognise, will find hard to understand. But a future nonetheless that will include Heartsease, and the Trent family, and the villages, going onwards. So, my children, and that's not an expression I use all the time like some priests, but I feel it's apt here, especially with all the children we see here today . . . my children, let us pray for Alexander and Lara, for their family, and for the future.'

Everyone lowered their heads. Booth did too.

He listened emptily to the prayers, waiting and waiting. He had been there and done this, and these words were mockery to him now.

Finally, they all looked up.

'Our first reading,' said the vicar, 'is by an honoured guest, Mr Booth Hawtrey, who has come all the way from London at the request of his own employers. I hope that on Capella they'll be interested in our wedding ceremony, and that Mr Hawtrey will be among those taking pictures.' More laughter. 'Mr Hawtrey?'

Booth smiled quickly at the vicar, and turned to Alison. 'Oh, I left my notes in the room, could you go and get them?'

'Since when did you need notes?'

'Ally, just go and fucking get them, all right? I'll improvise until you get back.'

She smiled at him. 'All right.'

She got up as Booth did, and hurried away to the door as Booth shook the vicar's hand, nodded to the happy couple, and took up his place behind the lectern. He found the bookmark in the gilt-edged Bible that indicated the passage from the Revelation of St John the Divine that he'd selected. And he looked down at the passage for a moment. But he found that he just couldn't bear it.

He looked up again. 'I'd just like to say a few words of my own, if I may?'

The vicar smiled and nodded.

'What you were saying earlier, about seeds, green shoots, renewal. Well, you would think that, wouldn't you?' The chapel fell silent. Very nearly the whole staff of the house, all wondering what they should think, all taking the easy option. Two stunned families, struck dumb. The vicar's smile held for a moment, as he tried to work out just what Booth meant. It looked for a second like he might argue, so Booth dived right on in. 'But I can see the big picture. And, you know, there really are no green shoots. There is no hope.' The bride was staring at him, open-mouthed. Anger was stirring on Trent's face, but it was clear the man was working out how much it would take before he leapt on Booth, made the break with the forces he represented, betrayed the bigger cause for his one little hope. That calculation was still continuing. 'We are never going to get back to the Union Jack, to Britain, to one government over this island,' Booth continued, projecting his voice towards the back of the chapel. 'History and tradition and pageantry have royally fucked us over. We can't start anything new, because we keep trying to build new things in the image of the old. We can't get out of that mind-set. We are still too British, when there is no Britain to be British about. I see new movements arise, and I see them fall, because each of them is rooted in the past. Each of them displays some bit of the past and tries to fasten the future on it. We don't think there's a world out there any more. It's just us. It's the British hell. And we are stuck here. For ever and ever. Apart from us, that is.' He took the button from his pocket. 'We're out of it. Now.'

He pushed the button, and completed his last act for the Aurigans. He didn't know why they'd told him to do this. He'd enjoyed the idea so much, he hadn't asked.

Beneath the slab, far below, he knew the ten-second countdown on the explosive pack he'd taken from the quarry had begun.

But up here, they didn't know that. He'd wanted this time in order to relish it, to see their expressions, to have one last opportunity to try and understand the people this meagre time had created.

They thought it was some sort of joke, or that the button hadn't done anything. Some of them were laughing nervously, some wholeheartedly, still playing the game, making him welcome, enjoying his joke.

Alex Trent took a step towards him. 'I don't think I understand,' he said, his expression neutral. His bride had started to sob.

Booth had been counting in his head. Now he looked to the vicar. Who was looking back at him with the first honest expression Booth thought he'd seen in decades. It was a look of incredulous contempt and horror. He seemed to have got the idea.

But then Booth realised he was looking past him.

He turned around.

Alison was closing the door of the chapel gently behind her. She glanced over her shoulder and made a grimace to Booth. Couldn't find them.

Booth opened his mouth to say something. And found that he could not.

He raised a hand, trying to make his mouth form a warning. A low sound began in his throat.

She frowned at him. Perhaps she began to understand.

And then there was a sound.

The chapel exploded.

The fireball burst out of the ground and through the building, erupting from windows and bursting the roof and splintering the doors.

The building bulged with the impact, folded in on itself in the fire. Dug a crater underneath it as the roof fell.

Until in seconds there was just a hole in the grass, and a bloom of smoke curling hugely above it, and a sound that smacked against the walls of the house and the hills and the trees and then came resounding back, sending every bird cawing and cartwheeling out into the summer sky, to swirl above the ascending darkness.

Forty-Three: The Dolorous Stroke

Rebecca sat with her back against the stone of the folly, holding the cardboard-thin body of Simon Trent in her arms as he sobbed blindly into her neck. She bit hard on her lip, trying not to let the tears come herself. He had started to sob as he finished his story, and now the tears were coming madly out of him, a great torrent of them.

His body was only slightly warm, and she felt she would freeze in the night, but she couldn't let go of him.

Booth's separated eyes stared past what Ruth was doing to him. They were locked in horror, unable to cry. He was glad of the pieces his body was in now. He deserved it. He deserved everything and nothing.

He experienced the huge pain at a distance, and bit on it to keep himself hurting. Now he remembered everything.

Simon Trent walked through the empty house.

He had watched three servants running towards the explosion. One of them was the boy Henry, who was malformed and would shout things, and had been told to stay away from the wedding. He was shouting things now as he went. Big painful yells of not understanding.

His world was about to come to an end.

The world of all of those who had been under Simon's protection. So much for that.

He reached the bedroom Booth Hawtrey had taken, and found all the new things that he had brought to the house. That was how he found the favour and note, sitting on the bedside table, having been crushed under a phone. Alison must have taken that with her when she ran back to the chapel.

Simon had watched her run, feeling the bittersweet joy of distant proprietorship. His family were celebrating, yet he could not join them.

And now he could never join them. He felt, distantly and numbly, the stillness in what remained of the chapel. He could not clean it up. He must bring them all back to life. He must reverse this evil. But he had told himself he would not do such things.

He would not give in to grief again. He would keep his hope.

He picked up the note and read it. Then he looked at the favour.

He put them back on the table, his whole body shaking.

'The selfish . . . bastard!' shouted Simon in Rebecca's arms. 'He killed them all for . . . for how he felt! For his principles! But he *has* no principles! Because he had no hope, we had to be hopeless too!'

Simon swept his hand over the table.

And the note and the favour were gone.

'No history for him! No explanation, I thought! Let people think what they would of him!'

Simon wandered aimlessly through the house and gardens, watching from the shadows as the remaining servants fled. They were already telling their stories, and with a whisper here and there, he managed to make those stories into the atrocities of Booth Hawtrey.

'Apocrypha, I realised, as time went on and I heard mention of him on the radio. The stories people tell when they're drunk and they've already heard a tale about something brave or noble he did. These few folk started those other stories of him, of what he was *really* like. I'm proud to have started that.'

'Everybody's heard stuff like that,' said Rebecca. 'But why isn't Alison's death in the chronicles? I've read about her. The diaries say she left Booth because of mutual differences. Didn't anyone get to write this history down?'

Simon slipped his parched fingers through hers. 'Apparently not,' he said.

For the first time in decades, he went and tuned the radio to Alisdair, hoping for some comfort, some recognition that this new pain was exactly like the old, that being who he was, he would even get over this, in time.

And indeed, for the first time, there seemed to be something in the message that he heard washing about on the AM band in the room high up in the emptied house.

'You must build a maze,' Alisdair whispered to him. 'On the very spot. Here are the measurements.'

And Simon found himself writing down coordinates once more and then sketching them out.

'But this time I needed no help. I forced myself to go and look at what the explosion had done. Nobody had tended to it. The housekeepers had all fled, and the villagers had not dared to come and occupy the house. They had made some initial visits, to try and find their own dead, but the complete destruction of the chapel, and the other end of the tunnel, had frustrated their efforts. They finally brought a priest to bless the whole site as a mass grave, and returned home. They were already getting ready for the hard winter that would come, without Alex's organisation. Indeed, several villages decamped that very autumn, headed to Warminster in great convoys. This was before the epidemics hit, when the towns seemed better places to be.

'I stood on the lawn one night, and raised my arms over the pit, and willed the entire pattern to life. And there it was, as I swept my palms before me. The circuit of hedges and space. A thing of joy, I thought. A hopeful thing for children to play in. And spurred on by that hope and wanting to damn Booth Hawtrey, and hoping that my God would concede me this blasphemy, I swam my hands again, hoping to bring them all walking out of that maze, alive and healthy and joyful in their miracle.

'But I could not. I tried and tried, and pushed and pushed. But all my efforts were lost in the web of the house.

'I tried to unmake the maze, to get at them better, but I found I could not do that either.'

Simon stared at the wall, at the face that was forming in it.

He could barely keep from spitting in disgust, the face meant so much horror to him now.

It was Booth Hawtrey, his head appearing moment by moment out of the plaster, a hand pushing steadily out of the wooden lintel above.

'You will not!' he hissed. And he ran to the wall and put his own hands on the large and ugly face and shoved it back into the plaster. It receded, and the plaster rippled for a moment, but there it remained.

*

'I found him everywhere, moment by moment. I no longer slept, for if I had but a few hours away from tending the house, he would grow somewhere, like the seed of some awful weed. He and the house were made of the same dreamstuff, and it felt like the house wanted to grow him back, that for the first time I was fighting the house over the issue of him.

'I should have understood when he first came to Heartsease, when I saw him moving books and furniture. Doing those things that Alisdair had always insisted I do. I should have realised then that he had a bargain with the house.

'That is why I fear the conflict that has started now. The Campbells and the Hawtreys, at each other's throats in my house. Why is Booth Hawtrey here, but that he has a hand in that?'

Rebecca gently stroked Simon's hair, feeling how thin it was under her fingers.

'I'm sorry,' she said. 'But he isn't like that now. I've never seen him do anything terrible or cruel.'

Simon turned his stretched face up to look at her. 'I would have killed him when I realised he had returned,' he murmured. 'I would have killed him, except that my faith forbids me to do so. So I watched you, hoping that he would not hurt you like he hurt his Alison.'

Rebecca closed her eyes.

From out of the maze one night, something came walking.

It looked like Alisdair Trent. It wore his uniform, and carried his rifle over its shoulder.

Simon, shivering, met it outside the front door. He'd been aware of its approach since it started to form in the maze, three nights before. He had guessed what it would look like when it arrived.

'Father,' it said, 'I'm back.'

He restrained himself from going to it. 'Is this what all this was for?' he said. 'Were the lives of those people taken only for you?'

'Father,' it said, its mouth half smiling like Alisdair had half smiled. 'What do you mean?'

Simon closed his eyes, and raised his palms in front of him. 'Go back to whence you came,' he said.

'I'm your son.'

'My son is *dead*.' His hands fell and he put them to his own head, feeling the ghost at work inside him.

'Father, you don't understand. I'm working for higher things now.

We have to make sacrifices. You have to let Booth Hawtrey come to life again. You have to bring back the note and the favour.'

'I will not.' He managed to say that through gritted teeth. And then bellow it into the face of this presumptuous, parasitic creature. 'I will *not*!'

Alisdair grabbed him by the collar and shoved him inside the porch. He hammered him against one of the walls, screaming.

Simon ripped himself from his son's grasp and punched him in the face, feeling his hand reel with complicated sensations as the blow connected. Alisdair staggered back and then, a moment before he could have, launched himself forward again, his hands outstretched for Simon's throat.

Simon stepped back through the wall and let Alisdair hit it.

Simon fell through wall after wall, rolling through hallways, marshalling the house as he went. He could feel the intruder cajoling the space of the building to be on its side, but he was the master of habit here, and the space bowed to him.

Alisdair caught him in the kitchens, and blazed at him like light, reflecting off all of the copper pots as he tried to enter his father's body and mind. But Simon made the space between them into a wall, and deflected the suggestions and the fire.

They fell through the floor and Simon hit the granite slabs of the cellars hard. He was up in a moment as Alisdair formed again out of the shadows and held him back against the wall, their strengths matching.

Simon watched the far wall, as the shadows there stretched into the shape of the hated one. In his hands he carried the note and the favour. 'No!' Simon bellowed. 'I will not let this happen!'

Their strengths met again, and Booth halted, a shadow puppet made of the silhouettes of two competing hands.

Alisdair murmured, 'The dead own this house, Father. And this world. We have to do as we will, and you cannot stop us.'

'I must try!'

'We will take Booth Hawtrey from here. We will let you live on here. We will not torment you. Allow us this. Allow your son this. All will be well. Father!' And this time it sounded like the true voice of his son, breaking through the ruddy face that was struggling with him. 'Father, this is all for the best, like in my book, I swear to you! Father!'

And the sound of the voice made Simon relax a moment, in pity.

Booth fell from the wall, fully formed once more. In his hands he clutched the piece of paper and the scrap of cloth.

Alisdair turned to make terms with his father.

But Simon had already gone, off through the walls to some hiding place.

'When I emerged, hours later, they were gone. There was no sign of Booth in the house. I gather that he had wandered away. There was a BBC news report of the Hawtrey family joyfully welcoming him back a few weeks later.'

'Yes,' whispered Rebecca. 'He'd been wandering in the wilderness. That's when Alison left him, he'd become too spiritual for her.' She met Simon's haunted eyes. 'So now we know what really happened.'

'I could not find the note or the favour, either. And of . . . the thing that called itself Alisdair, there was no sign. In the decades that followed, I was sometimes aware of a presence, when the house was occupied. The occupants would always fall afoul of a bad ghost, in horrible ways. I supposed that was him. So I played the bad ghost too, to warn them away, to scare them and make them aware of the danger. When most of all I wanted company, and a house that would welcome people because I wished it to. I drove them all away, against my own nature, until the priest came. I thought perhaps she could deal with the ghost. But I suspect I was wrong.'

Rebecca shivered. Slowly, she got to her feet, helping Simon rise with her. 'You've kept that story inside you for so long. How could you bear that?'

'My faith bore it. My faith in God and my faith in the future. I created another chapel, since I could hardly visit the one where all my bad memories lay in wait for me. I am not Lutyens, and the style, so I hear, is strikingly not his. But it is where I make my worship, in my own quiet way. And that abides.'

Rebecca held him close to her breast, and put her hand on his head once again. 'It's all going to be all right,' she said.

She was surprised to find that he'd started to laugh. He brought his head up to look at her with that smile fully formed, open and joyful. 'Well, yes!' he said. 'That's it exactly!'

Alisdair took the favour and the note from Booth's spasming hands. He looked at them for a moment, and then he opened his hands and they were gone.

Their energy wasn't released at one time in one place, but was smoothed out around the globe in a flash that made radio reception jump and hiss for a moment. The ghosts of electromagnetism remembered every detail of the objects, translated them from material into thought, kept that thought in mind in spikes of spiralling interference, a communication exchanged between many ghosts.

And then, one hundred and fifty-eight years later . . .

Ruth Crawshay broke the Campbell seal on the last packing case, and opened the lid.

She was ten. Her parents had left her to finish the last few boxes, while they went into Chester to get supplies. Ruth knew nothing about the history of her family apart from what Dad said, which was that they'd once lived in Hawtrey country, but that his granddad had been exiled for spreading slander about the big family. This move to the town, so that Mum and Dad could apply for positions in the Campbell court, had happened because their farm was failing. They'd had livestock stolen three times in the last year, and they weren't on good enough terms with their neighbours to do anything about the continuing threat.

A new start. Which had made Ruth feel good too, because she'd always thought there must be a better way to live than the farm, which had made Mum and Dad so unhappy all the time. They'd sold it for a steam truck and a big net credit, which could only really be spent in a town, so from that point they'd been committed to Chester.

Ruth pulled blankets out of the packing case, slapping them on her legs to knock off moth eggs.

Something fluttered to the ground. Two things.

Ruth bent to pick them up. A small piece of embroidered cloth: a favour! She'd never seen one before. Was it one of Dad's? From Mum, or from before? He should never have kept it! She wondered if the piece of paper with it was a love letter. She opened it, and started to read.

After a few moments, she fell back on to her knees, and had to put a hand on the case to steady herself and make sure she was still in the same world.

A few weeks later, Booth Hawtrey came to visit Chester.

Ruth watched him from the ranks, as he shook hands with Clifford, the new commander of the Ensign Campbell Militia. Ruth had joined the organisation a week before. Her parents were now a chambermaid and an underbutler in Campbell service, and they were very proud of her.

The children all around her stared at Booth as he went along the lines, suppressing smiles and giggles.

But Ruth kept her silence, staring at this terrible man, the incarnation of everything she hated, of all the things that had hurt her mum and dad.

'And who's this?' he asked, stopping in front of her.

'Mona Flint, sir,' she said, using the name of a friend from the next farm.

Clifford didn't know them well enough yet to realise she had lied. He never recalled that, in fact.

And Ruth allowed herself a little smile, as the monster called Booth passed by, knowing that in his huge memory there was now stored one little lie.

The first step on the long path that would allow her to approach him and then kill him.

Booth, newborn from the material of the house and naked, staggered up the driveway of Heartsease towards the gates, not understanding what had happened to him, knowing only that he had to get away from this place. The memories of what had happened just before he died were rolling around and around in his head.

When he got to the gates, Alison was standing by them.

He looked at her long and hard. But he knew that she couldn't be real. 'What are you?' he finally asked.

'I'm the ghost of Heartsease,' she told him. 'You see it as me. Others see it as their own ghosts.'

Booth clenched his teeth in pain. 'I can't die, can I? She . . . you . . . were going to be my saving grace. But I killed her. They told me I was going to die. But I can't.'

'They told you about total destruction. They didn't say you were going to die.'

'So how can I go on? What can I do now, with all this . . . life ahead of me?'

'You can forget.'

'That's the one thing I can't do.'

'I can let you forget, sweetheart. Come here.'

She reached out for Booth, and he didn't resist as her hand touched his forehead. Then moved inside. Her fingers slid into the blue.

He just stood there, mouth open, as he felt a terrible tension grind his neck. Pain flared in many small places throughout his body. He cried out, and the cry was answered by birds and peacocks.

'Have a dream,' she said. 'I left you because we were too different—'

'No, I was hurting you.'

'Because I could do better, then. Because I needed to grow, away from you. You can't have the luxury of pain or guilt, and especially not about this house.'

She withdrew her hand, clutching something she'd taken from Booth's flesh in her fist, and Booth felt happier.

'Well,' he said. 'I suppose I have been a bit of a bastard to you.'

'Not at all. I just need to be myself, and not Booth Hawtrey's biographer.'

'I understand. You just try and be happy, wherever you end up.'

She kissed him gently. 'I'll be in touch. Oh, and you're going to need this.' She opened her fist. Sitting there was a silver ring.

Booth thought he'd seen one on her finger a moment before, but it seemed to be gone now.

'For the next biographer,' she said. 'I managed to get it off. Perhaps that's a sign.' She dropped it into his palm.

'Thank you,' he said. 'She'll have to try hard to live up to you.'

'Right. Now, shouldn't you go and put some clothes on, get your baggage, and go and get into your car?'

Booth nodded.

'I have to get on. We all have to get on. The wedding's over and it was lovely.'

Booth nodded, and set off back down the driveway.

Halfway to the empty house, he looked back over his shoulder.

But Alison was gone.

Ruth slipped Booth's eyes back into his head, and held it in her hands over the bubbling pot, intrigued for a moment by the steam furling around the cords of blue material at the base of the neck. She'd found the bullet famously lodged there, and had thrown it away.

Booth's mouth started to move. 'Sorry,' he said. 'I did it all. I really did. The buried chapel. I'd forgotten. I want to forget again now. If I hadn't forgotten I'd be a different person.'

Ruth increased her grip with one hand to hold on to the mobile shape in her hands, and with her other reached inside her jacket pocket. She took out the favour and held it in front of Booth's eyes. 'Everyone is who they are because of something. With me, it's this. I came on this mission to find out if who I was was real. To find you here as well was wonderful. This can be the end of me as well as the start.'

And she dropped his head into the pot.

*

Rebecca and Trent walked arm in arm down the forest path that led back to Heartsease.

'I saw everything that happened, from here,' Trent was saying. 'I saw the bargain between Booth Hawtrey and Alisdair, as it was sealed there by the gate.'

A thought had struck Rebecca. 'So this ring I'm wearing . . . the ring that's supposed to pass from one biographer to the next . . .'

'Is part of him. Made of dreamstuff. Yes.'

She fingered it for a moment. It felt exactly like a ring. She knew what she had to ask next, but she also knew what the answer was going to be. 'Simon, I have to try to rescue him. Will you help?'

Simon looked at her, his eyes blazing in the darkness. They kept walking together.

'All right,' said Rebecca after a while. 'I understand. But this is going to make things so much harder.'

Jane looked slowly upwards, trying to take in the whole sky at once. She stood on the white sands, feeling every soft grain beneath the bare soles of her feet. She had clambered down from the mountain that was a warren of little caves, found her way by ledge and chimney down to ground level. Now the mountain stood as an unlikely peak in the midst of emptiness all around, two hours' walk behind her.

It seemed small now, in comparison to what was above.

Two giant suns shone overhead in the pale yellow of the sky. The largest of them took up half the sky, looming over the horizon, bathing the desert in gold with long red shadows. She couldn't even begin to guess if this was morning, evening or the middle of the day, the star was so huge. But it wasn't so bright, she could look directly at it. Red swirls and flares and details on its surface were endlessly, slowly changing. A loop of a solar flare was hanging in its sky, collapsing back into the surface. Tiny elements of it were changing every moment.

After a while, she made herself look at the other sun. It was hidden behind a low bank of clouds, but it showed through as a red disc, much duller than the sun as seen from Earth.

Even against the light of these two brutes, a bright morning star sparkled in the yellow, low on the horizon, its light fluttering in the atmosphere. The sight reminded her of nights staring up into the sky of Earth, of Jupiter at midnight and Venus glimpsed from carriages in the early morning. It reminded her of all those sights at once, and she lived through them again in that second, revisiting them all.

The man her calling was named after, Giordano Bruno, had been burned at the stake in 1600 for daring to imagine worlds such as this. And now here she was.

The spectacle above her was so awesome that it took her a moment to realise that she was hearing something above the gentle wash of the wind on the sand.

A high, whining noise, steadily rising in pitch.

She saw something dark in the sky overhead. Black dots, getting closer.

Jane suddenly realised that her body was starting to run, that she herself was familiar with exactly what was going on here.

Those were shells – and they were falling towards her!

She ran across the desert, over the top of a beautiful swordlike dune, rolling down the other side when she lost her footing, clouds of sand billowing up over her until she stuck at the bottom, vulnerable.

She struggled to her feet. The noise was all round her now. The shells must have been falling from some incredible height—

She looked around for shelter.

There was none.

She threw herself into the sand, her hands over her head.

The explosion blasted the top of the dune over her head. She felt the shadow of the sand rush over her in a great wave. A second blast and a third hit to her left and right. The darkness grew darker. She cowered in her arms, trying to burrow into the sand.

And then there was silence.

After a few moments, Jane dared to look up.

She didn't understand what she saw.

The sand from the dune had been frozen in the blast. Three wings of flying dust hung in some glassy material above her. She wondered if time had stopped, but when she got to her feet she could feel the wind blowing against her skin, diverted by these new shapes, shifting sand into the gap underneath them.

She reached up to touch the nearest surface, the first one, that had passed just a few feet over her head.

'No!'

She snatched her hand away. The shout had come from nearby. Not that she'd heard it as 'no'. She'd heard a high, hooting grunt, and her mind had immediately known it meant danger and withdrawal. Someone was approaching from behind her, from the direction of the mountain. She could hear the sound of something struggling to move across the sand, little muscular noises of exertion.

Three figures appeared on the dune behind her, silhouetted

against the orange, reflecting bulk of the mountain. She couldn't tell if they were men or women. They looked exactly like her, white and thin. And their eyes! She hadn't had a reflection to see her own as yet. Their eyes were a dull red, large orbs bulging out of gaunt, pained faces.

So these were her fellows in Hell. She hoped they weren't here to hurt her.

They slid down the dune towards her, gesticulating wildly that she wasn't to touch the glassy sweep of sand that had been solidified above her. Jane stepped back, her hands folding between her legs in modesty, despite the fact that neither she nor they had anything to hide.

The leading figure came right up to her, and looked her up and down. What it could possibly be looking for, Jane had no idea. To her, she and the newcomer looked exactly alike, apart from the fact that it, like its fellows, was wearing a weapon of some kind over its shoulder, and a belt slung with various unfamiliar tools. Finally, in the alien tongue she somehow knew by heart, it said:

'Are you the Reverend Jane Bruce?'

'Yes.'

The figure incongruously stuck a hand out towards her. 'Thank goodness we found you, Reverend. You're expected back at base. I'm Major Alisdair Trent.'

Forty-Four: A Mad Sort of C.S. Lewis Thing

The four white figures marched across the yellow land.

'Where are we?' asked Jane. 'Is this—?'

'A world orbiting the twin suns which, together, the astronomers of Earth know as Capella. Or, so I'm told, Alpha Aurigae.' Alisdair sounded enthusiastic. 'Light from that old monster up there takes forty-five years to reach home.'

'So we're—'

'Aurigans! Capellans! I don't want to explain too much. Stealing the thunder from my CO, you see. We're taking you to meet him. Suffice it to say, Reverend, that everything's fine with the dear departed!'

'Right . . .' Jane managed to return his thin smile. The other two 'men' in Alisdair's patrol were also managing a rough approximation of a grin, their face muscles stretched by the effort. They had been introduced to her as Captains Eric Sandicott and Harold Finch. Finch had an odd way of talking, very eloquent, so flourished she could hardly follow it. Sandicott, on the other hand, hadn't said a word.

They had taken her at speed from out of the shadow of what had turned out to be three frozen splashes of a silver material, over-lapping around her. Very precise shelling, Alisdair had explained. She had been walking towards some distant cannon, and the bombardier, faced with only one dimension to take into account, had calculated her position.

Even so, she wanted to spend a moment examining the plumes of sand, trapped in the moment of explosion. But the patrol had rushed her off, moving in a hasty zigzag across the dunes. The shells, Alisdair had explained, were full of some sort of adhesive, designed to trap her like a fly in amber.

'At least,' she'd said, 'they weren't trying to kill me.'

The whole patrol had laughed like drains at that, for some reason. Which had led to her irritated questions about just where they were, and what the nature of this post-death existence was, exactly.

Questions which were still unanswered.

They ran over a rocky ridge that stuck up out of the sand, covered with white mineral deposits. On the other side of it, shielded from distant gunners by the rock, lay a curious vehicle.

It looked like a bedstead, made of rough metal, blackened and eroded by time, with four seats, two or three controls only and a big engine at each leg. Some sort of small gun was mounted at the rear, accessible from one of the rear seats.

Sandicott leapt into that one, with Finch beside him. Alisdair took the pilot's seat and Jane was instructed to get in beside him in the front. 'The air's too thin for wings,' he said. 'You wouldn't notice it, of course. That's what your new body's used to. So we use rockets.' He pulled a lever on the panel in front of him. 'Here we go!'

An extraordinary noise erupted from the four corners of the bedstead, and a cloud of sand rose to form a mist about them. It took Jane a few seconds to realise that they were moving forward, faster and faster.

They sped out from under the rock ledge and swept straight upwards, so fast that Jane shrieked as the ground fell away beside her naked foot.

Alisdair laughed. 'You'll get the best possible view from here, Padre. We'll fly parallel to the lines for as long as it's safe. Take a look.'

'The lines?' Jane was looking down at a landscape of yellow and white, the mineral deposits writhing over the desert like the courses of rivers or the icing on a ruined cake. The mountain she had awoken inside was an ugly eruption in the midst of all that, part of a completely different geography, falling behind them. They were heading, she realised, in the direction of the gun that had fired at her. She hoped Alisdair knew what he was doing.

She studied him for a moment as he concentrated on banking the craft, smaller rockets bursting from along one side of the frame with explosive noises. How could this creature be the same boy who had been in the rowing team, been photographed ready for battle?

How could she be Jane Bruce? And how could he know her?

Mind you, if this was Hell, then Alisdair seemed very cheerful about his situation.

The craft swept around, so that Jane's viewpoint was tipped towards the ground. She gasped at what she saw in the far distance.

A black band ran across the land, stretching off as far as Jane could see in either direction, until it was lost in cloud and in a range of mountains. It was higher than the desert: Jane could see clouds snagging on various features amongst it, and the shadow of its escarpment on this side. The edges were rough, and in some places burst forth from the band like the banks of some huge river overflooded.

'Use the telescope,' Alisdair advised.

Jane found the instrument stowed in a pocket by her foot. She swung it to cover the black band, and was startled by what she saw.

Hundreds . . . no, surely thousands of trenches, all filled with Aurigans, stationed at weapons points, standing guard, in one case suddenly leaping up from their trench and running out across the bare, blackened land, their weapons ready.

She swung the telescope to cover the other side, and was shocked to see that the enemy was identical, composed also of Aurigans, who also filled their trenches attending to their various duties. The ground between the two forces was covered in metal spikes, black residue, the blooms of the adhesive, in some places forming great forests of the stuff, which had in turn been broken by explosives or blackened by fire. Sometimes one kind of blemish lay across another, as with a mass of adhesive blooms covered in pink foam, with balls of black metal spikes littered upon it. The entire landscape suggested geological change, the pain of the movement of glaciers across a valley, or a river eroding its way into the rock, but done by the hand of man. The two fronts and the space between them must have stretched across twenty or thirty miles.

She found the advancing Aurigans once more as they sought cover in a garden of adhesive blooms. Explosions suddenly turned the ground about them into black dust, and they fell, to her horror, or were blasted upwards.

But shortly, as the dust subsided, she could see them getting to their feet, moving on once more amongst the white of the new craters, only for another barrage of shells to land amongst them. This sprayed the pink foam into a river that engulfed them, swelling around them for a moment like it would wash them back to their own trenches. Then it froze in a second, caught on the swell, and Jane could see the troops stuck in it, some of them waving desperately, some of them visible only as individual limbs.

And then she saw the object of their expedition, just ahead of them. One Aurigan had been caught in such a mass of foam before, snagged only by his foot. He stood as a scarecrow, his body full of holes, his head smashed in on one side. The ground around him had become so brightly coloured with the hues and striations of battle that he was an obvious target. Jane was moved for a moment by this attempt to retrieve a corpse, but then the scarecrow moved, its mouth forming some call back to its fellows.

Jane lowered the telescope. 'This *is* Hell,' she said.

'It's war,' said Alisdair. 'This section of the front we're just passing has seen action since the Combined Advance of 1963.'

'How far does the battle extend?'

'The battle? The war front encircles the planet. The particular battle down there is the Battle of Geoffrey Muir.'

'Geoffrey Muir?'

'The poor bastard with his foot caught in the tarbaby. You saw him, surely? He's been stuck like that for fifty years.'

Jane put a hand to her mouth, feeling an urge to cry or vomit, and frightened by not knowing what would come out if she did.

Alisdair swung the flying machine back in the other direction. The look on his face said that he was aware that he'd shown Jane too much for her sensibilities. 'Sorry, Padre,' he said. 'Always a bit much, one's first sight of that. But it really is the war to end all wars, you know. Nothing futile about this one. Absolutely good against evil, and we're on the side of the angels.' He leaned closer to her. 'I was horrified to die in that gas attack, you know. Absolutely petrified. Soiled myself. And it all seemed so meaningless. The poor horses! But when I came here, and when this war started . . . well, it all made sense. My life as well as my death. And it'll make sense to you too. Because that's why you're here. You've got a part to play in ending the war. So cheer up. It's all going to be all right.'

Jane managed to nod once more.

Alisdair angled the craft away from the lines, leaving the scar in the landscape far behind them.

The cluster of buildings was etched deeply into the land, so much so that Jane initially thought they were descending into a stretch of featureless scrubland. As they turned to head for a small landing area, however, she noticed a couple more of the strange rocket craft, then a compound where ground vehicles were standing, then a series of large buildings, linked by walkways and bridges.

There was less dust on landing than on taking off. Jane stepped on to the hot surface of the landing pad exhilarated despite herself. That had been her first flight in anything other than a dirigible.

Alisdair bent to check the motor on the left front foot of the contraption. 'Just in time,' he said. 'Nearly out of fuel. We'd have had to walk home.'

'This "CO" of yours . . .' Jane didn't really know how to put the question that had been brewing in the back of her mind. 'Is he . . . ?'

Alisdair straightened up, and put a hand gently on her shoulder, his eyes meeting hers. 'Yes.'

'Oh fuck,' said Jane.

She approached the low blockhouse with a sinking feeling in her throat. All of this might well have been the deliberate creation of hope within her, a very apt beginning to Hell, considering what she had done to Rebecca.

She hadn't asked if she was about to meet God or Satan. Both seemed equally fearsome, considering her sinful condition.

The three soldiers opened the door in front of her, and ushered her inside into a pleasant coolness out of the sun. The interior was dull white, big fans swinging in the ceiling. Notices on boards fluttered gently, kept there by pins. She was marched silently through a hall, past an Aurigan guard who nodded to Alisdair, and then down a very clean corridor, with offices leading off it.

They turned a corner, and walked into a more open office space. Desks and chairs sat around, under a huge fan in the middle of the room. A map showed the black gash across the globe, running at an angle to the equator, Jane noted, so the war must take place in every climate this planet had to offer. 'Welcome to Field HQ for the north-north-east sector,' Alisdair said.

'Oh. So this isn't—?'

'Not at all. He's come here to meet you. I keep anticipating you, don't I? After all this time, guess-the-question is one of our favourite games.' He flashed her another narrow smile, and went to knock on an office door. 'Before you get to meet him . . .' He called through the door. 'Matthew? Someone to see you.'

The door opened, and an Aurigan hesitantly stepped out. 'Reverend?' he said.

And somehow, Jane knew who it was. There was nothing familiar about the face, which seemed to be like that of every other Aurigan she'd encountered. But something in her senses recognised him. 'Matthew,' she said. 'Matthew the gunner.'

'Matthew James Richardson of 2248, Chester,' Alisdair reeled off quickly. 'We're very particular here. Matthew will be taking you through to see His Nibs.' He looked quickly between them. 'I'll, erm, leave you be. See you later.'

And he marched off.

'Matthew,' whispered Jane, taking his hand in hers. 'What are you doing here?'

He nearly took the hand away. 'So you think I should be in the other place?'

'I meant . . . I'm sorry! I'm not used to this. Matthew, I saw Mary kill you! I'm so sorry . . .'

He seemed to forgive her. At any rate, he held her hand more gently again. 'I don't know who Mary is. I was killed by . . . well, I thought it was my mother.' Matthew looked at his feet for a moment. 'And no . . . there's no need to be sorry. Everything's fine now. There's nothing to be angry about any more.'

'I really meant: why are you *here* here?'

'Oh. Right. I was being debriefed by the leader, and we've been here waiting for you.'

'They were expecting me?'

'And they wanted someone you knew to be here when you passed over. The leader wanted to know everything that happened in Heartsease, and listen, the ghost . . . my mum or your Mary or whatever it looks like . . .' Matthew couldn't resist an excited conspiratorial glance around the room, though he didn't seem to be afraid of being overheard. 'It's working for him!' He looked at his watch. 'We'd better move. He'll know you're here by now.'

Jane felt something in her stomach contract. She let Matthew lead her back along the corridor and up a flight of stairs. 'So don't you feel . . . bitter? About the manner of your death? About being killed by . . .'

'No! Listen, Rev, they needed someone, okay? They needed some intelligence about how the situation was developing. And, typically, they chose me.' He stopped at a corner and turned to look at her seriously. 'I ran away, you know. I broke my Campbell oath. But he just cleared the phone on that, just said it was okay as soon as I admitted it. He gave me some of his stuff and I got it, like everyone gets it. Once you're briefed, it's obvious. What we do back there . . . on Earth . . . it's not important. It's just getting us ready for this place. For the war.'

'I see.'

'You will. Through here. This is the main planning centre in this manor.' He stepped forward and knocked on a door. A call came back from inside and he swung the door open, bidding Jane enter.

Jane almost stumbled inside. She looked back and saw Matthew closing the door, heading off again, flashing her an encouraging smile before he left.

The door closed.

Jane turned to face the room, trying to suppress her shuddering.

The chamber was packed with technology: screens showing the battlefields; computers larger than any she'd ever seen; a big central map table showing an ever-changing view of the black scar that circled this world. But immediately Jane could also see that this wasn't the silvery new technology of net novels, but equipment that had been used and repaired many times, like that of her own world. There were open panels everywhere, new modules roughly connected to old. It looked like the war was taking its toll.

In the middle of it all, alone, stood a tall Aurigan, his back to her, studying the screens.

Now he turned around, and smiled that painful smile.

She got the impression that he hadn't adopted the pose to intimidate her, that that had just been where she'd found him.

He was staring at her, Jane was certain, though all the inhabitants of this strange new world seemed to be staring all the time.

Then he came to her, and put his hand to her cheek, touching it as though they were old friends. As if she was the most precious thing he had ever touched. 'Jane,' he said, his voice deep and gentle, his tongue giving her name more consideration than anyone had ever given it. 'I've been waiting for you. I'm Grey Namer.'

Forty-Five: Rebecca's Third Birthday

You're sitting in the middle of the potato patch, behind the bean poles, talking under your breath, hiding from Mum and Dad. You're in your rough trousers, and wellies that have been sealed with tape and spray so many times that they shine.

You're talking to your friend who nobody can see.

She's really fat and lovely. She's much older. She talks in a really slow way. When someone's told you something that's true she'll repeat it to you and make sure you remember it. She gets an extra bit at tea to keep her being really beautiful.

'Shh,' you whisper to her. 'Shh. Quiet, quiet, quiet!'

You bounce up and down on your knees with excitement.

You've just realised that Mum and Dad *really* don't know where you are. That you've *really* hidden from them.

'I can see you!' calls Dad, from over by the house.

'No he can't,' says your friend.

And Dad's pointing in the wrong direction, at Maggie the scarecrow. You think, with horror, for a second, that he's teasing you like he does with every game, just pretending for a moment that you might really be winning.

Dad goes over to Maggie and suddenly leaps at its base, flipping up the plastic sheet that protects the shaft of the scarecrow. He stands up, looking suddenly worried, and puts a hand to his brow against the low sunlight, peering around. 'Rebecca?'

Your friend was right. She dances up and down and has to sit down and pull open her collar to cool down, she's been dancing so hard.

You have to put your fingers in your mouth to stop yourself squealing with delight.

Mum appears, marching towards the bean poles. She's wearing her big warm fluffy hat and gloves. She has a warm smile on her face.

She's glad you can hide.

She squats down to peep between the poles.

Delighted, you rush forward and thrust your hot little face into hers. 'Boo!'

'Boo,' she replies, and reaches over to pick you up, and calls to Dad.

Forty-Six: You Only Live Twice

Jane knew immediately what she had to do.

She dropped to her knees at the Aurigan's feet, and closed her eyes. 'My Lord,' she said.

'Jane,' said Grey Namer once more. 'The Reverend Jane Bruce, of the Reformed Church of England.' He laid his hand on top of her bald scalp. 'Please, open your eyes. There's something you want to tell me, isn't there?'

'Yes. I tried to kill someone. In the most terrible way. I was driven to it. But that's no excuse.' Jane felt the words jump out of her, like she had been waiting to admit this for so long. She felt utterly vulnerable to the Namer, but it was good to be vulnerable to him. She felt his love and trusted him.

'Hush.' He bent to kiss the top of her head. 'I know what you did. Because it was my will that you did it. If you'd succeeded, you know,' he laughed kindly, 'things would be a lot easier for everyone right now.'

Jane looked up at him. 'Your will . . . was for me to torture some-one to death?'

He sighed, took both her hands and helped her to her feet. 'For us . . . for human beings . . . death is just a door. There's no reason to fear or hate the process, unless you come through on the wrong side, and are reborn on the Morningstar. As for the torture . . . we can soothe that, take the memories away. You did a terrible thing to Rebecca. That's my fault. But look around you. Translate it into this. If you'd succeeded, Rebecca would have been here to greet you instead of Matthew, and I promise you, she would have been just as happy to meet you. I would have talked to her. She would have understood.'

'Let me understand. Tell me everything.'

Namer pulled out a chair for her at the big central table, and, shaking, Jane sat on it. He sat down beside her, and waved a hand over the table. The display changed. Now it showed the globe of the planet as a diagram, with great voids visible inside.

The display zoomed in on the voids, and Jane could see fine structure, millions of lines and squares and circles. It was an architectural plan, she realised.

'Living spaces,' Namer said, his gentle red eyes fixed on the display. 'For every human being who has ever lived. Eight billion people here. And almost another eight billion *lost* souls on the Morningstar.'

'Lost? You mean this is Heaven, and this other world you speak of is Hell?'

He shook his head. 'I wish it were that simple. Because I wish these were not material worlds. We're still in the universe my Father created. If you could journey far enough through spacetime, Jane, forty-five light-years, you would come to the Earth once more. I say I wish it were otherwise because of the pressures we're under. This is a large world. Bigger than Earth. You don't notice the change in gravity because of your new body. The Morningstar, which orbits the other sun here . . .' his finger touched a subsidiary display showing the planets' orbits, 'is large also. But both worlds are quite hostile environments. It's much more comfortable for a human soul to live underground. And we're simply running out of space.'

'How do people come here after they die? Why? What are *you* doing here?'

Namer chuckled again. 'Well, I'm everywhere. Or I can be.' He leaned closer to her, a child divulging a mock secret. 'I've been born three times. Twice on Earth, then once here. Listen.' He rubbed his fingers together for a moment, then split them to reveal a tiny ball of flesh. 'Take my memory. It's easier when you can see what I've seen. I do this with everybody. Not one to one like this, I don't have the time! Usually, I just give the memory to all those in my house, when they arrive. It comes back to me after you have the information. You're not eating me up.'

Jane took the pea-sized ball from his hand.

'And now may I have your memories in return?'

'I . . . don't know how to . . .'

'Let me.' Namer reached out and placed his hand on her arm. He rolled his finger slowly against her skin. There was a tiny moment of pain. A similar ball of flesh was rolled off into his hand. He showed it to her, holding it between finger and thumb. 'There,' he said. 'We'll come to that later. For now, take my memory into yourself. See things as I see them.'

Jane looked nervously at that calm, unfamiliar face, then took the lump in her mouth and swallowed it.

She didn't expect it to act instantly, but it did.

She was in the river, the interlocking pieces of human thought coming together in her mind. And for a moment she thought she'd dreamed all of her old existence.

Then she was sitting by the sea, hearing the distant chants, thinking of doors and keys.

Then she was hanging in absolute pain, her wounds open for the world to see.

And then she was here, looking right at herself. The shock of seeing herself as an Aurigan. She raised her hand an inch, and saw this strange being raise a hand too. And she knew that the person looking at her loved her unconditionally.

And she knew everything he knew, now.

Now she could see him through her own eyes again.

'Walk with me through the memories,' he said.

They were in the river, lying on the surface, staring up at the sun as it rippled through the forest canopy. 'Here,' he said, 'I thought of myself as Grey Namer, though I never got to say that name aloud. I was the first of my kind, the first *sapiens sapiens*, though within my lifetime I met others like that who were not my kin. I use that name again now for the pleasure of hearing it, and because my second name, Jesus son of Joseph from Nazareth . . .' he reeled the name off as Alisdair had named Matthew, 'feels presumptuous here, with all the expectations that people attach to it. I'd rather they knew me as the Son of my Father than respect me just because of a name.'

Jane lay back, luxuriating in the water. She was trying to sort out everything that had suddenly been placed in her head, but, her brain was saying to her, even with her training, it was going to take decades. She had a huge, persuasive human experience now sitting in her own, now unlimited memory. Finding her way round it would be a task that it would take her more than another human lifetime to complete.

It felt like she had been invaded, in a gentle way. It was easier to ask about what she couldn't find. 'So why do human souls come to Auriga?'

The Namer ducked into the river, spun underwater, burst up out of the surface and laughed again. 'I don't know. I'm a human being, Jane, simply a dead human being! I have to guess at my Father's plan and have faith in it like everyone else. But I think we're starting to see how it all might fit together now. Everyone who ever lived is in the Alpha Aurigae system, apart from those who still are alive on Earth. And we've been put here in bodies that are indestructible, that can't die again, no matter what happens to them.'

'Can't die?'

Suddenly, they were walking through the battlefields at night. All around them, Aurigans hung, groaning and calling, from hardened masses of adhesive and foam.

'These bodies,' Namer whispered, 'hang on to our souls and *cannot* let go of them. That's what makes us think this is the last chapter. We're stranded here, we're here forever, we have to make this world *right*.'

'How can anything natural be immortal?'

He came to a head that had been split from the body of a man, the body being lost somewhere in the warped and burnt lands, and bent to touch its forehead. 'We have so many scientists and theologians, with so many ideas between them. Such a torrent of voices, such a commotion. Especially since a lot of the earlier ones have to catch up with the later ones, and a lot of them can't, but still they insist they know best.' He straightened up again. 'Very human! My favourite idea of theirs is this: the Aurigans, these creatures we inhabit, still exist as animals, living down in the depths of both planets . . .'

They hung from a wicker basket on the end of a long cord, watching Aurigans in the depths of a cave below wrestle and compete, growling like kittens, rolling over and over in the dust, bounding away and then bounding back, by instinct rather than decision. 'They seem,' said Namer, 'to have arisen on one world and journeyed to the other. We often captured these beasts, in the first days here, to study them. They seem to live by instinct, breed and stay alive in competition with several predators, as small-minded as sheep.'

They watched a group of Aurigans, with instruments in their hands, studying one of this lower form of their kind, who was beating on the bars of a cage, its teeth bared.

'Then, when they reach maturity, a sort of trance comes over them, their sexual organs are absorbed into their bodies, and they make their way to the surface.'

Jane watched an Aurigan stumbling out of a hole in the ground into the light, looking around wildly, as if it didn't understand its own actions. It cast around for the right place, still driven by something that frightened it, and then frantically kicked up a circle in the sand. There it lay down, and gradually its jerking movements became slower, until they stopped.

'They fall into a coma, and wake as one of us. With a human mind inhabiting their brain, just as you did.'

The Aurigan opened its eyes. With a new purpose in them.

'We've studied their evolution. They're based on sulphur-eating bacteria, but at some point in the distant past, a mutation emerged which allowed them to exist on zero-point energy . . . The meat of the universe, so I'm told, the fundamental essence. That which fed my faith, through grace, while I was in the wilderness.'

They watched Aurigans walking through rock, it parting before them.

'Once they had chanced upon that foodstuff, they were able to roughly create the caves they now live in, deep beneath our own living spaces. They were able to remake their environment through thought, as you sometimes find you can control a dream. From that point they were immortal, yet they continued to breed. Which resulted in them dominating their ecosystem, almost destroying it, the point where we are now. Human minds may turn out to be *their* salvation. Their consciousness, not that they were even sentient, was linked to the universe, to my Father's work. Many of my folk now think that in doing that, the Aurigans attracted dead human minds to them in their dreams.'

They walked through a market in Galilee. The Namer stopped to take an apple from a stall and weighed it in his hands. 'My Father seems to have placed Auriga at the bottom of a slope in the universe. You're a Brunian, this shouldn't be so hard for you. Many of your calling have started to think that the human memory is too large to be contained within the human brain.'

'Yes, that's been the subject of some debate.' Jane was looking around her, wondering at the people walking past. There were gaps in her vision, things that Jesus hadn't looked at when he'd originally been here. She could follow, she saw, children in detail, and whenever some cry of a vendor came up, her head swung to catch the excitement, against her own volition.

'What if humans are on the same path as the Aurigans? What if we store memory *above* the universe? With a knot of it inside our brains, connecting the ifs and thens of pseudo-objects, of what my scientists call monads, to us?' He seemed to realise that Jane didn't understand. He took the apple and held it up, then dropped it into his other palm. 'When we die, the knot unfurls, the fruit falls from the tree. The memory slips off down the slope and ends up on Auriga. It becomes a symbiotic parasite on an Aurigan, allowing it to come to the surface, allowing the mind to continue, allowing my Father to fulfil his purpose.' He saw Jane nodding, smiled, and bit into the apple, placing a coin from nowhere, a coin that must once have had a material existence and come from a purse, into the hand of a fruitseller, who suddenly animated into a nod of thanks and moved on. 'We think that's why Aurigans look so much like humans: the arriving minds have reshaped their bodies.'

'You talk,' Jane said, 'as if all this happened recently. But haven't you all had millions of years to—?'

'No,' said Jesus, shaking his head. He took a moment to finish the apple. 'The first of us became aware of our existence here all at once, in our billions, all the human dead of all the hundreds of thousands of years before. In the year 1917.'

'Nineteen seventeen?'

They stood on a great open plain, with Aurigans as far as the eye could see, all thrashing, all screaming, with more and more of them rushing up out of holes in the ground, a great torrent of bodies, flinging themselves into the mass ecstasy.

'Perhaps it was the sheer numbers of dead minds coming through in the battles of that war. The log jam broke, and we all slid down the slope together. We created the civilisation we have here in the three hundred and thirty-one years since then.'

'So why—?'

'Is it so weak and wretched? When we could change the universe to make it how we wished? Well, when we first arrived here, only I could do that.'

They stood smiling amongst a group of enthusiastic Aurigans in a cathedral, a dome of brilliant glass shining in the sunshine high overhead. The Aurigans were looking at them in awe, some of them down on one or both knees.

'The resources of the Aurigans seem to have been bequeathed to me. That's how I, and those who follow me, came to realise that I was once, and still am, my Father's son. I recall those twenty-seven years of development and growth as a golden age, a true heaven.' They walked about the cathedral, Jane able to observe every detail of the simple but profound architecture, the vaulted ceiling, the millions of panels of brilliant glass. 'A celebratory place, that they might worship my Father still, in the world after,' said Namer. 'I worked miracles freely and at large, finally able to give to my people everything I always wanted to give them. I thought my Father had put us all here so I could reward them. I even began to reach out with my newfound communion with the universe. I learned to move above the cosmos, and to touch the Earth once more. That's when I decided to bring everyone to my Father's house, to finish his plan.'

'In what way?'

'Later for that.' The Namer turned on his feet, raising his hands to the ceiling. 'I enjoy the memory of these times so much. My perfect twenty-seven years.'

'Why did you have only that?'

Namer paused for a long time before answering. Then he waved a hand.

Suddenly, Jane was watching the Namer shaking another Aurigan by the hand. This one seemed to have something about him. A presence, an authority that she suddenly realised none of the others had.

'In 1944, the mind of the Adversary, the master of Morningstar, arrived. Initially, he came to me and we were friends. He would not accept that I was who I said I was, a matter of hard faith, even after I had shared my memories with him. But there have been many like that, and in time I was used to winning them all over, so, we agreed to differ. He went to live on the other world, the one we now know as the Morningstar. There he built his dwelling. And in doing so, he discovered that he also held the power of miracles in this world.'

Namer suddenly looked up from where he was standing, his finger held above a rock, replaying the memory of the moment, Jane realised, that he became aware of another mind working in his domain. His eyes flew up to the bright star she had observed in the sky when she first came here. Another world, she now realised, going around the other sun. Namer's expression grew worried.

'It was not long before we locked horns,' he said. 'He seemed to take more and more offence at my identification of myself as my Father's son. Everyone else saw the truth before their eyes, but he would not. And then, to my horror, others started to come, arriving around him, who did not see it either.'

They walked down to a natural amphitheatre where the Aurigan that Namer called the Adversary was speaking, surrounded by interested Aurigans. It looked like he was preaching, almost, but his words didn't carry to this distance, and Jane found she could not move any closer.

'Swiftly, the Morningstar became *their* world, and all my pleas could not prevent them from opting to live in the darkness.'

Explosions, earth flying up in violent concussions, Aurigans running everywhere.

'My folk began to struggle with them on their world. Then they invaded this one. So both worlds are divided now, at war.'

Jane watched the battle unfold. The gash across this world grew steadily larger as the war escalated.

'More than that, I now have to struggle with him for everything I try and create through my will alone. Which means neither of us have miracles except at great cost, and that all our people suffer. Minds arrive now according to that grinding contest of wills, either here or on the Morningstar, to swell one side or the other.'

The battle lines enlarged for a while longer, and then faded into clouds, as Namer mentally withdrew from the fray.

They were back sitting at the table, her hands now both clutched in his, his eyes gazing at her, full of pain.

'Can you imagine how painful it was for me, Jane, finding that such things were to be here, as well as on Earth? I had a crisis of faith. I felt that I could not understand what my Father could possibly mean by this. I felt that I had no Father.'

Jane was astonished. 'You?'

Namer nodded. 'And during those years, these worlds were truly hell. But I walked through it. I grew in understanding. I found the path once more.' He broke into a smile again. 'I came to understand that there was *purpose* to this battle. That out of it, something better was to come, though I know not what. So I decided to continue with my plans for *all* of humanity. As I mentioned before. I would fight to bring them *all* to my Father's house. I collected together those builders of things I needed, and I stored my own strength.' He pointed to the table, and a great machine appeared on the surface, shaped something like a cannon. It slid up out of a crater, and swept around the sky, its blunt tip seeking something. Finally it stopped, aimed at its target, a distant star.

'I could not reach *over* the universe to do such an enormous thing, not now the Adversary was fighting me for control. So my scientists created a device to send a message *through* it, across the light years. It was a maser, if you understand the name. They called it the Infomeg.'

The device fired. In an instant, a complicated lightning of fluttering shadows connected the cannon to the sky. Then it was gone.

Namer's eyes fixed on hers, driven now, as if he'd recounted this to many people, many times. 'I rewrote a piece of the universe, what people of older times might have called a spell, and had the maser send that message. It used fully half of my power, reduced me to battling the Adversary every day, thinking about his every action and

360

countering it consciously with one of my own. It made me so mortal, so tired. But it was worth it. The beam altered the electromagnetic atmosphere of Earth. Something that in my golden twenty-seven years I had been able to do without its help. In those days, it seemed like I might have been able to proceed with my plan directly. Perhaps that was why my Father allowed the Adversary to arise, so that my work would not be so simple, so that I would know challenge.'

Jane had started to frown. 'So this was the beam that hit Earth in 1998?'

'The beam which transformed Booth Hawtrey. I chose him because he was such an ordinary man, a man who would accept the honour and despair of his position. He became an Aurigan, giving him the time necessary to work for my purpose.'

Jane let go of Namer's hands so she could rub her forehead. 'Booth Hawtrey. You created Booth Hawtrey. I never thought . . . Look, does he *know* he's working for you?'

'No.'

'Why do you ask him to do so much that's . . . foolish? Sending him to photograph things . . .'

'His duty is mostly to wait, and people aren't good at waiting. So I gave him something to do.'

Jane put her hands in her lap, her mind still racing with all this new information. She knew Namer was telling her the truth, she could see glimpses of everything they'd talked about in the river of new memory that was rushing around her head. She would have to start arranging it into her memory theatre. She would need to build a new one, one the size of that cathedral. Which had been destroyed, she suddenly realised. Ripped apart by bombs. She could see the ruin of it.

And that was when something startling leapt out of the memories at her.

She turned back to Namer, blinking. 'You started the Brunians.'

He clapped his hands together and threw back his head, laughing. 'Well done! See, you're starting to organise it all already! Having put so much data into the Earth's EM field, I needed people who could read it. Most ghosts are a sort of recording. The field takes an impression of a mind as it slides out of spacetime, and that can stay around for a long time. But now there were more important ghosts, with things to do. They whispered in the ears of Swansley and Kemp—'

Jane had her mouth open now. She was aware of her pupils rushing back and forth. It felt like she was reading the new information that was rushing in to answer her every question before she asked it.

Some of the answers were starting to horrify her. 'You gave Swansley a stroke!' she whispered. 'To open him up. To make him—'

'Sensitive to the field, yes.'

'And Georgina Campbell!' Jane's eyes widened as she chanced on the detail. 'Her dreams . . . You influenced them . . . got her to send . . . *me* . . .'

'To Heartsease. Yes.'

'And I heard it! I heard this ghost of yours. Talking! Over the radio that night! And it seemed to talk to *me* . . . it said *Jane* . . .'

'It learnt your name from whispering into your dreams. From becoming part of who you are. It followed your life to make you go to Heartsease, as I followed your life through all those that knew you and passed on and came to me here. I know you so well, Jane.'

Jane could hardly see him. Her mind was making conclusion after conclusion, faster than she could think. 'And Mary . . . This ghost came to me as Mary, because it knew that was just the figure I'd obey. And Mary made me do—'

'My will on Earth.'

'You needed a Brunian to go to Heartsease—'

'So I could get this.' Namer held up the tiny ball of flesh that contained Jane's memory. 'A first-hand description of the current state of the house, compiled by an expert.' He put it into his mouth, swallowed it and closed his eyes.

Jane raised a hand without thinking. As if some part of her wanted to stop him doing it. Her mind was burrowing through to something vast. Something terrible, that lay under the surface of all these connected facts. 'Heartsease is . . .' Her brow furrowed. She couldn't quite get there. Something was coming between her and the information. It was as if she held contradictory thoughts in her nature. She couldn't be both things at once. Her two memories, her two . . . personalities . . . fought for a moment, then settled on something smaller they agreed on. 'Heartsease was dictated to Simon Trent during your golden years. Alisdair did that for you. You reached out over space to put his voice in the Earth's EM field.'

The Namer, his eyes still closed, nodded.

'Every detail of Heartsease has to be perfect.' Jane felt the memories fall into place, saw the faces of the people she was talking of rush by. 'Simon was supposed to do that. But he stopped. Booth was created . . . to replace him . . . to come back and look after Heartsease, keep it ready, and make . . . Mary . . . make Mary . . .'

She saw fire, the chapel exploding, the bodies, the pieces of bodies falling with the rubble into the ground. And then she saw Mary . . . Alisdair . . . she could see them as both the same thing . . . striding out of the ruins, out of the maze. 'Make Mary to protect the house,' she whispered. She could hardly make her mouth say the words in front of Namer. 'To kill. To kill and keep on killing.'

'To bring those who would disobey my will to me,' Namer emphasised, still concentrating on his own new set of memories.

'That was the other reason for me to be there. To bury Rebecca. To give Mary new strength. To boost her power. To . . .'

'Move everyone who is arriving at the house in the ways I willed them to move.'

They said the words together: 'To complete the plan.'

'But I failed,' Jane said alone.

'But the plan will be complete,' said Namer.

'And the plan is—' Jane began to stammer, her teeth chattering. 'The plan is . . .'

'Heartsease has been absorbing and compiling the electromagnetic radiation of the planet Earth ever since it was completed.' Namer whispered the words like a prayer, letting out, Jane knew now, the creed that had kept him on the same course for hundreds of years. 'I designed so many things to bring emotion and conflict to the house. To add to its architecture. When all is ready, very soon now, it will release that energy in a moment, in a burst that will switch the magnetic poles.' Namer joined his hands, tying a knot tight in the air. 'That will kill every human being and bring them all here to my will. The shock will make the Adversary reel and lose control. His folk will become mine. We will win the war. Then my Father's will shall be done. Then the destiny of humanity will be complete.'

Jane's head slowly fell to her chest. She knew it all to be true.

'Ah,' said Namer. He opened his eyes. 'I now have the last few things that need to be done. Thank you for the details of your memory.'

Then he closed his eyes again.

Jane clutched the table as she felt the universe bend around Namer.

Forty-five light-years away, David squatted by the compiler in the dawn, his temples pressed against the metal. His eyes were closed.

Then he opened them. 'Yes,' he said. 'Oh yes.'

Namer stood, and smiled at Jane. 'Soon,' he said, 'will come the victory that we've always wanted. The work of God shall be done. Evil and conflict will vanish from the human mind. Then we will have Heaven.'

Jane raised her head to look at him. She had stopped shaking. Her mouth was set in a thin line. 'I have only one question now,' she said, hoping that she could keep her voice steady. 'Where is my father?'

Namer paused for a moment. 'If you can't find the answer in my memories,' he said finally, 'it's because you don't want to. He's on the other side. In Hell.'

Jane balled her hands into fists and pressed them together into her chest, her eyes never leaving his. 'Thank you,' she said. 'Now I understand.'

He led her to the door. 'After the victory, I look forward to talking more with you. We will have all the time in the world for conversation. As will all mankind have. But now you must give me a while to myself, to finish the preparations. Alisdair and Matthew will look after you.' He held her hands again for a moment, then opened the door and eased her through it. 'For all our sakes,' he said, 'I'm about to do my Father's will.'

The door closed between them.

Jane waited a moment, then let her face crease into the expression she had been holding in for so long. 'Bollocks you are,' she whispered.

Forty-Seven: Going Over the Wall,
Going Round in Circles

Rebecca had been surprised not to find David in his room. So she'd explored everywhere inside the perimeter, not wanting to call his name in case a Campbell sniper was hiding around some corner.

Outside the windows, dawn was in the air. The corridors looked washed out and wan. As hungover from emotion as she was.

She couldn't help the feeling that she was searching for her love. But something else was overlaid on that. The feeling she'd had when she first arrived at Heartsease. The shape of a house of disasters and fear, without any of the fear. It was as if the bricks had come from a haunting, as if this house was the curtain behind which atrocities were being performed.

Now she knew the truth about that feeling.

Simon had led her around to the rear of the house and opened a tiny wooden door for her to enter. He had taken her by the hand, and looked for a moment like he was going to ask her not to rescue Booth. But finally he just shook his head, and walked with her up stairwells and down narrow little corridors, until the defences parted before her again, and like magic, she was in the Hawtrey zone of the house once more.

Then, without a word, he let go of her hand, and headed off down those same narrow corridors.

He looked back at her once, with an expression like he was amazed they'd talked, like the tears he'd shed had made an understanding between them.

And then he was gone, and she was left alone with the house again.

What Simon had told her should have made her feel better about the place. He was the friendly ghost here. These long corridors had been his only friends. But it didn't feel as if his kindness was the master here. It felt as if the house, the power of the bad ghost, had mastered him. That was the threat she felt behind the walls. The ghost that had called itself Alisdair.

It was probably, she knew, preparing horrors for them all now. Which meant that the Hawtreys had to get out as soon as possible.

But first: Booth.

She found David sitting on the table in the dining room. She had done the little leap over the threshold to safely enter without even thinking about it. 'There you are,' she said, running to him. 'I've got so much to tell you! Listen, we have to get Booth out! We're running out of time!'

'Yes, yes, we are!' He held her with his eyes, nodding seriously. 'Come here.'

They embraced slowly, and he lifted and rolled her over on to the dinner table. They upset table settings and candelabra as they tumbled over and over, him throwing his weight on top of her, her shifting it off once again, enjoying the closeness of the man she loved, the man who had saved her, but needing to get him to just listen to her. 'No,' she said. 'We have to— We have to—'

'Here,' he said, in the exact centre of the table. He used his strength to halt the roll with him on top of her, those deep and lovely eyes staring down into hers. She tried to push again. He held her. 'I've been waiting for you to come here. It's time.'

'Time for what?' She laughed over the words, because his hand had moved inside her coat and his fingers were smoothing at her nipple.

'Time for this place. This room. This house is so beautiful. It's perfect.' He was whispering hotly in her ear. 'I want us to stay here until the end.'

'The end of what, sweetheart?'

'The end of the world.'

'Whatever . . . you . . . want. But we have to get out of here. We have to rescue Booth.'

He shook his head violently.

He lifted himself up, and started to unbutton her trousers.

'Not now!' she laughed.

'We've never done this. It's perfect. Perfect history. What we do here is important. Finally, something we're going to do is important, Rebecca. What if you conceive a child? What's he going to be like?'

She realised what he was talking about as he pulled down her underwear with her trousers, so that they were both around her knees. 'No,' she murmured. 'I love you, but we haven't time, there's going to be a better time . . .'

'I love you, too, but this is exactly the right time and this is the right place. The compiler says so. The waves are getting bigger and bigger. You can start to feel the pattern.' His fingers were urgently separating her, prising at her. She was getting wet for him, and she knew he'd find that in a moment, and think she really wanted him, which she did, she wanted him inside her, but not now, not exactly now . . .

'No,' she said. 'David, wait—'

He didn't stop. He was looking down at her, enthralled by her reactions, waiting for something she didn't understand. Holding her down with one hand, he started to use the other to unzip himself.

She started to seriously struggle now. This was an inconvenience. This was not the right thing at not the right time. Why was he being so stupid? 'David!'

And then she saw the look in his face. The look of satisfaction. Her struggling had been what he had been waiting for.

She suddenly felt a thump of fear in her stomach. 'Oh, David, come on. What are you doing? It's me. Rebecca. It's us.' His fingers had made her wet now, and she was half inclined to grab his head and just kiss him and let it happen, still, but his eyes had that thing in them which was making her afraid.

He *wanted* her to be afraid.

She bucked suddenly as she felt his cock against her leg. His grip flew from her, but he grabbed again. They struggled and she heaved.

They fell off the table.

She landed on him, hard on his balls. He cried out.

She scrambled to her feet before he did, falling and stumbling to try and pull her trousers and knickers back up.

He got up. He swiped for her, but his arm missed.

She pulled them far enough up to trip away, back towards the door, turning to watch him as he glared after her, his eyes fastened on her like she was getting in the way of something trivially important, like all his things were trivially important.

'Come back,' he said. 'Rebecca, I want you. I want you here. Come back.'

He sounded so plaintive, like a little boy. His cock was sticking out of his trousers at an angle, vulnerable and funny.

She took a step towards him, and then she stepped back again. 'No,' she said. 'I love you, but we have to get Booth.'

'Why do we have to get Booth?'

'Because there's something here that's going to hurt us.'

'That can't be true. You *know* that can't be true.'

'You tried to . . . You wanted me to be afraid.'

'Fuck!' He swept his arm in the air as if he was swiping plates off the table. 'Why can't you be afraid if I want you to be? It's really important that we do it now!'

He nearly persuaded her. But she managed to stay on the threshold. 'David, the compiler . . . It's getting to you. It's changing us both. David, if you keep doing things like this, when it's switched off I might not still love you.'

'It's not going to be switched off. Not until I've felt the whole pattern.' He started to wander towards her, his hand stroking his cock. 'Come on, Rebecca. Come here. You want to. I'm telling you you want to.'

She couldn't quite contradict him. But she could take a step back. So she did.

She looked down at the pressure on her foot.

Her heel had pulled on the tripwire. The one attached to the bomb on the ceiling.

Here's the instant, somewhere down the strata of seconds and milliseconds and nanoseconds, down to the gap between actions. The gap where the pseudo-objects of boot heel and tripwire are either apart or together.

Something decides whether they're apart or together. Moment by moment. Whatever moments are.

Either something conscious. Or something random.

Most of the truths of physical reality have no explanation.

This time it was Rebecca who decided that there was no pressure, after all, of boot heel on tripwire.

The situation solved itself.

The moment was created.

And passed.

And the boot heel was on the other side of the tripwire without having tugged on it.

David stared at Rebecca, the look in his eyes saying he never expected his girlfriend to do something impossible.

He rushed at her.

She jumped back.

Through the wall.

He hopped instinctively over the wire and hit that wall. Slammed his fist on it, stumbled off back into the dining room.

'Fuck!' he yelled at the wall which he couldn't help but think was there. Because to him it was all the history and architecture and weighty pride of this damned beautiful house.

He zipped himself up, and headed back to his troops.

He was going to wake them all up.

Rebecca fell screaming down the chimney.

She hit the ground and went straight through that too.

She fell through cellar after cellar, feeling only darkness as she passed through each block, then light when she came out.

She thought she would fall forever, to the centre of the Earth.

So she just thought: stop! Stop falling!

And she did.

She hit the ground with a deadly—

No. The ground softened under her and buoyed her back up like a big cushion.

It sprang her back to her feet.

She was standing on the walkway beside the waterwheel. It was still churning away, in the early hours of the dawn. She put her hands on her body, and found that she was still solid.

She looked at the ring. That was what had let her do this. The ring, made of Boothstuff, the same stuff the house was made of. Stuff that was connected to the magic of the universe.

Fantastic.

Now she could save Booth from the enemy, and David from whatever the compiler was doing to him.

She headed for the door, but then she stopped.

She decided to leave through the wall instead. And this time she successfully, deliberately did so.

The Campbells had left on their dawn attack. Booth swam back out of his memories to find a numb emptiness where his head used to be. All his senses were gone, finally burnt away.

He had been trying to enter the false memories he had had of Alison leaving. He had never been there before, and now he knew why. Every time he tried to get there, his thoughts slid off. The memory impressions existed only to paper over a gap. To keep his narrative intact. He had never even thought of going back there before. Had that been some sort of defence mechanism at work, or just a subconscious desire to keep the reality of those lies alive?

This death might last forever. He'd have to cut the present off, at one end of his memory circle, and only live in the past. If he could. Now parts of his past were infinitely painful too. The lies of how his life with Alison had ended, still taunting him, teasing him to go back and live in their perfect nobility.

All the time, he had been the monster they might have thought he was. He had even been given the luxury of living without the guilt. He was darkness inside darkness, a nothing having to live in the shape of something. Having merely to keep on living. With no reason outside, or inside, now he couldn't pick up his phone and follow his list.

It took him an eternity of memories to realise that he was experiencing something new again. The gaps in him were being filled in. He started to hear distant noise. Then to smell sudden, overwhelming odours. Tea. Vanilla. Blood. Cars. Tyres.

He suddenly realised that he could see.

He saw Rebecca, standing in front of him, talking animatedly, blue stuff in her hands. He gradually realised he could hear her as well. ' . . . can see your eyes moving now. They grew out of this stuff in about thirty seconds. I hope you can hear me. Those bastards. We'll kill them all, Booth. We'll kill them all.'

He found that he had a mouth again. He split open the lips and felt them part. Felt something give between them. A great gulping gap suddenly erupted down his throat and right into his middle, a cavern blooming and setting its own shape in one explosion inside him. He groaned. All the pain was gone, but his body still had the memory of it, like an overcoat of ache.

He tried to move an arm, and found he could. He reached up to touch his own face. There was a gap, an awkward shape, around the corner. Where Rebecca was working. She had been throwing Cortex from ripped-up tyres on to him, in a pile, and his body had been pulling it into the shape of itself, remembering its own details.

He reached out and touched *her* face. She didn't stop working, she just smiled at him complicatedly. It took him a moment to remember how to speak. 'I don't deserve this.'

'Thank you for saving me, Rebecca,' she muttered. 'Thanks for getting a lump of Booth soup out of a saucepan, shaking it in a colander, and then rolling it in Cortex until it started to grow. I had to make you a new dick, you filthy bastard.'

He winced at the familiar sound of her voice. He didn't want to be close to anyone he loved now. He wasn't even sure he wanted to be remade. 'If you knew what I know . . .'

'I do. I know everything.'

Booth didn't know what to say. He let her finish off the side of his head, and watched as she stepped back from him, nodded at her handiwork, then went to wash her hands at the big white sink.

He sat up. Only when he did did he realise that he'd been lying on the Lutyens table. He slid his new, naked legs down on to the floor, watching as they changed from blue to pink, and grew skin, and tiny hairs.

He saw that Rebecca had turned to watch too. 'I can see it happen now,' she said. 'I can do the trick too.'

He took his weight on his feet, and looked around the room. He felt himself starting to shake, fighting off the avalanche of memories. He was suddenly terribly fearful that Ruth would come back and it would all start again. 'We have to go,' he whispered. Miserably, he looked around him, and laid his hand on his phone, which had been left on a worktop. 'We have to leave. I have to finish my list . . .'

'No!' Rebecca shouted. She marched over to him, shaking her head ferociously. 'No, no, no! You must *not* do that!'

'Why?' murmured Booth, lost.

Rebecca stared at him, as if she was suddenly puzzled at her own insistence. 'Because . . .' She searched for a solution and couldn't find one. 'Oh, fuck, I don't know. There are more important things. I'm missing something. Something really huge. We have to get out of here. Before the ghost gets us. Before the Campbells get us. Come on!'

She grabbed his hand and ran straight at the wall.

Booth didn't have the energy to think they couldn't get through it. So they did.

David was sitting around in the Switching Cupboard with Steven, Little Bob, Frank and Jacko. As they'd sat around in barns and haystacks and tents and mess halls in many different places.

They were listening to the compiler clicking away as the light formed longer patterns across the floor. Jacko had opened a window, and the cold dawn air was touching their skin, making them rub their eyes and do stretching exercises, ready for the day.

'They're on the move,' said David, referring to the Campbells. 'Very slowly. They're coming up one of the stairwells, taking our stuff down. I can feel them walking.'

Little Bob pulled his gun from his belt.

David waved a hand out. 'No. Wait until they're in the right rooms. We've got hours.'

He became aware that suddenly, all his men were looking past him.

He turned to look. Rebecca was standing there, proudly hand in hand with Booth Hawtrey. Who was naked.

Jacko was the first to his feet, hollering a Hawtrey whoop as the others began to react.

'Bex!' cried Steven. 'Bloody hell, you got him!'

David watched as they ran forward, embracing Rebecca and Booth both, though only Steven had ever met the man before.

David kept his distance, his eyes meeting Rebecca's over Jacko's shoulder.

She wanted to talk to him. She would say they *needed* to talk.

She probably wouldn't want to do that in the dining room.

He needed to know how she'd left through the wall. Maybe she was feeling the way this house was going too. The way it was inviting them all to complete the picture, to make things right. He felt jealous under his love. She knew things he didn't.

He went to her. She disengaged from Jacko. Booth stumbled into the room, and was helped to a chair by the others. Little Bob took his phone from him, and David immediately took it on from him and slipped it into his pocket.

He looked on for a moment as his men fussed over the hero of his family, giving up a coat for him here, a pair of boots for him there.

Then he turned back to Rebecca.

'We need to talk,' she said.

They walked a few feet up the corridor. Rebecca was trying not to make eye contact with him. As soon as they'd got within a few feet of each other, the teenage feeling of need and stupidity shoved its way up into her chest again, despite the fact that he had tried to rape her. *Despite* that . . . How could there be a despite? 'We have to leave, David,' she managed to say, trying to hold on to that certainty. 'As soon as possible.'

He managed not to laugh at the absurdity of the suggestion. 'Absolutely not. We've got Booth here now.' She could hear the mockery in his voice at that. 'Nothing can hurt us.'

'We *have* to leave!' To her despair it came out as a shriek.

He spun on his heel, grabbed her and slammed her up against the wall, his hands around her head, his lips against hers.

And after a moment, to her horror, her lips parted, her muscles relaxed, and she kissed him back.

'I love you,' he said. 'Sorry about the dining room.'

He was sorry. The lovely old thing was sorry. Her heart went out to him. She could never stay angry with him for long. She put a hand gently to his cheek, and stopped him from kissing her again. 'No, I mean . . . not *no*, but . . . Oh shit, I'm missing something. I'm missing something so *big* . . . It's the compiler. What it's doing to us. It's cooperating with everything else. David, it's—'

He kissed her again.

'We have to leave!' she muttered under his kisses. 'We have to!'

But David just kept on kissing her.

She loved him.

Under all his kisses, she started to cry.

Jane ran across the sand, her heels throwing up tufts of dust behind her. Ahead of her, the huge sun was setting. The more distant star had already set. She had no destination in mind. Right now, she was just running. Away from Grey Namer and his army.

Matthew and Alisdair had left her in a room with a window. They hadn't even seemed to consider the possibility that she might not have agreed with everything the Namer said.

She had pulled open the window, and leapt the twenty feet or so to the ground. Then she had walked out of the main gate, making eye contact with the guards as she left. So much trust! This must be an extremely clear-cut war, to have no spies, no traitors, no threat other than that of the enemy, who were always to be recognised. Just what a war in Heaven should be.

Not that they were in Heaven.

She became angry again at the thought. The arrogance of Grey Namer! The great I Am! She could feel his memories stewing inside her, still.

He had been born twice. And the second time he had taken the form of Jesus of Nazareth. Jane felt unworthy to bear those memories of passion and calm, had barely touched them, they felt so precious.

There was no experience of God in the memories, only faith, a familiarity with the Holy Spirit. Which should have been no surprise. Jesus was a man. There was no physical resurrection in the memories. His birth seemed to have been ordinary, as confused as the birth memories were. There were miracles, some vastly different to what was written. But what were miracles, after what she had learned here? There were details of his existence that had never been recorded, and perhaps should have been. Throughout, he was the lamb, the gentle one, the perfection of man on Earth, while being fully a man.

There was the Crucifixion, almost supernaturally identical to the way it had been recorded.

But.

She knew that if he had been the Son of God on that second occasion, he was not so now. Or perhaps he had never been the Son, just a powerful and loving man, and history had mistaken him for the Messiah. As he had. No, she decided, she could not bring herself to believe that. But that left open an even more terrible prospect. The Son had broken with his Father. He had wilfully or mistakenly misinterpreted his Father's plan.

She recalled the distance between those expressions on his face, now that she could read the body language of Aurigans from what had been in his memory. In his cathedral, he had been that joyous young nation, delighting in his power to restore and help. Back in the control room, as he recalled all those trivial human details of his plan, he had been an empire, a dictatorship . . . and just one small man.

The Namer had gone insane. Perhaps when he conceived his plan, he had not been. But in completing it, he had been brought low. He had bent beneath the weight of three lives and the responsibility of half the Kingdom.

And how did she know that all this was true? How did she know that despite all appearances, and the love and trust of a full half of the human race, this was not Christ enthroned?

During the interview with him, while she heard his huge plan that was also so mortally small being spelt out, she had realised the most wonderful, central thing about her life. She had realised it because of the direct comparison with what it was not.

She knew, as the Namer put word upon word, that her God was something more than these words. That He was not in the room with her.

She had realised where her God had gone, just as she was supposed to be meeting Him.

In the corridor outside, she met with Matthew and Alisdair again, and they had walked her off, talking of victories and grand schemes. They had taken her to a room alone, to rest. The room with a window. They had left her alone there.

And there she had got down on her knees, closed her eyes, and offered herself up to her God.

That was how she ran, without a moment of uncertainty, out into the desert, trusting to Him to show her why she was really here. Why they all were here.

The others, she thought, were bent double by Christ's memories. Were swallowed by the power and truth of them. That was what held them in certainty.

But she had reached. She had reached up a hand to her God.

And in the room with the window, He had grasped it.

The joy of love. Complicated love. The love for a life. For a country. For the green. For the world. For a whole existence. That was not limited and did not have an ending. The ending that had been written was wrong.

Suddenly, as she ran, the Namer was with her. He asked if she was not the arrogant one, to assume that only she had seen the truth, of all the humans that had walked with him.

Jane told him to walk out of her sight, behind her. She was with her God.

The Namer said that it was just because of her father not being here. That she could not accept that painful truth. She had constructed her sudden faith in a false impression of God just so she would not have to believe in her father working for the Adversary, so she could continue to believe in the shooting accident. What a tiny, human failing. What wickedness, to want to betray your Lord just so you could feel better.

Jane denied the Namer again. She told him about lines and circles.

Her father had liked to walk with her, when she was small, in all the different seasons. They had watched dewy things growing in spring. They had sat on green banks split by light and shadow in summer. They had crunched and caught falling leaves in autumn. They had walked on the points of hard mud in winter. And Dad had always delighted in telling her that things would all come round again. That the seeds of each season were visible in the one before it.

She had grown in cycles. She knew the truth of her path, as it had come to her gradually in buds and birds and the filled-in impressions of shod horses, as a circle. Of birth, death and resurrection.

Instead of this circle, the Namer saw a line. An ending. A completion. A crude race from one side of existence to the other, for all of humanity.

She told him now that could not be true. She had faith that that was not how her father or her Father in heaven saw it.

She could take pleasure in all the seasons. She was alive with everyone else in the light evenings and cursory nights of summer, anticipated through all of spring. When she walked in autumn, she didn't feel death coming, as she knew many of her folk who got sullen and depressed in the darkness did. She felt joy that the world was bonfire-red and falling, and that she was still alive and of faith in it.

In the midst of death, she said to the Namer now, *we are in life*.

He fell behind and was lost in the desert. He could do nothing to stop her run now.

She had found her Father.

Now she was going to find her father.

Forty-Eight: Fall and Rise

She ran for what seemed like hours, the countryside around her unchanging and steadily less visible in a darkness that glowed red and yellow at levels just at the edge of her vision. She ran according to her faith and her instincts, following what seemed right, though she grew colder by the moment, and the sand had started to fret at her feet with a continual, throbbing pain.

After a while, she became aware of a noise gathering in the sky above her, amongst the unfamiliar constellations.

She looked up, and saw dark shapes forming there.

Figures. Aurigans!

They were falling towards her from a great height, spinning as they came.

She looked around for somewhere to hide.

The first Aurigan hit the ground behind her with a yell, and rolled for a long distance. Jane started to run away from him, but just then the other two landed in front of her, rolling off in blooms of sand, all of them yelling.

For a moment she was surrounded by flying sand, not knowing which way to turn.

And then they were on her. The three figures came at her all at once, from different directions. They grabbed her by the arms and midriff, and held her expertly and tightly, silencing her desperate wrench to get away.

'Wait,' one of them said. 'Jane Bruce, wait!'

She stopped and looked into the face of the Aurigan who'd shouted at her.

And she realised somehow that he . . . it was, or had been, a he, she had learned how to understand that implicitly . . . was unlike any of them she'd previously seen. He was . . . of the enemy. A soldier of the Adversary. There was no physical sign of it, but she knew.

'You know my name?' she said.

They let go of her. 'I'm Captain Andrew Standish of Dorking, 1975,' said the man who'd spoken previously, and offered his hand. 'Sorry to manhandle you. We couldn't let you get away. We only have a matter of seconds before the Namer tracks us.'

Jane noted that the other two wore bulky backpacks, which they were swiftly ripping apart. Inside were pieces of a machine, which they began to assemble with practised speed.

'You work for . . .'

'For the Adversary, yes. Bloody hell. Tell me I'm right in thinking that that doesn't fill you with horror.'

'You're right. Do you know—?'

'Your father? Yes, he's waiting for you.'

'Would you please stop—?'

'Of course.' He turned to his men, who had now finished assembling the machine. It was a box on tripod legs, with computer controls and what looked like a fuel tank, which one of the soldiers was swiftly filling with fuel from a separate tank. 'Right, we're nearly ready. In you get.'

'In?'

'In there.' He led her over to the box. 'This is your way to the Morningstar.'

'Oh!' Nervously she allowed herself to be lifted by the three men into what now was obviously a very flimsy cannon. 'Are you going to fire me back over the lines, like the way you came here?'

'Ah, rather more than that.' Standish stepped back and glanced at the controls at the base of the cannon, making a couple of adjustments.

Jane felt the floor move slightly beneath her. She crouched down. 'Now wait,' she said. 'Is there anything I have to—?'

There came a sudden whistling noise from overhead. 'On target!' Standish shouted. 'No time. Fire!' He hit a big button.

There was a concussion that knocked Jane's jaw upwards like she'd been punched.

A moment later she was aware of the pain. A terrifying level of pain.

It felt like her skin had been ripped off in a single sheet.

She cried out, and realised that her eyes were closed.

She couldn't open them. A blowtorch was roaring down on top of her head. She tried to raise her arms to protect herself, but they were held down by her sides. Her stomach had compressed, and every muscle in her body was hammering against every other one.

The blaze of grandiose pain went on for minutes. Jane vanished into her own memories, spun around and around with the golden twins, went catching leaves with her father.

And then the pain swiftly died, retreated, became a dull throb.

Only to be replaced by another sort of pain. A deep cold that swept into the depths of her and made her fear even more greatly than the heat had.

She could move her limbs. They were moving of their own accord.

She could open her eyes.

She did.

She looked down.

She was standing over the world, floating in the sky. Or above the sky, because she could see the curve of the horizon far beneath her. The yellow clouds compacted with distance, making it a sweep of eggyolk around the planet.

The great stripe of war slid away directly below, its blackness becoming more stark and less complex every moment. She tried to pick out where she'd come from, but had no idea of where anything had been.

She became aware that the planet was getting smaller beneath her. It was an awe-inspiring image, like the photos of space from the 1970s that could be seen on the net. She was falling upwards away from it.

She was startled by a burst of light. The smaller star had appeared from behind the curve of the world once more. She could now only look away from it. Or down at the dawn that was breaking across the plains and deserts below.

She was falling in a curve, an arc.

She wondered if the Namer knew she had gone, if he felt her presence slipping away over to the other side.

She wondered if the three soldiers had dodged the shells that had been falling on them when she had been blasted into the air.

She felt the pain as a distant friend now. Something that kept the idea in her mind that this was real and not a dream. That all this was happening within the universe she knew.

With that, and her faith, she would survive.

She curled into a ball, gripping her bony ankles with her hands, and let herself drift off into memory, enjoying all the good things of her life.

The next time Jane was aware of now was when the hot pain started to clip at her feet.

She looked up from her reverie and found herself suddenly terribly afraid.

She was plummeting down towards the globe of another world. The horizon had nearly swallowed her already. The heat was starting to make the lower half of her body glow.

How could she cope with this? How could anyone exist through such a fall?

The hissing heat started to climb her body, started to roar in her ears.

She couldn't look for much longer.

She hid her head in the curl of her body. 'Our Father,' she said inside herself. 'Who art in heaven . . .'

The Adversary stood on the lawn of his house, a pair of binoculars held to his eyes, watching the sky.

A distant boom rumbled across the valley. He clicked his tongue in pleasure. Right on time!

He was certain he had the right area. Surely by now . . . His eyes found a point of light against the deep yellow. There!

He gestured to the soldiers around him. 'To the boats! Ready, but don't launch them! Here she comes!'

He turned back to the sky, aware of his people running to their posts all around him.

The speck of fire was becoming bigger and bigger, a new star in the sky.

Jane couldn't help but open her mouth to cry out.

The heat rushed inside her, entered every part of her.

The pain was immense, a system that connected every open surface to every hidden one by means of difference. If she could be all pain, that would be better. But there was comparison.

The horror had grabbed her by the heart. The fear was in every atom of her. Her whole self was in terror.

But she knew she was going to survive it. She knew that fear and horror and pain were beside who she was.

She stayed in the now, not in her memories. She wanted to have this as a memory.

God was in her also, at her side, in her sight of the ground below.

The last layer of cloud flashed past, parting as if burnt away by the thundering heat and vapour that had cocooned her.

She could see details now. This world's band of warfare was far away. Amongst the desert, beneath her, there was green. Squares of green. And a patch of blue.

A lake. A house by the lake.

The speed with which they leapt up at her.

The blue flung itself.

A view from a height. A normal view. Possible only for a moment. Buildings and boats and people and a whole world.

She hit the water.

The water hit her like a hammer on every inch of her body.

The heat parted the water.

She hit the lakebed.

The lakebed hammered at her.

The lakebed parted.

She flew at and was matched by the solidity of the world. The mud pressed back at her. Gave way, gave way, gave way : . . . Ceased.

Stillness.

She was lying face down, underwater, with pain echoing in every part. She could feel the ooze start to shift around her, and she became afraid again, thinking that it would collapse on her and she would be lost, caught in this world's sort of death, struggling forever.

But then strong hands grabbed her, slipped, held on. Mechanical hands. Grips that dangled and then flexed, pulling her up out of the mud.

The water was full of mud, she couldn't see.

Then the water became clearer, she was near the surface.

The shadow of a boat.

She broke the surface, and the winches pulled her on board.

She started to howl uncontrollably, like a baby. The pain soared through her, making her wish she could die. She swept in and out of her memories as figures clustered around her, shadowing her, cooling her. Tiny lost pains of things were applied to her skin.

There were noises at a lower volume, under the roar, which was continuing as . . . memory alone. Speech noises. She knew those.

'You're going to be all right.'

She managed to raise her head slightly, and look up. The boat was approaching a docking place. In the near distance, there was a familiarity, a shape that made her doubt where she was.

A house. She was looking at a house. With a Union flag on its roof.

She was looking at Heartsease.

Forty-Nine: Rebecca's Second Birthday

You're standing in front of the television, in a paper hat, both small palms flat against the screen.

You can see that pictures are made of little dots.

Each one's a different colour. Put them all together—

You take a step back.

And you've got pictures! Magic!

'Beck-y!' calls Mum from across the room. 'Come away from the telly!'

'Come and eat your cake,' says Dad, more impatient. He knows that the loop that connects the five farms has put *Armitage's Land* on as a treat for the community after the storms of the last few weeks. The scene you're standing in front of is the pivotal moment, where Rebecca (who you were named after) forgives the bandits who took her father's farm, and allows them to develop the stables and the lands around them.

In the book it's a trick, but in the movie, made a few years later with lots of goodwill and a tiny budget, it's the last beat, the point where one person declares an end to the violence.

It could have been worse. They could have called you Alice.

The movie was the last one anyone had ever heard of. The last movie to be made, over a hundred and fifty years ago. But you don't know that yet. You don't have context for anything. All you have is a bit of you that knows the things you don't yet.

You can see the dots, and there's the pictures. Do you remember all the things you have to remember? You're going to keep it all safe, aren't you? You're going to keep it all inside you until one day it pops out.

You nod seriously.

Then you turn and run, one straight leg tripping over another, back to your Mum, muttering, 'Becka Becka Becka!'

Fifty: Martyr

Jane lay in a bed for a time, she didn't know how long. Light and darkness swung past. She attended services in her head at various times of day, listened to her favourite speakers. Suckled at her mother's breast.

In time, she became aware of a figure sitting beside her bed, and realised that he was looking back at her, and that she could speak to him. 'Hello,' she said, weakly.

'Hello,' he replied. 'I won't shake your hand. Still rather painful for you, I gather.'

She raised her head a few inches, and got a good look at him. It took her a moment to realise what was strange about him. Then she understood. She still hadn't got used to the way things were here.

He looked like a human being. He was clothed. In a dark suit and tie.

He was a balding, tall, energetic-looking man, his eyes sparkling at her through unwieldy spectacles. He looked like an owl about to pounce, but there was something about him . . .

Jane realised she was smiling. 'Are you the Adversary?' she asked.

'Err, yes,' he said. 'But I'm also Edwin Lutyens. Please call me Ned.'

Later that day, they went walking out around the house. Jane could feel every pebble of gravel under her feet. The big sun stood over the building, painting every flower and bush red. The effect startled Jane. It was like this world was doomed already. She gazed at the shape of Heartsease, wondering at how strange the tan stone looked against the huge red bulk of the sun and the shimmer of the surrounding desert. Here the weathering of the house made it white rather than dark. The grounds and the lake were kept intact through a system of watercourses that led deep down into the interior of the planet, and it was a battle, apparently, to keep the desert from intruding.

'It's all so green here,' she said. 'It's like home.'

'That's our job writ large. To stop not just the desert, but those who'll get their just desserts. To play ring-a-roses with the god of the sandpit up there.' Lutyens gestured irritably towards the world Jane had initially appeared upon, hanging as a bright star in the primrose sky, high above the roof of Heartsease. 'To war with him until he sees sense.'

'Oh. What about the men who came to rescue me?' Jane asked.

'They didn't make it back,' said Lutyens. 'They'll be trapped, more flies in the ointment. They knew what they were in for. We were all quite eager to get you here.'

'Why?'

'Because you could tell Namer how to finish his own Heartsease. How to complete his final weapon. We haven't got long.'

'I know, he told me.'

'I fought like blazes to have you come over to this side, but Namer was ready for that. You were too important to him. I had hoped, when I felt you escape, that perhaps you hadn't shared your memories with him. A fleeting hope. Possibly our last, only I don't believe in last hopes once they're gone.'

'I'm so sorry.'

'Not your fault. Sorry I can't absolve you, but that's the Namer's own patented brand of arrogance.'

'I've been such a fool.' Jane wrung her hands together. She felt like the whole victory of Namer was down to her stupidity. 'I failed every test. It took so long for me to find my faith again, and it was only after I would have needed it most.'

'Yes, well, it wouldn't be special unless it was hard to find, now, would it? That's why I built houses. Because it was fun and it was hard, and you could visit afterwards and see folk enjoying them. I've had tests of my own faith. My wife and I didn't really live as a couple for many years. She was a Theosophist, you see.' He saw that Jane didn't understand. 'A member of a spiritual society. They believed they had their messiah, Krishnamurti, and that his divine love was going to take over from our plain old human love.' He shuffled his hands behind his back as they walked on. 'And dear old Emmy followed them as far as they went. Just for twenty years or so. She had her life and I had mine. Me and my buildings and my clients. All my own fault. Madame Blavatsky was in charge of Emmy's life. She's here somewhere. Won't hear of the Namer being her saviour, of course. I say of course, but it's surprising, those that do. Emmy won't go near her now. Forgive me my little smile. Water under the bridge. That's why I put a bridge across the river by the lake, just so I can say that! And the lake is so Emmy can have some seaside. Oh, and Emmy wants to meet you. You must have some of her cakes. If we have time left for that. Anyhow!' He started to laugh at his own meanderings.

Jane thought it was wonderful that he could take such time with her in the face of such a desperate situation. 'Why do you wear clothes and look human?' she asked.

'Because I can. It's not that I want to be special. I'd give everyone their bodies back if I could. But I can't. Too complicated to keep on . . . spinning out all the details. Tried it. Couldn't get anything else done.'

'So why is it you? Why are you the special one who's fighting the Namer?'

Lutyens sighed, his hands dropping to his sides. 'He thinks it's because I'm his fallen angel. But I think it's an accident. On Earth, Heartsease was always a bit of a mystery to me. I saw it as a darling riddle, right from the planning stages. I kept running it through my brain. There was something about the system of it . . . An architect, Reverend, holds in his mind the shape of a house and the way it will function together and equally. And Heartsease, as set down for me by dear old Simon Trent, was a system like no other. From time to time, I considered the possibility that Simon might be the world's greatest architect, come to tempt me. But I gradually realised he knew nothing about the building I was making, only that I should make it to his demands.' He swung his arms around in front of him like a small boy. 'When I woke up here, when it was supposed to be Heaven, and everyone was living like they were swimming in golden syrup, I thought after a couple of years: here's fun. I can have another go at that building I never got to understand. So I started building it again. Lots of chaps joined in. Local materials. The power of the mind over matter. Big lightning strokes of geometry. Vivreations all round.

'Namer visited so often. In those days, I'd bow and scrape and all that, because I really thought he should be in charge. But he seemed so worried about the new building. As if it was something I shouldn't really be doing, but he couldn't quite see any reason to stop me.

'I ended up having my friend MacSack look after him when he came for his tours of inspection. Not a pleasant feeling for me, feeling socially embarrassed around Jesus.

'So finally one day, the day before we put the last stone in place, he took me aside, and said there was only one way to show me why I shouldn't complete this house. He did what he does with everyone nowadays: gave me a piece of his mind. I suppose you've had a slice?'

'Yes.' Jane nodded.

'Wonderful that you haven't been swayed, then. That only happens once in a blue moon, would that we had one. Anyhow, when I understood what he planned to do, to bring all of humanity here, using the original Heartsease, I was horrified. What sort of behaviour is that for a saviour? I said to him. Look at this place. Only one bit of green, and we can't make any more as yet, but you want to deny all those people on Earth the sight of any more of it?' He stopped, and waved his hands at the house. 'Why, they might, in time, cease to be mortal. They might conquer death. All kinds of brilliant futures might await. What kind of shepherd are you, who's planning a Sunday roast?'

Jane was laughing now at Lutyens' inflatedly pompous turn of voice as he described his own anger.

'He wasn't used to being argued with, but give him his due, he told me we'd talk further, and didn't ask me not to finish the house. I think he thought that was all I wanted to do, and that I was getting angry to allow myself just to do that.

'So I slid the final brick into place, and finally I understood. I understood all this bunkum about having the Saviour here and now and not in the hereafter as complete . . . sorry, Reverend: balls! I found the same power that the Namer has, and it's just universal bricks and mortar, and if I can have it too then it can't be divine, can it? So I sat down and thought: what are the choices here? And it was Emmy who sorted it out for me. I gave her back her old body for a week, and we spent the time extremely married, working out what we should do. Silly of me to choose this version of my body, eh? But still.

'We were in a boat on the lake, and she said—'

Jane realised that there had been someone walking behind them for a good while now, and jerked around to see an Aurigan, who jumped forward to grab Lutyens around the waist and join in with the conversation at the same moment:

'She *said*: "You're for the future, and going everywhere, and doing everything, not just this one thing. You're for human beings and what they need. You're for usefulness over mad old tradition. You're for God, for trying to find him and not succeeding." '

Lutyens laughed. 'I think I'd remember that even if I couldn't remember anything else. Emmy, you're my inspiration. And we seem to have hit upon something, because now half of the newcomers pass over to us. Oh, Emily, this is the Reverend Jane.'

'That is how my husband became Satan,' said Emily, kissing Jane on the cheek. 'All my fault. The crosses some wives bear.'

'I have always been keen on you baring all,' Lutyens replied archly. 'Here is Heaven for me in that regard, anyhow. Was there something you wanted, or did you just come here to take credit where it's due?'

Emily took Jane by both hands. 'Your father has arrived,' she said.

He stood in the hallway, which here was illuminated by dozens of new windows cut into the stone, at the nexus of a star of sunlight on the tiles.

He was a tall, thin Aurigan figure, his eyes red and worried as he turned to look at her.

But there was no doubt about who he was.

Jane ran to him, and embraced him. 'Daddy,' she whispered into his unfamiliar shoulder.

'Jane,' he said.

They went to see the chapel, here undemolished and perfect, while they talked. From the outside, the building shone in the sunshine, its whiteness topped with a golden bell inside an open tower. The bell was tinkling gently in the wind.

They both dipped in front of the altar, then went to sit in one of the front row pews. Jane was luxuriating, both in the feeling of her father's presence, and in the perfection of the chapel, the presence of the Holy Spirit inside her, and inside it. The stained-glass windows filled the chamber with rainbow light, projecting their vision of Christ and his companions. The golden eagle lectern sparkled. Even the Trent family Bible was intact, here on the other side of forty-five light-years of space and hundreds of years of time.

Dad cleared his throat awkwardly, and let go of her for the first time since they'd met up. 'I left you alone so long. Bloody idiot of a lieutenant. I told him there was a round in the breech when I gave him the rifle. I've had a word with him since. He's on our side! Not in my lot, I tell you. Wouldn't trust him with the glue.'

'I knew it had to be an accident.'

'As if I'd leave you.'

'Is Mum here?' She hadn't even hesitated to ask the question.

'Oh yes, and she sends her love. We're not together again, or anything. She's with somebody. Couple of somebodies, actually. Which is easier, when you don't have to consider you-know-what. She wants to see you. If we get the time.'

Time again. Jane put a hand to her brow. There shouldn't be time here. There wasn't going to be time for anything. 'I haven't thought about this kind of thing. Having to meet everybody. Do families stay together, in big clans, with all the ancestors going way back?'

'Probably someone's tried it. These are big worlds, they've tried everything. But most of us around here like to live with people we don't know that well. Or people from our own times we're not related to. More natural. Not that anybody gets to do much of that, with the war. We're all soldiers now.'

Another thought came to Jane, an image that rose up out of her perfect memory. Dad appearing through the wall. 'You tried to stop me, didn't you? You tried to tell me to get away.'

'Didn't pay any bloody attention, did you?'

'How did you do that?'

'I tried to kill myself off. This body, anyhow. There's a whole unit of them, his Necronauts, Ned calls 'em. When he found out you were the one who'd been called to Heartsease, I went to him and told him it ought to be me to try and talk to you.'

Jane was astonished. 'But why do you have to die to do that?'

Dad meshed his hands, a wonderfully familiar gesture when he was thinking hard about something. He'd always loved to talk about things he didn't really understand, to try and work them out in front of her, or with her help as he'd always put it. 'You have to try and get back up the hill, you see. Back up the hill in the universe, back to Earth. The Necronauts think that if you could successfully kill off one of these bodies, and they're tough old monsters, you might go back. That's what Aurigans see, when they're really pushed, when they really might die. They see Earth waiting for them. 'Course, none of 'em ever got there, as far as we know. I certainly didn't.'

'What happened?'

'Bloody body wouldn't give in. I could just about touch the concept of Earth, in my coma. I could see the EM field. I managed to imprint myself on it. Sent that message to you. Not a very good one. But then I fell back. I didn't have the will to get there. I woke up here again. I was so frustrated, angry with myself for not saving you.'

'What do you mean, you didn't have the will?' Jane's thoughts were racing.

'We're supposed to be in charge of these bodies. The Necronauts have sorted out a nerve poison that should kill an Aurigan, if only they weren't living off this zero-charge-thing stuff. If only they weren't plugged in. Well, one of us ought to be able to tell one of these bodies to bloody well switch off. But so far we can't. You'd need some kind of saintly willpower to do that. The faith of a martyr, my girl.'

Jane's eyes had slid from her father's face to the stained-glass portrait of Christ. Now she inclined her head slightly. 'Oh,' she said. 'Now I see.'

Ned, Emmy, Jane and her mother and father took an electric train out from a barnlike station at the rear of the house. Heartsease was, Jane had been told, shielded from the front line, by Lutyens' abilities as well as its own shape and the range of hills.

Jane felt uniquely displaced, watching the house recede from the little carriage she sat in. She felt like everything around her had been translated to here, dropped on to the landscape like random bricks.

Except here nothing was random, and everything meant something.

She was certain in her heart of that.

She needed to be certain for what she was about to do.

Her father had argued with her for a while. Her mother, when she had come from the north to meet her, had also not wanted her to do this. But for both their sakes, she had to. They would meet once more, she had told them. The circle would be unbroken. No matter what happened. And if she succeeded, she might get the chance to deny the Namer his victory.

Now her parents sat on either side of her, both holding her hands.

They journeyed for half an hour, further down the valley, during which time the ground became more like a desert again. Jane saw low hillocks of passageways, places where the native Aurigans sometimes came to the surface, low red domes against the white sand.

A meaning, a progression, a great circle. If the natives could be saved from the great plague of humanity that was about to rain down on them.

Finally, they came to an elegant tower, another Lutyens design: a bigger recreation of the folly of Heartsease. With walls that were so smooth they shone in the red sunlight.

Ned saw her looking, and winked at her.

Inside the tower, it was cold out of the sunlight. Sparkling blue and white corridors rested the eye, and reminded Jane of the lake. That was the purpose of the water, she supposed, to keep the memory of Earth in the mind of this community, to stop them from despairing.

'This building is where the Necronauts do their work,' Ned said, leading her on to a bridge that spanned the centre of a high-ceilinged chamber.

Below them was a laboratory, with, jarringly, comfortable-looking couches at its centre. Dozens of Aurigans were working with chemicals down there, back to back, doing their best not to get in each other's way. There was an air of desperation about them. The endgame was being played out. One or two of them glanced up at Ned, and he waved calmly back to them.

They proceeded through into a small amphitheatre of white stone, with a blackboard and lecturer's table in front. On the blackboard was written: 'Gods of the Old Testament. Magical practice. Summoning rituals. Human sacrifice.' They seemed to be rough headings for a discussion. 'Practical theology?' Jane asked.

Ned laughed. 'We've tried everything, over the years. But now we're down to the only real hope we've ever uncovered, pushing for a success there. You see, our friend Namer spends a lot of his energies interfering in the radio band between here and Earth. So we can't get a message through to anyone, or alter any of his ghosts. Mind you, even if we could it'd take four decades to get there, and that's been too late for quite a while now. That's one problem.'

Emmy took up the story, sitting down opposite Jane. 'On top of that, Ned can't match the Namer's strength. Ned's tapped into the power through Heartsease. He can't influence things on Earth, like Namer can sometimes when he wins the arm-wrestle for a bit over Ned.'

'So,' Lutyens finished, 'we had to find a way to get over space, rather than through it. We heard from various people who'd had extremely close shaves in these bodies, scientific accidents, that sort of thing, that they had visions of Earth when it looked like they might die. Initially, we tried to find more efficient ways to kill these bodies. But that all came to a screeching halt when Edward Grey returned.'

'Poor Edward,' Emmy noted.

'One of our earliest proper Necronauts. He asked to be fired into the sun we orbit, using one of our launch cannons. It didn't destroy him. He spent ten years wandering inside the star, in unimaginable pain. He came back as a shooting star, a mass of plasma. We managed to get his body reassembled, in time, but his mind never really recovered from the experience. No, as your father told you, it's about willpower, about having the ability to throw yourself over the fence.'

Jane gave her parents a reassuring smile. 'I have faith,' she said.

*

Booth was sitting in the corner of the bedroom, his eyes fixed on the opposite corner.

Rebecca was walking up and down, her arms wrapped around herself. She felt battered, like she'd been jostled in the playground. Like she'd been pushed from one person to another. She could feel the wood of the planks on top of her face. Feel her reaction to the bullets bringing Jane down. Feel David's weight on top of her, the look in his eyes saying he wanted her to be afraid. She had abiding love, which should have solved everything. But it didn't. She thought the love must be only coming from the compiler. So did she want it to be switched off? Because if it was like anaesthetic, wouldn't she fall apart now without it?

She was missing something, the solution to all this. She was missing the distance between how she was and what she wanted to be.

David entered, holding Booth's phone in his hand. 'We're just getting ready to capture the Campbells,' he said. 'Then we have to make some final adjustments from your list. And then we have to kill the Campbells in a couple of particular rooms.' He went to Rebecca and put his hand gently on her shoulder. 'I'll use the Campbell woman for the dining room. You don't have to worry.' He turned back to Booth. 'I was wondering if you'd both like to join us?'

Booth looked at him blankly for a moment, then said, 'Why?'

'You're a hero to my men. They . . . we'd all like to have you along.'

'I'm not a hero,' Booth whispered.

'Ah well, that's your decision, of course.'

He turned on his heel and was about to leave when Rebecca grabbed him by the sleeve. 'David . . . please. Turn off the compiler.'

'No, sweetheart. The ghost is our friend. It's helping to complete the pattern. To let the wave come. It doesn't hurt people who want to do the same thing.'

'My love for you won't vanish if you turn it off.'

He looked at her for a moment, a half-smile flashing awkwardly across his face. 'Well, no. No. Of course not. But why take the chance?'

He kissed her quickly, then headed back for the door.

'I'll see you after the world's done,' he said, his words dull with feeling.

Then he was gone.

*

Lutyens and Emily stood beside her couch, looking down at her in concern. Mum and Dad held her hands.

'Your first aim is to alter the EM field,' Lutyens told her. 'Try and knock things over to stop Heartsease from working. If you can't do that, try and get a message to anyone you think will listen. Either directly or by radio. Get them to stop Heartsease from being charged up and readied for firing.'

'I understand,' said Jane. 'But what if I get up the hill? What if I die?'

'We don't know,' said Ned. 'Nobody's ever done it.'

'Let's get on then, please,' said Jane. 'Before I chicken out.'

As the Aurigan beside the couch prepared the syringe, Jane's mother and father held her close and whispered prayers and love for her.

'Certain?' said Lutyens.

'Yes,' nodded Jane.

The Aurigan slipped the needle into her arm and pushed the plunger home.

Rebecca had asked Booth to come with her. But he had shaken his head. 'I don't know why I should do anything now,' he said. 'Considering what I've done in the past. I'm . . . evil. I'm a terrible person.'

The look in his eyes had said to Rebecca that there was no point in arguing.

She stepped out into the corridor and headed for the Switching Cupboard. As she went, she listened to the sounds of the house around her. There were distant low whistles. The two armies, moving into place, each intent on the other. But as yet no gunfire.

She descended one of the servants' stairwells, stopping and listening again at every third step. She was still safe. The last thing she needed was to be fucking shot at this point. When she was missing something. When she was certain about everyone and everything, that was when they could put her up in front of the firing squad.

She would hum, then. And read from her collected works. And not care at all about death. Because you wouldn't, would you, not if you had everything sorted out? If you either were utterly loved, or did not love, and either had religion or didn't. Then death would be just an inconvenience.

What the fuck was she thinking about?

She came to the short dark corridor that led to the Switching Cupboard, and scampered along it.

She was after one little bit of certainty for herself. And maybe she wanted to do something for the rest of the house too. At any rate, something inside her told her that this was what she had to do.

She stuck her head round the door.

Nobody here. Just the stubby black cylinder of the compiler, clicking away in the corner.

She could feel it, bathing her with nostalgia. She felt it lacing her closer and closer to David. To warmth and security and womblike feelings for him. She wanted him in her womb. She wanted to be in his arms. The past rolled over and over.

The past. She suddenly thought of the look in Augustine's eye as the knife had gone in. All the birthdays and the four o'clocks.

Fuck the past.

Rebecca walked quickly over to the compiler, followed the connections, and found the relevant fuse box.

She put her hand on the switch that would kill the power.

Why was she doing this? Just to solve her own question? Or was there something more here? Something she didn't get yet?

Then maybe she would in a second. She clutched the lever. Oh bollocks. It always came down to something like this.

The darkness was on Jane instantly.

Her whole body had switched off. She remembered the instant. The frightened expressions on the faces of the others.

She was in darkness. Not aware of her body at all.

Then there was something ahead of her. A nebulosity, a vagueness on the nothingness where she thought her eyes should have been.

She willed herself towards it.

She was suddenly back in her body, slamming against straps they'd fastened around her, screaming.

And then back here, as if that was a fantasy.

The light and the screams.

The darkness.

She rode wave after wave of it, pushing herself towards whatever was ahead.

This was what she was born for, she urged herself. This was what she had to do, because of what she'd done to Rebecca.

'Guilt?' said the Namer, gently, in the back of her head. 'What use is guilt?'

'It's not guilt. You think what I did to Rebecca was okay, because it'll all be worked out here. You think life on Earth doesn't matter.

You just see the start and the end. You don't see anything of what you're trying to rush through.'

'I just want to be with my Father.'

'But it's not the consequences that matter. It's what was going on inside of me when I tried to hurt her. I want to make sure I *don't* have guilt at the heart of me. I want to make things right. I'm going to make amends.'

'You're not. You can't. Nobody can swim upriver.'

And then she felt the pain cut through into this dying space in her brain. Once. Twice. And then it broke through in a scramble of memories, her own and the Namer's.

She was staring up at the sun, so long it reached back into her eyes and burnt them. Her hands were being torn up by her own weight. The tiny cracked bones being mauled into a mass of flesh, hour by hour, every day. The pressure building on your chest. The way what's inside you changes into shapes that don't feel they could live inside you any more, if impossibly you were cut down. You're in death already. The sun in the morning. The darkness at night. The world that would go on, blind to you. That was the horror of what was staring her in the face, out of the faces of all those that gathered around to blithely watch, distant from your pain because it wasn't happening to them. The world will go on and you will be out of it. No, says some spark of faith inside. And it says it on the first day, and the second, and the third.

Can it keep gently saying it, or will it vanish into the weight on your chest? Will you accept this death? That's the horror, the fight, the keeping on just one more inch of flesh, just one more day. I will not accept this death. I will not accept the judgement of those watching. I will die my own death, just with this body, but I will go on and mark the face of history.

I will save you all.

'I will save you all!' screamed Jane, smashing at the table with her fists. 'I will save you all!' Her teeth snapped into her tongue. A foam of blood, real blood, miraculous blood, kept spitting the words. Spitting them out.

Rebecca took a deep breath.

She slammed down the lever.

The noises from the compiler stopped.

Jane saw the lights ahead of her. Heard noises from home. Recognised the smells.

Her body slammed into a spasm, every line of it stretched hard.

This was the moment. The difference between the future, and an ending. An ending was just the past, over and over. And a sacrifice was to close the circle, to pull the world out of an ending, to send everyone off into the world of what might be. The sacrifice was for something more. To reach for a divine impulse that could not be reached.

Jane reached for it.

The remains of her mouth opened in a scream.

Rebecca realised, with her mouth wide open, exactly what it was she had been missing.

And on the couch, Jane's body arched and collapsed.

And then Jane was gone.

Fifty-One: Rebecca's First Birthday

You've forgotten where you came from, but you know that it was somewhere else, far from here, and that you weren't you then, but became you at the instant you got here.

You were dropped here from the great abode of memory above the universe, like an apple falling from a tree. You fell.

You still want to be called Jane. Because everything about you now is still Jane.

You haven't yet learned to look up when they call you Rebecca.

But you will.

Dad holds you up, and bounces you gently up and down so that your feet squirt and stumble beneath you. You're one year old. 'Daaaaaaa!' you blurt, and huff a series of deep breaths.

But you know you used to be able to walk. You remember something more. There's a solid mass of stuff in your little head, information that this small body and brain aren't able to deal with yet. It's important. It's the you stuff and the stuff you have to pass on to save everybody.

But you have a terrible knowledge that you're going to forget it.

You can learn a language. You're going to. Not by working your way through it. Just by looking at it once, for a long time, and getting it. If you could count, you could say how many curls of pasta were in that jar, instantly.

But you can't do either of those things yet.

You remember the bullet bursting into your brain and you struggle. Was everything between here and there a fantasy?

You will never even realise *which* Rebecca you are. You won't quite recognise yourself when you meet.

Mum is trying to get the booties on to your feet.

'Hold her still,' she says to Dad. 'He's not holding you still,' she explains to you. 'Silly Daddy. Isn't he a silly daddy?'

You know that Mum is the most beautiful thing you will ever see. You laugh everything out at her.

You cough, squeeze up your face, and casually throw up down one shoulder.

It's good to be back.

'Shit,' Dad says, and pulls a tissue from a box. He starts dabbing at your mouth with it.

'Careful,' says Mum. 'She can understand everything. It's all filed away in there. I really believe that.' To you again. 'You'll repeat it all to Grandma, won't you?'

You live in the centre of your head, and are numb around the edges, and when you try and reach for something, the thought doesn't quite get to the hand, but slides off the physical world in a clumsiness which is the essence of frustration, where frustration is defined. Damn damn damn bloody damn. Fucking fuck.

This world is wrong for you. You have no place here at all. Not until you can tell everyone the things inside you have to tell.

If history makes people who they are, Jane Bruce made Rebecca Champhert.

So thank goodness, Jane, that really, it doesn't have to at all.

Fifty-Two: Lie Back and Think of England

Rebecca fell off her feet, and sat down so hard it hurt.

Switching off the compiler had pulled out the supports. Something had fallen away. Those things that the compiler had made her believe . . . When the dam of driftwood had burst, and all of those ideas had been washed away, something else must have have gone too. The thing that had been Rebecca, Rebecca, Rebecca.

She was Jane.

She had built Rebecca on top of Jane.

Jane was her history, her past.

She felt drunk with the idea. Panting with it. It was too huge to hold inside her. She had swallowed a drug which she now wanted to unswallow. She had a faith in her chest she didn't want to have. A big angular shape sat in her stomach.

So everything she was had been . . . a disguise?

No. No, it couldn't be. She was Rebecca. She had written books.

But what did books say? Books were like little intelligences of their own. They didn't say who you were. Jane could have written exactly those books.

Jane had had faith. Rebecca had only faith in herself. Faith that she would fuck up and then survive, faith that more pain would be along in a moment.

Or had that been Jane's faith, inside her, transformed into poison, leaking out?

She had the whole journey Jane had been on, the whole story, in her head. But that was what it felt like. One of her stories. A novel that sat there and was the thing that you always referred back to, that changed who you were. But only a novel. Was it real? Should she act on it? Had she only taken on some kind of religious allegory? Where was Jane now to tell her? Gone in baby talk. Washed under into the currents of Rebecca, she was seen just here and there as every ninth wave. She couldn't tell her the truth of all this new material.

But what was any history or belief except a book, a story to live by?

She became aware that someone was standing in the doorway behind her. It really didn't matter who it was. Nothing in the world was big enough now to bring her back into it. She was an odd beast from somewhere else.

She got to her feet unsteadily, and saw that it was David.

He was pointing a gun at her. As if that was terribly important.

'You did it,' he said. 'I knew you would.'

It took her a moment to realise what he was talking about. When she did, she just nodded. Her thoughts were racing.

'Rebecca Champhert,' he said. It sounded like the first line of a death sentence. There was a hard look on his face, that look that would sometimes turn violent and sometimes burst into laughter. 'You and I have shared everything. We have *history*. I have saved you from your past . . .'

'I doubt that, David.'

'I've given you your future. Helped you recover from what we *did* to save you from your past. I have been there on every birthday, and the thought of me has been there at every four o'clock . . .'

'David, I—'

He shouted it. To stop her from derailing him. 'Do you still love me?!'

She paused. 'No, David,' she said. 'I don't love you. Not without the compiler.'

David stood still for a moment, as if he'd been slapped in the face. Then he stepped quickly towards the compiler, as if he was intending to just switch it on again and have another go.

And suddenly Rebecca knew that Jane didn't make a damn bit of difference. That she had to do things *now*, that *then* didn't matter.

All those things she thought had made her hadn't made her at all. She had been made by *different* things. But if those things had meant anything, either, she would surely have realised, would surely have discovered them, a long time before now.

Whatever had made her, it wasn't here now.

Now there was just Rebecca.

And there were urgent things she had to do now. Things bigger than either of them. She had to act on what she'd learnt.

'You bastard,' she said. 'You killed me.'

She launched herself at David, and grabbed his arm, twisting the hand with the gun away from her.

'No!' he shouted. 'You will love me! When the wave hits. When everything's real!'

They struggled for a moment. Then his strength overwhelmed her. He threw her aside and she hit the floor with an impact that blew the breath from her lungs.

She looked up, aching, and watched him grab the power switch and push it down. She steeled herself, tried to crunch up all the love inside of her, ready to fight the waves of emotion she expected to wash over her as the compiler hummed back into life, making its little thinking clicks once more.

But the wave did not come. She could feel Jane inside her, an ancient hatred for this man. She could never love him when she could decide that, for that moment, the priest was who she was.

She was in charge of her history now.

David turned back to her, grinning at who he expected her to be.

She smiled back at him. Not a smile of love. But one of triumph.

For a moment, she thought he was going to cry.

But then he leapt at her, a high-pitched yell breaking from his throat. He grabbed her by the back of the neck and dragged her to her feet. He shoved the gun into her face. 'You will love me,' he said. 'When completion comes and everything's perfect, you will.'

He dragged her out of the door.

Booth was sitting with his back against the wall of the bedroom.

His thoughts were going round and round in very small circles.

He had killed all those people. He had killed Alison.

What sort of person was he, to have done that?

He felt like he could never be happy again. Or could never allow himself to be happy. The memory of his terrible actions would sit in his head, perfectly, forever, ruling him.

He was no longer part of the world. He was just himself, locked off. Locked away.

So he barely looked up when the door of the room was jerked open, and Rebecca was thrown in. David Hawtrey stood at the door, shaking.

He watched as Rebecca sprang back to her feet and ran straight at the militiaman. But he'd already strung trap wires across the doorway with one practised swipe of his hand.

Rebecca wasn't wearing the biographer's ring any more. Her finger was red and bruised from where it had been wrestled off her.

'Not long now,' David said. 'Soon we'll have reached the end. Then we'll all be free. Goodbye for now, Rebecca.'

He closed the door.

Rebecca turned round and looked at Booth as if he should have done something.

'Had a row?' he asked, hating himself for the automatic urge to make a joke.

Rebecca slammed herself against the wall beside him, and slid down it to his level. 'He's going to kill everyone.'

'We should form a club.'

'Everyone on Earth.'

'I see. You've snapped under the strain.'

'Shut up. Booth, I *know* now. I know who I am.'

He looked at her for a long moment. She did seem different. Full of purpose. Just at the point where he wasn't. 'Me too,' he said. 'Shit, isn't it?'

'No . . .' She shook her head strongly. 'No, it isn't. I *am* feeling like shit now, but who I am is the good bit.' She took a deep breath. 'We have to get out of here. And quickly. But right now there's something you have to know about me. I murdered—'

He sighed. 'Augustine Campbell.'

Rebecca stared at him. 'How long have you known?'

'Before we met. I hear and remember every story. I thought you might need looking after.'

From the look on her face, he thought she was going to shout at him. But instead she just let her head fall sideways on to his arm and closed her eyes. For some reason. 'You are such a fool. Knowing I did that, how can you feel guilty about what *you* did?'

Booth felt himself bridling at the implication. 'Because my crime is much worse!'

'No, mine is.'

'Mine is!'

'Uh-uh. Mine. I decided to do that. You were led astray.'

'And you're just a . . . a product of your culture!' he bellowed. 'Of this awful fucking time! Where *everyone* is ready to give you a fucking history lesson at the drop of a fucking hat about what their fucking enemies did a hundred fucking years ago, and how it's all *their* fucking fault! Christ, if I'd wanted to live in Ulster, I'd have gone there! This is meant to be the *future*, for God's sake! So why did none of you sadistic, jingoistic, isolationist, paranoid, fucked-up little suburban warlords ever start thinking about fucking *making* a future?'

They both got to their feet at the same moment. 'Well look at you, you fat fucker!' she shouted into his face. 'You can't lecture us about the past! You had to forget who you fucking *were* before you could start living! And when you did, you were the best thing in this whole fucked-up world! Only—'

He grabbed her hands. 'Don't say that. Don't say I was good.'

She held on to him, thinking for a moment. 'You were the *only* good thing. I look back at my life, at all those birthdays, and I wish I'd lived in your time instead. I wish I'd had those chances, those—'

Something inside him snapped. 'Stop!' he shouted. 'Stop living in the past! You can still have a future. We can build something better, something that—'

'We?' she said.

He closed his mouth. He felt like something had filled the space behind his eyes. He didn't trust himself to say anything. Because she'd let something go in him. Something that was true.

The look on her face told him that she understood.

'All right,' said Rebecca, squeezing his hands in hers. 'Let me tell you what's going on here. Because we have to save the world.'

Ruth, Joe, Morgan and Davey crept up the stairwell. They had spent two hours slowly negotiating their way through the various traps and devices that the Hawtreys had left there.

They had just got past them.

Now they were the wolves at the edge of the forest, feeling the warm closeness of their victims. They were going to dive in and catch them unprepared, and take the whole house.

Ruth had in her mind only what she was going to continue to do to Booth Hawtrey when she returned to the kitchen. She was in an ecstasy of planning: planning to put him back together again in order to once more take him apart. She would keep him with her, keep him in hell, to let him know what suffering was like. So he would hurt like her family had hurt. So his eyes would one day look like her mother's eyes at the breakfast table, haunted because they had been cast out and had no master. When the Campbells had this house, they would move here, and use it as a base from which to expand into the Hawtrey country. They would take Ealing and Chiswick and Charlton. They would make Ben Hawtrey suffer too, for as long as he held out.

In the end, Ruth would get a home of her own.

Joe Purchase had not always been ugly. He had been the most junior of the engineers in the apprentice school at Alderley.

Competition was fierce. To get his first certificate he had had to endure a panelling by the other apprentices. In his case, that meant being thrashed across the face by a pan, until he bled. He was happy, because he had made that grade and had gone on to be a militiaman and had the badge of his trade on his arm.

Morgan Carter had left a wife and two sons in Wales, when there was clearly no hope for the farm. He had said he would be back when he had found a position, and, now, six years later, he still firmly believed he would do that one day. When he had his next promotion.

Davey Clarke had worked for three of the big families. When he was a child, he had always said he was going to start a big family of his own, and unite the whole island. As he got older, he had fallen into the service of the Mandervilles, but when he was ordered to get up out of a trench and attack the enemy, he didn't see why he should, and had run off in the opposite direction instead. He had journeyed by riverboat to Singh county, and had worked for them until the same point. Which had brought him to the Campbells. He was certain he was not a coward. There just didn't seem to be anything big enough for him to believe in. Apart from God.

These four stepped to the top of the stairwell now, and spread out, each taking a few steps down a little bloom of corridors.

David stepped quietly out from a doorway along one of them, watching Morgan from behind, calculating.

He took a couple of steps forward, his gun raised.

Then he fired.

Morgan's head exploded.

The other Hawtreys leapt from their places.

The corridors echoed with noise.

Rebecca went over to the dressing table, and looked at it for a moment, thinking. She had told Booth her whole immense story, as fast as possible.

'So I'm here to kill everyone,' said Booth. '*Everyone.*'

'Or save them. But we have to get out of here first.' With a sweep of her hands she sent everything on the table flying against the wall. She flung the table itself over, kicked at the mirror until it broke, grabbed a chair and hurled it at the other wall.

The wall behind where the chair landed wobbled.

Through it, glaring at Booth as he came, stepped Simon Trent.

The Campbells ran down the corridors, firing as they went.

The Hawtreys pursued them individually, splitting up and chasing them as per the schemes David had written on their phones.

Ruth waited around one corner, and leapt out to slash at Steven's throat with her knife. He dropped his gun and fell to the floor, slipping on his own blood, his hand trying to grab his neck to hold it in.

Ruth ran back the way she'd come.

Elsewhere, David reacted, feeling the beating heart of the house swell in a sudden, unexpected direction. 'Nearly there,' he whispered. 'The wave's coming.'

'Why should I help *him*?' Trent said.

'You must help *me*,' Rebecca insisted. 'You can feel what's happening, can't you?'

Trent slowly nodded, his eyes never leaving Booth. 'The house is readying itself for something. Something huge.'

'Right. There should be spikes everywhere now, but I'm sure there aren't. It's all being kept in.'

'But it's getting too much.' Trent seemed to listen to something distantly. 'The house can't hold. It's going to let it out.'

'Simon,' said Booth, suddenly. 'I'm sorry.'

Trent looked at him for a long moment. 'That's not good enough.'

'Then I'll give like for like. If I have to. If I can.'

Trent closed his eyes. 'Where do you want to go?'

Joe jumped up from behind the snooker table and swung his machine gun across the room.

The shells smashed Frank and Little Bob, who had been running through the room on their way to the hall, into the far wall, making their bodies dance with bullets.

Joe laughed at what was left of them and ran.

David fell against a wall, thinking the wave would sweep over the house at that moment. But it didn't. They were just on the edge now. He could see the deaths on the map in his head, blooms that made the whole house sing with colour. 'One or two more,' he said. 'Just one or two more.'

He couldn't hear anyone moving anywhere. His gun held above his head, he rushed off to find them.

Jacko swung with a shout, to cover Rebecca, Booth and Trent as they stepped out of the wall.

He stood between them and the compiler.

'Jacko,' said Rebecca, 'get out of the way. We have to switch that thing off.'

'No!' Jacko yelled. 'Bex, I can't, even for you. I can't—'

Booth walked straight at him.

Jacko fired three times into Booth's chest. The bullets broke chunks of material off him. Booth ignored them.

He went to the compiler and wrenched it violently from the wall, pulling all the leads out in a sparking, trailing mass.

The compiler kept clicking and humming.

Jacko lowered his gun, looking wildly between them all. Then he bolted out of the door.

'How can it do that?' Rebecca grabbed the black cylinder, and together with Booth, they swung it and threw it against the wall.

It broke open, and fell in pieces to the floor.

And then, as their eyes flickered aside from it, it was once more whole and ticking where it fell.

Trent went to it and raised a hand. He frowned. Tried again.

Then he lowered his hand. 'I can't get rid of it,' he said. 'It's part of the house now. The house is protecting it.'

'How long have we got?' asked Booth.

'Any moment.'

'In that case,' said Booth, 'it's time for you to get your revenge.'

And he sprinted out of the Switching Cupboard.

Rebecca and Trent went through the walls, and met him at the threshold of the dining room. 'No,' Rebecca said, stopping him just in time. 'The bomb.'

'That's what I'm here for. I heard the Campbells talking about how they were going to get past it.'

'What are you going to do?'

'Set it off.'

'But that'll help what David's trying to do.'

'Not if I can . . . oh, just get out of the way.'

Booth took a couple of steps back and prepared a run-up.

Trent grabbed Rebecca and swung her back through the wall.

Booth ran into the room, kicked his way through the tripwires, jumped on to the table and leapt for the bomb on the ceiling rose around the chandelier.

David had run up two flights of stairs randomly, and burst into a room at the apex of the house.

A little window looked out over the driveway.

He couldn't find anyone.

'One more life,' he said.

It was worth it to complete the world.

He ran for the window.

As Booth's head came level with it, his eyes locking on it—

The bomb exploded.

The centre of the house collapsed.

Stairways unreeled in one smooth motion, bringing loops of masonry and brickwork falling with them. Chasms opened in corridors. The upper floors toppled into the lower, statues and suits of armour being smashed at high speed across the lower rooms as if they were caught in a tornado. The windows buckled in their frames and burst outwards.

Joe, running, was caught by a thunderous, flattening slab of ceiling that detached from the sky and slammed him into the floor.

A great cloud of scraps and shreds and dust and debris burst into the air from the centre of the building. The flagpole fell. The cracked floor of the rooftop swimming pool disintegrated.

And down it all fell. Down into the increasing pit at the heart of Heartsease.

And then it stopped.

David was sliding down the floor, away from his window, his mind holding on to the ideal of releasing the beast.

Ruth was yelling as she burst through a curtain of wrecked furniture, wanting to kill.

Jacko was dragging his shattered leg out from under the remains of a wardrobe.

Davey was huddled in a corner, praying feverishly.

Trent and Rebecca had leapt into Jane's bedroom, and Rebecca had her hand inside Jane's bureau. She grabbed what she'd been looking for.

All halted, and for a moment their movements stuttered, slid, warped across the structure of reality as the house desperately tried to hold its image of itself together.

But in every pore, between every brick, in the strands of plaster and the lines of electrical power, a new intelligence fought it.

Booth Hawtrey was part of the house now.

His consciousness impacted the desire of the house to shrug off the bomb and become complete, and met it with his own will. The building shook. Time and space shook. Booth heaved on the rules of reality and the walls started to sway, to teeter out over the edge, to collapse into what would be their final destruction.

But then the maze twisted open.

The hedges overlapped, realigned themselves, and the ground beneath them knotted too.

A sharp, final scream came from the earth and was cut off as the maze sliced closed again.

Mary walked out into the sunshine. She was Alisdair, and Alison, and every facet of the ghost of Heartsease. She had her orders. She marched towards the endlessly collapsing house, where a knot of space and time was rippling the air, sending violet waves of light rainbowing from the windows.

From the forest all around the estate, the animals came, rushing in to Mary's boot heels, the wolves and the tigers and huge, spiralling flocks of birds. All descended with her on the house. The ostriches and the sheep and cows ran in towards the collapsing building, tripping over their hooves to throw themselves into the destruction, to add their small deaths to the cause of reforming the weapon, of holding it steady for the moment it would take to explode it.

Mary walked to the wall of the house, put her palms to it and *shoved*.

Rebecca saw Simon Trent stagger.

She was suddenly aware that something was happening. The house was falling down. Or was it? It felt like she was waking from a dream. The concussions threw her from one side of the room to the other.

'Are you all right?' she shouted.

'No,' he shouted. 'He's trying to destroy the house. But I . . . I have to help him!' He ran to a wall and braced himself, his thin muscles stretching against the crumbling plasterwork.

He started to scream. 'Get out!' he shouted. 'Get everybody out!'

Rebecca hesitated for a moment and then ran for the door.

Ruth fell down the remains of the main stairs and rolled into the hall. The chamber was full of birds, flailing in the air and battering themselves to death against the walls. Hundreds of tiny, blurring sacrifices.

She saw that the door was open ahead of her. She could see a distant, dusty horizon of green and blue through the gap.

It was time for her to get out of here. She had not secured the house for the Campbells, but she had done the next best thing. Nobody else would be able to use it. That was the way of her world.

She would go back to Chester and tell the stories of those who had fallen in her service. She would promote war with the Hawtreys, who had killed her people so cruelly. Their armies would head south-east, and she would be at the head of them, keeping these wild emotions the compiler had raised in her close to her heart. They would split the country in two with their war. To finally unite it. That was the way. And if Booth Hawtrey somehow survived this, she would live to split him in two again as well.

She saw that the favour was coming out of her top pocket. She took a moment to stuff it back inside. It was her badge, her own little flag. She was going to need it in the future.

She got to her feet and ran for the door.

She heard the sound from above her just as she took in her first breath of clean, grassy air.

She just had time to look up.

The portcullis slammed down.

It caught her across the back of the neck and carried the axeblow down with her body into the floor beneath.

The wood hit the tiles with a crunch.

Ruth's head bounced down the steps and rolled out into the sunshine.

Booth felt himself as the walls and the roof and the floors of the house as it was both demolished and whole. He tried to collapse himself, to will himself permanently apart. Trent pushed with him, willing his own destruction with that of his property. Mary pushed against them, the sacrifice of every creature of the woods adding to her intense insistence that everything was fine, that the building still stood.

When the building did still stand, the pulse would be released, the door would slam, every human being would die.

Rebecca managed to stagger up the stairways as they veered from there to not there, stepping into space like she was in a cartoon and never looking down to realise she would fall.

She had found Jacko, eaten in half by a saw-toothed floor, the weight that lay on his leg having trapped him. And though she knew her emotions would add to the weight of Mary on the walls she had started to cry at the sight.

She had searched as best she could, and found nobody else. But she wanted to make sure that none remained alive before she got out. Who she was, she felt, was enough to protect her. Who she was now. Which was simply her. Rebecca. Moment to moment.

Now she heard a shout from a high place, and tottered through the storm up the stairs to Alisdair's room, swaying on the rigging of the house as it went down.

She flung herself through the door, and leapt to grab David's feet. He had nearly made his way out of the window.

She pulled him, fighting against his strength, back inside the house.

'No!' he spat at her. 'If you win, it'll all be a mess again. Such a mess . . .' He was sobbing too, she realised. 'Rebecca, let me die. I can't live without you. You're the only thing that makes this world any good.'

'What did I ever do to deserve that? You can't live *for* me, David.'

'But it's all shit!' He fell to his knees in front of her, the tears streaming down his face now. 'Every year, every afternoon, it's just us *doing* things! It's just something to do to keep us going! There's no bigger meaning except you and me. Killing Augustine was just something that happened! *There's no point!* Only there *will* be, if we can just get to completion!'

They were thrown against the wall and rebounded, Alisdair's certificates flying off the walls, his desk sliding across the floor.

David managed to grab a paper knife from the contents of a drawer that had slid into his hand, and unbuttoned his cuff, the knife poised in the other hand.

Rebecca threw herself at him, and landed on top of him, the knife angled in the air above them both. She wrestled for both his wrists.

They stood like that for a moment, heaving against each other, balanced.

And then an eruption of fear, fear like the small creatures feel in the mouth of the owl, burst up through the floor of the house.

David dropped the knife and curled into Rebecca's arms. 'It didn't need me!' he screamed. 'It's closing! It's closing! Mother!'

Rebecca shook along with him, and held his head to her breast.

She could feel that what he said was true. Booth and Simon were losing.

The ghost had brought all its attention to Heartsease, from every storm and every signal across the world. The Van Allen belts turned a significant turn. The ghost brought its hands together around the building.

Simon Trent felt his heart gripped by something again. 'At last,' he said, ecstatic and despairing at the same time.

Booth felt the pain across the whole estate. He felt the house start to reassert its shape, to crush his consciousness out of it. To conquer him.

Davey stood by the fountains at the front of the house, watching the destruction happening and unhappening at once. His prayers had sustained him as he crawled to the hallway, heaved open the portcullis, and scrambled over the body of his last commander to run out into the light, panting at the clean air as it swept into his lungs.

He watched dismayed as the animals continued to be drawn into the vortex, flocks of birds forming huge spirals in the sky that led down into the building, the trees of the forest too bending in the direction of Heartsease. It was warping faster and faster, every brick in motion now, an explosive cloud bursting and unbursting from its centre.

He realised that watching from here was a bad idea.

He turned and started to run up the long driveway that led to the gates.

Rebecca slapped the floor with her free hand, cradling David with the other. 'Booth!' she shouted. 'There's no chance! Your mouth! Open your mouth!'

A wooden mouth loomed out of the floor beneath her and gaped, in pain, an unreal darkness beneath it.

Rebecca, her fingers skittering against the metal, fumbled with Jane's pill dispenser. She managed to spill several greens into her palm.

Without caring that the others were falling all over the floor, she made the handful into a fist and threw the greens into Booth's mouth.

David cried out into her, one last time. She held him tighter.

The moment had come. She could feel it rushing down at them.

She was Rebecca Champhert. She was never going to have a twenty-first birthday. No more birthdays. No more four o'clock. She was going to die as herself.

Thank God.

Booth's memories flooded in on him, and he was swept up by them, away from the battle in the house.

Why had she done that? Why had she made him let go?

He saw the pieces flying together as he rushed off down the corridor of memory.

Behind Davey, sprinting up the driveway, the house rippled.

Then suddenly it was whole again.

The pulse took Rebecca and David together and instantly.

Their bodies fell to the floor, wrapped around each other.

Davey fell an instant later, his momentum pitching him forward on to the gravel, as his feet folded over themselves.

The wave of death swept around the world inside a heartbeat.

The last heartbeat.

Every compass needle spun south, and before the needles had juddered to a stop, the intelligence of Earth was dead.

In the little market towns, the stalls went flying as the people toppled into them, shut off in a second as the electromagnetic pulse snipped off their minds.

In the cities of the families, the courtiers with their luncheon dishes crashed to the ground, and the families themselves tumbled into each other and dropped.

Every single human being, from all the disparate communities around the world, perished in an instant.

The last were several members of a New Guinea tribe, who had never known the last civilisation that had risen and fallen around them. They were sleeping around the remains of a fire.

Then they were not asleep, and had gone.

The animals of the earth moved amongst the dead humans. The farmyard creatures started baying for help within a day. The scavengers and birds and insects and fungoids and microbes began to swarm. The others moved by the smell of death, as it swam again from the places that, for a while, it had avoided.

A fox stopped at the top of the great field in front of Heartsease, and stared at the peaceful monument for a moment, whole and solid and casting a shadow at autumn noon.

Then it wandered back into the forest.

'I just need to be myself, and not Booth Hawtrey's biographer,' said Alison.

'I understand,' Booth said quietly. 'You just try and be happy, wherever you end up.'

She kissed him gently. 'I'll be in touch. Oh, and you're going to need this.' She opened her fist. Sitting there was a silver ring. 'For the next biographer,' she said. 'I managed to get it off. Perhaps that's a sign.' She dropped it into his palm.

'Thank you,' he said. 'She'll have to try hard to live up to you.'

She turned and headed back into Heartsease, pausing only to look at him one last time, and give him a sad smile. Then she was gone.

Booth smiled back, and got into his car.

He was sitting there when he suddenly remembered.

What had happened at Heartsease. The struggle for the house. The house that was standing in front of him.

He'd taken greens. He'd never done that. Why would he?

Had all that been a dream? He felt the wheel of the car. It was as he'd expected it to feel. He got up out of his seat and looked around. The great house, the long driveway, the gates shining distantly in the sun. It was a lovely winter's day.

He thought of other winters. Other seasons. Summers. Willed himself to think of them.

And suddenly he was in one summer from his childhood, racing naked down the beach, his tiny genitals bouncing. He was three.

He splashed about in the sea water, feeling the waves lift him up and put his toes back down on the sand. Such control! He could stay and live in any of his memories. The green had given him the ability to fix to one time, to stop being swept along and stay in one place if he wished. If he wanted to, he could live his whole life again.

Which was a good thing, he thought, laughing at the taste of salt on his tongue. Because he must have died with the rest of the human race at Heartsease. He felt forward in his memory, and saw that there was indeed an ending now. A point where the stream ran out. It was no longer connected in a great circle.

And yet he was here. Bit of a contradiction in terms, that. Still, as long as he never went there . . . But he was going to be alone. He felt a sudden great sadness for Rebecca and young Ben and for all the rest of humanity.

He peed into the ocean.

It was then he realised. Alison. The memory he'd first clung on to when he'd been thrown off the warping house.

That hadn't really happened.

He swept back to it, lived in it again for a moment, sitting in his car, looking around. He had never been able to visit this memory before.

The greens.

Was that why Rebecca had given them to him?

No. There must be something more to it than that.

He turned the key in the starter and the engine of the Bentley Electric purred into life. He released the handbrake, slid into first gear and took the old girl gently up the drive, then faster and faster. The gates were open.

He sped through them, and turned on to the road of many curves which led up out of the valley and through the forest. Heartsease and the shining lake beside it slipped away beneath the tree line. He must have done this in the false memory. But what if he went somewhere he'd never been?

He suddenly spun the wheel of the car and sent it into a high-speed turn off down a little byway. According to a sign, it had once led to the estate's forestry management facilities. He had no idea what was down here.

He sped down the dark little wooded road, the road whipping away underneath him, and the trees becoming a blur on either side. Bloody long road. He pushed the accelerator down, went faster and faster.

Then he understood. The road and the trees were never going to change.

But a moment after the realisation, the scenery did.

Booth brought the car to a skidding halt, looked over his shoulder, and slowly reversed back.

The man was still standing there. Or rather the creature. He was tall and painfully thin, with bulging red eyes.

'Grey Namer,' said Booth.

'Yes,' said the strange figure. His voice was like honey. 'Let's go somewhere more sensible.'

They sat at a corner table in the military club that Jack had often taken him to, while he had still been alive. Military men and women, out of uniform, passed by without looking or stopping to shake his hand, which was the attraction of the place. That and it was dark. The memory of a very particular night, this one, when Booth had come here alone for the only time, and been surprised to find that they still let him in.

'Thank you for all you've done,' said the Namer, both his hands on the table.

'I fought you,' said Booth, taking a swig of Laphroaig while he could.

'In the end. But you did a lot before that: creating Mary especially.'

'Cheers, that makes me feel a lot better. So why are you here?'

'Because all of my Father's children are now in his House. Except you. I came to tell you that you can come home.'

Booth frowned at him. 'I am home.'

'I mean my Father's home. The new home of all humanity. You can come and join us.'

'Why?'

The Namer looked perplexed. 'Why? Because you're the last. The missing piece.'

'Thanks, but I'm quite happy here. I'd be letting the side down if—' He stretched out his arms in a yawn, and bumped into a man passing by with a tray of drinks. The man tripped over his feet and went flying, the glasses smashing in a sudden concussion that generated applause.

Booth's head snapped back to Namer. 'That didn't happen when this happened last time. Neither did this conversation. But I thought that must be something you were doing.'

Namer looked coolly back at him.

Booth couldn't read the face very well, but he was sure the creature looked tense. 'But I can do it too . . .' he murmured. 'Can't I?'

The man was getting up off the floor, starting to yell abuse at him. Booth thought for a moment and raised a finger, about to ask another question.

Namer leapt at him.

They rolled down through Booth's memories, Booth trying to haul the Namer's hands away from his throat.

There was a point in his life that Booth was trying to get back to, but Namer knew exactly where it was, and every time they rushed towards it, Namer would use his strength to shove Booth away again.

They crashed and staggered through Booth's playground life as a child, on to the sports fields where he had been kicked and punched and had his face shoved through the mud, into the falls and collisions of adult life, and then on into all the terrible torments of immortality, into the world of pain that Ruth had made for him.

They fought above the great fall to the ground in the Whispering Gallery of St Paul's.

They were struggling in the boiling water of the pot now, Namer as the gusts of water that brought new pain to Booth's skin.

Booth knew the battle could last forever. That Namer had his strength and more. That he wouldn't give up until Booth had surrendered and died and been brought within his paddock.

But he knew also that Namer must be desperate to stop him reaching his goal. That he was fighting for everybody now.

So he thought the unthinkable.

He brought the flame of now back in front of his eyes. He grabbed Namer and forced him towards it. They were going to walk from the shadow of now right into now itself.

Namer struggled, fought with all his might. 'Sacrifice your small concerns!' he was yelling. 'For the sake of all humanity! You have to! Think of it, Booth! All of us, living as one! The grand picture! The ending! The climax! The world unchained!'

But Booth kept going, holding the Namer with both hands, roaring at him, yelling himself on into the furnace of creation.

He forced his way towards the glowing, shattering, world-devouring now. He pushed them both forward with all his will. They were going. They were going—

Namer let go.

Booth Hawtrey thrust himself into now.

Something fluttered past.

There were no photons to freeze in his memory, he was told.

He was standing in a round, dark corridor. He was alone. There was just a small patch of light around him. He took a few steps forward. The patch of light moved with him.

Time, he was told, had turned into space.

Booth Hawtrey started to run.

December 1998. Bill Parkinson ran out on to the pavement outside the Forum, Kentish Town, displaying a pink feather boa like it was the World Cup. 'I got it!' he shouted. 'I got Sarah's boa!'

An audience was pouring out of the venue from all four doors, the bouncers leaning back against the brickwork and letting them through. The heat of the crowd's bodies bloomed into steam in the winter air. People were carrying their coats, still hot from the concert. The lights of the street glared messages about many different kinds of fast food, and amongst the laughter and the singing there were conversations starting about finding the car in the backstreets and getting some chips and somewhere Cher was singing 'Do you believe in life after love?'

'Stop whirling it about,' muttered Booth. 'Somebody'll nick it.'

Amanda, Bill's sister, looked sidelong at Booth, obviously pissed off. It was probably because he'd just tried to take her arm and she obviously didn't want him to behave like that when people could see them.

Bill carefully finished slipping the boa into his record bag. 'Anybody sexy for a kebab?' he asked.

'Do you know what they put in—' began Booth. Then he stopped. 'Oh bollocks,' he said. 'Sorry, it's taken me a moment to catch up.'

Amanda and Bill looked at him, perplexed.

'Run!' he bellowed at them.

He grabbed them around the shoulders, and heaved them out into the street, shouting: 'Fire! Fire! There's a fire!' As madly and loudly as he could.

People started to pay attention to him, the crowd bursting off away from the pavement, not quite sure what they should be reacting about, but—

Booth stuffed the boa into the ears of his friends and himself, and threw himself down on to the ground on top of them.

The beam hit.

Booth felt it reach for him. Miss him. And in missing him, smash through . . . something. He had an image in his head for a moment of the wind in an orchard. Of all the apples falling.

The empty pavement blazed with light, roasting air into rainbows.

The roar hit a second later, smashing car windows and upending food carts, a giant fist that smashed down into the street corner.

And then a few instants later it subsided.

Booth got to his feet, rubbing his ears. They were ringing, but then they had been after the concert. He helped Bill and Amanda get to their feet too.

There was a striated, multicoloured blast mark on the pavement where he'd been standing a moment before. And nearby there were several bodies. And several more wounded.

All around them, shocked people were standing up, pointing and starting to mutter to each other. Across the city there started to echo a continuous blare of crashes and collisions and screams.

Amanda looked oddly at him. 'What are we doing here?' she asked. 'Who are you? What's that?' She was pointing at a black cab. 'What's all this stuff?'

Booth turned to Bill. The man was looking around in wonder as well, his eyes wide like a child's. 'Yeah,' he whispered. 'What *is* all this *stuff*?'

Booth started to laugh. He wandered about through the crowd, helping people up.

None of them could remember a thing. About anything. They were all asking questions.

He grabbed Bill and Amanda and ran off with them into the city, pointing out things and naming them. He told them that they were Bill and Amanda and asked them to make up everything else about themselves. They came up with some good ideas. Everywhere there was chaos. Nobody could remember even their name, let alone who anyone else was.

In the early hours, Booth learnt that that was how it was internationally too.

He stood in a callbox on Cricklewood Broadway, all the cars still all over the road, because nobody could remember how to drive them, the noise of people wandering the streets making him put a finger in his ear, trying to find out the number of an uncle of his, the only relative he hadn't called. Several of them hadn't picked up the phone, probably because they didn't know what the ringing sound was.

That was when he realised. He was trying to find out the number . . . because he couldn't remember it.

He started to laugh harder than he'd laughed all night.

'My God,' he cried out. 'I've fucked the entire world!'

Epilogue One: Rebecca's Twenty-First Birthday

Autumn, Year 250

After Booth changed the past, of course, the future went in all sorts of ways. The pseudo-objects formed and reformed on a random basis, and many different paths were taken in the space they mapped out between them.

But still some of the pseudo-objects were connected by non-local entanglements from time to time. The monads inexplicably produced magic every now and then.

And that was how Rebecca Champhert came to have her twenty-first birthday, and how on that date she paid a visit.

'I'm writing a book about the first century,' said Rebecca. She was sitting at Jane Bruce's coffee table in her flat in Salisbury, the autumn sunshine making everything russet. The clock on the mantelpiece was just striking four. The walk through the Cathedral Close had been glorious. The street sweepers had whirred around her feet, polishing every stone, their tiny voices advising her of tonight's choral concert. A tea stall had had a bunch of tourists from the Russian Area gathered around it, listening to the news coming over the radio. Another alien civilisation had contacted Earth, the third in the last year, and the President was making a speech at the Congress about it. Congress was in Africa this year, and it was odd getting used to the different times of the televised sessions. Everyone was complaining that they were missing out on their scheduled links with their representatives.

Although it was October, and the wind had a fresh promise of snow inside it, the taste of it had reassured her of the coming spring. Perhaps that was because it seemed to be spring for the human race as well, all these others saying hello, as if the Earth was good enough now for it to compare itself to all its wonderful neighbours.

So Rebecca felt happy, glad to exist, on this day.

The reverend slid a coaster under her teacup before she could stain the table top. 'I see. What sort of book?'

'A historical novel, set just before and after the Forgetting.' Rebecca watched for the usual reaction, a little resigned sigh. There were a lot of these novels, about all the people who had to relearn their identities, and those who didn't have enough to go on and so chose something new, and those who were actually in the first category, but for one reason or another had pretended to be in the second. 'There's a lot of autobiographical stuff in there too,' she added quickly. 'About why someone becomes a writer, things like that.'

'And why do you need the services of a vicar?'

'Well, I really need the services of the cathedral archives. The Bishop's already agreed, and he recommended you as the best guide. So I popped straight over. I could have done it over the net but it's kind of complicated. But I'm in a bit of a hurry, I have to catch a train. It's my birthday party in London tonight. And it's going to be really wonderful.' She realised that this might not be the best impression to give Jane, and killed her smile. 'This is only my first visit. Of many.'

Jane smiled herself. 'So who are you after? We have identity records and proofs going back to then, certainly.'

'Well.' Rebecca took a quick sip of her tea. 'There's a guy in my novel called Booth Hawtrey. I thought I made him up, but then I found an entry in one of the family directories of the time. I was just wondering what the real Booth was like.'

Jane got up from her seat and took a bunch of keys from her pocket. 'Let's go and have a look,' she said. 'I'm sure we'll have birth and death. And perhaps something more.'

A few hours later, of course, Jane ended up at Rebecca's birthday party, wearing a funny hat.

Epilogue Two: This is a Young Country

Winter, Year Ten.

The door to the kitchen opened, and Booth cautiously stepped inside. Nobody about. He took a chance, and switched on his torch.

The sight of the kitchens, perfect and gleaming in this European Trust property, made him very scared again. The sight took him back to his time spent suffering here. But not literally. He missed having his memories to surf through, sometimes. But not now.

He needed to breathe. He pulled off his balaclava and ran a hand through his hair. The curls were starting to grey now, not at all gracefully.

He'd told his wife that he was going to be away in the country on business for just this one night. And that after he returned, everything would be all right. He needed to be back at his company tomorrow morning. He hadn't bothered naming too many things for the forgetful population of the world. It was more of a joy to watch them create sparkling new systems and organisations themselves. It looked, from his vague grasp of economics, like the GEC wasn't going to happen this time. Things seemed to be very different already. All the new growth. All the new systems. Anything that fell apart just got replaced by something better.

He'd gone into the export business, with trade contacts all across the European Nation. It was still a bit of a shock to Booth that his wife trusted him so much. But then, she had every reason to. She'd said that she would spend the evening he was away visiting Fee and her husband.

A sound behind him made Booth turn round. But it was only Simon, stepping through the wall. He carried with him two more cans of fuel, to join the two Booth had brought down here, their contents carefully splashed to link up with the others all through the house.

They had met last summer, when Booth and Amanda had taken a guided tour of the place. Booth had slipped away into a quiet corner and upset a salt cellar.

Simon, of course, had had no idea who Booth was, or what his plans had been. So Booth had had to buy an amateur radio set, and learn how to use it, and spent the next few months communicating with the old man, and letting him know what had happened, or rather what had never happened, when last they met.

They had become friends in the process. Simon seemed to relish the idea of what Booth was about to do.

Together, they splashed the fuel everywhere it could go. Simon dealt with Alisdair's room himself, soaking every little thing.

As he sloshed the liquid around, on to carpets and furniture, throughout the house. Booth started to sing.

> '*It was on the good ship Venus,*
> *By Christ you should have seen us . . .*'

The two men bumped into each other, back to back, as they returned to the main hallway, their trails of explosive meeting.

They turned in surprise, shook hands, and walked to the door together, Simon joining in the chorus.

> '*Frigging in the rigging,*
> *Frigging in the rigging,*
> *Frigging in the rigging,*
> *There was fuck all else to do!*'

They stood by the van outside, watching the house stand there in the crisp autumn darkness for a while longer, illuminated in its grounds to be seen for miles beyond.

Then Booth clicked the electrical trigger.

The first gout of flame burst up inside the ground floor, visible through the windows, sending a flickering pattern of new light out across the gardens. Soon it was joined by a second and a third.

Booth glanced at Simon. 'Still going strong?'

'I'm fine. As long as we've got that with us.'

They both looked to the round Lutyens table with the tortured surface, that stood next to them by the van.

'I'm going to get it renovated,' said Booth.

Then before the security guards got the chance to see them, they opened the back doors of the van, swung the table inside, then got in themselves.

They drove off up the valley, watching the flames rising higher and higher from the old house, the smoke sending streamers into the forest, the reds and yellows blanketing the parched light of the illuminations. Booth wanted to stop and see the final collapse, but Simon insisted they get a move on.

He had a place in Booth's company and his house. He was excited about the future.